For my readers on Wattpad who encouraged me to take that
first step.

For my mother, my number one cheerleader, who has
challenged me and saved me from the darkest parts of
myself.

For my best friend Jo, my other half, who has helped me
become not only the writer I am today but also the person I
have always wished I could *be*.

Glossary

Blessings of Blood - Synonymous with magix user.

Consorts - Life companions of the King/Queen/Heir.

Consort King/Queen - Out of the five chosen Consorts, the first to impregnate or be impregnated by the heir.

Haise - A feeding of lust and sexual energy for S-Level Incubi and select Succubae. Happens once a month but can be induced if exposed to high levels of pheremones. Intended to increase fertility and fortify the womb.

Hora(s) - Hour(s) (latin)

Magix - Abundance of wild magic energy.

the Orb - magically engineered projection device

Potentials - Suitors in the running to become the heir's Consorts.

S-Level - Androgynous Incubi equipped with a womb and the ability to carry offspring.

Tick(s) - Second(s)

ASTORIA

THE
CONSORTS

N.A. MOORE

Prologue

For twenty-three years, these sheets have caressed the skin of my body alone. Never holding the entangled limbs of lovers or saccharine sweet kisses of a heat familiar to frenzied physical contact. This emptiness has held me firm in its embrace, soaking my bed with the loneliness that seeps from my dreams to my waking reality.

Soon...that will change.

For I am Prince Killian Innis, heir to the throne of Incubi, future ruler of Astoria, and today I will meet my Consorts.

Chapter

I

At the age of fourteen, Killian Innis was brought before an Incubus and a Succubus. Both were tall and imposing, bare of all but thin white robes.

King Ellis Innis of Astoria watched his son with an attendant by his side. He asked his child, voice careful but expectant, "Which of the two calls to you?"

Killian knew his father referred to his *Haise*, a feeding of lust and sexual energy that all S-Level Incubi and the rare few Succubae endure. It was the curse of their species that few were forced to bear.

As beautiful as both were, Killian found something alluring about the lean muscled Incubus with tawny skin and squared features. He ogled the male's impressive frame and intoxicating scent, feeling his chest tug him in the Incubus's direction. The prince stood with a crown too big and lips parted in wonder. His choice had been made and he would soon grow to resent it.

"Ah, the Incubus. Very well," the King said simply, then gestured to the attendant who began writing. Killian had no idea that this choice would define his future, having been more concerned with the frivolous desires of a child.

The choice determined the pool of suitors he would choose from to be his Consorts. King Ellis had chosen Succubae. The five females that made up his Consorts played a part in raising all four of their children. Jessa, the first to be impregnated and the King's Rank One, was the Queen Consort and Killian's mother.

It was incredibly important for the Royal family to reproduce as quickly and plentifully as possible. They were an example to be followed. A task with that much weight proved to be more of a burden than an honor.

Succession in Astoria was a competition of sorts. A tradition shared across all species...who could provide the heir first. It did not matter if the current heir was the carrier or the breeder. It was the responsibility of the chosen Consorts to plant or accept the seed that would bring about the next ruler.

But most species were allowed one Consort, two at most. Only Incubi and Succubae were allotted five based on the Astorian hierarchy put into place by the first rulers of Ancient Astoria. It kept the Incubi numbers inexhaustible and limited the repopulation of other royal lines.

None were able to compete against the strength and power of the Incubi race. Some tried but most learned to adjust.

The Gods above, in their sacred home amongst the Clouds, willed it so. They watched but did not interfere, showing their blessing. Incubi would not have been built for success had it not been the plan of the divine. They were chosen.

As firstborn, Killian was heir and it was his duty to maintain order after his father stepped down as well as continue the line of ruling. From the moment he was born, Killian became sacred. His body and his virtue were of the highest value and to compromise them in any way was treason. He understood why, purity being of the utmost importance when aiming to please the Gods, but it still left him isolated and trapped. There were so many things he could not participate in because of the risks, while his siblings could do as they pleased. And it had been that way for twenty-three years, six moon cycles, and fourteen days.

At times, Killian wished he hadn't been born first or that he was a normal Incubus. Sure, S-Level Incubi were revered as precious and special--those who experienced the *Haise* were the purest of their kind--but he didn't care about that. He wanted to be free like his siblings, making his own choices and not dealing with the complicated mess that made up his biology. He could see no benefit in enduring a monthly *Haise*.

It was awful, especially when spent alone. Even more so when an audience was present, which occasionally included family members. Due to his status as an S-Level, he was pressured with the task of giving birth to the next heir.

As if ruling an entire Realm wasn't scary enough.

"Are you ready to be dressed, Your Highness?" a voice called from beyond the grand door of the bath. Killian moaned as thick heat wrapped around his body like an embrace he'd never had. It would be the last time he bathed alone.

"I will be out in a short moment," Killian called in the soft, even tone he always maintained.

He climbed out of the bath slowly, letting the steam kiss his flushed lavender skin. The bright maroon curls he inherited from his mother, swayed with the weight of the water pouring from it.

He padded over to the drying station, leaving a trail of puddles in his wake. Killian grabbed a fluffy heated towel from the rack and began to rub himself down. When he was dry, he slipped into a silk red robe.

When he opened the door, Ethel and Kara, his attendants, were waiting for him. They had his clothes ready once they ushered him back to his room. It was a special occasion which meant the outfit was incredibly intricate.

Killian pulled on his undergarments, which consisted of a thin white thong with sheer lace that kept his genitals neatly tucked and allowed for a comfortable breeze. White shorts made of soft silk followed so the skirt could be fastened.

The front strip of the skirt dipped down to Killian's ankles, lightly brushing the floor while the back strip trailed on the ground behind him. They were strung together with a web of rubies encased in gold. The family crest, resembling four horns wrapped in vines, rested in a circular pendant that sat at the buckle of the skirt. A thin strip of rubies connected the buckle to a jeweled collar, resting gracefully on his chest.

The attendants slipped him into a tight white sleeveless vest that exposed his upper hips before attaching a long white mesh cape to his shoulders. Three gold armbands were placed on his biceps and forearm before a crown was gingerly placed on his head, carefully avoiding his four black horns. He gasped softly as his thin maroon tail was pulled through the hole in the back of his ensemble.

It was the most revealing and daring outfit he had ever adorned. His stomach filled with agitated little flutters at the knowledge of anyone other than his attendants seeing him this way. He had never been so exposed before, but it suggested that he was finally reaching a new point in his life where this was okay, something that never had been before. It was the first step toward that tiny sliver of freedom he so desperately craved.

The attendants stepped back and smiled in approval at their work. A knock interrupted their admiration.

"Come in," Killian called.

A servant poked her head in and informed the room that it was time for the prince to make his way to the main hall to be officially announced.

Nervousness settled in Killian's gut. Was he ready for this? Truly?

He had never been around other Incubi aside from his brothers and father. Once his attraction to Incubi had been declared, the ones that worked in the palace were forbidden to come anywhere near him. No exceptions. He only ever had Succubae as his servants or attendants. He was terrified.

"Don't be frightened, this is a joyous moment in your life, Your Highness. One that you have been eagerly waiting for," Ethel said sweetly to the quivering Prince. She was older, with gray hair cropped short and pale blue skin. Killian adored her. When he was younger, she would sneak him pastries before dinner and always told the most amazing stories before bed. She was closer to him than his own mother, and he had five.

"I am worried they may not find me appealing. I do not wish to force any to be my Consort if they do not have feelings for me," Killian admitted. Worry shone raw in his red jeweled eyes.

"Nonsense! You are kind, gentle, smart, and absolutely beautiful. There are none who would not fall to your feet. Do not fret," Ethel insisted, her smile even wider than before.

Killian let himself be reassured by her words. The tightness in his chest eased and the clenching in his gut became less intense. He let out a soft breath before smiling at the older Succubae, finally ready to meet his Potentials.

As they made their way to the main hall, Killian's heart began to thump rapidly again. He doubted anything could be said to make him calm down at this point. It was so loud he could hear nothing else but the blood rushing in his ears.

He was in shock. This was really happening.

Killian didn't know if he was ready. What if he couldn't decide? What if he fell for all of them?

What if they didn't love him back?

When they finally approached the tall double doors that led to the main hall, Killian was close to fainting.

"You'll be fine," Ethel whispered just as the doors opened.

Killian couldn't hear the attendant announce his arrival over the beating of his heart.

He saw his father standing before his throne with his birth mother right beside him. Killian's siblings and Consort mothers were standing a little off to the side, whispering to each other. He didn't want to look, but his eyes couldn't help but drift over to the line of Incubi, at attention with their legs slightly spread, wings exposed, and hands clasped behind their backs. All twenty-five males waiting for his perusal.

Each one wore a small black loincloth that would expose everything with the slightest movement.

Killian swallowed noisily, averting his gaze. Lisa, his third and least friendly attendant, shot him a warning glare as they proceeded forward.

Killian and his attendants bowed respectfully as the King came to greet his son. The King looked as regal as ever, with his long chocolate brown waves plaited and body draped in a magnificent red and white tunic and trousers. His gray eyes sparkled with pride and excitement. One might mistake this for his Consort Ceremony.

"Father," Killian said softly.

"My precious Killian! You look stunning. A spitting image of your mother at my Ranking Ceremony. Wouldn't you say so, Ethel?"

Ethel nodded in agreement. "Yes indeed, Your Majesty."

The King winked at her.

"Come, meet your Potentials. If you see one you do not like they will be discarded at once," King Ellis announced, loud voice booming.

Killian gulped and hoped he wouldn't throw up. That would make for one awkward first impression.

They turned toward the line of Potentials. Each one was huge; tall and incredibly muscular. They towered over the prince by at least a foot. Their faces were void of emotion as they looked forward and not at the Royals as was instructed.

The prince was to inspect them, not the other way around.

The King put his hand on Killian's back, gently leading the group to the front of the line, beginning the inspection.

As they approached each Potential, the King ordered them to state their name and region. It was important for the King's Consorts to be diverse in background, that included where they were raised. It was preferred for each Consort to be from a different region.

Killian was sure not to remember all of the information, but it would give him a slight idea of the Potential's upbringing.

Some Potentials were not attractive while others were absolutely gorgeous to Killian.

"Go on Killian, you can touch them. See what you're working with," King Ellis said. Killian's eyes widened at his father's audacity. It shouldn't have come as a surprise though. King Ellis had always been...eccentric.

The King stepped up to a Potential with bright green skin and hair like spun gold, tied tightly in a ponytail, bound with a worn red ribbon. He looked at the Potential intensely before grabbing their genitals through the cloth and giving them a squeeze, then pulled the material away to peek.

A collective gasp of surprise came from the servants and attendants watching while Killian's mothers all giggled knowingly. To Killian's surprise, the Potential didn't even flinch. There was no outward change to his stance, expression, or demeanor.

The King turned to his gaping son with a wide grin.

"This one's got a nice package." He jerked his thumb at the Potential he just groped before ordering, "Name and region."

"Drek Leon of Gemp, My King," the Potential replied in a low, even tone that made Killian shiver in delight.

"I like him, keep this one," King Ellis laughed before continuing down the line of suitors.

Killian vaguely heard his birth mother scold him. "This is Killian's Ceremony, not yours, Ellis."

The prince blushed, ducking his head as he passed the Potential.

Drek snuck a glance at Killian, bright green eyes twinkling, and smirked, causing the prince to blush even harder.

They walked slowly down the line until Killian found himself transfixed by a Potential with onyx skin. He hadn't realized he stopped before him.

The prince admired the Incubus from his solid black eyes to the four pointed horns protruded from his forehead.

The Consorts

Most Incubi and Succubae had two. Stronger ones leaned more toward three. The exceptionally powerful had four like King Ellis, his children, his brother, and nephew. Very few Incubi had four, less than twenty total. To think this Incubus was one of them...

His face was carved like the gem his skin mimicked with a sharp jawline, elegantly slanted deep-set eyes, a wild mane of long black hair, and sinfully full, luscious lips. His ears were pointed, another sign of power and his body was incredible. He oozed authority and masculinity. Killian was left in awe.

"Found one you like?" King Ellis mused, then addressed the Potential, "Name and region."

"Rem Brangwen of Tenebris, My King."

His voice was a deep baritone that coaxed a soft moan from Killian's lips. He hadn't realized his eyes had fluttered shut until they popped open again and he was staring into pitch-black depths. The Potential had him locked in his gaze; the prince was unable to tear himself away.

The King smiled knowingly. "Why don't you touch him, Killian?"

Killian knew his father would keep pushing until he did it at least once. If there were ever a male he wanted to touch, it was the one before him.

Killian swore his father enjoyed making him uncomfortable.

With a deep breath, Killian stepped up to the Potential with a sputtering heart. He didn't have it in him to be as daring as his father but he did tentatively place a hand on the Potential's chest.

His skin was warm and soft. There were raised symbols pressed in his skin. They danced around his upper chest favoring his left pectoral and trailed their way down his upper left bicep. Killian brushed his fingers over the marks, feeling every raise and dip, embedding it into his memory.

This close, Killian could smell him. It was an intoxicating scent like cinnamon and myrrh. Killian shivered, involuntarily stepping even closer. The tips of his fingers grazed the Potential's impressive pectorals again. His left nipple was pierced with a silver hoop.

Killian wanted to touch it but held himself back. Instead, his hand traveled south, down every ripple of his abs. Killian could feel the Incubus' dark eyes boring into him unwaveringly.

"Your wings," Killian whispered a little breathlessly, unable to make his voice any louder in fear of what embarrassing noises might escape.

The Potential immediately unfurled his wings. The spines were black like the rest of him, but the webbing was a dark bloody red. Killian could see the tiny dark veins, pulsing with blood as the sunlight tried and failed to pierce the wall of them. His wings were magnificent; majestic as they dipped and stretched.

The waves of power radiating off him were almost enough to call Killian's *Haise*.

Killian backed away from the Potential feeling dizzy and disoriented.

"Are you well, Prince Killian?" Ethel asked, appearing beside him.

"Y-yes, I am fine," he answered shakily.

"Rem, what is your combat specialty?" The King asked, continuing the assessment.

"I have no specialty. I am equally proficient in all weaponry."

Killian shivered as he spoke again. The King's eyes widened, clearly impressed. Killian's Consorts would not just be his lovers; they would be his protectors, advisors, best friends, and his family. It was required for them to be highly skilled in combat.

"Lisa, take note of this one," King Ellis commanded.

"Yes, Your Majesty," Lisa obeyed, writing on her parchment pad furiously.

"Come, Killian." His father pulled him away from the Potential. He followed reluctantly.

The prince's eyes lingered on his black skin before they slid to the next male.

This one was the stark opposite of the previous, with bright white skin as vibrant as freshly fallen snow with long straight white hair to match. His eyes were as black as the previous Potential's skin, completely consuming his sockets. He had two pointed black horns to match. He was stunning with long and symmetrical features, small mouth, and an elegantly sloped nose.

"Name and region," the King said when he noticed Killian had stopped again.

"Faust Akili of Sapientae, My King."

His voice was soft and gentle like a soothing lullaby. Killian wanted to hear it again, knowing the Potential must have an amazing singing voice.

"Take note of this one too, Lisa."

"Yes, Your Majesty."

They continued down the line and found a couple more that fascinated Killian before they were all dismissed.

After briefly speaking to his parents, Killian retired to the lounge with his siblings. The room was specifically kept for familial bonding.

"Killian, you are so lucky! They were gorgeous! I wish I was heir," Gilra sighed dreamily as her eldest brother sat gracefully on the couch across from her, back straight but unable to keep his composure completely intact. He nervously fiddled with the jewels in his ridiculously gaudy belt, only stopping when he looked up to address his sister.

"But then you'd never be able to sing at galas," Killian said with a gentle smile. His tone was sweet, conveying none of his underlying bitterness.

Gilra, the second youngest sibling, was born to their father's Rank Five. She had a Cloud given voice and frequently sang at banquets and galas in town. She made numerous friends and almost always had company over. Killian was rarely allowed near her.

"I like that Orion guy, he looks like he's good with a sword," Pierce said with a grin. "Pick him, brother, so we can spar."

Pierce was still in his training uniform with his short white hair slicked back and blue eyes glowing with excitement. He was the youngest of the four siblings, born to their father's Rank Three. He was always with the Warriors, training in combat. The King said it would most likely be Pierce who took over the mantle of lieutenant or General of the Astorian Army.

"That Rem guy looked like he could take them all without breaking a sweat. If you want someone with skill little brother, that's the one you need to spar with," Ian pointed out, lounging comfortably on the chair, resting his arms casually along the back of it.

Killian was elated that Ian came home for this. Ian was the second oldest, right after Killian, born to their father's Rank Two. He spent his days traveling the world, establishing relations with foreign Kingdoms, and learning new languages and cultures. It was something Killian would never be able to do. Astoria was too large. He needed to be in Heltzig at the main palace at all times. If there were ever an emergency in the fifteen regions, ambassadors needed to know where he would be. They came to him, not the other way around.

Ian arrived last night from Tarr, crossing three seas just to get here. Killian knew Ian's mother had a lot to do with it, but the gesture was still appreciated. He looked just like her with navy shoulder-length hair and bright green eyes.

"I think Rei has my heart already," Gilra giggled.

Pierce whacked her on the head.

Gilra pouted while the rest laughed.

"Who do you like, Killian?" Gilra asked. When three pairs of eyes fell on him, the laughter died from his lips. His mind immediately went to the black-skinned Incubus. Killian shuddered in pleasure just from the thought of that deep voice and soft skin.

"We already know the answer to that. You saw how long he stayed with that Rem guy. Only one he touched too. I was almost certain he would bust a *Haise* right then and there."

Killian glared at his youngest brother.

"You are so crude, Pierce!"

Pierce shrugged and grinned.

"I do not know what to think. This is the first time I have been around Incubi that I am not related to. It is...overwhelming."

"Well, whoever you don't pick, I'll take them," Gilra sang.

"I second that," Pierce piped up.

Killian rolled his eyes and laughed with them, but a part of him was annoyed. They always wanted what little he had when they had what Killian did not, the world at their feet.

They had billions to choose from for suitors, but they wanted his twenty-five.

He pushed the ugly thoughts away and continued to jest with his siblings until Lisa entered the room.

"Your Highness, Lord Ian, Lady Gilra, Lord Pierce, it is time for dinner."

The Royals rose and headed for the dining hall. Killian sat next to the King across from his birth mother while the rest of the Consort mothers and siblings filled out other available seats.

Food was served immediately after seating.

"Killian, what did you think? Who was your favorite out of the males presented?" The King asked as they all devoured their food.

"Well, we all know the answer to that. It was clearly the Incubi with skin as black as coal," Consort Mother Mae smirked.

Killian ducked his head and blushed furiously before uttering in a small voice, "Was it really that obvious?"

"Yes," everyone chorused.

Killian groaned in embarrassment.

"There is nothing wrong with that. He looks strong, capable, intelligent; an excellent choice for a Consort and even better for a King," King Ellis said.

"I do not know what I want. I am utterly flabbergasted."

"It's okay, sweetheart. You take all the time you need to figure it out," Queen Jessa said gently, regarding Killian with red eyes that mirrored his own.

After dinner, Killian had a few lessons with a history scholar before it was time to retire for the night.

"Did you want to take a bath before resting, Your Highness?" Lisa asked.

Killian knew some of the Potentials would be in there right now and while he may be required to wear his robes now when he bathed, he knew they were not. He was definitely not ready for that.

"You can try all you want to avoid them but now that they are here, it will be impossible," Lisa tsked before leaving the prince to sleep. Killian collapsed in his bed, thoroughly exhausted.

Almost immediately he fell asleep, dreaming of waking up in someone's arms.

The next night there was no way out of it. Killian managed to evade bathing that morning and avoided the Potentials all day, but now he had no excuse. He had to bathe before the day ended. Ethel and Kara were practically giddy this evening when they were escorting him to the bath. He wanted the world to swallow him whole.

"Have fun!" Kara whispered as they approached the doors to the bath. Loud male laughter and chatter could be heard from where they stood. Killian gulped before they opened the doors and he was given a not so gentle push inside. His heart was pounding as the laughter stopped. He could feel all of the eyes on him, burning into his skin. He tried to ignore them as he walked further into the room and over to the water spouts.

One of the Potentials, Caspian, was in the booth beside him. Killian tried very hard not to look at him. As he washed, he tried to reach his hair in the back but couldn't manage to rinse the soap out. The prince huffed in frustration.

"Would you like me to pour water in your hair to wash the soap out, Your Highness?" a rich, low voice asked.

Killian looked up and saw Caspian had finished washing and was watching him struggle with amusement clear in his expression.

He was tall and fit with gold skin that complimented his long wavy red and orange hair. His eyes were a startling yellow and his features were almost feline.

"Yes, thank you. That would be helpful," Killian answered shyly.

Caspian reached toward the spout to cup water in his large hands before pouring it over the hard to reach areas on Killian's head. The Potential took care not to touch the prince in the process. When the soap was all out, Killian thanked him again.

"You are most welcome."

"Goodnight, Caspian."

"Goodnight, My Prince," Caspian grinned before giving a dramatic bow and leaving. Killian rose and made his way over to the bath. He stepped into the water, descending down the stairs. The water reached up to his hips, he waded through it slowly.

There were about fifteen Potentials still bathing, all spread out within the main section of the bath. Killian knew he was supposed to be socializing with them, but he couldn't bring himself to do it.

As he passed them, a low murmur started to fill the room.

Killian hurried around the corner where an area was hidden from view. He breathed a sigh of relief with his hand to his chest, trying to calm his frantic heart. He took a step further then froze when he realized he was not alone.

It was him.

He was sitting on the inner ledge submerged in the water, stark against the pale backgrounds. He wasn't looking at the prince, but Killian knew he was aware of his presence.

He turned in Killian's direction. His face blank but gaze intense.

"Your Highness," he greeted with a bow of his head. His hair flowed around him like a dark oil spill. Killian wanted to touch it, sink into it, drown in it.

"Rem," the prince greeted but the words came out breathless. Blush colored Killian's cheeks as he sat down on the ledge opposite of the dark male.

It was silent for a long while. Killian wanted to say something but could not find the words.

"You are nervous," Rem pointed out. Killian tilted his head back against a pillar and let his deep voice wash over him like a slow breeze on a hot day.

"I do not know what to say," Killian admitted, hating how inexperienced he sounded.

"What is it you wish to know?"

His job was to get to know them. If they were to be lovers, he should know what they take pleasure in. It was a valid question, right?

"Something you enjoy," Killian blurted.

"Hunting."

Killian blinked at the response. He didn't know why but a part of him didn't expect the Incubus to answer.

He could imagine it though; seeing him throw a spear into an elk. Every bunch and coil of his muscles were ingrained in Killian's mind. He wished to see the reality.

Killian gazed at Rem's chest, what he could see above the water at least. He was fascinated. He hadn't realized he drew closer until he was kneeling before the male. His eyes tracing the swirls and loops that decorated his skin.

"You can touch them again if you would like," Rem offered.

This was a chance Killian could not pass up, no matter how embarrassed he was. He touched Rem's chest again, loving the sensation of the ridges in his skin.

"What do they mean?" Killian asked in awe.

"They are a blessing of blood. The symbol of a gift and a curse."

Killian's head jerked up in shock. "You have magix?"

Rem nodded once.

Killian should have known, but it amazed him anyway. It was rare to find any in his species with magix. It was a sign of ultimate power. He remembered reading about them in his father's books but never thought he'd get to meet someone who had it. He was sure they never left Tenebris.

Killian scooted closer to get a better look, aiming to balance on the Potential's leg but touched something else entirely. His cheeks flamed as he stumbled away, splashing Rem in the process. Rem wiped the water from his face casually.

"I d-did not m-mean to--" he couldn't finish the sentence, unable to say it out loud. He had mentally scolded his father about this behavior and here he was acting just the same.

"It is not against the rules for you to touch me, Your Highness," Rem replied.

"Despite what the rules permit, your body is your own. It is not right for me to take advantage of it," Killian snapped sharply.

Rem raised a dark brow that nearly blended in with his skin. "Is it not? My consent did not seem to matter yesterday," he challenged.

Killian backed away, flustered and unable to come up with a quick response.

"I must go now. Goodnight," he muttered before wading through the water toward the steps.

There were fewer Potentials in the bath now, but they stopped talking once he emerged. It was a bit unnerving.

He climbed out and grabbed a towel to dry himself off. He slid behind an enclosed booth to swap his wet robe for a dry one, slipped on his cloak, and nodded at the other Potentials before taking his leave.

"So how was it?" Kara asked giddily as they walked back to Killian's room.

Killian grimaced. "Nerve-wracking. They all just stared at me. It was awkward."

"I didn't see your favorite in there, were you disappointed?" Ethel grinned.

"I do not have a favorite," he lied quickly. Ethel and Kara shared a look. "But if you are referring to Rem...he was there. I exchanged a few words with him." Killian said indignantly.

Ethel and Kara squealed.

"Did you get to touch him again?" Ethel asked.

Killian looked away guiltily before giving one sharp nod. The attendants squealed even louder.

"My Prince! So naughty!" Kara laughed.

"It is not like that! I just touched his marks!" Though that was a lie too. He most certainly touched something else. "He has magix."

Ethel's eyes widened. "Magix? How rare."

"Makes sense. He's from Tenebris," Kara remarked.

When they were inside his room, they dressed him in his nightclothes. As he was about to retire, there was a knock on his door.

"Come in!" he called.

King Ellis appeared in the doorway wearing his own nightclothes. He entered, sitting at the edge of Killian's bed.

"How do you feel, Killian?"

"To be honest, I do not know what I am feeling. I do not know what to do or what to say around them. It is uncomfortable."

"That's normal. You are just getting used to it. It will become easier when you narrow down your options. Are there any that do not appeal to you?"

Killian thought about it and felt ashamed to admit that there were a few that did not call to his *Haise*. He didn't want to eliminate a candidate because of aesthetics but he wondered how they could ever be Consort King if they could not call his *Haise*. It was necessary if they were to ever fill him with an heir.

"There are a few," Killian admitted.

"Tell me," his father insisted.

Killian rattled off a few names and descriptions.

"They will be gone before morning," his father promised. "Pleasant dreams, Killian."

The King kissed Killian's head before departing. He watched him leave and was once again left alone.

It hurt now, but soon; he would not be alone anymore.

Chapter 2

The next day the Potentials were to prove themselves with their first test in the art of combat. With twenty Potentials left, they were split even in pairs to spar. Each Potential chose a weapon from the Royal Armory. If they did not impress King Ellis or Prince Killian with their skills, they were dismissed immediately.

In the Arena where most of the Royal Guard and Astorian Army trained, sat two massive silver thrones with the Innis family crest embedded in the backs. The King and Crown Prince sat side by side in them at the head of the large dirt plane, elevated above all. Just below them sat the King's Consorts and their children. The Potentials were lined up in the center of the plane dressed in dark leathers while General Lee of the Astorian Army, gave them instructions.

It was difficult for Killian to hear what was said to his future lovers. He chose to study them, read what he could from their body language, expressions, and emanating energy. Most listened carefully with blank expressions, bodies tight on full alert.

Killian spotted Caspian leaning lazily on a bow, which to others might seem as if he were not taking the test seriously but Killian caught the steely glint in those feline eyes and the tenseness in his frame. He was like a cat slinking in the brush, ready to pounce the moment his prey let their guard down. Those dangerous yellow eyes flickered to his.

Killian stiffened.

Caspian's lips quirked into an easy grin before he winked, then wiped all expressions from his face, blending in with those around him. Killian's gut clenched as he fought to keep the heat from his face.

Forcing his eyes away, Killian's traveled down the line of glistening muscular warriors. He found his eyes drawn to another Potential with light blue skin and long navy hair with white streaks. From where he sat, Killian couldn't see the male's eyes but assumed they were light and bright. The Potential was twirling two short swords in his hands. He was smiling, manner eager as if he couldn't wait to start.

"Lisa," Killian whispered. "Who is that?" He pointed to the blue-haired Incubus.

"Zev Lane of Tarr, Your Highness," Lisa said from her spot behind his throne. Killian hummed with interest.

Zev.

Killian kept his eyes glued to him. He was paired with a black-haired Potential. They were the first to spar. While the other Potentials retreated to the outskirts of the arena, the chosen pair remained in the middle awaiting the signal to start.

During the battle, the Potentials were not to deliver any fatal blows. The goal was to incapacitate their opponents for sixty ticks.

Killian practically fell off his seat as he leaned forward in anticipation. When they began, Killian's anxiety grew. The black-haired Incubus wielded a morning star with power but not agility. He was sloppy with his movements making it too easy for Zev to get the upper hand.

The sound of metal clashing reverberated in his ears as they battled. Weapons swinging; bodies dodging, turning, lunging, grunting. Much too soon, it was over. The black haired Incubus left his side open, allowing Zev to land a swift roundhouse kick to the sternum, forcing the air from his lungs. Once sufficiently distracted by trying to breathe, Zev repeated the move to his head, knocking him out cold.

Zev stood over him, nudging the male with his foot to see if he would move. When the Potential didn't budge, he pouted before waving servants over.

King Ellis grunted in approval, then dismissed the unconscious Incubus, unimpressed by his skills...or lack thereof. The servants carried the male out of the arena to receive medical attention.

Zev turned to the Royal family to give a small bow with a wide grin before returning to the outskirts with the other remaining Potentials.

The next pair Killian knew to be Valen and Orion. Killian had found Valen attractive in the initial line up while his younger brother Pierce mentioned wanting to spar with Orion. Killian was a little excited to see them face off.

Pierce eagerly leaned forward as he watched Orion. The tall red-haired Potential with bronze skin twirled a long blade expertly in his hands. Valen held a spear. Killian thought he looked like he knew how to use it but was poorly mistaken. The fight was almost embarrassing with how quickly Orion won.

The same results occurred with a few more pairs leading to the dismissal of four additional Potentials. There were some that were equally talented and both were able to stay. The prince did take note of one Potential with curly blonde hair close to yellow that wielded an ax with amazing skill but his interest was fleeting.

With only one pair left, Killian's heart fluttered in his chest.

Rem walked calmly to the center of the arena with a single-edged sword. Caspian met him there with a quiver of iron-tipped arrows and a steel bow in his hands. Rem was stoic while Caspian grinned.

When the fight began, the onlookers struggled to keep up. One tick and the males stood motionless, watching each other intensely. Another tick and their forms blurred in motion. They were both unbelievably fast. Neither stayed still long enough for the other to land a blow. From what he could see, Killian admired the way Caspian used his bow and arrow to its fullest ability. Vicious in his fighting style, he even used his bow like a sword to block and strike.

Killian was surprised to see that Caspian was keeping up with Rem. Both were holding back considerably but he could tell both males were almost evenly matched. The prince raised his hand to stop the fighting. It was a battle of stamina at this point.

"I have seen enough," Killian announced in a clear voice that echoed across the vast space. Rem and Caspian turned to bow to him before returning to the line of remaining Potentials. Only fourteen were left.

A feast was served afterward. After being given a moment to clean themselves, the Potentials joined the Royal family for dinner.

The King sat at the head of the table with Killian and Queen Jessa on either side. Killian's Consort mothers and siblings were absent.

"I am thoroughly impressed with your skills in combat. Caspian, I have never seen a fighting style quite like yours. Where did you learn?" King Ellis asked.

Caspian grinned slowly, yellow eyes sparkling which made him look even more catlike.

"I was born in Faltaire. Making use of your entire weapon is something we learn early on," he answered.

Killian couldn't help but notice the slight bitterness in his tone. No one else seemed to pick up on it. He frowned.

"And Zev, you handle a sword better than my general!"

General Lee, who sat at the other end of the table sipping wine quietly, let out a small snort.

"Thank you, My King," Zev said with a cocky smirk. He glanced over at the prince with confidence in his smile. Killian averted his gaze quickly.

"Now that the number of Potentials has been reduced significantly, my son will be more available to you. Spend as much time with him as you can," the King announced.

Killian choked on his food, fighting not to openly glare at his father. Ethel appeared beside him with a goblet of water which he guzzled down greedily.

"This is your chance to stand out, don't pass it up," King Ellis continued. "Though some of you have already caught his eye." The King winked at Rem. Those black eyes flickered to the prince whose stomach quivered at the attention.

"I want to make sure you all understand, you must follow the rules or you will be eliminated. If you break the number one rule: touching the prince without permission, the penalty is death by decapitation."

Killian looked down at his half-empty plate. To die for touching him? He never liked that rule and didn't understand why it was enforced in the first place.

The rest of the dinner was spent with idle chatter between the King and whichever Potential piqued his interest. The prince remained silent, keeping his head down, thankful the conversation never forced him to participate. When dinner was finished, Killian was a little nervous going to the bath. There were sure to be a lot of Potentials in there after a day of sweating and no real time to sufficiently clean.

"Don't be nervous," Ethel said as she slid on his bathing robe.

"How can you always tell when I am nervous?" he asked her.

"Because you freeze up and start shaking like a leaf," she laughed. Killian sighed but smiled. "And this time, talk to them. The bath is the best place to get to know them. They'll be relaxed and so will you."

"Easier said than done," Killian muttered, causing the blue attendant to laugh again. Kara, slightly younger than Ethel with pale yellow hair and peachy pink skin met them at the door of the bath. Her periwinkle eyes were gleaming with delight. She and Ethel grabbed the handle of each door calling out, "Good luck!"

They took Killian's cloak and disappeared. Killian inhaled deeply before raising his chin and striding inside with false confidence. The candle lights flickered, setting the room in an intimate dim. He didn't know which of his attendants ordered it, but he would definitely be having a word with them about it.

He glanced around the bath after doing a quick scrub underneath the water spouts. There were thirteen Potentials present. All except Rem. Killian tried not to be disappointed. This was the perfect opportunity for him to check out the others.

Your Consorts are out there right now, Killian thought to himself, trying to calm down and work up the courage to approach the others. He waded through the waters, letting its heat caress his skin. Zeroing in on Zev sitting near the steps with his arms propped on the ledge as he lounged, laughing with Gunner, Rei, and Titus. They all stopped as the prince approached them.

Killian looked at Zev, finally able to see those mesmerizing eyes up close. He was right in assuming they were bright. They glimmered a light teal color, mischief swirling in those cool depths. He was transfixed.

"My Prince," the males greeted with a bow of their heads. Killian nodded at each of them before returning his studious gaze to Zev. He did not enrapture the prince as Rem did, but he was certainly interested.

"I wanted to commend your swordsmanship. You are exceptionally skilled with your blades. I only wish that I might have seen you fight longer," Killian said with a gentle voice.

"Many thanks, My Prince."

Killian shook his head at him. "You do not have to call me that when the King is not around. Killian is fine." He looked at the other males. "The courtesy and compliment extend you all as well. I was impressed with your skills."

He diverted his attention to Gunner, a handsome Incubus with wide, pronounced features and a head full of wavy gray hair. Half his head was shaved with jagged designs trimmed into the side, adding intensity to his squared bone structure. His eyes matched his hair and skin, both an even gray, not dark or light, right in the middle.

"Gunner, your skill with a spear is unlike any I have ever seen."

"Thank you, Prin--er--Killian," he corrected with a slight blush.

Killian complimented the other two as well. They engaged in an easy conversation. The whole time, Killian's eyes kept traveling back to Zev. Trying to remain fair and focused, Killian questioned them all about their home regions, their families, and interests. Killian was pleasantly surprised by the ease of it all. A part of him expected the Incubi to laugh at his awkwardness. Instead, they welcomed him and his quirks. Being included was not something the prince was used to. It made him feel warm inside.

When the bath started to clear out, Zev and Prince Killian remained soaking in the water, close to pruning. The prince found himself drawn to the easy smile and perfect white teeth of the blue Incubus. There was utter confidence in every breath he took. He was everything Killian wanted to be. He was having such a great time; he did not realize they were not the last ones in the bath.

"Haven't you been in here long enough?" Zev growled looking over Killian's shoulder.

The prince turned in his confusion, spotting another Potential lurking across the bath with curly blonde hair and fair skin.

"I was hoping to get my turn to entertain the prince," the other Potential said smoothly. His voice made Killian's stomach twist, a sensation he was unfamiliar with.

"As you can see, he is preoccupied," Zev growled. His expression was hostile and body stiff with tension.

"And I am patiently waiting for my turn."

"Could you remind me of your name?" Killian asked, interrupting their squabbling. Zev tensed even further.

"Jax," the blonde Potential said with a smile.

"Jax," Killian repeated. "I will speak to you soon."

"As you wish, My Prince," he bowed before leaving the bath. When he was gone, Killian focused his attention on Zev who stared after Jax with a bitter scowl.

"Zev? Are you well?" Killian asked, not sure why the blue Incubus had such a negative reaction. It did not seem like it was due to the competition. After all, Zev had made friends with the others. Killian was at a loss.

"I do not believe he is a proper suitor for you, Killian," Zev gritted out, fixing his intense blue eyes on the prince.

Killian frowned. "Saying that will not sway my affections in your favor--"

"It is for your own protection," Zev interrupted. He quickly stood, bowed, and left the bath, leaving the prince confused.

Killian was still in a daze when he dressed for bed thinking back on the earlier altercation.

What did he mean 'for my own protection'? Killian thought. His father would not allow a suitor for him that was dangerous in any way. Zev must be mistaken, there was nothing for him to worry about.

It did please him that Zev seemed to care about his well-being. That was a positive sign of his affections, right? Or was he just trying to narrow the competition? Was he after Killian or the throne? Killian didn't want to be gullible.

The prince huffed in frustration before slipping out of his room to seek out the questionable Potential. He would speak to him and draw his own conclusions.

Two Succubae Warriors stood outside the prince's door. Killian put a finger to his lips and urged them to stay put. One opened her mouth to protest but Killian shot them both a pleading look. They sighed and remained outside his door. He grinned and snuck down the hall, barefoot in his nightclothes.

He would see Jax and prove Zev's suspicions were for naught. His father had chosen these males for him and his father only ever had his best interests in mind. There was no cause for alarm.

Killian wandered down the hall to the wing where the Potentials stayed. Each Potential had their names etched on a golden plate outside their door. He read Rem's name on one of the doors and froze.

Was he there?

There was a curfew at night. He had to be.

Would he be awake?

Killian shook his head as if to clear his thoughts before continuing down the hall. He was just about to turn the corner when he nearly bumped into the very Incubus he was looking for.

"Killian," Jax greeted.

"Hello, Jax. I was coming to find you." Killian's words died off as the Potential took a step closer toward him. He was still wearing the tiny loincloth that King Ellis required all of them to wear in case Killian ever wanted to 'check the package' as his father crudely put. Just thinking about it brought color to his cheeks.

"You are so beautiful when you blush," Jax whispered, caressing Killian's cheek tucking a stray maroon curl behind his pointed ear. Killian's big red eyes grew wide in surprise and mouth parted in shock. Jax brushed his thumb along Killian's plump bottom lip. Stunned to silence, Killian made no move.

Jax was not supposed to touch him.

But...he only touched Killian's face...there was no harm in that, right? Nothing he should *die* over.

Killian cleared his throat uncomfortably and took a step back to put some distance between them. Only, Jax advanced on him, backing him up against the wall.

"Jax--" Killian began, a warning in his tone. Big hands grasped his waist through the thin fabric of his nightclothes, slid along his body until they reached the edge of his tunic to grope his bare butt. A shocked gasp left the prince's lips. His head snapped up to find himself staring into brilliant blue eyes.

They were nothing like the warm teal of Zev's. These were cold and slimy. His gaze made Killian feel sick.

"Jax, you are not supposed to touch me. It is against the rules. The punishment is severe," Killian warned firmly, trying to keep his chin raised and the discomfort off his face. He didn't want to cause a scene and get the Potential in trouble. A misunderstanding wasn't something to lose his life over.

Jax smiled.

"The King wants us to break those rules. How else are we supposed to prove our worth? You are practically a child, Killian. Let me show you how to be a lover."

His hands dipped lower, grabbing each mound of Killian's butt, spreading them apart.

Killian wasn't used to being handled so forcefully. No one had ever touched him aside from family and attendants. Even then it was restricted. They *never* handled him as Jax did.

"Stop this at once, Jax!" Killian tried to push the Potential away, but he was pure muscle and did not budge an inch. His fingers swiped against Killian's puckered entrance causing tightness in the prince's gut and a tingling sensation up his spine. Killian fought to keep the roaming hands at bay while trying to understand the way his own body was behaving.

Killian tried to reach within himself, to the endless well of power in his core but there was something blocking him. Like a wall of granite had risen in his way. There was no way over, none around.

Jax's lips pressed against Killian's ear. "You want to know why the King chose me? Because I have a power that none can compete with. I can nullify all power. Keep reaching little Prince, you won't grasp it."

Jax shoved him harder against the wall, forcing the smaller Incubus to yelp. "Besides, you do not want me to stop. Your slick is starting to drip." He pulled the finger that was just touching Killian's anus to show the prince the clear liquid coating it.

That was from him? But why?

Killian stared, mortified when Jax licked the slick off his finger before returning it to the source. This time, he pushed the finger past the tight ring of muscle. Killian tried to clench his body to push the offending digit out, but it only succeeded in allowing the finger deeper.

A sound he had never made before forced its way from his lips as he fell against the chest that held him hostage. The tingling became burning. His stomach began to quiver again.

It was almost like his *Haise,* but different in its intensity. He could not tell if the feeling or sensations were entirely pleasant.

Confusion led to tears. They gathered in his eyes as the finger pushed and pulled out of him.

"Stop, stop, stop!" Killian sobbed, clawing at the male and trying to get his voice loud enough to draw the attention of the Warriors a few halls overs. He regretted not letting his Warriors accompany him.

Jax shoved his hips against Killian. The prince could feel the hard length of the Potential stabbing against his stomach.

The feeling that drew confusion grew stronger and more intense until Killian's throat constricted as he fought to *breathe.*

Jax brushed against something within the prince causing him to snap. It was the push he needed to scream.

Several things happened at once. Jax was no longer touching him. He heard a loud thud, tiny gasps of air, swords being unsheathed, and the creaking of doors.

The invasion had ceased abruptly.

Why?

Rem had Jax by the neck. Doors had opened while the Potentials in the hall poked their heads out to investigate the noise. There were Warriors everywhere.

Killian hadn't seen any of them appear. His eyes were locked on the blue ones before him. Jax licked his lips, slow and deliberate.

Killian stumbled back, wrapping his arms around his own trembling frame trying to hold his disheveled tunic together. He fought hard to keep the tears that had gathered in his eyes from tipping over, desperate not to show any weakness.

He *touched* him.

He wasn't supposed to *touch* him.

It was against the rules.

"It is against the rules," Killian whispered brokenly, trying to understand why someone...*anyone*...would break that rule.

Rem watched the shell-shocked Prince as the Warriors took hold of the choking Potential and hauled him away. Before Jax could disappear completely, he tossed his head back and laughed. The sound raised the hair on the back of Killian's neck. "You're mine, little Prince, and I won't ever let you go."

Killian's stomach roiled. He thought back to the warning Zev had given. He should have listened. Zev had been around him, around other Incubi. He knew how they thought. He *knew* Jax would break the rules.

"Killian," Rem murmured. Killian looked up at him as he hugged himself against the wall trying to hold himself together as his very foundation crumbled. He hadn't even noticed the hall had cleared aside from his two Succubae Warriors who must have been called over. They remained silent and in the shadows, no doubt cursing the prince for making them abandon their charge. The Potentials had closed their doors. There were none but Rem to witness him fall apart.

"He was not supposed to touch me. I told him to stop. He did not listen. He broke the rules." Killian felt like he had to explain, as if that would somehow make sense of everything. He was awarded no such clarity.

"An Incubi's urge may lead to poor decisions. Not all behave in such a manner, but you must be cautious as if they do," Rem said quietly.

"Would you?" Killian asked, eyes as wide as saucers. If Rem were to say yes, it would crush any part of the naive prince that ever dared to hope.

"No. I would not," he said. Then more quietly added, "My faults lie elsewhere."

He stood there, strong and dependable.

He felt *safe*.

Killian threw himself into the Potential's arms. Rem went rigid in his grasp.

"My Prince, it is unwise to--"

"Please! Please do not let go. I want to be held by you. I want his touch to go away. I want to feel safe," Killian begged, knowing that it was beneath him.

Kings do not *beg*.

Kings do not *plead*.

Killian did both if it meant he would feel safe again.

"My Prince, I will be punished for such inappropriate behav--" Rem began to protest, bewilderment clear in his eyes. He tried to pull away but Killian clung tighter.

"I have chosen you," Killian said softly.

The silence was thick, suffocating. Rem stared at the small quivering Incubus in front of him. Every instinct in him screamed to protect.

The dark Incubus fought the power within him, threatening to take over. For a brief moment, the endless blackness in the depths of his eyes flared orange. It was gone as soon as it came.

The rigidity dissipated and the body encircled in the prince's arms began to soften. Slowly, thick muscled arms enclosed around Killian, pulling him into a warm embrace. It was everything the prince wanted. Everything he dreamed about.

"I do not wish to be alone. Stay with me."

Rem began to pull away again at the prince's words. They were moving too fast. The protest was on his lips, "Prince--"

"Killian," the prince interrupted.

"Killian," Rem amended. He opened his mouth to reason with the prince but once he saw the look of pleading in those pulchritudinous glowing red eyes, he caved. Not even a male with his control could resist the prince.

"As My Prince wishes."

Killian's gut clenched at the words that made his loneliness envelop him further.

Rem followed behind the two Warriors who began to lead the way back to Killian's room. They were on high alert now that a threat had been discovered and did not want to let the same thing happen twice. Killian started to follow but his knees were still shaking from the frightening encounter causing him to trip. Rem was there in an instant, catching him before lifting the prince into his arms and cradling him to his chest.

Killian snuggled closer. He was so warm.

The prince listened to the heavy beat of Rem's hearts through his chest as he was carried back to his room.

Rem opened the bedroom door and closed it swiftly behind them. He set the prince down on the bed, taking extra care to fix the crumpled tunic. When he climbed into the dark red sheets of the bed that had been empty for such a long time, Killian finally allowed himself to smile.

Rem's hair spilled across the pillows and blankets like ink. His blackness was a solid shadow amongst the deep sultry red.

Killian hurried to crawl beside him and into those capable arms. With Killian's face inches from Rem's, he could gaze into the alluring face that was now his forever.

Was it wrong to only want beautiful Incubi as his Consorts?

Killian reached to stroke Rem's cheek with his palm. "How did you know?"

Rem knew what he meant without having to explain it further. The male blinked at the prince with an expression on his face that Killian was unable to decipher.

"I sensed it."

"Sensed it?" Killian repeated, hoping he would elaborate, but the male said nothing else. They lay in silence.

Killian felt safe in Rem's arms and thought the unfamiliar feelings were gone for good. But they came back with vengeance, plaguing his dreams. The memory played over and over again until his subconscious could no longer bear it, waking the prince with a whimper.

Rem was awake and alert immediately.

Killian curled around himself, helpless little cries leaving his lips and concerning the Consort in his bed further.

"It will not go away. Why will it not disappear?" Killian whispered shakily. His voice quivered with tears Rem knew he would fight to withhold.

"What is it?" Rem asked, his normally deep voice even huskier with sleep. It made the tingles in Killian's body spread again.

"It will not go away!" Killian shouted, teeth clenching, making his jaw ache.

It was not the physical feeling alone that unnerved the Incubus Prince, but the lack of understanding that threw him. He was used to being in control of a situation. It was something he had to be familiar with as future King. But this? This was uncharted territory. The sensations overwhelmed him, taking control of his mind and his mobility. His fear of incapacitation was becoming a reality. It terrified him.

"What is it that you wish to go away?" Rem asked, but every time he spoke it only pushed Killian further over the edge. His anus throbbed and wetness trickled from within him, soaking his clothes. It was *disgusting*.

Slick, Jax had called it.

Killian's fingers dug into his palms, the nails slicing into the fleshy bit leaving crescent-shaped indentations.

"I do not understand what is happening to me. I wish for it to stop," Killian ground out.

Rem felt behind the prince to the wetness of his clothes before rising from the bed and leaving the room. He returned a few moments later with a dampened cloth. Handing it to Killian, he reached inside the armoire to pull out another tunic. He laid it on the bed beside Killian before turning to give the prince some privacy, though he did not need to now that he was a Consort. Killian appreciated the gesture.

Coming to, from his frozen state, Killian used the cloth to wipe himself clean and traded his soiled clothes for fresh ones. Rem grabbed the dirty cloth and tunic, leaving them by the door for Kara and Ethel to retrieve in the morning.

Guiding the prince back to the bed, Rem held him much tighter than before. His words were surprisingly gentle. "You will understand the feeling in time. It is not something to fear."

"Do you...know what it is?" Killian asked softly, murmuring against the muscular chest he was pressed against.

"Yes."

Killian relaxed, settling in even closer to his chosen.

He didn't think he could stop being afraid but if Rem understood...then he trusted it was nothing to fear.

Chapter
3

The morning was a bit of a mess.

When Ethel and Kara arrived to awake the prince for his morning routines, they were quite shocked to see him in the arms of one of his Potentials. The night guard must have switched otherwise they would have been informed.

"Prince Killian! This is--" Ethel started, her eyes wide with shock.

"He is my first chosen," Prince Killian reassured sleepily. His lavender body was flush against the dark Incubus, face tucked underneath the sharp jaw of his new lover. Rem remained unperturbed by the intrusion, staring only at the prince, running lazy fingers up and down his spine.

Killian shivered at the delicate touch which did not go unnoticed by his watching attendants.

"You haven't shared your *Haise* with him, have you?" Ethel prodded in a hushed voice.

Killian blushed heavily, "No!"

Kara and Ethel both gave a sigh of relief.

"Well, I guess we better start making the preparations. Kara, will you let Lisa know? I'll have to whip something up for his chosen."

Both attendants flitted about with purpose. Ethel sewed silk black pants with a gold chain belt and leather straps around the legs for Rem. It was amazing how fast she worked and designed.

Killian watched his first chosen after he was dressed. Rem held his gaze. The space between them crackled with energy like an electric current. The spell was broken only when Kara came rushing in to inform them that they were to see the King immediately.

When Rem was finished being dressed, he plaited his hair until the tip reached the end of his boot encased calves. He looked powerful, divine, and every bit of a King. Seeing him like this...Killian knew he made the right choice. This was a sign from the Clouds above.

The pair were escorted to the throne room quickly. The King and Consort Queen sat on their thrones while the Royal siblings and Consort mothers were seated on their lower pedestals.

King wore no expression, which was strange and alarming. Killian was used to seeing his father smile, this new serious look frightened him. The prince fought to keep his shoulders from hunching.

Rem didn't look shaken in the slightest. He wore confidence like a cloak. It seeped from his every pore.

"Father," Killian bowed. Rem following the gesture.

"I see you have chosen a Consort," King Ellis stated, gray eyes flicking to Rem before settling back on his son.

Killian's head dipped.

"Yes, Father."

"Excellent choice, but it is a bit soon, yes?"

Killian met his father's eye and held his gaze.

"I will not let him go, Father."

Finally, the King smiled.

"I understand. But you will do well in choosing your other four. Do not let your...*infatuation* with one prevent you from acknowledging the others."

Killian nodded, relief flooding through him.

The doors opened and twelve Potentials lined up beside the thrones. Lisa escorted Rem and the prince to Killian's throne, settled between his mother and father. Rem took his position at the prince's side, standing at alert with his hands clasped behind his back.

Another door on the opposite end of the room and guards came in escorting a battered Jax. Killian tensed at the sight of him, but relaxed when he felt a large warm hand rest on his shoulder. Rem offered the subtle comfort and reassurance he could without drawing attention to the prince's small moment of weakness.

Jax was stopped in the center of the throne room. A few servants rushed in, placing a large block in front of them with a battle axe leaning beside it before backing away.

The King's voice rang out loud and clear.

"Last night my son, Prince Killian Innis, heir to the throne of Incubi and future ruler of Astoria, was assaulted by this Potential: Jax Winnigh of Calla. The number one rule was broken, and he shall endure his punishment: death."

The attendants gasped and murmured. Killian was surprised that they were not already informed of all the chaos caused last night. Surely rumors must have spread? Killian felt ill at the memory.

There was something strange about the atmosphere. He couldn't quite place his finger on it, but he felt uneasy. There was something off.

Prince Killian ignored the focused leer Jax directed at him. Instead, his eyes were fixated on the axe. It felt significant to him somehow. What was it?

"Additionally, my son has chosen one of five Consorts. Rem, will you do the honor of executing the attacker of your future King and lover?" The King continued, gaze fixed and...expectant.

Rem stared at the King then briefly at Jax before he gave a firm nod, descending down the throne. The moment his hand left Killian's shoulder, the apprehension within the prince grew. Each step his Consort took away from him, twisted his gut.

Something was not right.

Jax's gaze was now trained on Rem. The hatred in his eyes burned, Killian could feel the scalding heat from several yards away.

He parted his lips to speak but had no idea what to say.

Rem reached the guards and the moment they moved to place the prisoner on the block, Killian remembered.

With Rem as the exception--and probably Caspian too even though he never admitted it--every Potential excelled with a specific weapon. Jax's weapon of choice was the axe.

Bright blue wings burst from Jax's back, spraying blood in the eyes of the guards causing them to loosen their grip. Jax made a grab for the axe.

Killian watched in horror, fists clenched at his sides, playing out the entire scene. Jax would grab the axe...he would slay Rem. Rem was unarmed.

Rem was unarmed.

The prince was tempted to cover his eyes, unable to watch his future lover be gutted right before him. But that was not how the scene played out.

Jax had grabbed the axe but his distraction in reaching for a weapon had cost him.

Rem was not unarmed. The Incubus was a living breathing weapon.

Before anyone registered the movement, Rem appeared behind Jax, grabbing each of his exposed wings with a bare hand. With one swift move, he tore the wings from Jax's back. The sound of wet thick gore splattering on the marble floor echoed in the room.

Jax howled in pain and rage.

Wings were as vital the Incubi as the blood in their veins. They were a direct connection to their life source. Damaged wings meant a shorter lifespan. No wings at all? It was the worst way to go. Slow and excruciating.

It was foolish of Jax to expose such a vulnerable part of himself, but Killian understood the strategy. Had anyone but Rem been down there, Jax would have slain them all. No one would expect him to expose his wings, it was the perfect distraction. The guards had been too stunned to move, blinded by the blood splashed in their eyes.

But Rem was not phased. Such a desperate trick would not deter him.

Killian frowned suspiciously. The rest of the room was transfixed by the twitching Incubus at Rem's feet. The pool of blood surrounding him grew in size by the tick.

The Consorts

It was strange that an axe was brought for the execution when a sword was the standard. Odd that the prisoner's weapon of choice was brought within grabbing distance of him. There was no way he would sit still and be executed. The guards had to have known that an Incubus with nothing to lose would try anything to escape.

Rem held the limp wings, skin slick with blood and gore. He was stared down at Jax. The look on his face was terrifying. Anger did not describe it, but there was something dark within him. It crept behind his eyes, lurking, waiting. And it was powerful.

The Consort reached down and plucked the axe from Jax's immobile hand. With grace and precision that could only come from years of vigorous training, Rem swung the axe high. Though bleeding out, Jax was still conscious. His eyes widened in horror as Rem brought the blade down so hard it embedded itself in the marble flooring with a loud crack. The stone split where the axe struck. Hundreds of fissures spread from the point of contact.

Jax's head rolled slightly. Muscle and bone shone through his severed neck and head. Eyes that were once bright blue now dulled.

The urge to vomit was overwhelming but Killian tightened his gut, refusing to make a fool of himself.

The spell cast over the room broke and suddenly the servants were in motion, cleaning up the gore and hauling away the body.

Servants rushed toward Rem, wiping away the blood.

The Potentials were uneasy as they looked on. All except one.

Zev studied the spot where Jax's body laid, then focused his gaze on Killian with an expression that was almost sad. Unable to bear the intensity of it, Killian averted his eyes.

Rem made his way back to Killian's side cleaned of all blood.

"I hope this dissuades any more attempts on my son without his consent," the King concluded then dismissed everyone for breakfast.

With his new rank as Consort, Rem ate with the Royal family.

The family couldn't stop staring at him, excitedly eating their food while sneaking peeks. Killian didn't know how anyone could eat after watching someone be slaughtered not even an hora ago.

"You will be weak if you do not eat," Rem murmured.

Killian nodded absently, continuing to pick at his food.

When breakfast finished, Killian ordered all Potentials to meet him in the library. He walked there with Rem at his side. They murmured quietly until Killian made his appearance. The prince had their attention immediately.

"This may come as a surprise," Killian stated, gesturing to his first chosen mate. "I assure you that choosing Rem will not impact the time I spend getting to know the rest of you."

"My Prince, it was no surprise at all. We knew he would be chosen," Caspian said with an easy smile. "As long as we have the opportunity to be chosen, it matters not. You do not owe us an explanation for every mate you choose."

Killian nodded, grateful for their kindness. But he was a bit unnerved that all could see his attraction to Rem, especially when he was sure it was one-sided. The affection he received could very well be the result of caution. No one would risk the King's anger and to reject his son would surely cause such a reaction.

But that meant he couldn't trust any of their affections. How was he to know who truly wanted him and who simply feared the King's wrath? Which did Rem fall under?

Killian felt hollow. He cleared his throat and returned his attention to his Potentials.

"Is there anyone here that does not wish to participate any further in the Consort Ceremony?"

Killian met silence.

"Being a Consort is not a task you should be shackled to. My Consorts will be my partners, my companions, my confidants, my *everything*. But they must *want* to be my everything. I do not wish to force anyone into this. If you do not wish to be here, if I do not appeal to you in any way, you will not be punished, and you may leave." Killian tilted his head in Rem's direction. "The same applies to you as well."

No one moved.

A Potential whispered, "Is this a test?"

Killian sighed a little sadly.

"Many of you, perhaps even all of you were forced into submitting your profiles by order of the King. And to defy our King is immediate execution. But I am telling you now, this is your out. There are no strings attached. If you wish to go home, you may do so, and I will send you off with well wishes. There will be no punishment."

Killian waited again.

Finally, a Potential named Jagger stood before coming to Killian and bowing.

"I am sorry, Prince Killian. I have a Succubus waiting for me at home."

Killian smiled at him kindly, thankful for his honesty.

"I wish you both the best."

Jagger left with another bow.

The prince returned his attention to the rest of the room.

"If you are not attracted to other Incubi, you may go home as well."

No one moved.

"Is it safe to assume that all that remain actually wish to be here. To be with me?"

The group nodded and though that was supposed to relieve him, he still felt lonely. The feeling grew with each passing moment. This wasn't how things were supposed to be.

"I will see you all this evening," Killian said before leaving the library, Rem following like a silent shadow. Before they made it back to Killian's room, the prince stopped his Consort with a hand to his chest.

The prince peered up at the Warrior with those big ruby red eyes of his.

"Rem, do you truly wish to be here?" he asked.

The Consorts

Rem's answer was immediate. "I would not be if I did not." His tone was flat and the answer seemed...trained. It made Killian question how his Consort felt. Who would actually admit that they did not want to be with him? Jagger was the exception because he had someone at home waiting for him. But what of those who were not already involved? What excuse could they give?

None.

Which is exactly why they hadn't. They said they wanted to be with him, but fear makes them speak. Not their true feelings. Why couldn't they just be honest with him?

"I think you are not telling the truth," Killian said firmly.

Rem raised a perfect dark brow at him. The dim lighting in the halls reflected off his pure black eyes.

"And you are able to tell?" he asked, the words a challenge.

Killian wanted to say yes, but he knew the real meaning of his words. And he was right. Killian did not know Rem enough. He did not know the male's habits or personality. He was a stranger even though he was to be Killian's mate for life. It was a scary thing.

"You are right, foolish of me to presume," Killian admitted with a hint of bitterness in his tone, looking away.

The rest of their walk remained silent. When they reached the room, Kara and Ethel were there, directing servants to bring in a small case of intricate gold collars.

There were several styles of collars in the case and Killian had the suspicion that they were not all Rem's. Were they making predictions on who he would choose next? Surely not.

But as he saw the older Succubus point and giggle, he knew that they were indeed.

Killian's fingertips brushed over the glass, admiring all of the different golds. Some were large, some tight and fitted. His eyes caught on a simple circlet with antique gold and one large ruby in the center. He opened the glass and pulled it out. It was perfect.

All Consorts were required to wear collars. It was Incubi custom. It showed their loyalty to the crown and the heir's or ruler's ownership of them. It was a small indication that they were off-limits. Of course, the crowns they would also wear would clarify as well.

Killian turned to Rem with excitement, only to pull up short when he noticed the look of distaste on Rem's face. It was slight and barely noticeable, as were all of Rem's expressions when he bothered to show any. It made Killian hesitate, smile faltering.

Ethel caught the look and scowled.

"Bow," she hissed uncharacteristically at the Consort.

Rem stared her down before slowly descending to his knees allowing Killian to clasp it around his neck. It fit perfectly. Killian gave him an apologetic smile.

"Lord Rem, your training as Consort begins within the hora. Come with me," Ethel said, leading the Consort back out of the room leaving the prince alone with Kara.

The attendant smiled at the prince warmly. "You should be with your other Potentials. They'll be eagerly awaiting which Consort you'll choose next."

"I do not think that is the case. I do not think any of them wish to be here, Rem included. They will not tell me so because my father threatened them. The grotesque display we witnessed earlier did not help matters either," Killian sighed.

The prince wilted as he sat on the edge of his bed.

Kara frowned.

"Nonsense, they will definitely wish to be with you. And sure, they may not be in love with you yet, but that takes time. You all will grow to love each other. You just have to give them a chance and they you. Love is difficult but so rewarding when shared. Be patient, Your Highness."

The prince sighed again before heading off to his own training, leaving his attendant humming a happy tune as she straightened up the room.

King Ellis was waiting for him in the study. Queen Jessa usually taught Killian's lessons on Royal customs. His father took over only when he wasn't too busy running Astoria.

He was seated at the head of a long mahogany table. A pile of documents were spread out around him. When the prince entered the room, the King smiled widely at him. When King Ellis noticed Killian's less than thrilled expression, the smile dimmed.

"You look troubled. What ails you?" he asked.

"I am finding it difficult to choose my Consorts when it seems none of my Potentials actually wish to be here," Killian answered with a sigh, joining the King at the table.

He ran his fingers through his maroon locks, huffing in frustration.

"Who said that? What was their name? I'll--" the King's eyes glinted angrily and Killian knew he was going to resort to violence again.

"No, Father. No threats. That is what started this in the first place. And it was not the Potentials who said anything, they would not dare and that is precisely the point. They refuse to speak in opposition of anything because they fear angering you. Because of that, I cannot be sure any will actually come to love me. How can I trap someone like that? It is cruel."

The King's brow furrowed. "Killian, love isn't something that happens instantly, it grows and it takes time. You must be patient, and you will all learn to love each other."

Killian rolled his eyes with an exasperated groan. "Kara said the exact same thing," he huffed.

The King's eyes twinkled and he winked. "Wise woman, that Kara."

Killian sighed again, not happy at his father's response which only made the King laugh. The King was the only one Killian was allowed to be informal with when they were alone. He could with his attendants too but not completely. He loved the time spent with his father. Where his siblings and mothers kept their distance, the King and Prince shared a connection. It was precious to Killian and he treasured it.

But the time for personal conversations ended and the Incubi delved into the lesson. It stretched for about four horas covering war strategies. The King always warned that though they were at a time of peace, war could be upon them at a ticks notice and they must be prepared for the absolute worst.

The throne is a scary place to sit, Killian thought.

He bet Rem wasn't scared. Or Zev.

Zev.

It surprised Killian that he thought of the blue Incubus as a Consort. Was that a sign? Should he be the next one chosen? He seemed to care for Killian's well-being. He would be considered.

When Killian left the study after his lesson, he had a quick bite to eat in the dining hall. He was heading to the garden when he noticed Faust in the library, reading a book. His paleness was stark against the deep green chaise he sat on. Killian couldn't help but stop to admire him.

Faust looked up from his book with startling black eyes almost identical to Rem's.

"My Prince," Faust greeted when Killian drifted inside.

"Killian," the prince corrected.

"My apologies."

"What are you reading?" Killian asked gesturing to the thick red leather book in Faust's slender hands. He tilted the cover so Killian could see the title.

Barren.

He had not heard of it before.

"What is it about?" Killian questioned curiously.

"A male who has lost his memories and struggles to find reasoning for his existence. It is a very interesting read, I would highly recommend it," Faust answered in that soft, lovely voice of his.

"Do you read a lot?"

"Yes, whenever I can. Back home, I ran the education system for the young. Most of my time was spent stationed in the library."

"Did you enjoy your work?"

Faust smiled gently. "Of course."

"Do you miss it?"

"At times but being stationed in one place limits my access to knowledge. I do not regret my decision to come here. In fact, I am relishing in the new information that I have acquired since leaving. It is a blessing."

Killian wondered if Faust felt forced to say that or if he truly meant it.

"Do you doubt my answer?" Faust asked with a slight tilt of his head and a knowing smile. Killian looked away guiltily.

"I do," he said quietly.

"Why are you so sure that no one wants to be here with you?"

"I cannot imagine a reason you would want to stay. I have been sheltered my entire life and do not understand some of my own emotions or bodily reactions. Who would want to be shackled to a person like that for the rest of their lives?"

"Is that not our purpose then? To teach you the ways of the Incubi and further your understanding of this species in order for you to better rule it?" he asked sounding sensible. It made Killian feel silly.

"Your purpose is to love me," Killian whispered brokenly.

Faust paused with a puzzled look. "We have only been here a few weeks; love does not come that quickly."

"I have fallen in love with Rem quickly," the prince protested with a matter-of-fact tone.

"You have fallen in lust with Rem," Faust corrected.

Killian frowned, confusion plastered all over his face. "Lust? What is that?"

"Instinctual physical and carnal desire."

"Desire? I am unfamiliar with the word being used in that context."

Faust smiled patiently.

"You were attracted to his looks, his aura, but there is no way that you know him as a person. You cannot love what you do not know. He is a very powerful and desirable person. I even find myself attracted to him." Faust's voice lowered at his admission. "But that is not love."

"How can you be so sure?"

"Experience. Lust is sometimes that first step to love. Just because you lust for him now does not mean you will not grow to love him later. You must be patient."

There it was again. It was starting to annoy Killian how everyone continued to throw the word at him. He had waited for twenty-three years already. He was patient enough; it wasn't fair he had to wait even longer.

Killian gazed into Faust's black eyes for a long time before asking, "Do you think that you could grow to love me?"

"I believe I could grow to love you," Faust answered warmly.

That was what Killian wanted to hear. He smiled at the Potential before taking his leave. If Faust could grow to love him, that means Rem could too, right?

Though Faust and Rem are two completely different individuals. Killian was unsure if he could put them in the same category.

Rem chose that moment to walk down the hall. Killian grinned at him, running to take the Consort's hand in his own. It was warm and calloused from years of rigorous training, completely enveloping Killian's. Taking it in stride, Rem held Killian's hand tightly.

"How was your training?" the prince asked as they continued on their way.

"Informative," he replied.

"Do you think it will be difficult? Ruling beside me, I mean."

"As it was only my first day, I cannot presume it will or will not be."

The Consorts

"I think you will do well," Killian said happily, giving the Consort's hand a little squeeze.

When they reached the room, Ethel was waiting to undress them for the bath. It had grown far later much quicker than Killian thought. He had forgotten about this part. He would be undressing in front of Rem. He was a chosen Consort and therefore, allowed to see the prince in the nude. It made Killian a bit self-conscious. Would his body please Rem?

Ethel began removing his clothes. The whole time, he could feel the heavy weight of Rem's gaze. It made Killian's skin heat up and groin tingle.

But Ethel quickly draped the robe over his frame, shielding him from Rem's intense stare. The prince peeked from the corner of his eye as Ethel began undressing Rem. His body was delightful, ripped to perfection. The raised marks of magix only added to his allure.

Killian refused to let his gaze wander past Rem's hips no matter how much his curiosity begged him. He was still too afraid to be that bold.

Ethel opened the door for the pair and led them to the bath. Fortunately, there were no Potentials bathing at the time. They had the entire bath to themselves.

"I will stand watch outside the door to make sure you are not disturbed. If you wish to remove your robes, you are free to do so," Ethel said shooting the prince a sly grin.

"Thank you, Ethel," Killian mumbled, face growing hot.

She winked before closing the door behind her.

The prince and Consort quickly scrubbed off at the water spout, keeping their robes on. Rem descended into the water with Prince Killian following close behind him. They sat beside each other on the ledge.

The water caused the thin material of the Consort's robe to cling to his skin, parting in the middle to reveal his glorious chest.

Killian ached to touch it again.

Rem watched him with knowing eyes. The prince was still so new to intimacy, he had no idea how to hide the unbridled lust in his gaze. "You may touch me," Rem told him.

Killian's plump lips parted in awe before he shook his head, uttering a small. "I do not wish to make you uncomfortable."

"I am not," Rem said.

Killian peeked at him from his long dark lashes before scooting a little closer to his chosen. His hand was moving before he could control it. Embarrassed, he started to pull back. Noticing his hesitation, Rem grabbed Killian's retreating hand and placed it on his chest. The prince's heart fluttered.

Rem's obsidian eyes never left Killian's. They bore into his being, tracing every move he made, pulling apart his soul with every tick. They played a dangerous game, close to igniting a flame that would rage and ruin.

As Killian's fingers dipped over Rem's skin, his breath hitched. Rem's face was so close. And his *smell*. Gods above, his smell was absolutely *intoxicating*.

Rem leaned closer, enough that the heat of his skin brushed Killian's. The prince panted at the close proximity.

"I am an Incubus and I am male. Even I cannot refuse to answer when you call me like this," he said, deep voice dropping several octaves making Killian's lower body clench. The tingling in his groin had returned sevenfold and the strange sensation was upon him again. Similar to his *Haise* but never this intense.

"Call you?" he whispered, unable to make his voice project. His own red jeweled eyes were transfixed on Rem's impossibly full lips. They beckoned him, throwing his body into motion until the prince sat atop Rem's lap, straddling his waist.

Killian wanted to be embarrassed--he *should* be--but his body was moving on its own accord and there was naught he could do to stop it. He just wanted to be close to Rem. He wanted to feel the male to an extent he did not understand. Why wasn't he close enough? He *needed* to be closer.

"Your nature as an S-Level Incubus is influencing your actions. You found a strong suitor and you want to mate. It is your instincts that chose me; urged you on. As your body calls, mine responds," Rem informed, grabbing hold of Killian's hip tightly.

Killian could feel Rem's body through the thin fabric of their robes. If only he could get closer, feel more of him.

Taking a chance, Killian nudged his robe apart, pressing his bare chest against Rem.

The Consort hissed, claws unsheathed, digging into the prince's skin. The new sensations of it all enraptured Killian. Distracted by his needs, he was unprepared when the tingles returned.

And the slick.

Memories he fought hard to keep down resurfaced, causing Killian to freeze up. Rem gently pulled the prince's hands back to his chest. He held them there, peering up at Killian.

"Do not be afraid. It is normal. What you are feeling is supposed to happen and will occur much more often now that you are around your future Consorts. Do not fear it. Embrace it. That is what it means to be an Incubus."

"It is dirty--"

"It is not," Rem growled firmly. Killian blinked at him, shock on his youthful face.

"I do not wish to dirty you," he choked, still afraid of the tingles that threatened to consume him. The heat and stickiness made him feel unclean.

"You will not. Embrace it," Rem coaxed.

Killian took a deep breath and let his hands slide up Rem's chest then around his neck. His fingers curled in the silkiness of Rem's hair as the male's breath washed over him.

It was just the two of them.

Their faces drew closer.

And closer.

"Do you desire me?" Killian whispered, just a breath away from Rem's lips.

"I do," Rem answered huskily.

"Do you think you will grow to love me?"

"Perhaps."

The air was thick. Heavy with tension. Killian's heart beat wildly. The only sound to be heard was their ragged breathing. Killian started to pull back, but Rem was swift, tugging him forward and connecting their lips.

Killian fell against Rem, full of passion and terror. Rem's lips melted against his own, taking charge. The prince moved his inexperienced ones against Rem's sloppily, trying to mimic the movements. He wanted to feel more of him. He wanted to be drunk on him.

The prince pushed Rem's robe off his shoulders and let it fall into the warm waters of the bath with a plop. Rem held him tighter. Killian's back arched toward him rubbing his lower half against Rem's. Gods above, he wanted to be *one* with him.

Rem pulled away, restraining the prince with strength Killian had no hope of contending. Killian's big red eyes were glazed over, breaths coming out in uneven pants. It took a moment for the confusion to surface.

Why did he stop?

"You are not ready to go any further," Rem told him.

"Yes I--"

"No, you are not. Had we gone any further, you would have felt sensations much more intense than what you felt with Jax. It will scare you. You must first understand your arousal before you can go any further."

"Arousal?"

"It is what you were just feeling. It is what causes your slick to produce. And it is the basis for your *Haise*."

"Will you teach me?" Killian asked with desperation. He hated not understanding these foreign feelings.

Rem stroked his cheek with his palm. Killian leaned into his warmth, eyes fluttering and lips parting.

"I will teach you, but it is not my job alone. It is the job of all your Consorts, so you must find them first before you gain a real understanding."

Killian nodded, feeling heavy all of a sudden. He slumped against Rem, cheek resting on his broad chest while he listened to the beats of his hearts, lulling him into a trance. The ridges of magix pressed into his skin. He hoped they left a mark.

They soaked for a few moments more before Rem carried Killian out of the bath easily, wrapping him in a towel after drying them off and proceeded to the bedroom. Ethel's eyes widened in alarm when she saw them, but Rem assured her that the prince was just tired.

Killian didn't want dinner, which meant he was left alone as his Consort went to the dining hall with the Royal family. He thought about how interesting dinner would be without him there--how Rem would react to questioning--but the curiosity was short lived.

Curling into a ball, he clutched the silky red sheets close. It was different now. He had something to look forward to. The moment Rem walked through the door and joined him. Rem would hold the prince close and Killian would fall asleep on his chest, listening to Rem's hearts beat in sync, knowing that no matter what; he would not be alone. Not anymore.

But why did he still feel as if this happiness was fleeting and soon, the males he had begun to adore would all leave him? Would Rem leave? *Could* he leave?

The possibilities left Killian restless, anxious for Rem to return but he hadn't, not for a while. Killian waited and waited until the anxiety won and he pushed the sheets off his frame, slipping out the door in the hall. There was still a bit more time before curfew.

Warriors followed Killian silently, disappearing into the shadows of the hall.

The floors were cold against the prince's bare soles, but he ignored it. There was no true destination, just the desire to clear his head; rid himself of these confusing thoughts. Waiting for Rem would only make them worse. He'd drive himself mad with all of his insecurities before Rem came back and would be nothing but an empty husk of self-doubt.

Killian hated being heir.

He wanted the freedom of his siblings' understanding. He was tired of being sheltered. Gilra probably knew what arousal was. Ian too. Pierce probably experienced desire. And who knows how far any of them got with other Incubi or Succubae. They were younger than him but knew so much more than he did. It wasn't fair!

But he had no right to complain. He wouldn't wish his fate on anyone. He was glad it was his burden to bear and not his siblings. It was his and his alone. No one could do it but him.

Killian inhaled sharply, fighting the burning in his eyes and constriction in his throat. He would not cry.

Kings do not cry.

"Prince Killian."

The prince jumped, startled by the voice.

It was Zev.

Somehow, Killian had wandered into the sparring room. It was a small space attached to the arena.

Zev stood in the dimly lit room, the glow of light bouncing off his pale blue skin. His body was impressively sculpted but still managed to remain lean. It was the body type that called to the prince the most.

Zev's long blue hair, streaked with white, was pulled back in a loose ponytail and a thin sheen of sweat clung to his skin.

This close, Killian could see a patch of white in his left eyebrow that he had not noticed before. The prince studied Zev's deep-set eyes, long lashes, and small beauty mark above his lip on the right side. He admired how Zev's bottom lip was fuller than the top, giving him a permanent pouty look.

He was incredibly handsome.

"Zev," Killian breathed. "I did not see you there."

"As I could tell," Zev chuckled.

He hadn't anticipated running into any of the Potentials. He glanced around the room in case there was another there, but it seemed as though Zev was training alone.

"I thought the Potentials were still having dinner?" Killian asked.

"They are," he replied.

"But?" Killian prompted.

"But I was not hungry."

Killian sank into himself a little before uttering a quiet, "Me neither."

"Did you come here to train?" Zev asked, gesturing behind himself to the sparring circle. Killian hesitated but nodded.

The smile Zev gave him was heart-stopping. "Would you like to spar with me?" He offered a hand.

He was giving Killian a choice but also asking permission.

Can I touch you?

Killian stared at the outstretched hand covered with hardened calluses. He almost accepted it until he remembered Jax. Feeling uneasy, the prince brushed past the Potential's hand and headed to the weapon storage. His answer was loud and clear.

No.

Zev didn't seem bothered though, perhaps understanding Killian's fear and hesitation after the last incident. Or so Killian thought. He did not see the brief flash of anger in those light teal eyes. He did not notice the arrogance that masked it. He had no idea how his small rejection hurt Zev.

Instead, Killian focused on grabbing a weapon. His choice was a double-edged longsword. He felt the most comfortable with it. His inherited sword had a similar weight and feel to it.

Zev grabbed his already prepped short swords, a carefully placed smile on his face.

Killian studied the male for a moment, as they stretched, then decided to make conversation. This was his chance to get to know him.

"Where are you from?" the prince asked, though he knew the answer.

"Tarr."

Tarr was three seas over from Heltzig in the North of Astoria. The region practically bred Warriors. The General of Astorian Army was from Tarr. No wonder Zev handled his swords with such expertise. It must have been hard for him to leave.

"I did not intend to force you from your home."

Zev's eyes slid over to Killian, but he did not turn his head. "I came here of my own free will, Prince Killian. King's decree or not, I wanted to be your Consort."

"Wanted?" Killian questioned with worry in his tone.

"Want," Zev amended, turning to face the prince.

Killian stared up at him with hopeful eyes. "Do you think you will grow to love me?"

Zev leaned toward him but did not dare touch. "Maybe I have already started."

Killian's heart thrummed in his chest.

"Father says that it takes time for love to grow. How can you love me in such a short time?"

"I can't say I love you, but I do feel this need to protect you and maybe that's where it will start. A seed that with enough nurturing will grow strong and plentiful."

Killian's chest constricted, making him inhale sharply. He felt guilty. If he had listened to Zev and stayed away from Jax, he never would have been attacked.

"It was foolish for me not to heed your warning before. I did not think anyone would dare to break the rules and put himself at risk unnecessarily. Thank you for trying to protect me."

"To be honest, I didn't expect you to listen. I just hoped you would. I had no real basis for my accusations other than my gut instinct and a few comments I heard him make. The whole situation does seem odd though."

"Comments? Like what?"

Zev sighed.

"I do not think they are entirely appropriate for your pure mind, but they referenced your body in ways strictly reserved for your chosen Consorts."

Killian frowned in confusion, curiosity piqued.

"It's okay, it doesn't matter now. It has been dealt with."

They both were silent for a moment before leaping into action. Zev seemed a little hesitant in his strikes, taking defense instead of offense but Killian was relentless. He may have a fragile looking build and calm grace, but he was highly skilled in combat. Most who fought him underestimated his small stature and innocent appearance, but he was the future King.

And he knew how to kick ass.

When Zev found himself defending in earnest, he switched from defense to offense.

The pair was surprisingly evenly matched. Zev was quick but Killian was quicker. What Zev had in strength, Killian matched in agility, contorting his body in way Zev could never hope to and would certainly dream of.

They sparred for what seemed like horas, chests heaving and bodies dripping with sweat, stopping only when they were too exhausted to lift their swords.

Zev was grinning. "My Prince, I am quite impressed with your skills."

Killian smiled back. "And I you. But you knew that."

They both laughed.

Killian noticed Zev's loincloth had a tiny tear in it. He frowned.

"You do not have to continue wearing that," he told Zev gesturing to his torn cloth. "I had Ethel stock your wardrobes with something more practical."

Zev smirked at him, "I want to. I'm still hoping that you might 'check the goods' as the King would phrase it."

Killian blushed furiously, "I--"

"It's alright, I don't mind. If anything, I encourage it. Drek may be a prize but I am no cheap competition."

Would it be okay to look?

The King would certainly think so.

Killian glanced around the empty room. The guards were just outside, it gave them a little bit of privacy.

"No one is around," Zev reassured. His voice dropped a few octaves, sounding deliciously breathy. Killian stared up into those light teal eyes and nearly drowned in their depths. He hadn't noticed the Potential get so close, swords discarded.

Zev's eyes were locked with Killian's as he slowly led the prince to the bench on the side of the room. He took Killian's sword, placing it on the rack without ever breaking contact. His body beckoned the prince closer as they sat on the bench. Killian stared at the fabric on Zev's lap. The thought about what lay beneath had his mouth watering.

Killian tentatively placed a hand on Zev's thigh, checking with him to see if it was okay. That lazy smirk stayed firmly in place as he stared Killian down.

Slowly, Killian's hand skimmed over Zev's thigh, brushing the edge of the loincloth.

"Why the hesitation? I'm sure you have seen Rem in the nude by now. Probably even placed your lips upon him if your body's reaction was any indication," he said, a hint of bitterness in his tone.

"I-I have not!" Killian protested.

"Have not what? Seen him? Or placed your lips on him?" Zev challenged, showing a little more of the ugliness beneath the arrogance. The prince was too distracted to notice.

While they may have kissed, Killian was sure Rem's lips were not what Zev was referring to.

"I have not done either."

"Interesting. Stiff even when he won," Zev muttered. Despite what was said, Zev's eyes still urged the prince to continue his exploration.

Killian peeled the loincloth away and sucked in a deep breath.

Zev's most private appendage was the palest blue of his entire body, with dark blue veins and an even darker tip. It seemed stiff, similar to Killian's during his *Haise*. The top shone in the flickering candlelight as if it were wet. It laid there still against his thigh but twitched occasionally. Some strong enough to lift his entire member.

It lay nestled above his soft looking sac, protected by a heavy bush of curly navy hair.

Killian wanted to touch it.

"You can touch me. It is not against the rules."

Those words were fast becoming Killian's favorite.

He let his fingers brush over Zev's length. The male's body trembled as his eyes fluttered shut. Killian held him in his hand, admiring how firm but silky smooth the skin was. His fingers rubbed along the skin in curiosity. They would not close around the girth no matter how hard Killian squeezed. The more the prince touched the blue Incubus, the darker the blunted tip grew, and the stiffer the appendage became.

Killian tapped the small slit at the top, letting the cloudy substance coat his finger.

"What is this?" Killian asked. He had not seen it before, not even from himself.

"Pre-ejaculate fluid, My Prince. It is what appears when an Incubus is aroused," Zev answered. His voice was low and raspy, eyes still closed.

"It does not happen to me," Killian pointed out.

"Your biology is different, My Prince. You are an S-Level Incubus. You produce what is called 'slick' from behind."

Killian was becoming well acquainted with that word.

"It comes before the release of semen which is what gets you pregnant," Zev continued. Killian gasped in horror, yanking his hand away. "But only if it is inside you," Zev chuckled huskily.

"Oh," Killian breathed, bringing his hand back.

The prince gently inspected the appendage with growing curiosity, trying to spot the difference from his own. Meanwhile, Zev fought to keep himself under control. The Potential fisted the bench's cushion, hips jerking up into Killian's hand periodically.

Killian tried to close his fingers around the width of him again, but something snapped in Zev. He grabbed Killian's hand, dwarfing it completely before squeezing it tight around himself. His hips thrust furiously. Killian didn't understand the sudden change, especially when white ropes of fluid spurted from the slit and splattered all over his hand. Some even managed to land on Zev's sculpted abs. This fluid was thicker and opaquer than before. Was this semen?

"What happened?" Killian asked with a frown, pinching the warm and runny substance between his fingers.

Zev was quiet for a few ticks, trying to catch his breath with eyes shut and mouth open.

When he was able to collect himself, he opened his eyes and grinned at Killian. "Sorry, I didn't mean to make a mess of you." He covered himself back up with the loincloth and brought Killian's messy hand to his mouth. Carefully, his tongue darted out to lick the stickiness off. When Killian's hand was clean of it, he let it fall back to the prince's lap and said, "You should wash your hands before going back to bed."

Zev stood and Killian followed. They smiled at each other before going their separate ways. Killian stopped to wash his hands before returning to his room, a wide grin plastered on his face as he tried to process his new discovery.

Rem was in bed.

His hair was a black sea amongst the pillows. Only the sheets covered the lower half, the top was bare and exposed. The Consort turned to look at the prince.

"Where were you?" He asked simply.

"With Zev."

The answer was enough for Rem. He raised the sheets for Killian, inviting him to bed. The prince crawled in beside him relishing in the warmth his body provided. Wiggling a leg between Rem's, Killian's knee grazed his Consort's scrotum.

Rem was naked.

That knowledge made Killian hot. His face heated and anus throbbed. Rem's arms came around Killian's waist as he held him tightly to his body.

"Rem," Killian whispered, longing in his voice.

His Consort did not reply, and it was too dark to see if he was staring at Killian, but the prince felt he had Rem's attention.

"I want to touch you," Killian said.

He managed to nudge a hand between them and grip Rem's member as he did with Zev, desperate to make that fluid appear. Rem was quick to respond, yanking the prince's hand away in a restraining grip.

"No," he growled.

"Rem--"

"No."

And that was the end of it.

Chapter 4

Gilra chattered away to one of her attendants. She smiled broadly, seemingly excited about some big news if the animated way her arms were moving were any indication.

Prince Killian made his way over to them.

The attendant saw him first and dipped into a deep curtsy. Gilra whipped around squealing in excitement.

"Oh, Brother! I'm so excited!"

"What excites you, dear sister?" Killian asked with a confused smile.

"Don't you know? Queen Jessa said we're having a ball! Everyone is coming to it, even those seven seas away! Can you believe it?" she laughed gleefully.

"This is the first time I am hearing of it."

Gilra's mouth formed an 'O' of shock, "I hope I didn't ruin a surprise. You know I can't keep my mouth shut. Anyway, Daddy said he thinks you'll have your four Consorts by the end of next week."

"Next week?"

That was much too soon. He had only chosen one thus far! Had they misled him in their insistence of patience when they meant to force his choices? Why was this the first time he was hearing of it? Surely he should be the first to know when it was his fate being determined?

"You don't look happy, Killian. What's wrong?" Gilra's tone softened as she looked upon him with concern.

Damn it all for letting his mask slip. He was being careless.

"I was not informed of the ball or the time limit on my choosing my life companions. The news is shocking."

"Oh no, brother dearest! There is no rush. The date has not been set; Daddy does not rush you. He just thinks you already have an idea of who you want. He estimates. Especially since your Rem was chosen so quickly."

Killian forced a pleasant smile on his face to hide the anger burning in his chest. How typical of his father inform all but him under the guise of keeping him pure and unbiased. Just the thought made him want to spit.

"But that is just it, sister. I have not the slightest inkling on who to choose next. I have not had the chance to know them all. It is not possible to make a decision so soon."

"You did it with Rem," she pointed out.

Killian sighed. "Rem is different. I was immediately pulled to him like I have been to no other."

"You could if you let it happen. Stop trying to be logical about this. Let your heart guide you. Our instincts never point us in the wrong direction."

He rolled his eyes in a very un-princely manner, but her words did resonate with him.

"Don't overthink it, Kill. Just do what you think is best," she continued before bidding him farewell.

Was that it? Was he trying to make sense of what he did not understand? Could it be that he was waiting for love with no comprehension on how it is received let alone given? Did he expect to fall in love first and choose second?

That would be ideal but was it realistic?

He stood there for a moment in the empty hall; forlorn.

"I do not know what is best, sister. And I fear I might make an irreversible mistake."

He took his leave then, contemplating hard before settling on the dismissal of four more Potentials, including Rei, the Potential Gilra was smitten with. Perhaps she would get what she wanted.

That left him with six Potentials and one Consort. He'd have to decide the four who stayed and the two that did not.

He liked Caspian. He was funny and entertaining. He always put smiles on others' faces. He was extremely charismatic. But there was something forced about his smiles. Whether it was good or bad, the prince had yet to determine. Was Caspian insincere?

Titus was warm and inviting, Killian felt comfortable around him, but he thought more like a soldier than a King.

Then there was Orion who was incredibly capable, and would make a great King. He was intelligent, skilled with many weapons, but there was a softness to him that was unsuitable for the viciousness of politics.

Zev and Killian shared a special connection. The Potential was confident and possessive, which he enjoyed, but could see it posing a problem in the future. One could not be possessive when they are meant to share with four others.

Killian hadn't spent much time with Drek but there was something that kept him from sending the male home. Something he planned on exploring. He was stunning without a doubt, but similar to Zev, there was an arrogance about him and in the way he carried himself. Killian had to be certain it would not negatively affect their future.

Faust was the kindest and most compassionate of them all. He was wise and charming. But Killian could not see the warrior in him that was necessary in becoming his Consort. Sure, Faust could fight, but he lacked the ruthlessness needed for victory in battle.

It was hard to choose and Killian wasn't sure he even wanted to, but there could only be five.

Who would be his next choice?

Maybe he could get some perspective.

Killian poked his head into the library to find Faust, but it was empty. Perhaps he was taking a bath?

The prince redirected his path in that direction. When he peeked inside, he did not see Faust, but the bath was not empty.

Caspian.

"Greetings, My Prince," he purred, reclining in the water. "You look puzzled. May I be of any assistance?"

His voice was rich and silky. Each word seemed to roll off his tongue.

"I am in search of Faust, have you seen him?"

Caspian raised an elegant red brow before a slow grin blossomed on his face. "No, I can't say I have."

He then draped himself over the edge of the bath, folding his arms and leaned his chin on them. He was still smiling with a mischievous twinkle in his yellow eyes. "You're not planning on choosing him to be your Consort, are you? I haven't gotten the chance to impress you yet."

Killian smiled at him.

"No, that is not it. I had a question, but do not worry. I have been paying attention to you all, even if it appears as though I am not."

"Are you close to choosing your next Consort?" Caspian asked.

Zev popped into his mind immediately.

"Maybe." Killian admitted and suddenly, his question for Faust was forgotten by the desire to see Zev. "Would you happen to know where Zev is?"

Caspian pouted, which surprisingly suited his handsome face. "My Prince, it seems you are looking for everyone but me. I am starting to get offended."

"That is because you are right in front of me," Killian grinned cheekily.

Caspian's pout deepened before it cracked, and he started to smile. "I won't let you forget about me, Prince Killian."

"Oh, I believe you." The prince retreated from the bathing room, listening to Caspian's honied laugh.

If he knew Zev, there were two places he could be. If not the bath, Killian would find him in the sparring room. He slipped into the room passing by the bench where they were intimate. Killian fought the blush threatening to consume him. Instead, he focused on the two males in the center of the room. One was a warrior from the Army. The other was Zev.

The Potential held his favorite twin swords in his hands. He was grinning. They both were as they waited for each other's next move.

Killian could see the spring in Zev's step and the excitement vibrating in his bones. He was completely in his element, loving every second of it.

The prince internally startled when they were suddenly in motion. The sound of clanking metal reverberated off the walls. They were quick and deadly. Killian was even graced with a glimpse of Zev's pretty light blue wings. When an Incubus is excited, translucent illusions of their wings may appear.

Zev had the Warrior pinned with a sword to the his neck.

Wow.

Zev grinned, sheathing his sword and offering a hand to the Warrior who was also smiling, a bit surprised that he was bested. Zev was an incredible fighter. They started laughing and talking animatedly about the fight, not realizing that Killian was watching them.

The Warrior happened to glance in Killian's direction and immediately his eyes widened. He fell to one knee with a firm, "Your Highness."

"You may rise," Killian said in acknowledgement. The Warrior stood, bowed, then ducked out of the room.

Zev stood there, sweaty and shirtless with a pair of tight brown leather pants. His hair was tied in a ponytail accentuating his sharp angular features, but not as sharp as Rem's.

"My Prince," he greeted, smiling more gently.

"Killian, Zev," the prince reminded in slight annoyance.

"Killian," Zev amended with a low and silky voice that did things to the prince's body. That made him react in a very certain way. And by the rotten smirk on his face, Zev knew it too. "What brings you here?"

"You," Killian said then blushed and tried to clear his throat. "Er...I was looking for you."

Zev's smirk deepened as he stood before him, leaning just a bit closer. Killian could feel the heat from his skin and smell his earthy musk, like sandalwood and pine. While the pull might not be as strong as the one with Rem, Killian could not deny that he felt something for Zev.

"And how could I be of service to you?" Zev asked, voice dropping lower.

Killian's lips parted as he stared up into his incredibly handsome face. His eyes kept slipping downward to those beautiful blue lips. He was so close.

"I... was just..." Killian couldn't get the sentence to form, his thoughts were scattered. One thing he knew for certain, he wanted Zev to kiss him.

"You were just?" he whispered, leaning even closer. Killian closed his eyes, thinking Zev would close the distance, but his lips remained cold. He blinked. "I can't touch you, Killian. It has to be you who initiates this."

Killian knew this, but there was no way he could be that bold.

To kiss him?

He wasn't even his Consort yet.

Yet...

Was he already chosen?

No. He couldn't be too hasty. He couldn't rush these decisions. He just had to think about this rationally and thoroughly.

Not yet, Zev. Not yet.

But to pass up this opportunity would be foolish right?

Killian leaned in, pressing his lips softly to Zev's. He practically melted into them. They were plump and smooth and everything he imagined them to be.

He moved his mouth carefully over Killian's. Gently, as if he were trying to memorize every sensation of the prince's lips against his. When the Potential's tongue swept over Killian's bottom lip, the prince panicked, confused on what to do next. When Rem kissed him, he didn't use his tongue. This was uncharted territory.

One of Zev's large hands laid on Killian's waist, pulling him closer to the curve of his body while the other cupped his cheek. He pressed the prince tightly to him, pushing his tongue through the barrier of Killian's lips and softly kneaded their tongues together. It was strange but oddly pleasurable. Killian's tongue caressed his curiously as Zev dominated the prince's mouth.

Killian's hands were pressed to Zev's chest, but slowly, he eased them up and around his shoulders, holding him closer.

This wasn't just desire.

It was passion.

It was everything he had ever wanted.

Killian jerked away quickly, almost stumbling in his retreat. Zev watched him with alarm but did not make a move closer to which the prince was grateful.

"Killian, what's wrong?" he asked.

"Nothing...I--" he was out of breath.

Gods, Killian almost caved. He almost asked Zev to be his Consort. It was on the tip of his tongue. He had to swallow it down. He couldn't, not yet. He couldn't make another hasty decision.

"I cannot," Killian breathed,

Zev's expression contorted from confusion to anger before settling behind a mask of arrogance. It was deeply set in his handsome features, from the tightness in his eyes to the stiffness in his jaw. He was hiding his true emotions.

"Zev--" Killian started.

"It's fine," he interrupted. "I must continue with my training, My Prince," he bowed deeply before grabbing his blades and leaving him.

What happened? What did he do wrong?

Killian screwed up and had no idea how to fix it. He knew nothing of love or relationships. He'd never had to deal with them before, not even with his own family. How was he to know what to say or do? How could he prevent something like this from happening?

He was too unprepared.

Killian took a deep breath and left the sparring room. It wouldn't do any good to linger and it might make Zev angrier. He needed his space and Killian needed to figure out what the hell he was doing.

One step at a time...

Killian continued on with his day, spending some time with Titus and Caspian but unable to give them his full attention. He still pondered over what happened with Zev. Confusion quickly became frustration and from that blossomed rage.

Unfortunately, Rem ended up on the receiving end. It started with a demand for a kiss.

"Kiss me," Killian whispered to his Consort.

Without any hesitation, Rem bent forward and pressed his lips to the prince's.

Kissing Rem was different from kissing Zev. Zev held nothing back, but with Rem? Killian felt like there was still a part of Rem that he couldn't reach. It was sweet and gentle, but there was a beast lying in wait, ready to devour him. Killian wanted to coax it out, but Rem was a male of control, making the task next to impossible.

Killian brushed his lips with his tongue the way Zev had done earlier, but Rem was stubborn and did not open his mouth. Instead, he began to pull away.

"Why?" Killian demanded, immediately furious but not really with the male before him. "You are my Consort! Why do you still withhold from me?"

He was so sick of it. He was angry with the distance, the estrangement. And he was lonely. He had been waiting patiently in solitude for twenty-three years. Now, when he finally had his reprieve, he was still isolated.

He wanted this Cloud forsaken loneliness to end.

Shoving away from his Consort and glaring at him, the prince released the anger swirling inside him. Hinges groaned as doors along the hall began to rattle. The subtle flames of the candles in the hall grew bright with fury, climbing along the walls.

"I must disgust you, since you continue to keep your distance. There will never be love between us, will there? I have waited my entire life to end this misery and you are my salvation, yet you abandon me. You keep away. I gave you a choice and you chose me, remember? If you did not want it, you should have left!"

Rem's dark gaze flickered to the doors and the candles before settling on Killian.

"Am I not good enough for you?" Killian seethed. "Too naive, too inexperienced, too needy!"

When Rem didn't respond, Killian deflated. The rattling stopped and the flames calmed. Not uttering another word, he walked into his room and shut the door in Rem's face.

Sitting on his bed, Killian shoved his face in his hands. It was childish of him to explode on Rem especially when he had done nothing wrong. He should say he was sorry but he remembered one of the first lessons he ever received from his father.

Kings do not apologize.

It showed weakness and Killian had showed Rem enough of that. He was still angry.

Angry at Zev for reacting in a way he did not understand.

Angry at Rem for putting distance between them.

Angry at his father for all these damn rules.

But most of all he was angry at himself. Because even after all of this, he still felt that crippling loneliness and it was close to breaking him.

Dinner was uncomfortable to say the least. He had cancelled the lunch in the garden and spent the entire day buried in his studies. Some servants must have heard the prince's outburst because the rumors had spread wildly. It was obvious when the family carefully approached him with conversation.

With his usual lack of tack, Pierce brought up the gossip.

Killian didn't rise to his younger brother's goading, but his fist clenched around his fork tightly enough to leave finger shaped indentations.

Queen Jessa quickly diffused the situation by remarking how close it was to Killian's *Haise* this moon cycle. His emotions were heightened.

That wasn't it at all, but Killian let her say what she wanted. He didn't have the energy to care.

Killian went back to studying after dinner, ignoring curfew. He found himself swept up in the history of fiver great Gods; Perseth,

By the time he put the books away and returned to his room, it was well into the night and everyone was asleep. Killian peeked over at the bed as he dressed in his nightclothes. Rem was fast asleep, displayed like a work of art amongst the spread. His black hair spilled around dark red pillows and matching sheets pooled around his waist. His arm was tucked under his head while the other rested on his sculpted stomach. He looked more like he was modeling than sleeping.

Killian crawled into bed, putting distance between himself and Rem. Enough that they would not touch in the night, even if they rolled over.

The prince curled into himself, feeling cold. He had grown accustomed to Rem's warmth in bed. It was yet another reminder that he did not have anyone but himself. He could rely on no one.

But he should have known the moment the bed shifted Rem would wake. Killian could feel the shifting of sheets and the slightest jostling of the bed. He was unprepared for the arm that had wrapped around his waist, pulling him into the warmth of Rem's body. The Consort's hair draped over him like a satin blanket, smelling of Rem's intoxicating scent.

Yet as tempting as it was, Killian was not so easily forgiving. He was still cross with Rem.

Shifting his body away, Killian restored some distance.

"Killian--" Rem started, voice deliciously husky from sleep.

"Keep your distance. You are good at that," Killian retorted with a petty huff, curling into a tighter ball.

"I am not disgusted by you," Rem said into the darkness.

Killian flinched but remained silent. When the silence between them grew longer, he thought the conversation had ended and settled into the bed.

That was not so.

Killian slid across the bed with force and suddenly his arms were pinned above his head, body trapped underneath Rem's. Killian shivered at the aggressive display.

Rem forced the prince to stare into his solemn black eyes.

"Where I come from, we are not accustomed to letting people in. We stay guarded to protect ourselves and those around us. Should we lose control, we would bring about devastation. We trust no one, are trusted by no one. We are beasts and it is our magix that makes it so. A few days is not enough to change who I am. Be patient with me and know that I am trying," Rem insisted with an edge of desperation coloring his voice.

That was the most emotion Killian had ever witnessed from his Consort. His mask was as impenetrable as Killian's and it made the prince question whether or not he was entirely honest with his words. Maybe he wasn't, but Killian could not tell, and it would be unfair of him to judge with no basis. Lack of expression did not automatically make one insincere.

"It hurts," Killian told Rem, feeling the ache gnaw at his chest.

Rem collapsed onto him, hugging him tight, burying his face into the prince's neck. "I know."

"Kiss me and hide nothing," Killian told him.

Rem hesitated, his body tense above him. As Rem pulled his head back from Killian's neck, he could see the uncertainty bubbling underneath his cool and calm mask.

What was he so afraid of? Why was he unwilling to reveal that part of himself? He had to know no secret would last forever and Killian would find out eventually. Why continue the torture, the suspense, and not just let it out in the open?

"Kiss me," Killian said again.

And this time he did.

He was aggressive in his initial contact, pushing his lips against Killian's in an almost bruising way. Then his fervor faltered, and he was more gentle. He was hiding in the way he lightly molded his lips to Killian's. He avoided entwining tongues. He was lying with his lips and Killian could tell.

"You are hiding behind your control, my Warrior."

He would let him in or they would be nothing.

"Again," Killian told him.

Rem kissed him again. He hesitated but was much more passionate than his previous gentle, controlled kisses. Rem was terrified of letting go.

Killian wrapped his now free arms around Rem's neck, opening his legs to let him fall between them. He fell against him like a wave crashing upon the shore. Their bodies moved like silk, gliding along each smooth surface. There was liquid grace with each grind and writhe to their bodies. They were alive. More alive than either of them had ever felt. As the intensity in their movements increased, Rem let go.

He was a male starved, hungering for the sweet taste of another. Of a lover. The beast inside him was ravenous, devouring the first lick of body heat.

Rem's body began to burn against Killian's, heating like sand in the sun. It was hot enough to hurt, but there was always a bit of pleasure in a little pain.

The raised swirls across his chest and arm were scalding hot, branding Killian's skin. The prince gasped at the feeling, not sure if the pain was too much or not. But Rem did not give him a chance.

He yanked himself out of Killian's grip and fell away from him on the bed. His chest was heaving as frantic breaths left on his lips.

His skin...was glowing.

His skin blossomed with thousands of colors. It was like a beautiful cloud of vibrance, moving against one another. His marks shone a bright orange, like lava slowing in the cracks of a volcano.

Rem was gorgeous.

"I cannot," he panted. "I beg for more time, My Prince. My control--"

"Killian," the prince interrupted. Rem sighed, then took another deep breath to calm himself. The glowing dimmed until he was as dark as the deepest shadows.

Killian's lips felt swollen and used. He gently brushed them with his fingertips, before looking to his Consort. "Do not keep me waiting for too long."

Rem nodded before crawling back beside Killian and pulling him close. The prince sank into the strong body and fell asleep, comfortable in his arms.

Chapter 5

The next morning, Killian woke before Rem. This gave him the perfect opportunity to gaze at his beauty without the self-consciousness that came whenever Rem laid those dark eyes on him. He was sculpted to utter perfection by the Gods, with chiseled features and smooth skin.

Killian trailed his fingers across his full lips. They were soft as rose petals at their peak. Killian's fingers drank him in, gliding down his chin, his neck, his chest. He traced the rings on his left pectoral. They swirled and circled around his nipple, pierced with a shiny silver hoop that was stark against his dark skin. Killian swiped over the nipple with the pad of his thumb, back and forth until it rose to attention.

A hand gripped his wrist.

He looked up startled and found himself staring into pitch black eyes.

Rem brought Killian's fingers to his lips before placing a soft kiss to each tip. Killian smiled at him before pushing his lips against Rem's. He kissed back gently, and Killian was okay with that.

"I did not mean to wake you," Killian told him as they broke apart.

Rem didn't answer, just leaned in for another kiss which Killian gladly complied with. Rolling on top, Killian straddled Rem's waist, their lips never parting. He cupped Rem's face in his hands as they kissed. Rem stroked the prince's back, fingers whispering along Killian's skin making him tremble in delight.

This male made him weak.

Killian's nightclothes slid off his shoulders, baring his upper half to his Consort. He had never been this exposed to another--attendants excluded--it was exhilarating.

Killian could feel Rem's length firm against the dip where his pelvis and upper thigh met. Killian rocked his hips slowly, creating a friction that had Rem groaning. The tingling sensation began in Killian's lower half as their kiss grew deeper. More frantic.

Rem chased Killian's lips, sitting them up with Killian in his lap. The prince dug his fingers into Rem's hair, sighing against his mouth. And for the first time...

Rem's tongue touched Killian's.

He completely overtook the prince's mouth, massaging his tongue against Killian's. It was different than the way Zev had done it. He was guided Killian without being forceful. There was precision and passion.

The tingling spread and Killian could feel himself grow wet. He was not afraid of it now. He wanted it. Begged it to come.

Everything halted abruptly when the door to the room opened and Lisa came barging in with Ethel and Kara on her heels.

Lisa didn't look at all apologetic for interrupting, but Killian could see the shock on the other's faces as they noticed how intimately the prince and Consort were entwined.

"It is time to get up. We must begin the day," Lisa said, writing on her parchment pad.

"We apologize, Your Highness. We did not mean to interrupt," Ethel apologized.

Lisa sucked her teeth loudly.

"I have a Consort now, Lisa. You will knock before entering," Killian snapped sharply.

She raised a brow at him before tipping her chin up indignantly.

"I am only--" she began in a haughty tone.

"I do not care. You will do as you are told or are you blatantly defying your future King?" he said with his normally soft and even tone, leveling her with a solemn gaze.

Lisa's jaw dropped before she fell into a deep curtsy. "Yes, Your Highness. Forgive my insolence."

Killian noticed Ethel and Kara grinning, the former giving a playful wink of approval.

"You may rise," Killian told Lisa then turned back to Rem to give him one last kiss. He pulled on his nightclothes and climbed out of bed. Once Killian and Rem were in their bathing robes, they made their way to the bath.

Faust, Caspian, and Orion were already there having a light conversation near the steps. They stopped once Killian and Rem entered.

"Good Morning," Killian greeted them.

"Good Morning," the males chorused. Rem gave a small nod in greeting. The pair sank into the water beside the other males after washing off at the spouts.

The group talked for a bit, laughing a little before the other Potentials bid their farewells. When it was just Rem and Killian left, Killian slid onto Rem's lap, pressing himself against the male. His wet hair caressed the prince's skin in the water, tangling with Killian's own maroon locks. Tucking his head under Rem's chin, the prince sighed in contentment. He did not want to move from this spot.

"If we stay much longer, Lisa will wonder."

"Let her," Killian huffed, snuggling closer.

Rem brushed Killian's hair from his face then pulled his head back so he could look at him.

"It would be unwise to do so."

Killian pouted but knew his Consort was right. But he was so comfortable, he didn't want to move.

Something had changed between the two of them and it was certainly for the better. Rem touched him more and was more comfortable in doing so. Killian saw more of him and it was making the prince feel like they actually had a relationship. He liked the feeling.

"The meeting with the Ambassador of Kappas is this morning. King Ellis requested our presence," Rem reminded him.

Killian groaned, falling back against Rem. Rem chuckled deeply, the sound vibrating in his chest. He stood with Killian in his arms, bringing him over to a bench where he dried them both off.

Ethel and Kara came in with their fresh robes before leading them back to the room to dress them. The pair were rushed off to breakfast and ordered to eat fast in order to make it in time for the meeting.

Rem finished his meal promptly, but Killian took his time, not in the mood for rushing. Ethel was not amused by his leisurely pace. Killian smiled at her before grabbing Rem's hand and heading off to the study.

They weren't late, but the King was not happy. They were meant to be early.

Killian took a seat and Rem right beside him.

When the Ambassador did come, the King had him wait a little bit before allowing him inside the room. Killian was told before in his earlier lessons that a King waits for no one and everyone waits on the King.

The Kappas were a peculiar looking race. The Ambassador was short, around four feet tall, with deep green scales. His eyes were huge in comparison to his face and bright yellow in color. There was not a single hair on his head or face. In fact, his face lacked a nose, only two slits that served as nostrils. He was a stout creature with a hunched back and inverted legs. The deep black webbing between his fingers revealed the origin of his race, somewhere deep in the lakes of the world.

"Greetings Kae, Ambassador of the Kappas," the King said as the Kappa hobbled in.

"Greetings King Ellis of Incubi," the Kappa hissed with a deep bow. His forked tongue, red dipped in black, flickered outside his thin lips. "Greetings Prince Killian, heir to the throne of Incubi and his Consort."

"Greetings," Killian replied. Rem remained silent as he was supposed to. Consorts did not speak unless told.

The smell of fish permeated the air. The prince kept his face neutral despite wanting to gag.

"Now I am running on a tight schedule so I would like to get this settled as soon as possible," the King began.

"Of course, My King. The imps in the southern region have been causing riots in the Kappa villages off the southwest lakefront."

"Riots for what reasoning?"

"I know not, My King. But I fear the chaos is spreading in the western forests and may anger the Nymphs."

King Ellis sighed, rubbing his temple. "We don't need the Nymph's priestess storming our gates...*again*...making an even bigger mess of this. I'll send the Astorian Guard to the southern region to gain control of the situation."

"I fear that may make things worse, My King. The Guard has not the best standing amongst the Kappas."

King Ellis raised a brow, eyes narrowed. "Are you implying that you do not trust my people?"

Kae shrank into himself, showing submission, knowing that he was treading dangerous waters here. "Never, My King! My allegiance is with you completely!"

"Very well then. I will send the General Leon of the Guard in three days' time. Prepare for their arrival. And in the meantime, find out what these riots are about. I want more information; riots don't start for no reason."

"Yes, My King."

The King dismissed the Kappa.

Grett, the King's attendant, leaned down to whisper something to the King. He sighed again and nodded before addressing his son and Rem.

"This next meeting you will not attend. Go spend some time with your Potentials. Rem, you have training."

Feeling slightly disappointed with having to be separated from Rem, Killian nodded and did as he was told. Both Rem and Killian departed, the prince heading off to find the other Potentials. Rem went to the library where his training would take place.

Killian wondered what they were teaching him. Would they be the same as his own?

He fought the urge to sneak into the library to find out. He had his own task to complete and it was a pressing one. He needed to figure out who he would choose next.

Zev crossed his mind again. Would he still be angry about before? He seemed like the type to hold a grudge.

He was beautiful, passionate, and extremely temperamental. Killian could see it being a problem in the future. But was it a big enough problem that he shouldn't choose him as a Consort?

This was much harder than he anticipated it would be. It took the fun and excitement out of the whole Ceremony.

Killian ventured out into the gardens. He found Caspian lounging on the branch of a tree, eyes closed, red tail swishing about. He was awake but resting.

He popped one eye open when the prince approached.

"Hello," Killian greeted happily.

"Hi," Caspian grinned, opening the other eye and angling himself to see Killian better.

"Do you sleep in trees often?" Killian asked.

"When your weapon of expertise is a bow, it's better to have a higher vantage point."

"But we are not in a battle."

"Are we not?" Caspian challenged and it made the prince stiffen, staring at the Potential with a furrowed brow. His expression grew suspicious.

Caspian tossed his head back and laughed, startling the prince. He clutched his stomach as he did so. "I meant that as a joke, My Prince. Nothing to be taken so seriously."

"Killian," the prince corrected.

"Killian," Caspian purred before fixating those glowing yellow eyes on him. The Potential's hair was a fiery waterfall, cascading off the side of the branch, jostling with the movement of his tail.

"I have a question for you, Caspian."

"And I may or may not have an answer," he replied.

Killian rolled his eyes at the response.

"What is it that you Potentials do when you are not with me or training?"

It was something Killian had been thinking about. Rem was no help at all. He answered with the one thing Killian knew he would.

Hunting.

"Most of the other Potentials like to spar. Faust likes to read. As for me, I sleep." As if to back up his answer, Caspian stretched, rolling his joints like a big cat before sinking back onto the branch, gracefully.

"And back in Faltaire, what did you do?"

Caspian sighed heavily. A look of dread passed over his usually lazy features before it was quickly wiped away. But Killian saw it and he could tell now that carelessness was a facade. He pretended like nothing bothered him, but Killian could see now that he was much more emotional than he gave the male credit for.

"Faltaire is a rough place. All who live there are unfortunate. It's poverty stricken and frequently caught between civil battles with different races. No one gets along and no one cares about anything other than themselves. It's a place where the strong and clever survive and the weak die, withering away without a trace. It's a place to get lost. And from an early age, you learn that you must fight to survive. Trust no one and always watch your back. Your own family could be your worst enemy."

He sounded empty when he spoke. Killian didn't even catch a hint of bitterness. It saddened the prince greatly. How could some place so terrible exist in their kingdom? Have they done nothing to stop it? Did his father know?

Caspian shook his head as if to clear it and smiled. "I know what you're thinking and there is nothing you can do. It's simply poor location. It's in the heart of four feuding territories. The King has tried but not even he could stop it."

"There has to be *something*."

Caspian shook his head.

"Doesn't matter now, I'm here right? Choose me as your Consort and I'll never have to go back again," he beamed.

And though he knew Caspian was joking, Killian almost did. Choosing Caspian would not be a terrible fate. Killian liked him. He was a good Incubus.

"Would you?" Killian asked carefully.

His yellow eyes widened in surprise. But then his expression calmed. "Ask me again when the reason you have chosen me is based on your actual desires rather your urge to protect me."

Killian was shocked by the rejection, but it only made the prince respect Caspian more. He knew now that the Potential did not have any ill intentions. He wanted to be chosen because he wanted to be Killian's Consort and that alone made the prince like him more.

"I understand," Killian told him before leaving him to his nap.

He found himself wandering back to the sparring room. Would Zev be there? Should he talk to him? He didn't know why he was so afraid of rejection from him. He was the Potential and Killian was the Heir. He shouldn't feel as if he had to answer to Zev, but there was a part of him that felt distressed being at odds with him. Killian wanted the Potential to smile at him again. He wanted to kiss him again. He just...*wanted* him.

And with that running in his mind, he pushed open the doors.

Zev was there of course, doing pull ups on some of the equipment. He had weights tied around his ankles and his waist, but he still managed to pull himself up effortlessly. His blue skin glistened with sweat and his navy and white hair clung to his moist skin. He was working out aggressively, pushing himself hard enough that Killian could feel the exhaustion radiating off of him in waves.

He still hadn't noticed Killian standing there. Or maybe he had and he was just ignoring him. The prince had never had the Potential mad at him before, but he figured it was very *Zev*.

"Zev," Killian called out softly.

He continued to pull himself up then down.

Up.

Down.

Yeah, he was being ignored.

"How long will you remain upset?" Killian asked him.

Zev stopped moving, then dropped to the ground with a loud thud. He bent over and proceeded to unlatch the weights. When he was free of them, he grabbed a towel from the bench and wiped the sweat from his face.

"Zev," Killian said again, reaching to touch the Potential's arm but he flinched away.

It hurt.

Why was he doing this? Didn't he *want* to be with Killian? Then why push him away? Why ignore him when the prince called out to him? He had done nothing terrible enough that he would behave this way toward him. Was Killian right in his assumption that Zev did not actually want to be here?

Why had Killian believed him before? It was clearly a lie!

"I understand," Killian said lowly. His voice sounded cold and detached. The emptiness grew in his gut, twisting and clenching.

Killian turned to go but Zev's voice stopped him.

"Wait!"

Killian turned to him, keeping his expression calm. If anyone knew how much he cared, they would use it to their advantage and he would be abused.

As much as he hated being alone, he hated being used even more.

Zev looked pained when he set his eyes upon the prince. His mouth opened and closed much like he wanted to say something but lost the words. Killian waited patiently for him to gather himself enough to speak.

"I am sorry. I know I should not be so upset with you. It's just..." he trailed off but stared at the prince as if he should understand what he did. As if he should feel guilty for his actions. Killian didn't like that look. He didn't like that Zev was expecting that of him.

Killian would be King, and he would not feel guilty for anything he did.

The prince narrowed his eyes at Zev not trying to contain his anger.

"And what exactly did I do to warrant such anger toward me?" Killian snapped.

Zev's eyes widened slightly in shock at the prince responding angrily, but Killian paid him no mind. He wanted Zev to know that he was not just some tool he could manipulate with emotions. He would not use his naivety against him.

"You rejected me. Rejected my kiss," Zev said.

"I was not ready to go further."

Zev's eyes flashed dangerously. Those light teal eyes seemed almost like polished silver. Killian had not known eyes could change so drastically in heightened emotional waves. They were like daggers, ready to strike him down.

"That is a lie you speak," Zev spat.

Killian gaped at him, appalled at the accusation. "How dare you? Have you forgotten that I was *assaulted?*"

Zev shook his head and an arrogant mask twisted his comely face. That ugliness didn't suit him. He was not meant to be so bitter. His gorgeous, near perfect face should not have been pulled so tight, so glacial.

"I know what you have done with Rem, how far you have gone. The servants *talk*, My Prince. They spoke of the embrace he held you in. The softness of your virgin body pressed against his planes. They spoke of your naked flesh bare to his gaze and the sweet smell of your soaking essence permeating the air! The servants *talk!*"

Zev lost all composure, breathing raggedly like a male gone mad. His words were formal, but his speech was anything but. He always spoke casually. Killian resented this icy verbiage.

And that's when Killian came to the conclusion: Zev was jealous.

Jealous of Rem.

It ate at his being and made him this hideous creature that stood before the prince.

Killian calmed himself down. It was no use arguing with him when he was like this, and in a way, the prince was flattered. If he was jealous, that meant he felt something for him and that was all the prince ever wanted.

"I was not ready at that moment because I was afraid my bodily urges would coax me into making you my Consort without properly knowing whether or not you should be. I cannot make these decisions on a whim, not like with Rem. I am trying to be more thorough in getting to know you. I want to *know* you before I bind you to me forever. If I had chosen you then, I would not have had the chance to see this side of you now."

Zev looked away, his arrogant mask desperately clawing its way back onto his face to hide what he truly felt.

Killian could tell he was worried though. Zev thought that with his jealousy he had destroyed any chance he had at being Killian's Consort.

But in fact, he had done just the opposite.

He had shown Killian a side of the Incubi that he would not have known. Faust was right, Killian did need them to guide him through the ways of his people, but he also cared for them. For Zev and for Rem. They were special to him and more than anything, Killian wanted them in his arms.

"Zev," Killian said softly, approaching him.

The Potential still didn't look at the prince, but Killian could tell from the tenseness in his shoulders that he had his complete attention. He was afraid of what Killian would say. He knew Killian was going to send him home.

"I care for you," Killian told him.

Zev cringed, waiting for the prince to say 'but'.

Killian didn't.

"I care for you and I care for Rem."

Zev turned his head toward Killian, confusion written all over his face.

Killian had thought about this and despite cautioning himself, he knew he wasn't being hasty or making a mistake. He was taking a chance and part of him knew deep down that he was making the right decision.

"Zev," Killian whispered.

He *definitely* had the male's attention now.

Zev was staring so intensely that it was hard to look away. Gone was the silver rage that swirled in those eyes and back again was the soft hopeful blues that managed to capture a special place in the prince's heart.

"Will you be my Consort?"

Chapter
6

Killian could not tell if Rem was upset with him or not.

The male had been acting a little strange since the prince had chosen Zev as his second Consort. When the servants were moving his things into the room they would share, Rem watched with a pensive expression. Killian was cautious but not worried. What worried him was when he went in for a kiss and Rem rejected it.

Then he proceeded to evade every initiation of physical contact.

It was frustrating. They had finally moved a step forward in their relationship only to move a step back again. Was it too soon to bring in another Consort? Should he have given him more time alone?

These men had to know they would be sharing. They knew he would choose five. Why were they behaving as if they did not like sharing? To be honest, he expected the behavior from Zev but not Rem. Killian wanted to be flattered but he was simply annoyed.

Things were like this with only two, how was he to manage three more?

But he had to admit, Zev looked good in his collar. It was pure silver and went perfectly with his dark hair and cool skin tone. He wore it with pride.

Father was pleased with the prince's second choice and welcomed Zev into the family heartily.

Killian was still worried about Rem.

When he finally managed to get the male alone in the bath later that day, he forced him to speak on the matter.

"Rem, what is wrong?" Killian asked, cupping Rem's cheeks in his palms, not letting him pull away. Killian was sure he could have if he truly wanted to. He was not strong enough to combat the male's physical might.

The Consorts

"Is it Zev? Do you not like him?" Killian pushed, searching his eyes for anything, but his expression was as blank as when the prince first met him. He couldn't detect anything, and it infuriated him.

"It is not I who has the problem," Rem answered calmly.

"I do not understand," Killian admitted. Zev hadn't shown any signs of not liking Rem in his presence. Maybe it happened when he wasn't around?

"Your previous disagreement with him hurt you deeply. I simply do not wish to see you in pain again if I can prevent it."

"You are hurting me now," Killian hissed, shoving his face into Rem's neck. "We have made so much progress. Do not further the distance Rem, I cannot stand it!"

Rem's fingers caressed Killian's wet hair. "He will be angered."

"If he cannot stand sharing, then he will be no Consort of mine."

Killian still had the right to revoke the title. He felt strongly for Zev but his feelings for Rem were on a completely different level. Zev would not drive a wedge between himself and Rem. He wouldn't let him. And if he thought he could separate him from his first chosen Consort, he would see a side of Killian that would make him wish that he had never met the prince.

Rem gripped Killian's waist tightly, diverting his attention back to him. His expression was as serious as Killian had ever seen it. He liked this attention.

"I do not like that look in your eyes," Rem said softly.

Killian pulled Rem's face in and kissed him gently. To show his appreciation for him. To show Rem just how much he meant to him. To show him that he valued every moment with him.

"Rem," Killian whispered, putting everything into that soft sigh. His eyelids dropped low over his ruby-red eyes as he stared into the black depths of his Consort's gaze. How could he show Rem how much he meant to him? How could he begin to explain what his mere gaze does to him?

Killian kissed him. Again and again, until his body was aching.

Gods above, he needed him. He needed him so badly it literally left him weak.

"Rem. Rem. Rem," Killian chanted between kisses, molding his body to his Consort. His lips moved from Rem's mouth to his jaw, and down his neck. He kissed, licked, nipped every inch of his skin within his mouth's reach.

Killian climbed on Rem's lap, digging his fingernails into his dark scalp and pulling him even closer. His hips moved in their own libidinous dance, rubbing his private center against Rem's thigh. The water slapped against their bodies and the edge of the bath wall from the furious motion of Killian's body on Rem's.

Killian swung his other leg around Rem's other thigh and forced their hardened members together, grinding against one another. There was a quick tenseness in Rem's body as he dug his fingers into Killian's hips just a bit harder. Killian knew what that meant and there was no way he was letting that happen.

"Killian," Rem said in a voice that told him he was about to end this.

No.

No, he needed it.

"Please Rem. More. I need more of you," Killian panted against his ear, rolling his hips a little more forcefully, letting him feel the thick shaft between his thighs through the fabric of their robes.

If they weren't in the water right now, he'd be dripping with slick.

He wanted Rem to touch him there. To teach him more about arousal and desire. He wanted to feel more of this and never let it end.

Pulling Rem's hands across his body, he let them rest on each buttock beneath his robe. Skin to skin. It felt wonderful.

"Touch me," Killian whimpered.

Rem hesitated and Killian thought he would stop, but much to his surprise, Rem groped each globe of his butt in his hands, squeezing and kneading the mounds until strange whimpers escaped the prince's mouth.

"There is nothing in this world more captivating than the sounds of your moans," Rem groaned.

Moans?

He was moaning?

Killian felt his cheeks get hot. It was silly but he didn't expect moaning to happen at a time like this. They only grew louder as Rem spread his cheeks apart. When the Potential's finger brushed the prince's entrance, Killian nearly lost it right then and there.

It was different than it was Jax. He felt fear with him. Right now? He was comfortable and safe in Rem's care. Above all, he wanted more.

Would he push it in? Would he feel him inside?

As if answering his prayers, that probing finger dipped inside the puckered ring of muscle, forcing a gasp of indescribable pleasure out of his throat.

Every part of him was set aflame, burning for his Consort. His body was humming, movements fluid as he bucked and writhed, urging Rem on.

"Oh! Mmf! More! Please more, Rem!" His was a breathy scream. He tugged his robe off and tossed it aside. Killian tried to take Rem's off too, but the Consort stopped him with his free hand, grabbing his wrist.

Killian stared at his Consort, pleading with his eyes until reluctantly, Rem released his wrist and let the prince tug his robe away.

Killian had never looked before. But now? He couldn't look away.

Rem was flawless and unlike Killian had ever seen. Everyone had flaws, he had plenty himself. But Rem? Not one. His shoulders were broad, pectorals defined, abs toned, and his shaft was long and girthy. It was longer than Zev's but not as thick. The tip was a deep dark red violet color, lighter than the rest of him. Killian could see through the waves of the water, prominent veins trailing up the sides of his length, just as dark as the rest of him that sprung from the thick bush of black hair. Nestled underneath was a large sac dressed with delicate wrinkles.

The prince's examination was suddenly thwarted by the incredible sensation of his Consort's long finger pushing and tugging inside him. He was overwhelmed with all of the new feeling. His body and mind became two separate things. The sheer force of it all might just kill him.

Subconsciously, Killian began pushing back on his digit, creating a more vigorous friction. Rem with his unmoving control, kept the flow of their movements to his pace.

Reaching between them, Killian grabbed the thickness of Rem, just as he had with Zev. Zev had lost control the more Killian touched him there. The same should work for Rem, right?

Rem grunted as soon as Killian made contact and groaned when he gave a squeeze.

"Feel with me Rem," Killian whispered, kissing him harder than before, stroking the length of him. His fingers lost their rhythm inside the prince but did not stop. Killian pushed his tongue inside Rem's mouth.

Rem's skin began to glow all of those lovely, vibrant colors. It fueled Killian. He wanted his Consort to grow brighter. He wanted the male to lose his rigid control.

Zev mentioned the prince putting his lips...down there. Maybe he should try that. He pulled away from Rem's lap, mourning the loss of his fingers inside him before urging the male to sit on the ledge out of the water.

Rem grew suspicious of the request but complied anyway. He was being obedient. It made Killian question if the male before him was really Rem.

Out of the water, Killian got an even clearer view of his impressive manhood. Kneeling between Rem's legs, still partially submerged in the water, Killian stared up the length of Rem's body, drooling at the bunching muscles in his abdomen. All of him in his wondrous glory.

"Do not stop me," Killian murmured to him, before placing his lips on his most intimate member.

Rem roared ferociously, his hands flying into Killian's hair, gripping the wet locks into a fist. Killian could feel the tug at his roots, but the pain set him off a little.

Carefully licking the mushroomed head, Killian took his time exploring his Consort. Rem tasted like...well...skin, aside from the random hint of saltiness with a strange flavor. He was so very smooth, like silk. Killian's tongue caressed every raised vein that twirled along his shaft and every dip and curve of his scrotum. The prince licked and lapped before gently blowing on the tip, curious as to the reaction he would get.

Rem's hands dug even deeper into his hair, pulling at his scalp tighter. Killian hissed before slipping the tip of him completely in his mouth. Much to Killian's disappointment, he couldn't contain much of him, only an inch or so. In his attempt to hold more of his lover, he ended up scraping him with his fangs.

Rem jerked in pain.

"Be careful of teeth," he told Killian before pulling him off of his member and bringing the prince up out of the water to sit in his lap again. Killian could feel Rem settling in the crease of his behind, softening with every minute.

The whole mood was ruined.

Killian sighed, falling against Rem's chest.

"I keep messing up," he muttered in defeat.

"Why are you in such a rush?" Rem asked.

The prince shook his head, refusing to answer. He wouldn't understand, he hadn't in the past.

Killian wanted to be closer to Rem. To all of his Consorts. He wanted to explore their bodies and understand how it worked. He wanted them to feel the pleasure the way that he did. He wanted them to be perfect together in every sense.

"We have been here for quite a while. We should leave now."

Killian held on to Rem's shoulders tighter. There were moments like these that made him question if any of this was even real. Was he truly going to have five Consorts? Was he really going to be King? Would he wake up and this all would be a dream?

Just the thought of that lonely bed and empty baths were enough to shake him. He clutched Rem even tighter, making sure he knew not to let him go. Desperation for affection and love made him bold. Now the entirety of his actions just moments ago came reeling back into his head.

Oh my Gods.

I cannot believe I just did that with Rem!

His face burned in embarrassment, making his lavender skin tinge pink.

This whole mess had him acting like a completely different person! Was it being brought out by the intimate interactions he had been having with his Potentials and Consorts?

No.

It started the moment he laid eyes on them.

He had changed. And he could only hope that it was for the better.

Rem pulled them out of the water and wrapped Killian in a fresh robe before getting one for himself. He held Killian's hand as they made their way back to the room to get dressed.

When they entered, Killian's eyes drifted over to the large bed covered in red satin, made to hold all five Consorts and himself. It had been Rem and him these past few days, but tonight, Zev would be with them. His bed was filling faster than he had imagined and it made warmth spread in his stomach. He was excited. Giddy even, at the possibilities.

Just as Kara was tying the sash of his belt together, Zev walked in looking as handsome as ever in his new clothes. He was dressed in navy pants that cupped his legs and backside perfectly. Tucked in was a black mesh shirt under a navy strappy vest. His calves were encased in tall black boots with laces all the way up the back. His silver collar twinkled in the dim light, but he wore it with pride. His hair was braided back with just a few tendrils curling in his face. His blue eyes were bright and lively.

He was happy.

When he laid eyes on Killian, he smiled. There was something about it that made the prince's chest hurt...in a good way, he thought.

"Killian," he greeted, coming over to him with a confident stride, before pulling him close by the waist and placing a sweet kiss on his lips.

Killian blushed, which made him laugh.

It seemed ridiculous to be blushing after everything he had done but he just couldn't help it. He was going to blame it on his approaching *Haise.*

"The collar suits you," Killian told him.

He smirked.

So fiercely confident. It was attractive.

Then he noticed something.

Zev's eyes slightly shifted past Killian and there was nothing playful about that look. It was aggressive and highly possessive. His light teal eyes glinted liquid silver. It was blatant show of dominance.

Zev really was trying to intimidate Rem as if he had the right to stake some claim on him; as if Killian were his and his alone.

A few horas as his Consort and he has already become a handful.

If he thought he could get away with monopolizing Killian, he must be put in his place immediately. There is no mark of dominance more powerful than that of a King.

Killian grabbed Zev's chin and jerked his face toward his, no longer smiling.

Zev's eyes widened in surprise.

"You must be a little confused. You wear this collar because you belong to me, but do not be mistaken. I do not belong to you. You do not get to puff your chest at my other Consorts. You are no better than them unless you are ranked higher. And until the ranking ceremony, you are all equals. But you are not equal to me. I will be King. And to you, I already am your King. To blatantly disrespect Rem, is to disrespect me. Knock it off and get used to sharing. Am I understood?"

Zev blinked at Killian in shock before wiping all emotion from his face other than that terrible arrogant pout. He nodded stiffly.

Killian sighed turning to Rem who was as stoic as ever. His pitch-black eyes slid from Zev to him and he saw a small flicker of approval.

Killian caught himself smiling at him then stubbornly forced himself to stop. He didn't need Rem's approval, Rem needed his.

He would have to keep Rem in check as well. He oozed natural power and authority. It might make others mistake him for King instead of Killian. That would be a dangerous thing.

Lisa came into the room--after knocking thankfully.

"Alright, it's time for the Consorts to go to their lessons. Chop chop!" she rushed.

Zev left without a word, but Rem stopped to kiss him lightly on the lips.

"I will see you soon," Killian told him.

He gave one nod before following Lisa out the door.

"I see you already have your hands full. Just think, you have to choose three more," Kara said, folding some of the scattered clothes around the room and tidying up.

Killian collapsed onto the bed with a groan.

"I know! I do not want to anymore."

"But you have to," she smiled matter of factly. "Now, up up up. I have to finish making the bed, and you're wrinkling your clothes!"

Killian pouted at her but complied.

She and Ethel were the only ones he let treat him like that because they were like family to him. He knew they only had his best interests in mind.

"Do you think I was too harsh with him? He is a bit sensitive," He asked her, hoping she'd be able to guide him down the right path, as she has had more experience in this department than him.

"I could tell. But if he wants to be your Consort, he's going to have to toughen up. I don't think you were too hard on him. You will be King, and he needs to accept that he no longer comes first, you do. It'll be a while before all of your Consorts grasp that, but they will eventually. Just as your Consort mothers had with the King."

Killian perked up at that information.

"You were there during my father's Consort choosing?"

Kara nodded.

"I was really young, just starting out in the palace as an assistant to the seamstress. Much younger than you are now. But the day the Succubae were brought in shines clearly in my mind. They were absolutely stunning, each Succubae that came into the palace. I saw them before the King did. I was told to get their measurements so that dresses could be made for them and I remember how arrogant Lady Mia was when she was first chosen to be a Consort."

"Mother Mia was arrogant? Wait, my own mother wasn't the first to be chosen?" Killian asked in surprise.

Kara smiled, her eyes crinkling around the edges, reminding Killian of her age.

"Yes, Lady Mia was very arrogant, but it was a front, much like Lord Zev. Your mother was very quiet and kind of shy. The King didn't take notice to her at first."

"What changed?"

"He did. There was a huge debacle with Lord Netter which led to King Ellis maturing much faster than before. I think that was the moment that your father realized that he would be King. And that's when he started to take the process of choosing his Consorts seriously," Kara told him.

"What happened with Uncle Netter?"

"That is a story for another time, but you should ask Ethel, she knows it better than I do. I was still a child at the time and didn't really understand what was happening myself."

"What drew my father to my mother?" Killian asked.

"She was smart and gentle. The King had quite the temper back then and Queen Jessa was the only one who seemed to calm him down and turn him into the joyful, carefree spirit he is today. She made him a better King and challenged him when no one else would. She was very compatible with him and that is why she is Rank One."

"I never knew anything about that time."

"Things are different now and so are your Consorts. Only you know who is best for you."

"And what if I pick someone I should not have?"

"Don't worry," she reassured, smiling sweetly at him. "You won't."

She seemed so sure. How could she have so much faith in him? He was completely inexperienced in this department!

As if she read his mind, she added, "The King was just as worried as you are. He was inexperienced and terrified at first, having never really been in the presence of Succubae, but he caught on quickly."

But Killian was not his father. He was not as sure of himself. His father was born to be King and oozed authority like no one he had ever known. Killian wasn't like that. He didn't have that natural ability.

"You need to have more confidence in yourself. You are your father's son. Don't forget that, My Prince."

That was easier said than done, but strangely, he did feel a little relieved. As if some of the weight had been lifted off his shoulders. Not all of it of course, but enough to notice.

He was his father's son. And he would be King.

"Now shouldn't you be heading off to your own lessons? I wouldn't keep the Queen waiting," Kara reminded.

Killian had nearly forgotten.

"Thank you, Kara."

"I'm always at your service."

The prince left the room and made his way to the study expecting to see his mother there but instead saw Ethel. His mother was nowhere to be seen.

Killian slowed his steps as he entered the room. He was sure the confusion was written all over his face as he approached Ethel.

"Where is my mother?"

"Queen Jessa wanted me to escort you to the *Haise* Chamber for your lesson today."

His brows furrowed even deeper, but he let her lead the way.

He had only been to the *Haise* Chamber once a month whenever his *Haise* struck him and left the moment it was over. While he underwent the cycle, he was so out of it, he barely knew up from down. The room was foreign to him.

He never had lessons in there. He didn't particularly like it there. Something about the place just made him feel uncomfortable.

N.A Moore

Ethel opened the large double doors that led into the cream-colored room with marble floors and towering pillars. There was a large four poster bed with gold covering and a small pool of water just at the foot of the bed. He never understood why there was a bed in the room in the first place. The water made sense because whenever his *Haise* came, the water would cleanse him and help the process along. The bed had no purpose.

His mother was waiting for him at the edge of the room where there sat a few chairs and a small table. It was intended for those who watched him experience his *Haise*. He shuddered at the memories.

His mother motioned for him to join her at the chairs then dismissed Ethel from the room.

Ethel left with a curtsy, closing the door behind her.

"Hello, my dear son," his mother greeted.

"Mother. What are we doing here?" he asked her a bit uneasily.

"I know that this room makes you uncomfortable but you are going to be spending a lot of time here so it would be best if you were to get used to it now. It also seemed appropriate for your lesson today," she answered softly.

"What do you mean?"

Mother smiled at him. He saw a reflection of his own bright red eyes and shiny maroon locks piled high on her head, framed by the elegant craft of jewels she wore as her crown. His mother was fair even with the lines of age etched into her features and he hoped that when he grew older, that he too would remain just as she was; vibrant.

"Let us start with the basics. As an S-Level Incubus, your genetic makeup is closer to that of a Succubus than an Incubus. Though your body is male, you are formed with the purpose of procreating. That is your body's top focus. And that is why as a child when you were given the option of a Succubus or and Incubus, you opted for the Incubus. Even at a young age you knew your purpose. With an Incubus you would be able to procreate."

"Wait, 'be able'? Are you saying that I am unable to procreate with a Succubus?"

"That is correct. You do not have the proper makeup to reproduce with a Succubus. Giving you the choice of the two was just a formality. You were going to be with Incubi regardless."

He let that sink in.

So it wasn't even a choice really? It was just instinct? Were the Consorts he chose instinct too?

His mother continued on.

"With S-Level Incubi comes the preparation. In order to be able to reproduce, your body must feed."

He knew that much. The whole point of the *Haise* was to feed off of the energy from the other people around him as they procreated. During the *Haise*, he tapped into the bodies of every living being that was consummating at that given time. He fed off of their fertility and sated the hunger within him along with strengthening his own body when the time came for him to procreate. When he fed from vast numbers that he shared no connection with, the feeding was...unfulfilling. He thought it was because he was forcing it. Once he had his Consorts, they would ignite that flame and hopefully make his mass feedings bearable. That was why it was important that he chose Consorts that called to his *Haise*.

"You must feed not only on our kingdom but also on your Consorts, but in order to do that, you must develop a spiritual connection with them."

"Why?"

"Because you cannot reproduce with them otherwise. You'll do it first with the two Consorts you have chosen thus far at your upcoming *Haise*, then again with the next three during your next *Haise.*"

"They are going to watch?" Killian asked, horrified.

He hated having people watch him during it. He knew it was important for his safety in the event that he fed too much or too little, hurting himself in the transference of power and energy.

"They will not just be watching; they will be participating in a sense. But you have to get over your aversion to having people present during your *Haise*, now that you have your Consorts. It is their job to take care of you during it until you are pregnant."

"You talk as if you want me to get pregnant as soon as I choose my Consorts," Killian said suspiciously.

"We do."

"Mother--"

"Your Father wants to step down. He's tired and he's had his run as King. He's trained you vigorously and he believes you're ready to take over. So yes, as soon as you choose your Consorts, we want you to aim for an heir."

A strangled noise left his lips as this weighed on him. They couldn't possibly believe he was ready to rule the kingdom, let alone raise a child! He could barely keep up with his Consorts, how would he deal with the entire Realm?

The heirs usually had a few months after their choosing before they had the mating ritual. Would that mean he would have it after the Ranking Ceremony?

"Mother, I am not ready," He told her, shaking his head. "I am not ready at all."

"You are Killian," she insisted.

His chest started heaving and his breath came out in sharp frantic pants.

He knew it was coming, walked around and acted as if he couldn't wait. He tossed it about again and again to others that he was King. Now that the moment was finally coming, he felt like a child playing dress up. He wasn't ready just yet. He needed more time.

But they were not going to give him any. He could tell by the resolute look in his mother's eyes. He would do it. He had to.

Killian took a couple of deep breaths and willed himself to calm down. There was no use fainting over it. He would shove that panic away until he had a private moment to himself, then he would panic.

The rest of the lesson continued and he learned a little bit more about connecting with someone spiritually. When they were finished, he nearly ran back to the room and into Rem's arms. He was in the middle of brushing his hair but dropped the brush to catch the prince.

He didn't say a word, just held Killian and that was exactly what he needed.

"Where is Zev?"

"He had additional lessons to attend," Rem replied.

"When he gets out, I want to have a picnic. The three of us."

Rem didn't say anything to that. He would go along with whatever whim the prince had unless it endangered him.

"You didn't have anything else planned, did you?" Killian asked, wrapping his arms around Rem's neck and relishing in the warmth of his silky black hair.

"No," he answered.

"Good," Killian whispered, kissing him.

He never tired of feeling Rem's lips on his. They were so full and soft. He felt like he was melting into Rem every time they came together.

Of course, Rem was the one to break the kiss, untangling Killian's arms from around him and picking up the brush to continue running it through his hair. For some reason, he didn't really like anyone else doing his hair, so he was left to do it by himself, the way he preferred.

Killian watched as he hesitated, staring at the brush for a moment, before looking at the prince and handing the brush over to him.

Was Rem going to let Killian brush his hair?

The Consort knelt on the ground and turned around, his back toward Killian.

Sitting on the bed, Killian opened his legs and Rem fell between them. Starting with small sections, Killian gently and leisurely ran the brush through Rem's hair. It was thick and soft with a coarseness he was unfamiliar with. It fascinated him and was actually quite resistant to his ministrations. Rem guided his hands in the beginning to help him through the section he began with until Killian finally got the rhythm of it. Killian repeated the process over and over. Rem had a lot of hair.

They were quiet the entire time, just enjoying the presence of one another.

When Zev came in afterwards, he looked a bit agitated. As he saw Killian brushing Rem's hair, the agitation seemed to grow.

"What upsets you, Zev?" Killian asked.

"Nothing," he snapped curtly.

"You should not lie to him," Rem said. His deep voice rumbled in his chest. Killian could feel the vibrations on his thighs, it made him shiver.

"Tell us," Killian told him.

Zev sighed, running his fingers through his hair.

"It is not something I wish to share."

"But it may help."

"You had dance lessons did you not?" Rem asked.

Zev blushed, then scowled.

Killian had never thought he would see that. The light blue of his skin became a deep purple as the blood rushed to the surface.

"Was dancing giving you trouble?" Killian asked.

"I don't want to talk about it!"

Killian took that as a yes. Turning his attention to Rem, he asked, "Did you have dance lessons as well?"

"It was not necessary. I am well versed in all dances."

Ah, that's why Zev is agitated.

"It is alright Zev, that just means the two of us will have private lessons," Killian reassured with a smile.

Zev perked up at that, then grinned.

It may be easy to upset him, but it was even easier to please him.

And suddenly, being with these two males didn't seem so bad.

Chapter 7

The picnic was a success...kind of.

Killian was able to get the two men to warm up to each other a little bit, maybe even enough for a friendship. Though he did start to get a tad jealous when Rem was more expressive with Zev then he was with him.

Afterwards, Killian sought out Faust. He hadn't seen him in a while, and he had to admit he was missing the Potential's presence. Faust was soothing with his kindness and wisdom.

Killian found him in the library with his head in a book. No surprise there.

He was perched on a reading chair with his gorgeous white locks draped over the side. His equally pale skin was stark against the deep red of the velvet chair. His loin cloth neatly covered his lap. Those pitch-black eyes flicked upwards toward the prince's approach before a sweet smile spread across his handsome face.

"Greetings, My Prince."

"Faust, how many times do I have to tell you to just call me Killian," Killian scolded but smiled anyway, taking a seat opposite of him. "What are you reading today?"

"Frozen Whispers. It is about a widowed Succubae who committed suicide and is searching for her dead husband in the afterlife. A very good read so far. I would definitely recommend it."

"I will keep that in mind the next time I'm looking for a good book to read," the prince told him happily.

Faust closed his book and gave Killian his full attention. "So, what brings you here, to me?" he asked.

"I have been missing your presence as of late. I wanted to see you," Killian told him honestly.

"Killian, you flatter me," Faust replied with a very happy smile.

"I also wanted to inform you, as I am not sure if you were aware yet, that I have chosen a second Consort."

"I had not heard. And who might your second choice be?"

"Zev."

Faust didn't seem surprised, almost as if he knew it was going to happen. Killian didn't think his attraction to Zev was that obvious. He was actually pretty certain that it would catch many off guard. Killian guessed he was not as stealthy in his affections as he had hoped.

"Congratulations," Faust said.

Killian nodded in thanks.

"I tell you this not to boast at your expense," Killian explained to him.

"I know there is more you wish to say. You are not the type to gloat."

The prince raised a brow. "How did you make that deduction?"

"Just as you have been watching me, I have been watching you. I would like to think I have a good idea of your character."

Knowing that Faust has been watching him made him feel warm. Silly, he knew. Of course he was watching, they all were. But just having that knowledge given to him so honestly filled his being with happiness.

"I wanted to ask you if you would be my third Consort when the time comes? I have to let the two I have get used to each other before adding another. Zev was already antagonizing Rem and Rem was getting really distant. I think they are starting to warm up to each other, but I cannot be too sure. I do not wish to ruin anything with hasty decisions. And I am rambling," Killian trailed off blushing heavily.

Faust smiled.

"Of course I will be your Consort."

Killian breathed a sigh of relief. He was nervous, which made no sense considering the reason they were there was to become his Consort. Maybe he shouldn't have asked? Kings don't ask permission. But it's Faust. He was so kind.

"Thank you. I will come to you with a proper proposition when the time is right."

Faust nodded.

"I'll be waiting," he answered, then pulled out his book again.

Killian stood and slipped out of the room heading to his private study, right beside his father's. He noticed a folder thick with papers left on his desk. Picking it up, a few pages skittered out. They were profiles of his remaining Consorts. A gesture from his father no doubt, to ease the process along with choosing his next companions.

How was it possible that these gorgeous Incubi existed? Could they really be his? It seemed like too much of fantasy to be real. There was no way he could have them all.

He had to choose.

He had already chosen three...he had two more left but four males to choose from. Four males who would make the choice incredibly difficult.

Orion.

Drek.

Titus.

Caspian.

Who did he choose?

Who did he let go?

Killian stared at their portraits hoping that in some way, they would tell him the answer...but they did not.

Who did his heart speak to?

He'd been sitting there for horas and night had settled quite some time ago. He gathered his things, carefully handling the portraits of his men, and hurried back to his room.

On the way, Killian bumped into Orion.

He was tall, with a slim build and lean muscles. His shaggy red hair fell into his face, curving around his three black horns. His skin was like polished bronze, glistening in the dim lit glow of the hall. He had very petite features, making him more 'pretty' than 'handsome' in a way similar to Faust. But Faust's features were just a tad more severe. Orion's eyes were like honey, glimmering.

"Hello Orion."

"Hello Killian," he greeted with a coy smile. A rosy color blossomed on his cheeks as his long lashes hid his ochre eyes from Killian.

"Where are you headed?" the prince asked.

"I was just about to take a bath before dinner."

Thinking about it now, he should probably bathe as well.

"I will join you. Would you accompany me to my room as I change?" Killian asked him.

Orion blushed even deeper.

"Of course."

Killian latched onto his arm, not waiting for him to offer it.

The Potential stiffened in shock, his skin hot, and the prince could see the blush spreading from his cheeks to the rest of his body.

Killian wanted to laugh, but that would probably be received poorly. It was funny though; Orion was even more prone to blushing than he was.

He had no idea he could make someone so nervous.

It was cute.

As they walked, Killian asked him arbitrary questions in hopes of loosening him up and getting him to calm down. It worked a little, but Killian could tell he was still nervous.

When the prince called him cute, he lit up like a polished ruby. His skin turning deep rose gold rather than bronze. Killian chuckled.

When they reached his room Killian told him, "Wait here." Then went inside to change into his bathing robes.

When he opened the door again, Orion averted his gaze but offered his arm. Killian took it with a smile and snuggled closer to his side.

All his blushing made him incredibly warm. He was like Killian's own personal heater.

The walk to the bath was short and when they got there, it was clear that there was a little party going on.

Titus and Drek were soaking in the bath already. Killian couldn't see them as they were hidden around the corner, but he could hear their loud boisterous laughs from where he stood.

Orion yanked his loin cloth off and neatly folded it before putting it in a cubby where towels were normally kept. Killian dropped his cloak and refastened his robe. Orion was in the water already, offering a hand. Killian took it gladly and descended into the water with him.

Together, they waded through the water, hand in hand, toward the sound of laughter. When they turned the corner, Drek and Titus were lounged on a bench in the water with their arms resting on the ledges outside the water. They stopped laughing when they saw the prince. Drek recovered quickly, green eyes sparkling but Titus was not so smooth with the recovery.

"Prince Killian wanted to join us," Orion announced.

"Hello Prince Killian," Drek greeted, voice smooth like silk. His confidence was a like a wave of warmth that washed over Killian, spreading down to his toes.

"You can drop the titles here. I am simply Killian. Do not give me any special treatment, I do not want to impose on your bonding. Act as you normally would," he told them.

"Of course," Drek said.

Titus looked a little uncomfortable. He glanced at Drek who was studying Killian. Then the green skinned Incubus looked back at Titus with a smirk and gave a slight nod. Killian didn't know what that meant, but he supposed he'd find out.

Drek offered the seat beside him. His golden locks were tied up away from his face with a red ribbon, bringing more attention to his three sharp horns that were normally hidden within those gold strands. His eyes were the same bright green as his skin, but his hair was such a stark contrast that even the slight beard he had looked much more full and plentiful.

He was a very handsome Incubus, there was no doubt about that.

Killian let go of Orion's hand and sat beside Drek in the warm waters. Drek draped his arm behind the prince but was careful not to touch his skin.

They were all so daring but so careful.

Orion went to take a seat next to Titus. Titus had a build much closer to Drek's and Drek was huge. By far the biggest of them all with broad shoulders and muscles wrapped all around his body. He was a masterpiece.

Titus, on the other hand, was smaller, but still larger than the average male. He had very dark but rich blue skin and silver hair. Three black prominent horns protruded from his forehead and his ears were slightly pointed, like Drek. But his eyes were whiter than Faust's skin.

He scooted closer to Orion. Their bodies were angled toward each other and he even pulled the slim Incubus snug against his side. Those white eyes flickered toward Killian then at Drek before returning to Orion.

Orion looked very comfortable in the embrace.

Killian cocked his head to the side, staring at the two in curiosity.

They looked close...like a couple.

He wondered...

"So Killian, we were just talking about our villages. Telling stories of our childhood. Titus was quite the reckless one," Drek said with a laugh.

Titus snorted.

"Like you were any better."

"You two are acquainted?" Killian asked, a little surprised by the knowledge.

They both grinned. "Trained together under my father in the Astorian Guard in Gemp," Titus said.

"He only kept me around because I was the only one he couldn't mop the floor with. Drek was the top Warrior in our class." Titus added. "He was a total asshole."

"Yeah, well, at least I didn't set the blacksmith's wife's dress on fire."

"No, you were too busy trying to peek under it," Titus laughed.

"Guilty," Drek sang.

Both Orion and Killian blushed.

"You guys are so crude," Orion remarked with a roll of his eyes.

Titus leaned into him, pulling one of Orion's legs onto his lap, his hand sliding around the redhead's waist. "Don't act so innocent. We both know how crude you really are."

Orion's eyes widened as he glanced at the prince, then back at Titus.

"Titus, knock it off," Orion scolded.

"It's okay. Killian said to act as we normally would. And is this not how we normally would act?" Titus's voice grew lower with each word, his lips lingering near Orion's ear. The red-haired Incubus's lips parted and eyes glazed over slightly, before clearing. He looked at him.

"Is it really okay?" He asked.

"Why would it not be? I care not if you are affectionate with one another. It is preferred if you are. My Consorts must share with one another."

Orion frowned slightly, but Titus nipped his ear causing a yelp from him.

Orion glared at Titus, who laughed.

"And I am still new to...intimacy. What better way to learn than from observation?"

"Oh, you will learn a lot tonight," Drek whispered. Killian wasn't sure if it was meant for him to hear. He ignored it.

They continued with their conversation of the various troubles the two Incubi got into in their village while Orion and Killian listened.

The prince watched the interactions between Orion and Titus. The blue skinned Incubus kept his hands on Orion the whole time. His hands stroked Orion's skin, caressing his thighs, his waist, his chest. Occasionally he would nuzzle into Orion's neck and Orion's eyes would lose focus. Killian couldn't see exactly what he was doing, but he was curious.

Rem and Zev didn't act that way toward him. Well Killian felt Zev might, but he never really gave him the chance. Killian guessed he was too scared. But it was like Titus couldn't keep his hands off Orion and that's what he wanted.

"Killian?"

The prince blinked and looked around to find everyone's eyes on him. A blush crept onto his face as he tucked a wet lock of his hair behind his ear.

"Did I miss something?"

"I asked what your conquests were like," Drek repeated.

"Conquests?" Killian asked in confusion.

"Fleeting relationships if you will."

He shook his head.

"I have never been around any other Incubi besides my family before you all. I am completely new to relationships."

"Really? I mean, it was always broadcasted that the Heir was pure of body and mind, but I thought it was just a facade. I mean, you haven't even been around other Incubi?"

He shook his head again.

Titus whistled.

"So, you've never had sex?" Titus asked.

Killian's face reddened before he uttered a quiet, "No."

"Do you even know how it works?" Drek laughed.

Killian shook his head again.

Drek's laughter died off. He looked at him in shock. "Wait, seriously?"

Killian nodded.

"Pure of mind, remember?"

"How have you survived? You're an S-Level Incubus. Your body literally needs it. How have you managed your *Haise?*"

"I don't know what you mean. Why would I need to have...intercourse...if I am not aiming to be pregnant?" the prince questioned.

"Killian, sex is not just for procreating. It's for pleasure too."

Well he knew that engaging in some intimate acts were just for pleasure, but he would never think to complete the act if the end goal was not to reproduce.

"But why?"

"Because it feels good. Right Orion?" Titus said. He cupped Orion between the legs and Orion let out a sound he had made only in the throes of passion with Rem.

"Yes," Orion breathed. "So good."

His legs widened, giving Titus more access to whatever it was that he was doing. Killian couldn't see through the waves of the water.

"Do you want to see?" Drek asked him.

"W-what?"

"Do you want to see them have sex? For pleasure."

He couldn't be serious.

But Titus did something else, forcing a loud moan from Orion.

And he couldn't look away.

Titus smirked.

"I'll take that as a yes."

Killian was nervous. Though not enough to look away. The curiosity was too great and everything he wanted to know about intimacy was right in front of him.

But he was afraid to know what he'd been sheltered from his entire life. The fear ate at his core, starting off with gentle nibbles until the gnawing became painful and relentless.

Orion was writhing with his eyes fluttering closed, creating small red crescents on his bronzed skin. With his head tilted back, the smooth expanse of his neck was exposed, and Titus locked in on it.

His dark gaze drove up Orion's stretched body with a look so passionate and full of carnal intention, it made Killian blush. Titus flicked his tongue against Orion's skin causing the Incubus' breath to hitch and stomach contract.

Drek watched the display with a sort of leer in his expression. When he caught the prince staring at him, he was quick to whisper, "Don't look away."

Killian turned his head back to the others.

Orion was yanked into Titus's lap. Titus's fingers brushed against Orion's dark nipples. He flicked and plucked them, drawing little sounds from Orion's mouth.

Didn't that hurt?

It looked like it would.

Killian looked down at his own nipples, hidden beneath his robe, and flicked them through the fabric. He winced as the pain shot through him.

He frowned.

That didn't feel good at all.

Orion whimpered, bringing the prince's attention back to him. He was a quivering mess in Titus's arms. Killian could see Titus's hand moving furiously under the water, but he had no clue what he was doing. He couldn't see anything.

Killian tilted his head in confusion. "What are you doing to him?"

Titus's eyes were slightly glazed but he smirked at the prince, fully aware of his question.

"Why don't you give him a better view?" Drek suggested amusedly.

Titus rose out of the water, tugging Orion up by the waist. He turned Orion around until his bare bottom was pointed in their direction. It was round and full. Tugging one thigh, Orion's legs spread and in between his round cheeks was a puckered circle of skin, dark like his nipples. It was twitching and crying as clear fluids dripped out of the opening and down his thigh.

A fluid that looked familiar to him.

Killian stared at it intensely.

Drek let out a small groan at the sight.

"Orion is the only regular Incubus I know who can produce slick," Drek said appreciatively. His grin widened as Titus licked the substance from Orion's thigh, causing him to whimper.

Slick?

Was that what Killian looked like when he made it?

Knowing that made his body tingle.

Titus licked and lapped at Orion's thighs before finally delving in the middle, sticking his tongue inside that winking hole. Orion cried out, nearly collapsing onto the marble.

Titus grabbed each globe of Orion's butt in his hands and squeezed it as he devoured the Incubus. When he pulled away, the skin was red and swollen but still producing that slick.

Titus stuck his middle finger into his mouth, sucking on it for a while before pulling it out with a wet pop and sliding it deep into Orion's hole.

"Titus!" Orion screamed, the front of him finally falling onto the marble but his backside was still in the air like an offering.

Titus grinned, before pushing his finger in deeper, then sliding it out, almost completely. Then he dipped it back inside, pushing and pulling, making Orion a moaning mess.

That's what Rem was doing to Killian? How could something so strange feel so good?

It was weird watching someone else go through what he had experienced not too long ago. It was almost as if he were watching himself through a mirror. He could almost feel Rem's phantom fingers entering him and leaving him over and over again.

The tingling in his body started to spread. It was a feeling he was becoming well acquainted with.

Rem said Killian shouldn't push this feeling too hard or else he'll lapse into shock again from the fear of his previous assault, but he couldn't help himself. Seeing Orion in so much pleasure that he was practically delirious, made Killian almost giddy for more. He wanted to know all about this level of intimacy. He wanted to push it with his chosen Consorts. He wanted to go further with them. Now that he had Zev too, he could only imagine how intense it would be.

Titus pushed a second finger into Orion's hole making the Incubus drool on the marble, his back arching and hips moving against Titus's digits.

Drek reached down in the water before him for a moment before turning to Killian and grinning.

"Why don't you sit here? You'll get a better view," he offered.

Killian looked at him curiously then at his lap.

It couldn't hurt right?

Killian sat in Rem's lap often. It was important for him to get close to his Potentials. He had to be the initiator of the contact since they could not. He wouldn't know if they were right for him if he did not put them in a position to show him what it was like to be together, right?

Killian scooched over, closer to the green-skinned Potential, before raising up a little bit and placing himself on his lap.

"Permission to touch you, Killian?" Drek asked.

Killian nodded hesitantly, before clarifying. "Not the way they are!"

Drek chuckled.

"Of course," he amended. "Just around the waist so you don't fall. Things might get a little intense and you'll want something to keep you in place."

He whispered the words just along Killian's neck making every little hair stand to attention. His face heated as he looked back over to the couple. Titus was now sitting on the ledge of the pool while Orion was draped over his lap, his mouth furiously working on the dark blue cock.

It was something he attempted with Rem, but he was not nearly as skilled as Orion seemed to be. Killian admired the way his lips fit over the bulbous head of Titus's shaft. How the very tip of his tongue traced one of the thick veins along the side of the shaft. How he moved his tongue ever so slightly over the little slit at the top. Or even how his cheeks hollowed when he plunged down, taking the length down his throat.

It was nothing at all like the prince had done. And from the way Titus's eyes were screwed shut and groans left his mouth, he guessed he should be taking notes on the performance.

Drek's hands slid around Killian's waist, tugging him back closer to his chest. Killian went with no resistance, sliding against his legs until something heavy bumped the small of his back. He knew what it was immediately and squeaked in shock.

"It's alright, I won't do anything," Drek told Killian. "And pay attention, you don't want to miss the best part."

Killian looked back at the couple again. Orion was climbing on top of Titus's lap now, and something big was about to happen. It looked like he was going to...

Killian's eyes widened and suddenly he was scared.

He wasn't going to put that in there was he?

It would hurt.

It would hurt really badly.

Jax's face flashed into his mind.

You're mine.

"Killian?" the prince heard someone call but their voice sounded far away. There was a thumping in his eardrums that blocked everything else out. It grew louder and louder.

You're mine.

Killian didn't want to feel this anymore. The tingling grew worse as he felt his body react. His insides felt warm. His butt was hot. It was burning.

He hated this feeling!

And it kept getting worse!

Jax.

Why did he keep haunting him? Why couldn't he just leave him alone? He was dead!

"You idiots!" Killian heard a voice in the distance shout.

The prince's vision was blurred. He could see Zev screaming at Orion, Drek, and Titus, but there was someone pulling him up out of the water.

Someone warm.

Someone that made the tingles spread even more.

Killian screamed.

"It is me, Killian. Rem. You are safe."

He couldn't process it in his mind. All he could feel was Jax's touch. His hands on his skin, the feel of him pressing up against him, the tingling sensation, the burning.

Please stop.

"You can't just expose him to stuff like that! He was assaulted! He'll go into shock if you push him too far!"

There was no way that Zev could know that, not without Rem telling him.

Killian could smell Rem's intoxicating scent and it made his shaft heavy and the burning increased much more than before. He wanted to cry.

"Make it go away," Killian whimpered. "I don't want to feel it anymore."

"We will make it go away, Killian," Rem promised.

Killian felt Rem scoop him up into his arms and hold the prince to his chest. Killian was dripping wet and shivering. His clothes were getting soaked, but he didn't seem to care.

"Zev, let us go," Rem command.

They were moving, and Killian could feel the vibrations of every step Rem took. He could hear his steps and Zev's beside them. The slick dripped down his skin and it made him choke.

Why did this happen?

Why did he feel so disgusting?

Why couldn't it just go away?

Zev opened the door to the room and Rem set Killian down on the bed, peeling off his wet robe and drying him off with a towel. The rough sensation of the towels sliding over his sensitive skin made the tingling that much worse.

He'd never felt like this before.

He thought he was going to burst into flames.

Killian screamed again, begging and pleading for the feeling to go away.

But with each scream, a new volume of slick gushed out of him. He cried, tears wetting his skin, as he sank into the sheets and pillows.

Rem's dark face hovered over Killian's.

"We are going to make it go away. I promise," he said before kissing the distraught Prince.

Killian loved kissing Rem, but right now, kissing him pushed another wave of slick from his body. He felt uncomfortable and he couldn't enjoy it much as he normally would.

But Rem was persistent, keeping his lips glued to Killian's, cupping his jaw in one hand to keep him in place. Rem's other hand restrained his legs.

He kissed Killian with passion, with determination. It wasn't like his normal kisses.

Another pair of hands glided along Killian's thighs, spreading his legs open. They were rough and calloused but warm.

Zev.

Killian tensed, trying to pull his body away, but Rem was strong and held him in place. The Consort kissed him deeper than before, planting his tongue into his mouth and coaxing him to follow his lead.

The hands on Killian's thighs turned to lips and the prince could feel them whispering along his heated skin, igniting a trail in their wake.

"No!" Killian shouted, writhing in their arms. "I want it to go away."

"We are going to make it go away, but you must trust us, Killian. Trust your Consorts to take care of you. We will protect you."

He cried harder. Sobs shook his body.

Rem kissed him again just as the lips on his thighs delved deeper. Killian couldn't contain himself or his movements. It was so strange, as if he were experiencing these crazy sensations but his mind was detached from it all. He couldn't keep his head and his body in sync. His body craved more but he was terrified in his mind.

He wanted it to end.

But he didn't want them to stop. He didn't know what he wanted anymore. Everything was blurring together.

Rem got hold of Killian's knees, pressing them into his chest as Rem kissed and sucked on his neck, bruising the skin and leaving marks in his wake. He was entirely focused on the act while another was inching closer and closer to that one spot that would throw him over the edge.

Rem kissed Killian's lips again.

Slick squirted out of him and onto Zev's face. What coated his lips, he licked away with a flick of his tongue before burying his head between the prince's cheeks.

Just like Titus did with Orion.

Killian knew what was going to happen, but nothing prepared him for the feeling of Zev's tongue on his hole.

"Mmffff!" Killian screamed against Rem's lips, bucking against him.

Zev held him in place while he worked his tongue against his hole, brushing the ridges with the tip of his tongue in gentle strokes.

It felt so good.

So so good.

Killian moaned, pushing his hips closer to Zev. He wanted to feel more.

Rem pinched his nipple, forcing a gasp from him. The pain was there but not like when he flicked his own nipple. What did he do that was different? How could they make this pain into something Killian craved?

How were they doing this to him?

How did they turn his fear into...this?

Killian quivered in Rem's arms.

Zev's thumb gently rubbed circles on Killian's ankle while he lapped at his hole.

His mouth traveled upwards, sucking Killian's sac into his mouth. He nibbled at the sensitive skin and it drove the prince insane.

But when his mouth enclosed over Killian's member...something in him exploded.

From Killian's shaft and from his butt, fluid spurted out, drenching his newest Consort.

Killian moaned louder than he ever had before, panting, sinking into the bed completely drained. The tingling had diminished, and the burning was now a faint sensation secondary to what he was currently feeling.

Killian was completely spent, and he had no idea what had just happened.

"Is it gone?" Zev asked in a soft voice.

Killian couldn't speak but nodded in reply.

Zev let out a relieved sigh before crawling off the bed and disappearing from the room.

Rem picked up Killian's limp body and laid him on a chaise while he removed the soiled sheets from the bed, replacing them with clean ones.

The bedroom door opened again, and Zev returned with a clean face and two wet cloths in his hand. He gave one to Rem and they both proceeded to clean Killian's body. When the prince was free of any fluids, they laid him on the bed again, Rem lying facing him and Zev cradling him from behind. The warmth of their bodies was comforting.

He felt safe.

Protected.

Comfortable.

Loved.

Killian's eyelids started to droop, but he fought to keep them open. He wanted to revel in this moment just a little bit longer. He didn't want reality to hit him in the face again.

"Sleep, Killian. We will be right here in the morning," Rem told Killian.

"You promise?" the prince slurred, fighting the fatigue with all of his being.

"We promise," Zev whispered.
He let his eyes close.

Chapter 8

Bright rays of sunshine bled through the thick folds of the deep red curtains that hung over the vast windows, looking over the wide expanse of the castle grounds. Trees towered nearly a hundred feet in the air. The leaves were a mirage of colors, from deep greens, to dark reds, and bright yellows.

Light trickled inside, highlighting the skin of Killian's sleeping Consorts with stripes of light. They danced across the smooth skin of Rem's cheek and Zev's muscled forearm.

Killian's breath left in a relieved rush, flooding out his nostrils with a soft whistle as his eyes forced themselves open.

They were still here.

It wasn't a dream.

Part of him was relieved and horrified at the same time. He couldn't for the life of him remember what happened, only the burning desire to wake up with his Consorts. His need for them both was stifling and a little frightening.

He expected as much with Rem, but Zev was slowly easing his way beside Rem in his affections.

The warm sensation of his deep, gentle breaths washed over the delicate skin of Killian's neck and made it flush with heat. The hard ripples of his abdomen were pressed tightly against Killian's back, not leaving any space between them. Zev's leg trapping one of his underneath him. His arm was a heavy but comfortable weight along the prince's waist over the sheet.

One of his own legs was hiked around Rem's hip while his cheek was buried into his shoulder. That first glance this close made Killian a little breathless. His breath was cool as it hit the prince's face softly in his slumber. His hair was tangled with Zev's, both creating a dark blanket along their skin. Thankfully, Killian's was still bound in a braid.

The prince watched Rem's chest rise and fall slowly, his arm strewn across it, surely leaving the imprints of his magix etched into his skin.

Killian shifted a little and almost immediately, Rem awoke. His eyes snapped open to reveal those dark depths.

Damn.

He wanted to watch him just a little bit longer but with Rem's awakening came Zev's.

The arm around his waist tightened. Zev's large hand expanded over the bare skin of Killian's stomach, slowly sliding up to his chest. Killian's stomach quivered.

He didn't think the act was intentional as he was still in the early stages of waking up, but it still had an effect on the prince.

Zev's nose skimmed along Killian's spine, before his lips settled against the back of his neck, placing a soft kiss there.

Killian trembled.

"Are you well?" Rem asked. His voice deep, husky. That husky morning voice almost had him busting a *Haise* right then and there.

Still a little dazed, Killian didn't answer right away.

It must have worried them both. They immediately tensed up.

"I am fine, but I am a little confused. I cannot seem to remember what happened last night," he admitted.

Both Consorts hesitated.

"You had an anxiety attack. Something you experienced triggered your trauma," Rem answered, his voice carrying a surprising and uncharacteristic edge to it.

Was he angry?

"Those idiots," Zev muttered, angry as well. His voice was a bit raspy from sleep but incredibly irresistible.

Killian could definitely get used to waking up like this every morning.

Morning...

It seemed a bit brighter in the room than usual when he woke up. He was actually surprised Lisa wasn't barging in here like she always did.

Killian frowned, sat up a little to glance at the window and noticed how high the sun was in the sky.

It was already noon!

Rem must have seen the alarm on his face and raised his hand to caress the prince's cheek. "It is alright. I have asked that you be excused from your morning duties. You needed your rest."

"But--" Killian started to protest.

Zev rose up to kiss his exposed shoulder.

"Rem is right. You need to just take it easy right now. You should lay back down."

Killian hesitated before letting Zev guide him back to the comfort of the bed. The prince sank back into the safe cocoon between his two Consorts. But as comfortable as he felt, he was a little worried. What happened last night that has them so concerned?

The Consorts

To cancel his morning duties, it seemed really serious. They said he was triggered.

You're mine.

Jax's face flashed into his mind again. He gasped.

The sound raised alarm for his two Consorts. Both of their heads shot up in worry, brows furrowed identically.

"Killian?"

Fear ran through his veins like ice, every little hair standing at attention. His chest tightened and his gut clenched.

What was this feeling?

"I am afraid," Killian said brokenly.

"You are okay, we are right here. Right beside you and we will protect you. Nothing will happen to you while we are beside you, okay? You are safe," Zev promised, kissing his chilled skin and rubbing his hands along Killian's arm as if to warm him up.

Rem tilted his jaw, forcing the prince to look at him before he kissed him on the lips. It was a fierce kiss that reaffirmed Zev's promise.

Killian let out a shaky breath.

The feeling was starting to dissipate but it rattled there, in the depths of his mind, reminding him that he would never be out of danger. That no matter what his Consorts' promised, they could not protect him from his own mind.

But he valued their effort and sincerity.

"He haunts me even in death," Killian whispered.

Zev and Rem said nothing but continued to caress him.

They lay like that for several moments until Killian's breathing finally slowed to a normal pace. He was strangely calm. It was as if these two men were the key to his contentedness. Where his emotions were a wild storm inside of him, his Consorts were the calm that laid them all to rest and he could see how important they would be in his reign.

It was amazing.

Was this how his father felt around his Consort mothers? Would it get stronger with every Consort he chose?

A soft knock sounded on the door.

"Come in," Zev called out.

Ethel cracked open the door and poked her head in. She looked relieved to see the prince awake. With a bit of caution, she entered the room.

"I was wondering if His Highness was feeling better?" she asked looking at Killian, buried under the bodies of his Consorts.

"I am fine, Ethel, thank you. I will be out soon."

"Would you like me to dress you? Or would you prefer to leave that to your Consorts?" she asked, glancing at Rem and Zev.

"My Consorts and I will dress on our own."

Ethel nodded.

"I have your outfits prepared."

Kara entered the room a second after with a rack of three outfits and tray with their shoes. Killian smiled at them both before dismissing them.

Rem was the first to get out of bed.

Killian appreciated the view of his muscled back dipping into low hanging red silk pants. His hair waved unbound down to his ankles in a wild mass of silky soft beauty. He glanced at Killian from over his shoulder, eyes smoldering, which should have been impossible with how black his eyes were, before he opened the curtains.

Zev rolled out of bed next. His own legs were clad in black silk bottoms. His navy locks gracefully curled down his back with blinding streaks of white interwoven in the delicate strands. His light blue skin darkening as the blood rushed to the surface in response to the heat of the suns' rays beating down on him.

His two horns glinted in the light and Killian could see the faint protrusions of his wing cartilage shifting underneath the skin between his shoulder blades as if they wanted to spring out.

They were both breathtaking.

And they were his.

The thought made him giddy.

His Consorts got dressed while Killian reluctantly pushed the sheets off his body and did the same.

Killian slipped on his boots before choosing a collar for each of them. Though Rem would never express it, Killian could tell he did not like wearing a collar. Killian contemplated letting him go without, but then knew that as a Consort, it was something that he'd just have to get used to.

Killian's stomach growled.

That was their cue to head to lunch. Breakfast for them considering how late they had slept.

No one was in the dining hall. The prince and his Consorts had the room all to themselves. They ate leisurely. When they neared the end of their meal, Lisa entered, parchment pad in hand.

"Glad to see you are feeling well, Your Highness," Lisa greeted.

Killian nodded at her.

"When you are finished with your meal, your Father wants you and your Consorts to join him in a meeting today."

"With whom?" he asked.

"Velma," she answered.

Killian's blood ran cold.

"Velma? And why exactly is she here?" he asked, keeping his voice empty.

"Lord Netter, his wife Lady Kendra, and your cousins Lord Bennett, Lord Filo, and Lady Marza will soon be visiting the palace."

Killian clenched his fork.

Rem's eyes flickered to the small movement before they flew up to the prince's face. "Understood. We will be in the meeting room shortly."

Velma was Uncle Netter's attendant. When she came, it usually meant that his family was coming to visit. Uncle Netter was a kind male and Aunt Kendra was sweet as well. He could not say the same for the triplets.

Killian's jaw clenched.

Lisa left the hall promptly, leaving them in silence.

"You are displeased," Rem noted.

Killian didn't reply, just finished his food.

The silence stretched on.

When his plate was cleared, Killian answered in a calm and composed voice. "Why would you say that?"

Rem stared at him blankly. His expression might have read as empty, but Killian could tell he was challenging him. Daring him to prove his assumption incorrect. How accustomed Killian had become to reading his near emotionless lover.

"Do you not wish to see them?" Zev asked.

"I am elated that my family is coming to visit," Killian answered mechanically.

Zev and Rem shared a look before looking back at the prince with empty stares.

Great...

Now they were both doing it.

Killian sighed.

"Come on. It is unwise to keep the King waiting any longer."

They may not understand now.

But they would...

The King waited at the head of the long oak table with a stack of documents before him and a goblet of steaming hot tea. His hair was unbound, waving down his shoulders. Atop his head was a golden crown interwoven with red rubies and linked to his four black horns, protruding from his lavender skin that matched Killian's own. Killian noticed it was a little paler than his usual complexion. His gray eyes were tight and focused on the documents in front of him. His brow crinkled in stress making the lines on the corners of his eyes more prevalent.

Killian was used to him smiling and laughing, full of life, that he was unprepared to see his father looking this worn and exhausted.

How long had he been ignorant of his state?

"Father?" Killian called to him.

His head lifted and the Consorts bowed to him.

"Oh Killian! Are you feeling better? Lisa told me you weren't feeling well this morning."

"I am well now, Father."

"Good, that's good," he murmured, looking a bit out of sorts. Killian watched him with concern.

He motioned for his Consorts to sit, which they did, obediently, while he approached his father and kneeled next to his chair. He was being pretty informal, something he would never do if anyone, but his Consorts were in the room. Killian grabbed his father's hand and clutched it between his own. Giving him a gentle squeeze, Killian sent a pulse of power through the King, just as his Mother taught him.

Fatigue.

Malnourishment.

Stress.

The causes came at him instantly and he frowned.

Killian had seen him eating; why was he malnourished?

His father blinked at him, confused for a moment, as if he didn't recognize where he was or why Killian was holding his hand.

"Killian, you did not have to go to such lengths. I am fine and well."

Killian narrowed my eyes at him.

"You are not fine. I can feel it. What is going on? You were not like this yesterday."

Father sighed, leaning back in his chair. "I've been a bit tired. Ruling is a taxing job, I will warn you of that now. And raising children is even harder."

"Raising a child is harder than ruling our people?" Killian asked skeptically with a raised brow.

His father grinned, pale in comparison to his usual ones. "That it is. You will learn that lesson soon enough."

Killian groaned but smiled at him anyway. Then he grew serious again.

"After this meeting with Velma, I want you to rest Father. Please. I can take over the rest of your duties for today. It will be great practice for the future."

Father shook his head.

"You have to focus on choosing your next three Consorts. Spending time with your Potentials. I can take care of the Kingdom."

Killian sighed. It was just like him to be this stubborn. He was notorious for it. But Killian guessed that's where he got it from.

"If I chose my third Consort today, would you let me take over for the rest of the day so you can get some food in your system and sleep? I know Mother and my Consort mothers must be worried."

His father frowned.

"Don't rush such an important decision on my behalf. These are the men that will be tied to you for the rest of your life."

"I am not rushing. I already chose my third Consort and informed them that they were chosen." Rem and Zev's heads snapped up at this. Killian's father's eyes widened in surprise. Killian continued, "I was just waiting until my current Consorts grew comfortable with each other before extending the formal proposition to my third chosen."

"And who might this third Consort be?" the King asked.

"Faust," Killian answered simply.

His father pursed his lips.

Killian glanced over at Zev and Rem.

Rem's expression was mildly interested while Zev looked impassive. Killian couldn't tell if the latter was unhappy or not as he had his arrogant mask set in place, keeping the prince from reading him.

"Faust. Not a bad choice," Father remarked.

Killian internally beamed at the approval.

"I even have my fourth choice in mind. But he has no idea yet."

The King looked surprised again. Zev looked suspicious and Rem was completely clear of any emotion. That he'd seen any at all in the first place earlier was abnormal.

"And will you share the name of that choice?"

Killian thought about it for a moment before shaking his head. He looked at his father meaningfully then darted his gaze over to his current Consorts.

The King's eyes narrowed in understanding.

"Another time then," he allowed.

"So, will you agree?" Killian pushed, squeezing his hand again.

The King nodded reluctantly.

Killian stood, kissing his father's cheek before taking a seat at the head of the table with his Consorts on either side of him.

At that moment, the large dark wood doors that towered high toward the ceilings, slid open reveal Lisa with a short dark-haired Succubae. A Succubae Killian knew quite well.

Her skin was a very pale green and her golden eyes were wide and bright. Her pupils were large, and she looked a lot like a cat. But not in the elegant way that Caspian resembled a feline. No, she was like a cat in their eerie way of blinking with those big glowing eyes and mischievous intent.

Her black hair was tied up in an elegant bun with a few tendrils curling around her two short horns and she wore a long navy dress. She bowed graciously toward the King then to Killian.

"Greetings, King Ellis Innis of Incubi. Greetings Prince Killian Innis, heir to the throne of Incubi and his Consorts."

Her voice was nasally and quite unpleasant, but Killian smiled anyway just as his father did.

"Velma," the King greeted.

"Velma," Killian repeated in greeting.

The Consorts remained silent.

The King motioned for her to take a seat at the table. The way she held her head high and aimed for a graceful stride. It was something Killian was used to seeing whenever Velma came to the palace.

She wanted to be one of them so badly that she'd pretend to herself that she was of royal blood, ordering others around as if she had the power and abusing it quite frequently. It irritated Killian. His loyal servants and attendants worked hard and did not need someone who had no business playing royal, barking orders at them nastily.

The staff here were not slaves. They were not lower beings. They were their subjects just as well and they chose to be here. It is not a job they are shackled to. And to be honest, they loved working there. The Innis's get millions of applications yearly, desperately wanting to be one of their staff.

To have someone come here and mistreat them like that...well it didn't sit well with Killian. Not at all.

It also didn't help that she was as vile as his cousins to whom she attended.

As she sat, Killian saw her golden eyes flick over to his Consorts. Her eyes wracked over Rem and Zev appreciatively before she turned her full attention to the King.

"My King, you look well."

Liar. He looked terrible.

"Thank you, Velma. I take it your arrival means my brother is coming for a visit?" he asked.

"Yes, My King. And he brings his wife Lady Kendra, and your niece and nephews, Lord Bennett, Lord Filo, and Lady Marza. They plan to come after Prince Killian has chosen all of his Consorts of course."

She shot another glance at his Consorts.

Killian held back a snarl.

"That's great news! They'll be here just in time for the ball we're throwing in celebration of Killian and his Consorts," the King boomed happily. His voice vibrated in Killian's eardrums.

"Father, we have not discussed a ball," Killian told him.

He managed to look a little sheepish.

"I was going to keep it a surprise but...I couldn't hold back," he grinned again, his signature smile.

"Father that is too much--" Killian started but the King interrupted.

"Nonsense! This is something to celebrate!" he cheered. "Isn't that right?" he turned to the Consorts for confirmation.

"Yes, My King," they recited in unison.

The King looked back at Killian smugly.

As if they would ever openly disagree with the King.

The prince wanted to roll his eyes. It was a physical effort not to, but he managed to keep his face clear of anything but slight--falsified--joy.

"It will be great to see the family again," Killian sighed in defeat.

The Consorts

"Please, discuss with Lisa the plans and accommodations you'll need," the King told Velma.

"Of course, My King. Thank you for allowing us into your home, you are so very kind."

"Family is family," the King said firmly before dismissing her. Lisa came to fetch her and immediately started discussing the plans for their future guests.

The entire meeting was short as it always was, but whenever there were guests coming to stay at the palace, they must send an attendant to the palace formally to request a visit and that always went through the King.

When she was gone, Killian sighed in relief but was very short lived considering he still had to deal with the arrival of his family.

The King never seemed to notice Killian's lack of enthusiasm whenever they came to visit. It was either that or he was ignoring it, but he couldn't imagine his father being that insensitive or careless.

"Remember our deal, Father. You get some rest and I will take over your duties today."

"Go find your next Consort and proposition him first. Then I'll get some rest."

Killian sighed again.

So stubborn.

"As you wish, Father," the prince said, then made his exit. His Consorts bowed to his father before leaving behind him.

It was when they made it back to their bedroom that they lost their rigidness and silence.

Zev was the first to break it.

"You chose your third Consort? Already?"

Killian nodded.

Zev looked like he wanted to be upset, but he only succeeded in being defeated. He didn't really have a right to be upset. He knew there would be three more, he knew that Killian did not have to discuss his choices with him, he knew he had to share, but he still couldn't help being jealous.

Killian didn't get mad at him this time because he could see Zev was making an effort to accept the dynamics of their relationship. It made Killian like him even more.

Killian touched his shoulder before leaning into his chest.

Zev's arms wrapped around his waist and pulled him flush against his hard planes. Killian peered up at him, gazing into those beguiling, piercing blue eyes.

"I know this is hard for you, but I know you will grow to think of my Consorts as your brothers. They will be soon. And we will all be family. I understand that this is new to you, it is new for me too, but we will get through this together and we will be stronger that way," the prince told him.

Zev sighed, then leaned down to kiss him.

Oh Zev.

He was already so precious to Killian.

Killian glanced at his other Consort.

Rem watched them quietly, keeping a slight distance.

Killian broke away from Zev's arms and threw himself into Rem's. He hugged him tightly with all his might, that which he returned gently and much less fierce than the prince.

"How do you feel Rem? About Faust?"

"I do not have a say," he replied automatically.

Killian rolled my eyes.

"I am giving you a say right now," he told him.

Rem was quiet for a moment before responding, "I am not opposed."

Killian tilted his head and narrowed his eyes at him.

"Would you be opposed to anyone I choose?" Killian asked him.

He surprised Killian when his eyes hardened.

"Yes, there are some," he responded.

Killian was too shocked to answer. But quickly, he shook his head and stepped back from him.

"Well then, I will be back. I am going to proposition Faust. Could you inform Ethel of my newest addition?"

Rem and Zev nodded while Killian left the room.

Killian sought out Faust and of course, as usual when he was seeking someone, he found Caspian first. Outside in the garden, surrounded by radiant flowers, he was in the tree again, resting on a low branch.

Killian walked up to him and noticed he was fast asleep. He looked innocent with smooth golden skin glistening, and full lips parted slightly. His red lashes framed his high cheeks gracefully and his dark reddish-brown horns curled around his temples. His red and orange locks spilled over his shoulder and the ledge of the branch.

He was stunning.

Killian knelt beside him, watching the soft rise and fall of his chest. It was soothing.

That is until his tail twitched and his face scrunched up as if he were in pain. The gentle fluctuation of his chest was now stuttering in panic. His breath quickened and the muscles in his arms tensed. Killian saw the contraction of his toned abdomen.

He was having a nightmare.

Killian moved to brush his face softly and wake him up, but Caspian's hand struck fast, clasping around the prince's wrist in a tight grip and his eyes flew open. His pupils were completely dilated, almost completely enveloping the glowing yellow irises in black.

He seemed dazed and disoriented until he blinked, focusing on Killian's face and realizing it who it was. His eyes darted to his hand which grasped Killian's wrist before widening in horror.

"I-" he started, but Killian cut him off with a soft caress on his cheek with his other hand.

"It is alright, I will not say a word."

He released Killian's wrist slowly, sighing in relief.

Killian glanced down at it and hoped it didn't bruise. He'd have a hard time explaining if it did.

"You looked like you were having a nightmare," Killian commented, stroking the soft tendrils of his hair from his face.

Caspian didn't say anything to that, just purred lightly at his touch. His eyes fluttered closed. Killian kept stroking his hair until he fell back asleep. Watching him a little bit longer, Killian waited until Caspian was deep in a peaceful slumber before he took his leave.

Caspian interested him. Killian felt like there was so much more to him than he let on and the prince wanted to know everything that made up the male before him.

That's why he would be the prince's fourth choice.

Killian finally found Faust in the sparring room, a place he definitely didn't expect.

His white hair was tied up in a tight ponytail, matching the very white of his skin. His black eyes were just as stark as the two small horns that protruded from his forehead.

He was wielding a spear with expert ease. His movements were controlled and skilled. It surprised Killian.

He'd seen Faust fight of course, during the first tests when the Potentials sparred against each other, but Killian had not known him the way he did now. It seemed out of character for him to be fighting, but as he watched Faust swing the weapon with precision, Killian became aware that Faust was a warrior, whether he thought him one or not.

Killian watched him train for a little bit before Faust noticed his presence and stopped. Wiping the sweat from his brow, he approached Killian with a smile.

"Killian, how nice to see you," he greeted.

Killian smiled back.

"I am surprised to find you here," Killian told him.

He laughed, the sound like bells. Killian could listen to the soft melody all day.

"I have to maintain my skills if I am to be worthy of the role of your Consort."

"About that...I am here to formally ask, would you be my Consort?"

Faust seemed a little unprepared for the question despite Killian telling him beforehand that he was chosen.

"I thought you were going to take some time to let your current Consorts grow comfortable with each other?"

Killian shrugged.

"They are."

For the most part...

Faust's smile widened.

"I'd be honored then."

He leaned in to kiss Killian's cheek.

It was kind and gentle, just like him.
Three down...two to go.

Chapter

9

King Ellis finally conceded and resigned to bed early.

Thankfully, the work he left behind was easy to deal with. There weren't many meetings, just a lot of paperwork.

Rem finished his lessons early and was able to stay with Killian, but Zev and Faust both had lessons that claimed them for the day. Zev was fast catching up with Rem's level of Consort knowledge but Faust had quite a way to go.

Killian was nearing the end of his last pile but as tired and outright irritated as he was, it became incredibly difficult to finish.

He huffed a sigh of aggravation, running his fingers through his hair. A few strands caught around the tip of his horn making it tug painfully at his scalp and succeeded to piss him off even more.

Rem was silent as he got up and brushed Killian's hands away and gently untangled his hair. His fingers were warm and as soon as they met Killian's skin, the prince sighed in contentment, visibly relaxing.

"Perhaps a break is in order," Rem suggested quietly.

"I cannot take a break; I am almost finished. My father would have finished this horas ago--"

"But you are not your father, nor do you have to be."

Killian scowled at him, but he returned the look unperturbed.

"Eventually, I will be," the prince reminded him, though he couldn't imagine that was something Rem had forgotten.

"No," he said.

Killian's brow scrunched in confusion.

"No?" the prince repeated.

Rem's black gaze was unwavering. "No," he repeated. "You will not be your Father; you will be your own King. You will be yourself and not an imitation. You will be King Killian Innis."

Killian stared at his Consort, feeling warm inside. The confidence Rem had in him was surprising but well received. Though, the pep talk was...unexpected coming from him. Killian figured that would be more up Faust's alley.

Faust.

Another sigh escaped his lips. He wanted to be there for Faust through his whole transition. Killian wanted to spend more time with him on his first day of being his Consort, but he'd been stuck in the study all day, doing paperwork. Killian could blame no one but himself. He chose to do this, volunteered for it so that his father could get the much-needed rest he deserved. Thinking about that made Killian feel a bit better.

Killian wanted to be a good King and a good son.

Rem's fingers smoothed against Killian's shoulders. He rubbed his skin carefully in a soothing manner. He knew what his touch did to the prince and was using it to calm him down.

He really was a wonderful Consort.

"Maybe a break would be best," Killian gave in.

Glancing over at his half-eaten dinner, Killian decided that food was not really what he wanted at the moment.

"Let us take a bath."

Rem nodded, standing aside. The prince rose. One the way out, Killian asked a servant to take away his uneaten food and make sure that no else entered the study as he would be returning after his bath.

Killian walked with Rem down the hall toward the bedroom to get ready for the bath. The prince noticed how the servants and attendants would stop and stare, whispering as they saw them down the hall. There were a lot more of them than usual and a mix of both Incubi and Succubae. Killian assumed it was because of the various guests they had and his choosing of Consorts. They needed more hands. But Killian could safely say that most of them had not laid eyes on him or his Consort before.

"That's him isn't it?"

"Is that his Consort?"

"He's so pretty! Like a Succubae!"

"That's the prince's first chosen, right?"

"Look at his horns!"

"I heard the prince's first has magix!"

The frenzied whispers stopped once they passed. The servants bowed in respect. Killian gave them all a slight nod while Rem remained stoic.

When they disappeared into their room, Killian turned to look up at his Consort. He touched Rem's chest, feeling his two hearts beat in sync. Killian hummed, stepping closer and lay his head on Rem's chest, twisting his fingers through that beautiful black hair.

"Your name fills the halls. They look upon you in awe."

Rem was quiet, but Killian could feel the whispers of fingers along his spine, slowly easing their way up and down his back.

"How do you feel about that?" Killian asked.

"I have no objections," he replied.

As Killian knew he wouldn't.

He wished that he could get a rise out of Rem. His unending control made Killian doubtful of his feelings, as irrational as it sounded. Then he immediately thought of the time when Rem almost lost control of his magix while they were...

A blush colored his cheeks.

Rem raised a brow.

Killian pulled back and hurried over to the closet, willing his blush away. The prince tugged off his clothes and draped the robe over his shoulders.

Rem was already dressed and ready to go. Killian latched onto his arm and led them to the bathroom. Soon, when all of his Consorts were chosen, they would be moved to a larger room with a private bathroom. He couldn't wait.

They were about to enter the bath when someone emerged.

From the stunning bronze skin, and vibrant red hair, Killian knew who it was immediately.

Orion.

He looked over at the prince, blushed, then looked at Rem.

He opened his mouth as if he were about to greet them but then another figure appeared behind him laughing loudly.

"Why'd you stop, Orion?" a familiar voice asked.

Killian's youngest brother, Pierce, appeared behind Orion. His white hair was grayed, wet from the bath. His blue eyes were wide and bright, and his lavender skin just slightly flushed.

When he saw Killian, his grin widened.

"Brother!" he greeted.

"Pierce," Killian responded with a smile. "Though we live together and eat meals together everyday, I feel as if I have not seen you for quite a while," he told him.

"Yeah, but that's to be expected since you're focused on finding your Consorts. Do not worry brother, your siblings are not offended," he smiled, knowing how terribly Killian felt for neglecting his family. Before, Killian tried to spend as much time with them as he could in between his duties as heir, which wasn't a lot. Since Pierce rarely left the palace, too engaged with training with the Guard, Killian saw him the most. He cherished his baby brother.

"I promise that once it is all over, I will spend more time with you all."

"I look forward to it." Pierce gave a wave before disappearing down the hall.

Killian looked up at Orion who was staring after his brother before turning his attention to the prince. He had a weird look in his eyes but it cleared and became gentle.

"Hello, Killian."

"It is nice to see you Orion. I am glad I ran into you," Killian told him.

Orion's face twisted into confusion, then as his eyes flickered to Rem's, fear.

"I'm sorry for before, My Prince. I did not know--"

"Enough," Rem cut him off.

Killian frowned at his Consort. The look he was giving the Potential was deadly. Orion became frozen, panic clear in his eyes.

"I just wanted to invite you have a private dinner with me tonight," Killian continued, unsure of what just unfolded.

Rem made a less than pleased noise, but it was very quiet, and Killian didn't think he was meant to hear it. He almost didn't and would not have if he wasn't so attuned to Rem.

"O-of course," Orion replied. "I look forward to it."

"Great! I will see you then," Killian told him with a smile.

He nodded before bowing and departing.

Killian glanced at Rem curiously and saw his expression was blank again.

The urge to demand to know what that was about grew, but he fought it back. King or not, Rem wasn't going to tell him.

Killian sighed.

Though he may be heir, it seemed ruling his Consorts was going to be harder than ruling the Kingdom.

They entered the bath.

Killian asked the nearby servants to make sure they were not disturbed as they were bathing. He didn't feel like keeping his robe on, though he knew Rem would. Killian would behave himself though. He didn't want to have another episode, it'd be embarrassing.

As he predicted, Rem kept his robe on, descending into the water after they both scrubbed down under the spouts. He looked back at Killian, waiting for him to undress and enter the water with him.

Killian slipped the robe off his shoulders before letting it slide to the floor, keeping his eyes locked on Rem's. Rem's eyes--if even possible--grew darker. Killian felt as if he were falling into those black depths like a bottomless sea. He was confused by the look and couldn't quite figure out what he had done to deserve it.

Cocking his head to the side, Killian raised a brow at him.

Rem looked away slowly but stuck out his hand.

Nearly tripping into the water, Killian rushed to grab it, submerging himself in the warmth. The sound of water splashing with their movements and sloshing against the walls of the bath echoed in the vast room.

Their path was short, but their walk was slow until they turned the corner and sat in their usual spot. Of course, Killian took his seat on Rem's lap as he rested on the bench within the bath. Killian's entire body seemed to relax against his chest as he tucked his head along Rem's shoulder, under his chin.

It had only been a few weeks since he chose Rem as his Consort. Only a couple of weeks since Jax's death. Since his assault.

How had time flown by so quickly?

And why did it feel like it was going on forever at the same time?

For twenty-three years, he would wake up, complete his duties as heir and go to sleep. He'd smile at his siblings as he watched them banter with each other and sometimes with him, though not often because he was heir and they had to be 'careful' with how they treated their future King. It was like he was an outsider, not their older brother.

His days were filled with diplomatic smiles and royal etiquette. He was kind and fair. He never raised his voice, never spoke out, never stepped out of line.

He was a shell of a person.

In just a few weeks, all of that changed. He became someone who stood his ground. Someone who took charge. Someone who voiced their discontent. But somehow, it didn't feel right. He was changing, yes. That much was very true. But he worried that he was not changing in a way that would benefit the kingdom, only in a way that would benefit himself.

As a King, he was to be selfless.

Did that mean the choices he made for his Consorts should benefit the Kingdom? Did his personal preference not really matter? Should he pick based on who would help the Kingdom flourish and not his own desires? Had he been selfish?

Being King is a lonely job.

His father told him this every day. It made him wonder...did his father actually love any of his Consorts? Did his father love his mother? Or was it all for the Kingdom?

Everything seemed like a lie now.

And Rem...Rem still didn't love him.

That one thought made his chest tighten and eyes sting. Gods above, he fought it with all his might. The bitter loneliness that always seemed to find its way inside him, festering like some kind of parasitic disease. He was a host for it and no matter how many Incubi entered his bed, this parasite would not let him go. It'd devour him until he was nothing but a husk again.

He didn't want to go back! He didn't want to be lonely anymore.

I do not want to be King, he thought.

The burning in his eyes grew. He clenched his teeth together and narrowed his eyes in determination.

Kings do not cry.

Killian's hands clenched into fists which did not go unnoticed by Rem. His hand smoothed the prince's open as he leaned to the side so he could see his face.

Killian hurriedly looked away, locks of his hair falling in his face to hide his expression from Rem's probing gaze. He was not fast enough, and Rem had seen all he needed to know that Killian was not okay.

"What is wrong?"

Keep it together Killian. You've shown too much weakness in front of this male already, don't give him any more reason to doubt you. You will be King dammit, he chastised in his mind.

"Rem..." He started, his voice only a shaky whisper and he cursed himself for sounding so pathetic, but he forced himself to continue. He had to know.

"Yes?" he answered.

"Do you--" Killian was still whispering. He cleared his throat and forced sound from his lips. "Do you think you will grow to love me?"

Rem's brows furrowed in confusion.

"You have asked this question and I have answered--"

"No!" Killian shouted, then clenched his teeth tight and squeezed his eyes shut. He tried so hard not to let it overwhelm him. He would not cry. "You have not given me a real answer. Please Rem, I just...I need to know. I need to know where this will go. Just please. Please Rem, answer me. I do not think I can..." Killian's voice broke at the end and he made himself stop talking. He wasn't going to make room for anymore weakness. Rem knew what the prince wanted. What he needed. He knew the answer Killian was looking for.

The prince was met with silence.

"Please..." Killian whispered not trusting himself to speak any louder. Not without letting himself succumb to that bitterness that was tearing into his chest.

Killian waited.

Rem did not speak, just gently shifted the prince on his lap until he faced him. He wrapped Killian's arms around his neck and leaned his forehead against the prince's until they stared at each other, unable to look away.

Rem's mask wasn't so unreadable at this proximity.

In his eyes, the prince could see the swirling colors of emotion, intensity, just swimming within those depths. The indecision, the uncertainty, the...fear.

Rem closed his eyes and inhaled.

"Do you know why I have two hearts?" he asked, his voice a low baritone that made Killian tremble as it always did.

Killian was a little caught off guard by his question but answered anyway. "All of those who have magix are born with two hearts."

"Yes, but do you know why?" he pushed.

"No."

"I have told you before that there is a beast that lurks within me. A beast that at times, has more control of this vessel than I. This beast has his own heart and I have mine."

"Is it...another person?" Killian asked.

"No. I am the beast and the beast is me. It is...difficult to explain but we are two halves of a whole. In some ways we are the same and in some, we are different. He does not talk but he feels."

The prince listened carefully, not used to Rem talking this much. Not used to him explaining. Not at all used to him letting Killian in.

"This beast...my beast...loves you."

Killian eyes widened and his mouth popped open.

Rem...loves him?

He swallowed the overwhelming happiness that he felt but it must have shown in his eyes because Rem's eyes narrowed in anger.

"Do not joy in hearing such news!" he hissed. "Be afraid!"

Rem's eyes were vicious...warm fiery colors rushing around in the darkness as if they were fighting a war before him.

"He has loved you from the moment we laid eyes on you. And this love," he sneered the word, sounding absolutely disgusted, "evolved into obsession."

Rem's eyes were practically glowing.

"I had hoped you would not choose me," his Consort said softly.

"Why?" Killian questioned incredulously.

"You do not want the love of a beast, Killian. You do not understand what he is. This beast is nothing but a monster!"

A tear finally managed to escape Killian's eyes, rolling down his cheek as he stared at Rem in shock.

"I do not understand," he whispered.

Rem tilted his head back and stared at the ceiling. His expression, once wrinkled in repugnance, was now calm and unreadable.

"He will hurt you. He is raw and uncontrolled. His love is too fierce, his obsession too deep. And you are so fragile...so delicate," the last words were whispered. Rem finally looked at Killian again. His expression soft. "You are so very delicate. He will break you."

Killian couldn't look away from those eyes. The intensity was overwhelming. They held him in an unbreakable gaze. He was trapped.

When he could finally find his voice, it sounded strange, breathy.

"You said that he loves me...but what about you?"

Rem leaned close and pressed his forehead against Killian's. There was little distance between them. Killian could feel Rem's cool breath on his skin, flooding his nostrils with that same intoxicating scent that drew him to the male in the first place. Dangerously sweet.

"I am afraid. I do not want him to hurt you. I do not want to succumb to his love. I am him and he is me. But you must understand, Killian," his lips were close, his scent saccharine, Killian's eyes fluttered. "If I succumb to his love...if I let myself love you..."

And then he moved, his lips traveling along the prince's jaw until they reached his ears. His voice a soft quiet whisper.

"I will tear you apart."

Killian gasped. His stomach clenched tight at his words. His breath came out in quick pants. There was a sudden change, but he wouldn't let himself call it fear.

He did not fear Rem.

No matter how hard he tried to get him to.

"I am not afraid," Killian told him.

Rem smiled and it was not a happy one.

"I can feel your heart racing," he said.

"Excitement."

"I can see your eyes dilate."

"Fascination."

"I can feel your body trembling."

"Desire."

He pressed his lips to Killian's in a kiss that rivaled everyone he had ever given him. There was aggression to it. He wasn't even sure it was Rem that he was kissing. The behavior was unlike him.

His soft lips were like rose petals, full and plush. His tongue was like honey, sweet and tender, slowly covering his own. His arms held Killian tight enough that the prince was crushed against his chest, his nipples rubbing harshly against the raised marks of his magix.

Was this his beast?

Was he trying to make him afraid?

If so, he was doing a terrible job of it. If anything, he was only making Killian want him more.

The prince whimpered, wiggling to get his lower body closer to Rem's succeeding in making him jerk away. Breathing hard, Killian stared at him confused. He was doing it again. Running away from intimacy.

"Why do you always stop yourself? You want me, do you not? Why will you not just take me?"

Rem shook his head, his expression tortured. It tore at Killian's chest. He never wanted to see such an agonized expression on his face like that, ever.

"I cannot."

"Rem please. I want you."

"I cannot!"

The shout made Killian jump.

Rem's eyes were fierce again, but his expression had calmed. "I cannot ever lose control with you. I can never let myself succumb to my instincts."

"Why?" Killian questioned, sounding embarrassingly like a whine.

"Because he will take over and I will never see you again."

The way he said it forced Killian to silence. He didn't question it or push him to explain. He just nodded and accepted it because he was starting to understand.

To love Killian meant to lose himself.

Killian would never let that happen.

But if he didn't, how could this love ever be?

After the bath, Rem and Killian went their separate ways. Rem disappeared while Killian finished the paperwork. When that was done, he had a dinner prepared for Orion and himself for later. Queen Jessa panicked after discovering the state the King was in and forced Killian to get examined by a Healer to make sure he too wasn't undergoing too much stress. Though the one she sent was not a typical Healer, she specialized in *Haise* cycles.

Killian was familiar with the pale-yellow skinned Succubus who wore her medium length bubblegum pink curls in a tight bun. She bore two large curved horns that strongly resembled Caspian's, and had dainty features. Her eyes were big and brown, very stark against the rest of her.

Lorn was her name, but most just called her Healer.

Killian wasn't most.

"Hello Lorn," he greeted.

She curtsied gracefully before replying, "Hello Prince Killian. How have you been holding up with your upcoming *Haise?* Any symptoms?"

Killian blushed at the question and the reason why was silly.

"It has been a little...difficult to keep myself under control," he admitted softly.

Lorn gave a knowing smile.

"That is to be expected as you are exposed to so many Potential Incubi as you near your cycle. Any mood swings? Headaches?"

Killian thought back to the several times he had cried--wanted to cry or lost his temper these past few weeks and frowned. "The mood swings have been quite frequent. Alarmingly so. But I have not had any headaches."

Lorn wrote that down with a nod. Then she looked up at him with a solemn expression. It made Killian worry about her next question and rightfully so.

"Have you fed on any of your Consorts or Potentials?"

He gaped at her. "I would never release my *Haise* on them without proper guidance! Who knows what would happen with my inexperience!"

Lorn smiled.

"Sometimes you may end up feeding in small doses without actually realizing it. Once you become active with your Consorts, particularly during the Ranking Ceremony, you will need to release your *Haise* often. If you don't feed, your health could decline rapidly. It is very important to keep yourself well fed."

Killian nodded.

"Have you felt energized lately?" she questioned.

"Quite the opposite actually. I've been a little drained."

She nodded her head again then jotted something down in her parchment pad. "It seems you have not been feeding. The feeling of fatigue may be stronger with your cycle nearing and the lack of sustenance." She did a thorough probing of his skin and general physical health. "I predict it will hit you within the next three days. I understand that originally you were going to spend it with your first two chosen Consorts, but from my understanding, you picked a third?"

Killian nodded. News traveled fast.

She notated it.

"As you are aware, the *Haise* is a very spiritual feeding. And as your Consorts are chosen, you will be tapping into them and feeding off of them, especially when you are pregnant. During this coming *Haise* it is very important to develop that mental and spiritual connection with them. It will make it easier to feed and keep you sustained, thus healthy, alive and well. So, as a precaution, I believe it would be wise for you, after tonight, to halt your interactions with your Potentials and perhaps limit your interactions to only your chosen Consorts. Just until the *Haise* passes. You would not want to feed on your Potentials."

Killian nodded again.

"Alright, I'll let Queen Jessa know of this and have the proper arrangements prepared."

"Alright."

Killian left her to her work and made his way to the garden where he would be having dinner with Orion. The sun was starting to set, and it was a little chilly outside but nothing unbearable. The warmth of summer was still present even as autumn began to seep into the air.

The towering trees rustled gently in the breeze, ruffling like thousands of feathers in the wind, light and flexible. They danced, casting dark shadows in the green grass. The flowers of the garden, giggled and blushed in response, flashing a vibrant range of colors.

He stared at them for a while in awe.

There was a table set up under a small gazebo with candles lit and plates spread. Orion waited for Killian patiently, looking a bit nervous to be honest.

When the prince approached the table, Orion jumped to his feet and bowed in greeting mumbling a "Hello, Killian."

"You do not have to be so formal when it is just us, Orion," Killian told him, waving off his bow and gesturing for him to sit.

The food was already prepared and ready to eat but Killian didn't pick up his fork. Instead, he placed his chin in his palm and rested his elbows on the table, eyes watching the male in front of him.

Orion was breathtaking.

With the flowers surrounding him, he blended right in. Killian could stare at him all day and not get bored. When Orion noticed the prince's attention, he blushed.

"I think you blush more than I do," Killian noted with a smile which only made the Potential blush harder.

Killian laughed.

"Where are you from?" Killian asked him, wanting to get to know him better.

"Rhettick," he answered softly, his eyes downcast creating a red crescent of his lashes on his shimmering bronze skin.

"Ah, the east or west? It's a big region."

"The west."

"That explains why your are so talented with a sword. My brother, Pierce, was enraptured the moment he laid eyes on you. He said you looked like you could fight well. He always has sparring on the brain," Killian chuckled.

Orion smiled.

"Would it be alright if I sparred with him on occasion?" he asked Killian.

"I am sure Pierce would love that."

They started to eat not wanting the food to get cold.

"I have to admit that it surprised me that you are so shy and mild mannered after seeing you confidently own your sword."

Killian hoped he didn't find insult in the prince's surprise. That wasn't his intention.

Thankfully Orion only grinned. "I am unsure about many things...but swordsmanship is not one of them."

"Did you spar often back home?" the prince asked though already knowing the answer to this based on where he was from. Tarr may be the top region for breeding warriors but Rhettick was definitely a close second.

"Yes. I lived with my parents and my younger sister Jo. My father pushed us to learn as soon as we could hold a short sword. We trained vigorously and eventually our father enrolled us in matches. It was how my family made most of our income."

The prince listened carefully. It was not uncommon for some to battle for money but young children doing it was heavily frowned upon. The King tried to ban it, but it only had a negative effect causing the black market to grow, so instead, his father created rules and regulations in order to protect the younger generations. Unfortunately, there were still some that slipped under the radar.

"Right now my sister is the sole provider for the family since I am here," he continued.

Killian frowned.

"How old is your sister?"

"Fifteen."

The prince's eyes narrowed, and he made a mental note to send someone to assess the situation and make sure that Orion's sister wasn't being harmed or in any danger.

He had to admit that he didn't expect such practices, especially not with his Potentials. How bad was this underground market? What else was going on without proper management?

He has his work cut out for him once he claimed the throne.

"Please do not worry. My sister is strong, and she loves sparring. It really is alright," Orion insisted, though it seemed very forced. Killian did not believe him for one second, but he smiled and pretended he did.

Killian was most certainly getting someone to check out the situation.

Orion looked nervous and twisting a lock of bright red hair around his index finger, biting on his full bottom lip. It reminded Killian of earlier when Rem had snapped at him.

Why did Rem behave that way? Did he not like Orion? Was Orion one of the Potentials that Rem did not approve of? Killian had to know.

"Orion."

"Yes, Killian?" he replied anxiously, not meeting the prince's eyes.

"Did something happen between you and Rem? I have not seen him act that way before."

Orion stiffened.

"I don't think he wants me to tell you--"

Killian cocked his head to the side, slightly irritated.

"Is Rem heir to the throne of Incubi? Will he be reigning King? Am I his Consort?" Killian asked keeping his tone even. He didn't want to intimidate him, but he needed to get his point across. He needed to make sure that he established his role and theirs. If they didn't obey and treat him as their all ruling King, then he would not have a Kingdom, he would have chaos.

One of the first lessons his father taught him was to establish dominance early on until it becomes natural for them to obey. Though obey sounded quite cruel and Killian did not mean it in such a way. He just needed people to trust him without question or hesitation as they do his father and as they had his grandmother.

"N-no, My Prince," he stuttered.

Killian waited for Orion to tell him the information.

"I do not believe Rem would want me to bring up anything that might trigger your trauma again. He worries for you."

Killian raised a brow.

He still didn't know what happened that night and no one will tell him. All he knew was that he lost it and it seemed to worry his Consorts.

Was it that bad?

From the look of terror on Orion's face, he'd wager it was.

"You will have to be patient with me. I am very new to certain things and I was not introduced to intimacy in the most...effective way."

Orion frowned. There was a bit of sorrow in his eyes.

"It is nothing to apologize for. I understand completely and it was unwise of us to put you in that position. For that I apologize. We were careless. Something that could be very detrimental to your reign as it is our purpose to protect you."

"Not your entire purpose," Killian corrected a bit thoughtfully.

Orion looked a little uneasy, but he smiled. "That is true."

The prince's brows furrowed.

"You do not want to be here?" he asked.

"No!" Orion insisted immediately. "That's not it! I do want to be here!"

Killian was startled by his insistence but didn't comment on it.

"I want to be here," he whispered more quietly.

They finished the rest of their meal in silence. Killian was trying to figure him out while it looked like Orion was mentally punching himself in the gut.

"I'm sorry," Orion said after the long stretch of silence. "I am not really good with words and I am easily flustered so it is hard to hold a conversation without some sort of awkwardness."

Killian could relate to that much more than Orion would ever know.

"It is fine. I am not upset. You did nothing wrong," the prince reassured him, smiling when Orion let out a sigh of relief. A little bit of the tension that had built in his shoulders deflated.

They stood and Orion offered his arm.

Killian took it gratefully and let the Potential lead him back inside the palace. They walked slowly and at a leisurely pace. It was quiet at first but comfortable. Killian was really relaxed in Orion's presence. It wasn't the same as the others. With everyone else he still had his guard up, but with Orion, his guard just seemed to drop and instantly he felt so content.

He liked how easily flustered he was. He liked how there was a sort of innocence about him. Killian liked how comfortable he was around him.

Killian just...liked him.

Could he be another one?

Could Killian have found his next chosen Consort?

Of course, the decision would not be made hastily. The prince still had to adjust to the newly acquired Consort.

Killian still couldn't help but ask.

As they reached the door to the prince's bedchamber, he turned to Orion and stared into his golden eyes.

"Orion."

"Yes?"

"Do you think you could grow to love me?"

Orion looked startled. His eyes widened and mouth popped open in shock. It might have been the directness of the question that tripped him up, but Killian didn't relent. He gazed at him waiting patiently for his reply.

"I-I don't know. I hope so," he answered.

Killian raised a brow before shaking his head, slipping inside the room without another glance in his direction.

He wasn't upset, but he didn't want Orion to see that.

It didn't bother him that Orion was unsure and that was strange. It should bother him, shouldn't it?

He didn't feel a bit out of sorts.

Strange.

"Killian?"

He blinked, not realizing he wasn't alone in the room.

Zev was staring at him with concern. His chest was bare and just a pair of navy silk bottoms covered his body. He was clearly preparing for bed.

Killian's eyes wandered around the room and he was a little confused.

Where was Rem and Faust?

"What's wrong Killian? You look troubled," he asked, approaching Killian.

Killian stepped into his chest and wrapped his arms around his blue waist, relishing in the warm feel of him. He was lovely.

His arms wrapped around Killian tightly.

"Are you alright?" he asked.

"Mmhmm," the prince mumbled against his skin. A sudden wave of fatigue hit him hard. His eyes drooped and he almost couldn't keep them open.

"You look dead on your feet," he said softly, placing a light kiss to Killian's forehead. He couldn't even argue that, he felt like it.

Zev quickly undressed Killian then pulled his nightclothes over his head. He pulled Killian into the bed and tucked him into the sheets, with his body curled around the prince from behind.

"Get some sleep," he murmured.

"But--" Killian started.

Rem and Faust, where are they?

"We'll all be here in the morning."

"You promise?" his words were beginning to slur.

"We promise."

He let his eyes close.

Chapter
10

The morning was awful.

It shouldn't have been a surprise to Killian. He wasn't unaccustomed to the feeling, as he had experienced it many times, but it was never this bad before. At least, not this early on.

His *Haise* was here.

And it was absolutely dreadful.

Killian awoke, but his eyelids were heavy and hard to keep open. A thin layer of sweat coated his body, but the ice in his veins kept the goosebumps raised on his flesh. Moving seemed almost impossible; he was so weak.

The warm bodies tangled with his own, shifted. Killian wanted to move with them, but his body was heavy, like lead.

"Killian?" the prince heard Zev murmur somewhere close from behind his head. "What's wrong with him?"

Killian blinked slowly, trying to desperately to keep his eyes open. It was a losing battle.

"It has begun," Faust said softly. Killian blinked again and saw Faust lying before him. His black eyes were calm and gentle. "He needs to feed, he's starving."

Though he was right in front of Killian, he sounded far away. Blood rushed loudly in the prince's ears and his head swimming.

He faintly heard the door open and a soft voice filled the room.

"How is he?"

It was Queen Jessa.

The Consorts

The bed shifted again, and he could feel the warmth of his mother's hand on his cheek. As soon as she touched him, a burst of power rushed through him and he finally had enough strength to open his eyes.

His throat was parched, and his saliva was thick. He tried to swallow but there was no way. Queen Jessa handed him a glass of water. He pushed himself up, with the help of his mother and Zev, before gulping the water down greedily.

Killian finished off the glass and two more that Rem brought him. They all stared at him. Even the King was in the room but standing close to the door and watching them carefully.

"I did not know it was going to come so quickly. I thought I had a little more time," Killian mumbled hoarsely.

"It happens," Queen Jessa told him, brushing his sweaty hair from his face. "We should go now."

She leaned off of the bed and headed towards the door.

Killian was still too weak to stand. Rem came and scooped Killian into his arms. The prince wrapped his arms around his Consort's neck weakly and fell limp against him.

The rest of his Consorts followed behind as they all made their way to the *Haise* Chamber. Once inside, Rem undressed Killian before depositing him in the pool of water. The water was warm and smelled heavily of nutmeg.

The moment his body hit the water and Rem's touch left him, the power started leaking out of him. It saturated his skin, pooling in the charged waters. Killian could feel the clarity started to break through in the fog in his head.

"Rem, Zev, and Faust, you will undress and enter the pool with him. From the moment your skin touches the water, you must not touch Killian, this first time. If you even brush against him, he will drain you dry of your life force and you will die," Queen Jessa told them. "Let him come to you."

Killian was vaguely listening but not really paying attention. His gut twisted with hunger. He just wanted to feed.

The water sloshed against the sides of the pool as each Consort slid into the water opposite of him, careful not to touch him.

When Zev put one foot into the water, Killian could see his body tense as the power ran through him like a knife. It was an aggressive force and quite painful. The prince watched him through hooded eyes, not taking his eyes off Zev until he was seated in the water.

"Now my sweet Killian, you know how to release your *Haise* but before you do it, I want you to reach for your Consorts with your mind. You know how to do it; we've been practicing for this very moment. You will feel more vulnerable than you have ever felt before, but you must not fight it, let it in. It will be scary, I know, but you must not fight it. Okay?"

Killian couldn't answer his mother, his body was too relaxed, but he looked at her, with just a flick of his eyes and it was understood. She nodded before backing away.

She and his father started to leave the room. Killian panicked, slamming the door shut with his power, trapping them both in the room.

The King looked stunned, but Queen Jessa simply looked at her son and smiled.

"You will be okay, Killian. You don't need us here. You won't hurt them."

The door started to creak back open and her smile widened. She and his father left the room, closing the door behind them. Killian thought he even heard the click of the lock going in place.

He looked back over at his Consorts who were staring at him.

"Is he really alright? It doesn't even look like anyone is home...it's creeping me out. Why is he just staring at us?" Zev muttered looking uneasy.

Upon hearing Zev's voice, Killian was thrown into memories of their intimacy. He could feel the smooth skin of Zev's member under his fingertips once more and the stickiness of his semen coating his skin.

His mind was already searching and with that direct thought, Zev didn't stand a chance. Killian's subconscious pierced through him. Zev jerked with the intrusion, feeling all of what he felt back then as if it were happening to him at this very moment.

Killian released his *Haise* on Zev, feeding off the lust potent in his body, evoking even more until it washed over him, the mild tingles spreading out in his body. Killian could feel Zev seeping into his mind, clear and purely him. It was warm and fierce.

Zev slumped over in the water. Faust looked over at him in alarm then looked back at Killian. Rem's eyes narrowed, turning to the prince.

Killian moaned, his groin burning. His skin felt hot, tingly, full of Zev. He felt energy course through him and he could finally move. Crawling forward, Killian headed toward Zev. Rem and Faust backed away from him, giving a wide berth watching him with caution. Killian ignored them, focusing on his precious Zev. He was unconscious but Killian could feel the male breathing in his mind.

Killian straddled Zev's slumped form, tilting his head back to look at his slack face. His eyes were open, but there was no one there. His essence was inside Killian.

The prince kissed his warm lips, putting Zev back inside his body.

He came to life in Killian's arms. His arms wrapped around the prince, gripping his waist, Zev's hips thrusting against him. He grunted, kissing Killian with more passion and aggression than the prince was prepared for.

Killian's nails raked across Zev's skin as his desire furiously pumped through the prince. He fed off it, drinking it in, feeling the energy fill him up.

He had to be careful. If he took too much, Zev would die.

Killian pulled away from his Consort with a loud gasp.

Zev chased him with his lips.

Killian shoved him back, breaking contact. As soon as he did, Zev melted back into the water, looking docile.

Killian sat back and waited, looking at his other Consorts.

Faust didn't have any sexual experiences with him yet, so his *Haise* had to search for his warmth and kindness, a target it was not familiar with. When Killian found his mind, it was gentle and inviting. He was welcoming the prince into him.

Killian grabbed his mind and sucked it into him, pushed all of his own desires for Faust to the forefront. Faust went slack immediately.

Killian thought of his voice and hearing him sing. He thought about all of the admiration he felt for him. He tugged on Faust's own desires, seeing himself clearly in his mind.

And...Rem.

It mattered not to Killian at that moment who the desire was for. It was all food to him, and he sucked it in, relishing in the sustenance it provided for him.

Faust was there, in Killian's mind, singing softly to him. Another moan left Killian's lips.

Killian cupped his cheek and kissed his warm lips, pushing his mind back inside him. He came to, gasping, hands gripping the back of Killian's neck and pulling him closer.

Killian kissed him again, gently, gaining a little bit more control over the process now that he wasn't starving and on the verge of passing out.

He broke away from Faust quickly, watching as he sank into the water contentedly.

Rem was waiting. He watched Killian carefully, but there was a tenseness in his frame. He was worried.

Killian watched him for a moment before bringing every intimate moment they shared to the forefront of his mind. Rem jerked harshly before slumping over.

His desires attacked Killian.

A scream of pleasure left Killian's lips. He squeezed his thighs together, slick gushing out of him in an alarming amount. His skin felt like it was on fire and Rem was there, in his mind, but...it was nothing like the male he was used to.

It was vicious, the desire for him. And suddenly, it wasn't just Rem, it was his beast and it wanted Killian. It was as if Rem and his beast were fighting each other in the prince's mind to gain control, but Rem's beast was a force on a whole other level.

Killian's head throbbed as his nipples hardened painfully, his legs spreading involuntarily.

Rem was supposed to be immobile like the others, but he was there, moving over Killian, magix glowing brightly underneath his skin. The prince gasped, trying to back away. He couldn't touch Rem yet, he'd kill him.

"Rem!" Killian screamed as the male fell on him.

His Consort shoved his legs open wider, grinding himself between them. Killian didn't feel his life force slipping away.

He was supposed to be...Oh.

It wasn't Rem, it was his beast. Killian could feel Rem in his mind, cradling him. He had won the fight in his mind, but his beast still had full reign of his body. Rem tried to protect him from the beast, but Killian had taken him from his body and there was no way he could control it.

Killian was surprised that the beast was unaffected. He seemed to have enough pent-up lust to keep the prince fed for centuries. It was overflowing in Killian. He was full.

He had never been full before.

The beast kissed Killian, devouring his mouth, forcing his legs over his shoulders. He kept thrusting, but Killian couldn't figure out what he was trying to do.

Rem panicked.

Send me back, Killian! Send me back now!

The command was screamed in Killian's head, making him wince in pain.

The beast's member slid along Killian's hole and the memories of Orion and Titus came flooding back to him.

The beast was trying to...

The prince shoved Rem back into his body, trying to push the beast away physically, though it was pointless when comparing their difference in strength. Rem's magix burned him but once Rem was back inside his body, it stopped. Rem fell away from Killian, breathing heavily.

The prince blinked at him, watching the swirling colors in Rem's skin start to dim before his vision clouded and everything went black.

Coming to, Killian noticed a few things. First, he was back in his room. Second, the room was dark, illuminated only by the moon's light gently streaming in from the open window. And third, Queen Jessa was sitting beside him, stroking his hair. Her red eyes were dim, not at all glimmering like they usually were, and tight with worry.

Killian blinked then tried to sit up. Surprisingly, he had no problem with the action. Energy coursed through him and he felt refreshed.

"Killian," his mother breathed, her voice tinged with relief.

He tilted his head, watching her. This was not the reaction he thought she'd have.

"Is everything okay? Did something happen?" he asked her.

She shook her head.

"I know it is pointless to worry but I am your mother, I can't help it. It was your first time without me, and you didn't wake up--"

Killian cut her off. "Mother, I always pass out after feeding."

"I know, I know. It's just you usually wake up within the hora but this time it took you six."

Killian thought about it, "It was a lot for me to digest. But I am completely full now. I feel great. I've never been full before, but after feeding from Rem..." he trailed off, smiling at the thought.

His mother sighed then frowned.

The smile fell from his face, "What is wrong?"

"I fear you may have some trouble with him now. He did not take so well to the feeding."

"What do you mean?" Killian asked slowly.

"Rem is a little upset with himself--"

Killian jumped up from the bed, "Where is he?"

His mother jerked her chin towards the window. He kissed her cheek, thanking her, then hurried out the door. He ran out to the garden in just his thin nightclothes and bare feet. The cold nipped at his skin harshly, but he ignored it, his eyes searching frantically in the night.

Killian almost missed him, he blended into the darkness completely. What gave him away was the small glint of his collar showing through the wisps of his hair.

He was sitting on a low tree branch, hunched over with his head in his hands. Killian approached him slowly, taking in his dark form.

"Rem."

He didn't answer. He didn't acknowledge the prince's presence, but Rem knew he was there.

Killian's eyes had adjusted to the night and he could see Rem under the faint glow of the moon. Crouching down, Killian put his hand against Rem's cheek. He couldn't see his Consort's expression, but when he flinched away from the prince, it said enough.

"Talk to me," Killian pleaded.

"Send me home," Rem stated clearly. His voice barely audible.

Killian froze, eyes widening.

"What?" he managed to choke out as soon as he was able to speak again.

"Send me home," Rem whispered.

"Why?"

    "I cannot do this."

"Do what?" Killian asked, trying to understand.

"Be with you!" He snapped, tearing his hands from his face. Killian could see his pained expression. Rem winced when he looked at him, horror spreading in those black eyes. His brows were furrowed and teeth clenched in agony.

It was the most emotion Killian ever seen from him.

He had shown the prince a little bit before, but it had never been unleashed like this. He looked like he would cry. It was the utter self-loathing in his eyes that frightened Killian.

"Of course you can--" the prince started.

"No," he growled. "I cannot. I thought I was strong enough. I thought I could handle this curse. That I could be exposed to others. To you. I cannot. I am weak."

"You are not weak--"

"I am weak, Killian. You do not grasp this! You are naive and innocent and delicate and beautiful," Rem's voice trailed off as he stared at Killian. "So beautiful," he whispered, eyes softening. "I fear the moment where we must mate. I fear what I will do to you."

"I know you will not hurt me," Killian insisted.

Rem shook his head in disgust. "You do not even know what almost occurred today. What my beast would have done to you."

Killian opened his mouth to protest but Rem cut him off sharply. "He would have taken you by force. He would have forced us inside you, bled you, made a mess of your virgin body and that would make me even worse than Jax."

Killian winced at the familiar name.

"Send me home," he said again.

The prince shook his head while tears gathered in his eyes.

"Send me home, Killian. I am not good for you."

"You love me!" Killian shouted at him.

"And the last person I loved died because of it."

Rem had loved another?

Jealousy coursed through Killian, but he fought it back. He had no right to be jealous, especially of someone who was no longer alive. It was an immature and pointless emotion that he refused to let himself feed.

Rem was silent for a little while but then took a deep breath and explained.

"It was my wife. Her name was Tara. She was arresting. Tiny and stubborn, but full of love, much like yourself. She lived in my village, one of the few families there that did not bear the curse of magix. She did not understand but she tried to. I do not know why she grew fond of me or why she insisted upon befriending me, but she was relentless. She believed that the beast was not something to fear, that it was something to embrace. And foolishly, I believed her. We married. It took a few years until I thought it safe enough to consummate our marriage, but I was wrong."

Rem looked haunted as he spoke, as if he were reliving the memories.

"That night I lost control...and I killed her."

Killian gasped.

"The beast loved her as well. He loved her too much. But the beast cannot comprehend pain and does not know how to treat that which is fragile. He is too rough. He bled her and did not care, did not treat her wounds, continuing to thrust inside her heat. She bled to death. The next morning that I was able to come back to myself. When I awoke, I was still buried inside her, my seed spilling out of her cold lifeless body. Bruises littered her skin, her hips shattered, her arms broken, her spine snapped, her brown eyes open, dull, and void."

A single tear slipped down his cheek. In the silence, Killian watched it fall, too stunned to say anything.

"My beast loves you too much, Killian. And I will not be the death of you," he swore. "I will not let it happen, not again."

The Consorts

Without another word, he stood and walked back inside, leaving Killian there, too shocked to move. The prince started to get up to go after him, but a voice stopped him.

"You should give him some time."

Killian jumped looking up at the source of the voice.

Caspian was seated on a branch high above.

The prince glanced back to where Rem disappeared, with wide eyes, wondering if he would be upset that Caspian had heard what they said. Caspian seemed to read the prince's alarm and responded.

"He knew I was there," he reassured, slipping off the branch to the one that Rem had just occupied. His yellow eyes glowed in the dark.

"You heard," Killian concluded dumbly.

Caspian nodded.

"What should I do? I do not want him to leave, I do not want to lose him."

He sighed. "To be honest, his mind is already made up. He loves you too much to put you in danger. The only thing that would probably make him stay would be if he somehow released his beast and it didn't hurt you. That might be impossible but if you love him, you'll get him to try again. If it doesn't work out, then maybe you really shouldn't be together. That might not be what you want to hear, but you can't ignore it Killian, and you have to acknowledge the reality and the severity of the situation. But then again, what do I know?"

"You know a lot," Killian mumbled feeling empty inside.

Caspian didn't say anything, seeming lost in thought.

"I cannot lose him," the prince said softly.

Caspian didn't reply.

Killian kissed Caspian on the cheek before going back inside. If Rem needed space, he'd give it to him. He needed to focus on his other Consorts anyway. His obsession with Rem had made him neglect them and that was something he wouldn't ever forgive himself for.

Killian found his Consorts being lectured by the King in the study. Killian didn't know why, but his father seemed upset. He spoke to them in a quick and sharp tone. The prince watched with a frown, noticing his Consort mothers, Mae and Thistle, standing behind his father. Thistle was gently rubbing his father's shoulder, whispering in his ear what seemed like calming words, shooting worried glances at Mae. Mae's white brow was wrinkled, and her blue eyes dimmed with disappointment.

What was going on?

Killian stepped into the room and almost knocked into his brothers Pierce and Ian. Pierce's blue eyes burned with rage.

"Pierce? What is it?" Killian asked his brother softly, reaching to touch his shoulder in comfort. But the moment Pierce laid eyes on him, his face morphed into an angry glare. He slapped Killian's hand away from him.

"Pierce!" Killian heard Mae shout angrily.

Ian was quick, slamming Pierce against the wall with his hand around his throat. He was so quick; Killian had only seen a flash of navy hair. Ian's eyes glowed like bright emeralds, focused solely on Pierce.

"You have forgotten your place, Pierce. Killian is not just our beloved older brother; he is the heir to the throne. You do not lay hands on him for any reason, is that understood?" Ian seethed.

When Pierce remained stubbornly silent, Ian tightened his hold on their brother's neck.

"Ian--" Killian began to protest but Pierce cut him off.

"Fine!"

Ian dropped his hands.

Pierce rubbed his neck and began to storm out of the room, but their father called out to him, stopping him in his tracks.

"Pierce, I will have words with you tonight," the King said.

Killian saw Pierce's eyes tighten and jaw clench before he turned to bow begrudgingly at their father and leave.

Ian sighed before turning to Killian, his eyes softening in concern.

"Are you alright, Killian?" he asked the prince gently.

"I am fine, it was nothing. I am just worried about Pierce, what happened? Why is he so upset?" Killian asked, feeling a sense of dread at his baby brother's unhappiness.

Ian looked uncomfortable.

"Father will tell you," he said after a pause.

"Ian, you will talk to me later, right?"

Ian looked unsure.

"Please?" Killian whispered.

The King would only tell him what he thought Killian should know, which meant a lot of it would be left out since everyone was so bent on keeping him clueless. Killian wanted to know the whole story and Ian would tell him.

With a slight nod, Ian left.

Killian turned back to the rest of the room who stared at him apprehensively. Looking at his Consorts, he tried to read their expressions, but they were intentionally keeping them blank.

"Father, what is going on?"

His father stared at him for a moment, then sighed, looking tired.

Killian waited patiently for an answer and was surprised when Mae stepped up.

"It seems my son is having trouble accepting a few rules in regard to his role as the next General," Mae said in her light and airy voice.

"Like what?" Killian pressed.

She opened her mouth to explain but the King raised a hand to stop her.

"Nothing you need to worry about, Killian."

The Consorts

"Father, I have the right to know. I am going to be King soon. You cannot keep me in the dark. I need to know what is happening. Especially with my own family," Killian told him exasperated.

"Killian--" Father started in a tone that said he was going to find some way to keep Killian out of it.

"Father, he is my brother!"

Killian hadn't meant to raise his voice, but he was just so fed up with being kept in the dark. It didn't make any sense. If he was going to be King, shouldn't that mean that he was supposed to know what was going on? How was he going to solve problems or rule their people if he was more clueless than they were?

The King glared at him, "Watch your tone, I am your King and your father."

Killian clenched his jaw in annoyance but bowed, "My apologies, My King."

"Take your Consorts back to your room and think about who you are choosing to be next. I want the fourth chosen before noon tomorrow and the fifth before midnight that night."

Killian's eyes bugged in shock and he choked on air.

"Father--"

Father slammed his fist on the table, his eyes full of stormy gray clouds. Thistle and Mae jumped. Killian didn't flinch and kept the slight fear internal.

"Yes, Father," Killian said evenly.

He glared, those frightening eyes never leaving his son, even as the prince looked at his Consorts and gestured for them to follow him. They stood and walked behind Killian like shadows after bowing to his father.

They didn't stop until they reached the bedroom. Only when the door closed did Killian let his shoulders sag. Zev and Faust were watching him warily. Killian took a calming breath before turning to Zev and burying his face in his chest. Zev's arms came around the prince, squeezing him tightly.

Faust came over to touch Killian's back, rubbing soothing circles over his nightclothes.

Killian breathed in his scent, using it to make him feel better. To feel loved.

Pulling back slightly, the prince peered up at him. His blue eyes were bright and full of devotion.

"Will you tell me what is going on?"

The blue clouded and Zev's face twisted with unease.

Killian sighed, looking over at Faust and asking him the same question.

"We are sworn. We cannot say a word."

"I am your King," Killian reminded him without much passion. He knew that if his father told them not to say a word, they wouldn't.

"I know," Faust said, cupping Killian's cheek. "And I want to tell you, Zev and I both do, but we are sworn and spelled."

Killian frowned. It was a serious enough secret that his father used magic?

"Killian, though we can't tell you, don't worry about trying to find out what it is. Trust me when I say this, you will find out and soon. It is not something that can be hidden for long. Not at all."

"Why do you two know?"

"To protect you." Zev answered this time.

"Protect me from what?"

Zev started to open his mouth, but he winced then shut it, shaking his head.

Killian didn't ask again. If they were spelled, then it would not do any good and he did not want them hurting themselves trying to go against the spell. He'd just have to wait until he spoke with Ian.

"Just be careful of who you pick to be your next chosen," Faust said with warning in his voice.

"Do you know who you are going to pick to complete the Consort group?" Zev asked.

"Caspian for certain, but I'm not sure for the last. I have someone in mind, but I don't want to say yet. I just hope the answer comes to me in time."

Killian pulled out of Zev's arms and hugged Faust.

His body was slimmer than Zev's. It was interesting to compare the two.

There was a knock on the door.

"You may enter!" Killian called out.

Ian poke his head through, before jerking his head as cue to follow him. Killian excused himself from his Consorts, before following his brother. They didn't speak as they walked, Killian simply followed his lead until he pulled them onto an empty balcony.

"I can't stay long; Father is looking for me. I think he knows I broke his gag order."

"You broke his spell?" Killian asked incredulously.

Ian rolled his eyes but smiled. "I think you have forgotten how proficient I am in magic, big brother," he laughed.

Killian had known Ian was good, but he had not known the extent to which he had improved. It made him sad that he was missing important moments in his siblings' lives because of how much time he spent dedicated to the crown.

"Tell me what you can," Killian said.

"I can't say much because I came in too late and missed a chunk of the conversation, but I heard that there was a residue of a forbidden spell cast in the Potential quarters and apparently it was cast by a Potential."

"How long ago was it cast?"

"That's the thing, no one can tell. They brought Magna in there, but not even she can figure it out, and she's the most killed caster in Heltzig. Though she might have determined that it was a cloaking spell of some sort. But because we can't tell when it was cast, we don't know if it was one of your remaining Potentials or one that has already been eliminated."

"Then why would my father want me to choose my Consorts quicker? Should I not be holding off until we can find out who the spell caster is?"

"I think Father and Pierce know who it is or have an idea. To be quite honest, I think everyone that was in the room besides you and me know who it is. I came in too late when they were discussing it."

Killian frowned then asked, "But what does that have to do with Pierce not accepting the rules as next General?"

Ian shrugged. "I don't know. I didn't hear anything about that. When I got there, Pierce was already angry."

Killian pinched the bridge of his nose with his thumb and forefinger.

It wasn't as if he could ask Pierce, who was furious at him for reasons the prince was still unclear about. This whole situation was frustrating.

"Just be careful, Kill."

"I will. Thanks, Ian."

Ian nodded. "Now I have to go, Father is probably furious."

Killian watched him leave then waited a few moments before leaving himself. When he got back to the room, all of his Consorts were in bed sleeping.

Even Rem.

There were three now, but tomorrow night, there would be five.

Gods above.

Killian climbed into bed after reading through a few history books. He should have slept beside Faust and paid more attention to Zev, but after what Rem had said, he couldn't help but slide in beside him pushing his face close. He gasped in fright when he saw his Consort's eyes open, watching him, empty and guarded.

"I did not know you were awake," Killian said quietly trying not to wake any of the others up. Rem remained silent and watched Killian. His expression was unreadable, but from the tenseness in his body, the prince could tell he would prefer he not lay so close.

Killian stroked his cheek softly. He was so unresponsive; it was like touching stone. Killian didn't stop though, gently caressing his face.

"Are you still planning to leave me?" Killian asked him.

Rem still didn't speak. A part of Killian expected that, but he couldn't help but hope Rem would open up to him like he had earlier. How could he make him realize that Rem was better with Killian than without him?

"Do not leave," Killian whispered, reaching up to kiss Rem's lips. He jerked back, eyes angry.

Killian tried to keep the hurt from his face, but he didn't think he was successful. Killian saw Rem's eyes immediately soften.

"If tonight is our last...will you hold me close?" Killian pleaded.

He looked pained again, as if the mere thought of leaving caused him physical agony.

He pulled Killian flush against his body, burying his face in the prince's neck, inhaling deeply before nuzzling the skin. Killian wrapped a leg over his hip, intertwining their limbs and tails. The sharp points of Rem's horns dug into Killian's jaw, but he didn't care. The pain was welcomed. It meant Rem was still there.

Like that, they fell asleep.

Throughout the entire night, they had not moved, remaining curled around each other. In the morning, Rem woke before Killian. Killian awoke to the sound of the door opening. Ethel came in quietly with an uncharacteristically somber expression.

"Lord Rem, your room has been prepared and your belongings have been moved. I will escort you now," she said softly.

Killian jumped up, looking at Rem in horror.

The Consort sat up in the bed and started to stand. The prince's eyes were wide as saucers, black cross shaped pupils dilated in horror as his heart beat furiously against his chest. The clenching in his stomach grew in intensity. He could feel the bile start to rise in his throat.

"Where are you going?" Killian asked him, panic evident in his voice.

Rem looked away from the prince's pointed gaze, avoiding having to see his terrified expression. Even Ethel looked down.

"Rem, you are not leaving me," Killian told him, a tremor in his voice.

Rem stood.

"Rem, do not leave me!" Killian grabbed onto his arm trying desperately to tug him back into bed. The other Consorts stirred with the commotion.

Rem easily untangled Killian's grip. He tilted his head in Killian's direction but did not look at him. Rem's lips moved and Killian barely heard the words at first. It might've been his disbelief and total denial that made it so hard to comprehend.

"Choose three Consorts today."

At that moment, it became as real as the stabbing in his chest. excruciating and true.

Rem moved toward Ethel who led him to the door. Killian could feel the familiar sting of tears in his eyes, blurring his vision, and slurring his speech.

"No! Rem, do not do this! You cannot leave!"

The hysteria grew and grew, tears completely blinding him as he stumbled out of bed and towards his dark hazy figure.

"Please Rem! Do not go, I am begging you! Do not leave me! "

Rem's steps did not falter as he followed Ethel out of the room. Killian screamed, trying to run to him, sobbing until strong arms wrapped around him, holding him close and pulling him back to the bed. He fought the arms for a while, before giving up and giving in to his grief.

Killian cried.

Zev held him tightly, sitting the prince on his lap while his legs rested in Faust's. Zev rocked Killian gently whispering again and again that everything would be okay. Faust's fingers moved gently across the sensitive skin along his inner ankle.

The Consorts

Horas later, when the tears had finally dried, Zev and Faust tried unsuccessfully to get Killian to eat something. Eventually, they decided he just needed space, so they left him in bed to wallow in his misery.

The wallowing lasted for a while but the determination to fix everything propelled him out of bed and down a few halls to the Potentials' wing. Rem's door was closed but Killian knew he was there. There were guards down the hall.

Killian knocked on the door.

No answer.

"Rem, please, let us talk about this." Killian knocked again. And again. Until the knocking became banging and the gentle pleas became screaming.

He wasn't behaving like a King, he knew this. But he loved this male and he would not let Rem leave him. Not like this.

Rem wouldn't open the door, nor answer the prince's calls. When the guards heard the commotion, they came and gently told him, "My Prince, Lord Rem has evoked his rights as Consort."

The prince's hand froze mid motion.

Consorts were allowed three days of solitude a month when they needed their privacy and not even the king was allowed to bother them. Unless of course, he issued a King's command. It was reserved for extreme situations. If Killian did that to Rem, it would only push him away more. That's not what Killian wanted at all.

Letting the guards escort him away from the door, he wandered back to his room.

Zev sat on the bed, waiting for him. Killian thought Zev was going to be upset that he was so torn up over another male, but he only looked sad. His brow was slightly furrowed and the corners of his lips were turned down.

"I don't want him to leave either," he said softly.

Killian didn't say anything, just walked towards him slowly. His confession surprised the prince. They must have gotten closer than he thought. Not too long ago, Zev was at odds with Rem.

"Will you talk to him? Bring him back to us?" Killian asked, cupping Zev's cheek.

"He's not going to listen to me, Killian. Not if you couldn't convince him. I don't stand a chance in changing his mind."

"You have to try. Please. Do not let him leave us."

Zev remained quiet, just staring at Killian with those bright blue eyes. There was so much emotion swirling behind them.

"I'll try," he said.

Killian sighed in relief, throwing his arms around Zev's neck. Zev hugged the prince tightly, tangling his hands in his maroon curls before pulling back to look at him with smoldering eyes. He leaned into kiss Killian. It was soft and pleasant. He was treating the prince as if he would break with the slightest pressure.

Killian don't know why his Consorts always treated him like that, but he wouldn't complain. It was nice not having to be strong. It was nice being cared for.

Before things got too heated, Killian thanked Zev and let him know that he was going to go officially propose to Caspian as it was almost noon. Zev gave Killian one last kiss before disappearing in the direction of Rem's room.

Killian really hoped Zev could talk some sense into Rem. If Rem left, Killian didn't think he'd ever get over it. A part of him would be missing right along with the male. With a sigh Killian ventured out to find Caspian.

It was no surprise when he found him lounging on a high branch, out in the garden. His bright red tail swishing about, dark horns glinting in the sunlight, his skin sparkling gold and hair, a waving flame, sprawled around him.

His eyes were closed but Killian could tell he was awake. The only movement coming from his tail. It stopped once Killian approached the tree.

"Caspian."

One eye opened as he peeked down at the prince.

A slow grin emerged on his face.

"My lovely Killian, what can I do for you today?" His other eye popped open as he spoke and his body shifted, muscles stretching, as he turned to face the prince.

Killian smiled up at him.

"I would like to formally ask you if you would be my Consort."

Caspian's smiled disappeared and his expression grew suspicious. "Are you sure about this?"

"I was sure the first time I asked you, I just figured you needed more time," Killian winked at him.

His grin returned, wider than before. "Well if that's the case, you don't have to beg anymore. Of course I'll be your Consort."

Caspian dropped down from the branch, landing on his feet gracefully, and Killian realized how much taller Caspian was than himself. Killian always saw him sitting down or lounging about, but now, standing only inches from him, Killian could only reach up to his chest. He was taller than Drek, maybe even Faust's height, who was the tallest of all Killian's Potentials and Consorts.

Caspian used his tail to curl around the prince's wrist, yanking him forward until the prince fell against him. Killian let out a startled gasp which only made Caspian laugh. Then suddenly his laughter died and he was staring at the prince vehemently with those bright yellow eyes. Killian got lost in them, he hadn't even realized Caspian was moving closer until his full lips touched Killian's.

Caspian kissed gently, tentatively, like Killian imagine Orion might have. Soon, he was pushing his lips against Killian's passionately, matching Zev's fervor.

When he finally pulled away, Killian was dazed with slightly swollen lips.

Caspian laughed again.

"Were you not prepared for my excellent kissing skills?" his eyes sparkled with amusement. A smirk tugged at his lips.

"I most certainly was not," Killian answered still a little breathless.

The Consorts

Caspian chuckled. His tail wrapped around Killian's. His red against Killian's dark maroon twisted and turned, braiding themselves together. The prince laughed, hugging Caspian close.

Caspian untangled their tails and offered his arm. Killian took it happily and they made their way to the bathing room. They washed each other, slowly getting to know each other's bodies without getting intimate. That would be for later.

Killian spent as much time with Caspian as he could before Lisa and Kara took him away to get him officially established as Killian's Consort.

Now that the prince was alone, reality was starting to hit. He only had eleven horas to choose another Consort. His final Consort. And with that final decision came the Ranking Ceremony--that was also being rushed. A total of fifteen days.

The first five days would be spent with his Rank One, tasked with trying to impregnate the prince. His Rank Two would have four days. His Rank Three would have days and so on. The first to impregnate him became the Consort King. If Killian was not pregnant by the end of the ceremony, it repeated until he was.

That meant tomorrow night, he would lose his virginity.

The thought scared him and excited him at the same time. He had waited so long for this moment, but the idea of being a parent, of raising a small child, terrified him to no end. There would be a piece of him running around the castle. Someone he was responsible for. Someone he had to teach everything he knew. Someone who would depend on him entirely.

It was frightening.

That wasn't his only worry. Who was he going to choose to be his final Consort?

There was no way he was choosing two more. Rem wasn't going anywhere. Not if he had anything to say about it. Killian had faith in Zev. He'd be able to convince Rem. Rem trusted Zev...he hoped.

Rem, Zev, Faust, and Caspian.

Who else?

Who could he choose?

There was one person that continued to flash in his mind. Only one that he could think of to be the fifth and final Consort.

When it clicked in his mind, he was running. Running as fast as he could down the halls, checking every place he might be. When Killian managed to find him, he was sitting in the library staring out the window.

"Orion!" Killian called to him.

He looked over at the prince and smiled warmly.

"Hello Killian."

Something was off. He wasn't his usual radiant self. He looked a little pale and Killian could see a thin sheen of sweat glistening on his skin.

The prince frowned.

"Are you well?" he asked him.

Orion looked a little uncomfortable before forcing a smile. "I'm fine, just feeling a bit ill. I'm sure it is nothing. Now what can I do for you?"

Killian took a deep breath.

"I wanted to formally ask you if you would be my Consort?"

His eyes were closed and his fists were tight as he asked the question. Killian waited and waited for an answer but was met with silence.

When he cracked his eyes open, he saw Orion's horror-stricken face. Tears began to glitter in his golden eyes before pouring over the rims and trailing down his bronze cheeks.

He covered his mouth his hand before looking away. His head was shaking in silent disbelief. Killian didn't understand his reaction. Was that a no? Did he not want to be?

"Was that a rejection?" Killian asked, confused and slightly worried.

Orion was quiet for a few more moments before he finally choked out, "I can't."

"Why not?" Killian questioned even more confused now.

"This wasn't supposed to happen. You weren't supposed to choose me. Mom said you wouldn't choose me; your instincts wouldn't let you. So why..." he trailed off.

"I do not understand," Killian admitted.

"I can't be your Consort, Killian."

"Why not?"

"Because I can't impregnate you."

His brows furrowed.

"What do you mean?"

"I'm an S-Level Incubus," Orion confessed looking guilty.

Killian's jaw dropped in disbelief. There was no way. He couldn't be. The King screened all of the Potentials. Only regular level Incubi were allowed to be Consorts since their main purpose was to impregnate him with an heir. How did an S-Level get past the screening?

"I was born into a poor family. My father has a gambling problem and always puts the family in debt. He has no regard for anyone but himself. He is a cruel male and would do anything for money. He's obsessed. So obsessed that my mother feared for me. She knew that if he were to find out I was an S-Level Incubus, he would sell me to the highest bidder. So instead my mother hid it from him. She told me to never show any signs of being an S-Level. She even taught me a cloaking spell to hide my level. When we received the order from the King to submit a profile to enter into the pool to become the heir's Consort, my father jumped at the opportunity. My mother was worried that I would be exposed knowing that S-Level Incubi were not allowed to enter, but my father insisted. My mother did not want my father to grow suspicious, so she let me enter. She told me that I would not be chosen. And I believed her, I did. But I was."

Orion took another shaky breath before continuing.

"When I got here and met you. I thought you were kind, beautiful, and I envied you. I wanted your purity, your regality. I didn't realize how much it cost you. I was foolish.

And then I found myself liking you. I liked you as a person and it became harder and harder to deceive you. Even now, I cannot deceive you. I cannot be your Consort, but I beg of you not to send me back."

Orion eyes watered again as he pleaded.

Part of Killian was angry at the betrayal, but another part of him pitied Orion. He didn't ask for this, he was just trying to keep himself from being sold. But still...

"Why can you not go back? I cannot choose you as a Consort, what other reason should you stay?" Killian demanded, showing his slight anger.

"If you send me back, he'll know!"

Killian shook his head. "There is no way to know. It is not as if he will know my reasoning for rejecting you as a Consort. That information is only known by me."

Orion shook his head growing paler.

"I can't go back."

"Why?" Killian demanded.

"I'm pregnant."

Chapter

II

"Pregnant?"

Tears continued to stream down Orion's rose gold cheeks, flushed and glistening. Killian's expression was stuck in a state of horror as he realized the gravity of his words.

Orion was pregnant.

But by who?

"Titus?" Killian asked.

Orion cried harder, blubbering something incoherently.

"I cannot understand you, Orion. Speak clearly."

"I don't know," he whispered.

Killian's eyes narrowed. "You do not...know?"

Orion shook his head.

"Who else have you been intimate with?"

Orion shook his head again, shoulders shaking violently. The prince watched him, eyes narrowing further into tiny slits.

"Who else?" Killian demanded, voice growing deeper, more authoritative. Orion could not disobey him.

"Lord Pierce."

His voice was barely audible, and Killian almost missed it, but there was no mistaking that title or that name.

His brother.

His seventeen-year-old baby brother.

Killian hadn't been angry before. He had understood, knowing Orion's circumstances and knowing what it was like being an S-Level Incubus. But there are lines that were not meant to be crossed. Orion lied to be there, covered up his identity and deceived them just to save himself from his father. That Killian could forgive.

But to consummate with his brother?

That was a betrayal he could not forget. It ran through his veins, thickened in his gut, sent his head reeling. It was almost hard to breathe through the constriction in his chest.

Completely at a loss for words, Killian stood there gaping at him.

"My brother..." he breathed. "You were with my...brother."

Orion wiped at his eyes aggressively, but it did nothing. New tears wet his cheeks almost immediately.

Anger finally settled in Killian.

"Have you no loyalty?" His voice echoed off the walls in the vast room making Orion flinch at the sound. "I do not care if you had been with other Potentials. I had not cared that you were with Titus! But my brother was off limits!"

"I'm sorry! I did not mean to, Killian--"

"Prince to you," Killian sneered.

"My Prince, I beg of you to forgive my treachery! I did not know that my *Haise* would strike me in that moment! I did not know how to control my power; I have not been trained in control as you have. I have little to no knowledge of what my status as an S-Level means. It hit me so suddenly in the bath and my body called to his. I did not intend it, this I swear!"

Killian couldn't even look at him.

"When did you first know you were pregnant?" the prince asked, looking down instead of at Orion. Killian was afraid he might hurt him if he did.

"Since this morning," he mumbled.

A low snarl left the prince's lips as they curled back over his teeth.

"Get up," he hissed. "And follow me."

Orion hurried to his feet. Killian did not wait for him, he stalked out the rooms and through the halls. They did not stop until they reached the study where Killian could sense the King, the Queen, his Consort mothers, his siblings, Ethel, Lisa, and Kara were present. His father was speaking sharply to Pierce who looked as stone faced as Killian had ever seen him.

Everyone looked up at the prince's entrance as he slammed the doors open. Immediately Pierce got to his feet, an angry snarl on his face. He started to leave the room, but Killian glared at him.

"Sit down," he commanded.

With a look of utter defiance and an exaggerated scoff, Pierce kept walking.

Killian's power flared out of him, throwing his brother across the room, slamming him forcefully into his seat.

"I said sit down," Killian's voice was low and cold. It was a tone he did not often use. His family knew him as even tempered and mild mannered. He was never aggressive or outspoken.

Things had changed.

Pierce gaped at Killian. He had not realized his older brother wielded so much power. The rest of the room was too stunned to say anything.

The King stared at his eldest son, surprise and worry clear on his face. Worried that Killian might know something he didn't want him to. Worried that the prince had snapped.

He was right to be worried.

Killian turned to Lisa.

"Bring Titus immediately."

Lisa did not even hesitate at the order, immediately jumping to the task.

"Killian--" Mae started. Killian could see the worry for her son written all over her face. She would say anything to protect him.

Killian's head snapped in her direction, "Silence."

"You watch your tongue when you address my mother," Pierce hissed.

Killian's eyes darted to him, power just itching to crush him.

Right now, he was not family. Right now, he was a traitor.

"You watch your tongue when you address your future King."

"Is that a threat, big brother?" Pierce grinned humorlessly.

Killian closed his power around Pierce's throat watching as his oxygen cut off. "Tis not a threat, baby brother, but a reminder. You will know your place."

"My Prince, please!" Orion begged from behind him.

Killian silenced him with a look but released his brother anyway. He wouldn't truly hurt him. But Pierce needed to be reminded that he could not do whatever he wanted. Killian was not only his older brother, but the next sovereign of Astoria. Pierce was under the impression that Killian was too gentle to put his foot down.

Killian turned his angry eyes on his father. "How long were you going to keep me in the dark?"

Lisa walked in with Titus who looked slightly confused. Killian paid them no heed and continued to focus his attention on his father who did not answer, just watched his son carefully.

"Imagine my surprise when I ask Orion to be my final Consort--by your rushed order might I add--just to find that he cannot because he is an S-Level Incubus like me."

No one said a word.

"And even worse, that he is pregnant."

Titus and Pierce wore identical expressions of both shock and disbelief.

"How long did you all think that you could keep this up?" Killian asked.

And when they didn't answer, the prince started to laugh. It was the hysterical and maniacal laugh that send shivers up the spines of everyone in the room.

"Do you all think I lack intelligence? That I would not figure things out eventually?"

"Killian listen--" Mae started again.

Killian stopped laughing abruptly and snarled at her.

"I said silence. Disobey again and I will crush your windpipe."

The Consorts

"Killian, you're not yourself right now," the King said.

"No, Father, I am not. I have not been for a while. I am glad you all are just starting to notice, maybe now you will realize that keeping me in the dark is counterproductive."

"So soon after your *Haise* your emotions are still heightened."

Killian shrugged. "Maybe so. But that is not important. What is important is that this Incubus," he pointed to Orion, "is pregnant with a child that either belongs to my brother or one of my Potentials. And you all tried to keep it from me."

Killian laughed again.

"As if I would not find out!" he laughed so hard his stomach ached as he clutched it, wiping a tear from his eye. "Unbelievable!"

The King's eyes darted behind Killian and the prince noticed him give an imperceptible nod.

Killian let his laughter die off and looked at all of them in the room. Really looked at them.

Killian looked over to his younger brother, his blue eyes wild, and white hair disheveled from the hand that ran through it, furiously.

"You have been given so much. You have your freedom, something I can never have because I bear the burden of the crown...for you. I have been shackled to my duties. Never allowed to make friends unless for political gain, never allowed to explore any further than the palace walls, never allowed to do anything because I am heir. And this one thing that I have waited for, my entire life, you have taken from me. My lovers are limited to twenty-five choices. But you...you have the entire world. So why, Pierce? Why did you take my Potential from me?"

Pierce frowned angrily. "He's an S-Level, you couldn't have him--"

"Do not take me for a fool Pierce. You were unaware of his level just as everyone else was," Killian snapped. Pierce fell silent but the look on his face had softened. He looked guilty.

Sighing, Killian turned to his attendants.

"Kara, please take Orion, Titus, and Pierce to the medical wing and have them take a paternity test," he commanded.

"Right away, Prince Killian," she replied with a curtsy then ushered his brother and his former Potentials out of the room.

Killian turned back to his father. "Why did you keep it from me, Father? For what purpose?" The anger dimmed and all the prince could feel was the bitter betrayal and utter loneliness.

"Killian, it does not concern you-"

"To hell with that!" he interrupted, baffled that King Ellis was still trying to keep him in the dark. He was so sick of all the secrets!

Killian's power licked at him, urging him to release it upon them all. It coaxed him to tear this room apart with no remorse.

N.A Moore

"Be calm," a deep baritone whispered along the skin of Killian's neck. Arms wrapped around his waist tugging him back into a familiar chest.

The heavy scent of cinnamon and myrrh Killian had come to adore, wafted through his nostrils, forcing him to inhale deeply just so Killian could get himself high off the smell.

The prince glanced up over his shoulder.

"Rem."

He kneaded Killian's hips through the fabric of his clothes. All of the anger drained out of him. Killian looked past Rem at Zev who stood a few feet back. Those blue eyes met his solemnly before he gave a barely noticeable nod. Killian breathed a sigh of relief, mouthing his thanks.

Rem was here.

He was here.

All of the violent emotions he felt just moments ago, faded away leaving nothing but pure exhaustion. The prince sagged against Rem letting him hold his weight.

"Rem, take Killian back to his room," the King said.

"We are not done talking about this," Killian warned, stepping toward him. But Rem's arms locked around him, tugging him back to his chest and holding him close.

"We will discuss it at a later time. Until then, you must choose your fifth Consort and prepare to rank them tomorrow morning. This little...outburst changes nothing."

Killian didn't say anything, too exhausted to argue anymore. Rem gently pulled him out of the room with Zev hot on his heels.

Faust and Caspian waited on the bed. They stood as soon as the others entered. Caspian sported a new warm gold collar that matched the color of his skin. Faust and Caspian wore identical expressions of concern.

"What happened?" Caspian asked.

"Killian proposed to Orion just to find out that Orion is pregnant with either Titus or Pierce's child," Zev answered.

Faust didn't look too shocked, but Caspian definitely did. Then his face mellowed out, "Well I guess that explains why he's been so ill lately."

"Enough," Killian breathed, not wanting to listen to it anymore. They quieted and looked to him, worry clear in their expressions.

"Caspian, Faust. Will you please tell Ethel that Drek will be my final Consort and to prepare his things."

They nodded and left the room.

Killian noticed how Zev's eyes narrowed at the name and Rem's hands tightened around his waist. They were both so tense that it frightened him.

"Do you not agree with my choice?" Killian asked them.

"Considering you have no choices left but him, I don't think we really have a say. It was to be expected," Zev replied, but there was an edge to his tone.

"But you do not like him," Killian said as more of a statement rather than a question.

"No," they both answered simultaneously.

Killian sighed.

"You will grow to like him."

There was a knock on the door and Killian called to let them in. It was Lisa.

"Sorry to intrude, Your Highness, but could I have a word with Lord Rem in regards to his room?" she asked, keeping her eyes low so as not to bother the prince. She was being incredibly subservient, it was very unlike her.

Killian nodded.

Rem released Killian from his grasp and stepped outside the room, closing the door behind him.

Killian turned to Zev.

"Is he staying?" he asked.

"A week, he says. Which means we have a week to convince him to stay."

"A week?"

A week to change his mind. How was he supposed to do that? It's not enough time. Damn it, Rem! Why was he doing this to them?

Zev cupped Killian's cheek and leaned his head against the prince's. "Don't stress about it, Killian. Just focus on the Ranking Ceremony. Make him King and he can't leave."

Killian gasped.

"I thought you would want to be King?"

Zev smiled gently. "We all know that Rem will be Rank One and he has the highest chance of getting you pregnant, therefore becoming King. I just want to be with you and make you happy. That's all I care about. If it means sacrificing my chance at the throne, then it's fine. As I said before, I don't want him to leave either. I'd rather him stay and be King than him leave and be King myself."

"Zev..." Killian tilted his head up to kiss his Consort tenderly.

"We'll have our own child. We just have to be patient," he told the prince as they broke away.

Killian hugged him close.

Rem walked back in the room. He watched them carefully, then looked at Zev. Killian could tell Rem wanted to talk to Zev but didn't want to say anything in front of him. That meant they would discuss in more detail the circumstances in which he was staying.

"I'm going to officially propose to Drek," Killian announced then left the room.

Killian found Drek in the sparring room working out. He was doing pushups in the middle of the ring. His bright green skin glistened with a thin sheen of sweat on his incredibly muscular body. His golden locks were tied up with his worn red ribbon in a messy ponytail with wet strands sticking to his skin.

His expression worried Killian almost as much as his furious movements.

There was something wrong. He seemed agitated.

"Drek?" Killian called to him.

He paused mid-motion. Killian saw his head tilted slightly in his direction. His green eyes glowed. He jumped to his feet in the most fluid and graceful movement, in a way one would hardly expect coming from a male his size.

He strode toward the prince with a confident glide, but his face was all wrong. His handsome features were contorted in frustration.

Killian's brows furrowed as he looked up at him. He towered over the prince unintentionally.

"I know that we have not had much time to spend together, but even so, I would like to formally ask you to be my fifth and final Consort. In time, we will learn to love one another. Do you accept?"

Drek's expression didn't change, but he gave a curt nod.

Killian breathed a sigh of relief.

"Your preparations have already been set in motion. Please find Kara or Ethel so they can take your measurements for your new clothes."

Drek nodded again then briskly left the room.

What was that about?

Killian stood there a little confused before he decided he was wasting time. It was almost dinner time. The results of the paternity test should have been determined by now. The process was near instant. Within the week of consummation, pregnancy could be detected and the parents recognized.

When Killian reached the medical unit, he found Orion sitting on a white infirmary bed, sobbing hysterically. As angry as Killian was with him, the prince couldn't help but worry for him. His hair was a mess on his head, his cries were broken and hopeless. He looked shattered.

Titus looked ill, standing away from the bed Orion sat on, pinching the bridge of his nose. There was a tension in his frame that mirrored that of Pierce who sat in a chair next to Orion's bed. His brother's head was in his hands and Killian could tell he was in a state of disbelief.

Killian looked over at Lorn who was looking at some papers with mild shock. Her expression scrunched in deep concentration as her eyes quickly scanned the paper she held.

She was so engrossed in her work she didn't even realize the prince had entered.

"Lorn," Killian said, gaining her attention.

Her head jerked up, mouth slightly parted. She looked startled, rushing to bow.

That was not a reassuring sign.

"What are the results?" Killian asked her.

Lorn gazed at the papers then took a deep breath. "It appears we have a case of *duplici paternitatis.*"

Killian's jaw dropped.

"A double paternity?" he questioned allowed, needing the answer to be clearly confirmed.

Lorn nodded.

"It's possible, just not very common."

Titus and Pierce were both the fathers of the child Orion bore.

Killian ran his fingers through his hair.

"He's going to sell me. He's going to sell my child," Killian heard Orion whisper through his cries. His eyes were wide but unseeing. He stared at the ground tugging at his face.

Orion started to shake.

"He's going to sell us."

Orion's eyes widened even further until Killian could actually see something snapped in him. He screamed, high and piteous, tearing Killian's heart in two.

No one made a move to comfort him at first and that aggravated the prince. Neither Pierce nor Titus did anything despite being just as responsible.

Disgusting and pathetic.

Despite the betrayal he felt, this Incubus was still Killian's subject and it was his job to take care of him. Killian rushed to Orion, pulling him into his arms and cooing to him. Killian stroked his hair and rocked him back and forth in a soothing motion.

"Shh, it is alright. I will make arrangements for you. You will be safe. Do not worry. Everything will be alright," he promised softly.

Seeing Killian act made something in Titus react. He seemed to snap out of his trance and grabbed Orion's hand in his.

"I won't abandon you," Titus vowed to Orion softly. "You are not alone."

Killian gave him an approving nod.

Pierce made no move.

As much as Killian loved him, at this very moment, he could not be more disappointed in him. He was going to have to step up eventually. And once Father finds out about this...he was going to be furious.

Orion eventually calmed down, settling into a trance. Killian was a little worried that he might have been going into shock but Lorn assured the prince he was fine and just needed to rest.

Killian had Titus take Orion back to his room and instructed that they share one from now on.

Pierce had the nerve to look upset about it. Jealous even.

Killian shook his head at his little brother and left him alone in the medical wing.

He didn't have time for this. Killian needed to prepare himself for the Ranking Ceremony tomorrow. He still had to figure out how he was going to rank his chosen.

When had everything become so crazy?

How could this happen?

Was it him? Had he done something wrong? He just wanted to know how to fix all of this! He wanted to be loved. Was that too much? Was he being selfish?

Shaking and crying was how Rem found him.

Killian hadn't known he was crying. He hadn't known how long he sat there in the library, slowly crumbling apart.

Horas, according to Rem's words.

"It is time for the Ranking Ceremony to begin."

Killian's body ached and his skin glistened with sweat despite being so cold.

A shudder ran through his frame, chattering his teeth.

"I cannot," Killian whispered brokenly. He can't face the kingdom like this. Not this shattered shell of a male, of a King. His people didn't deserve such a disgrace.

"You must."

Killian glared up into those black eyes.

"You do not have the right to tell me what I must do!"

"As your Consort, I do," he replied.

Killian slapped him, teeth bared in rage.

Rem's nostrils flared but he remained impassive.

Unable to resist, Killian reached up and forced his lips against Rem's. The male responded immediately, molding his lips to the prince's. Killian moaned before Rem broke away from him.

"I am sorry. I should not have struck you. That was very childish of me," Killian apologized.

"You are confused and hurting. I am not holding your pain against you. But you must prepare yourself, Ethel and Kara will be here shortly to prepare you for the Ranking Ceremony. The King has already let the people of the Kingdom inside."

"Where is Zev?" Killian asked, feeling the sudden urge to see him.

"He is being prepared for the ceremony as are all of your Consorts. I too must be prepared, but the King asked me to check on you. We all grew concerned when you did not show for breakfast and were not in the room."

Kara and Ethel came into the library, not bothering to usher him back to his room, with a cart and a rack of clothing.

"Lord Rem, Lisa is waiting to take you to the dressing chamber."

Rem nodded, before turning back to Killian and kissing his forehead softly.

"I will be waiting for you," he promised, then stood and left.

"Come now, Prince Killian, let's get you cleaned up," Kara said softly.

"My brother, and Orion, will they be there?" Killian asked numbly, letting them tug him around and primp him. They buffed and polished every inch of his skin, yanked and tied his hair.

"All of the Royal bloodline will be present as well as their...associates."

Killian climbed into the gold lace thong, tucking his genitals inside carefully, grateful for the silk pouch on the inside to cup his skin. A golden skirt, made of the softest satin, with two high slits on each thigh, was tied around his waist. Kara came around with a thick gold belt with thousands of dangling jewels, wound and linked together with chains of gold. It was heavy as it hung from his waist and the jewels dragged on the ground. He was dressed in a long sleeve white chiffon top that billowed around his arms. Over it was a gold-plated vest with his family crest encrusted with red rubies. A gold and ruby crown was placed on his head with the fallen curls from his braided bun cascading over the edges. Ethel attached gold links to his tail.

Kara and Ethel both brought a clear wrap and secured it around his body to protect his clothes from the blood. When the wrap was in place, he let his wings burst free from the skin on his back, blood splattering on the ground and some hitting the walls. The process was painful but well worth it. He hated having his wings confined but it was necessary. Wings were precious, a direct link to Incubi life force. If an Incubus lost their wings, they went mad. Most died from the loss. That is why the Incubi race keep their wings hidden unless around those they trusted.

Kara lightly cleaned Killian's sensitive wings until there was no trace of blood.

Ethel attached gold cuffs to his ankles before bowing. They both smiled at him.

"You've been waiting for this for so long, Prince Killian. Enjoy this moment. It will be worth it, that we promise you,"

He looked at the two females who had been kind and loving towards him for much of his life. He owed them so much.

"Thank you...for everything."

They bowed before opening the doors and escorting him to the main hall. The main hall was the biggest room in the castle. It was where all of the public thrones sat.

The highest level bore two thrones for the King and Queen. They were lavish gold thrones with gilded bronze and black marble.

The middle level held one red throne that glistened from the copious number of rubies embedded along it. On the left, sat two black marble thrones with velvet seats and on the right sat three more of the same style. The red throne was Killian's and the black thrones belonged to his Consorts.

On the lower level sat several wooden thrones where the King's Consorts and children sat.

On the main floor stood thousands of people from all different races that made up the kingdom. Nymphs, Kappas, Fae, Dragons, Pixies, Trolls, Shapeshifters, Elves, Mers, Sirens, Kelpies, Goblins, Satyrs, Kitsune, and more.

There was an excited hum of chatter as they mingled amongst themselves, eager to see who their prince had chosen and how he would rank them.

When the trumpets sounded, the guests kneeled. The doors opened and Killian made his way to the front of the hall. He kept his head held high and his expression complacent. Today was a special day. There could be nothing to ruin it. Killian knew how he would rank his Consorts. He was prepared.

N.A Moore

"Prince Killian Innis, heir to the throne of Incubi! Long live the prince!" The attendant announced.

"Long live the prince!" The crowd shouted gleefully.

So many people.

So many hopeful faces.

So many lives that he would soon be responsible for.

Sickness threatened to overcome him, but he kept his composure. He would not embarrass himself.

"I thank you, my loyal subjects and wonderful people of our Kingdom. Today marks the day that I welcome you, my Royal Consorts," he said clearly and fiercely, looking out into the crowd.

The crowds of people clapped and cheered at his words. He smiled at them all. The King stood and took a stand beside his son.

"Today we will witness the beginning of a new Reign and the start of a bright and fortuitous future! Now, let the Ceremony commence!" King Ellis's voice rang out above the cries and whistles from their people.

Dressed in black leathers and furs, with interwoven lace and silver jewels, Rem was the first to step out before the crowd. They gasped in awe as his first chosen Consort spread his powerful wings wide, letting his magix flare beneath his skin for an instant. His silver collar glinted in the light as his wild black mane fluttered around him. Killian's own wings quivered in response to his great show of power.

He kneeled before Killian.

"Rem Brangwen of Tenebris," the King announced.

Zev was next, stepping out in dark navy leathers and a silver mesh top with sleeves made of the finest silk. His hair was done up in an elegant braid, showing off his handsome facial structure and accentuating his impressive jawline. His silver collar nearly blended with the mesh of his top. His shimmering blue wings were a sight to behold. He knelt before Killian, just as Rem had.

"Zev Lane of Tarr."

Faust stepped out dressed in white gossamer and leather. His silver collar lay stark against his white skin. His hair was curled elegantly but pulled back into a high ponytail. Though he was more delicate looking than the other men, he was still blindingly handsome. His wings were white with iridescent swirls shimmering in the light, capturing the awe of the entire crowd. He knelt beside Zev.

"Faust Akili of Sapientae."

Caspian strolled out with grace. His body was encased in red leather pants and a dark red and orange vest made of chiffon and leather. His hair poured around him like flames, waving with every step he took. His skin glistened like freshly polished gold and his fiery red wings flickered with red streaks, imitating the movement of his hair. His gold collar blended in with his skin completely. He was absolutely breathtaking as he knelt beside Faust.

"Caspian Rafiki of Faltaire."

Last but not least, Drek emerged, looking like a God with his golden hair waving to perfection. His body shimmered as if glossed. His impressive chest was bare, and he wore nothing but a dark green satin sash across it. His lower half covered in dark green leather pants. His gold collar shimmered adding to his fantastic glow. His large golden wings stretched out gracefully. He was emanated power. Killian was impressed, as was the King.

He knelt beside Caspian.

"Drek Leon of Gemp."

The crowd clapped at the conclusion of the introduction of the five Consorts. The King settled them quickly with one raised hand.

"And now I leave the choice to my son, Prince Killian."

Killian took a deep breath.

"Rank One: Rem Brangwen," he stated clearly.

Rem stood, bowed before the King, then the prince before Ethel came and placed a small crown on his head. The crowd clapped vigorously. Killian's ears began to ring at the volume. Rem went to sit upon the first black throne.

"Rank Two: Zev Lane."

Zev stood, bowing to the King then to Killian before leaning down so Ethel could place the small crown on his head. He smiled briefly at Killian before going up to take a seat at the black throne beside Rem.

"Rank Three," Killian took another deep breath, and carefully let it out before continuing. "Caspian Rafiki."

Caspian looked slightly surprised before raising and bowing to the King and Killian. His eyes were wide as Ethel crowned him. He took the throne on the other side of Killian's red throne.

The choice to pick Caspian as third was difficult. Both Faust and Caspian were equal in the affections Killian held for them. But Caspian was more tenacious. Killian had to take into account decision making if it ever came to a war or battle. He needed someone as cunning as Caspian to take control if there were ever a need. Rem and Zev could easily have their hands tied and his third ranked needed to be able to step up.

"Rank Four: Faust Akili."

Faust smiled at Killian warmly before bowing to the King and Prince then accepting his crown from Ethel.

"Rank Five: Drek Leon." Killian concluded. He was starting to sound a little breathless. His heart beat rapidly and his face grew hot with the reality of this moment.

He just chose his Consorts. He had them now. All of them.

Killian watched Drek be crowned before taking his seat at the last throne. Standing back, the prince stared at all of them. He could officially call all of these beautiful and incredible males his, and one of them was going to be his Consort King.

The people broke out into roars of happiness. Some even cried as if they were the ones choosing their Consorts, but Killian knew the real reason behind their tears. Many of them had witnessed his father's Ranking Ceremony and the announcement of his mother's pregnancy with him. They had been there from the moment he was born and as he grew. They had watched him become the male he is today.

His people were his family and they had been there every step of the way.

Something about that made him even more emotional. He tried not to show it, but he was beaming with happiness.

"For fifteen days, my son will seal this Ceremony and strive to bear a child. Let us pray for fertility and strength. My son will not be disturbed in these fifteen days and will work hard to bring us the next heir."

The crowd clapped.

"Let the Ceremony commence!"

Killian turned toward his waiting Consorts and offered his hand out to Rem. He stood with all of his dark glory and strolled to the prince's side with confidence and grace. He grasped Killian's hand tightly before leading the way through throngs of people who parted, throwing white rose petals for purity and red rose petals for...well...that was obvious.

Rem clasped Killian's hand tightly as they ducked out of the room leaving the roar of cheers and well wishes. Guards lined their path to the bedroom where they would consummate. It was a room prepared just for the Ranking Ceremony. It was dimly lit with candles and scattered rose petals. The bed was covered in dark red silk and the canopy above framed the four posters with red chiffon fabric.

Lisa was there waiting. She asked Rem to step outside while she dressed Killian. Once he was out of the room, Lisa worked quickly, stripping him of his gaudy clothing and slipping him into something he would not consider clothing. His body was exposed in several places and others were covered in see through lace, with straps and bows. Killian couldn't understand the positioning of the fabric but didn't waste time asking questions. Lisa covered him in a satin robe and told him to take it off once he was alone with his Consort, then left the room quickly. A guard brought Rem back in.

"We will leave your meals at the door," a guard said then moved to close the door behind him. But Rem stopped him.

"If you hear a scream, you come in immediately. Anything suspicious at all, you intervene," he ordered solemnly. The guard raised a brow in amusement.

"As you command, my Lord," he said then backed out of the room.

Killian watched Rem carefully. He was tense, looking at Killian with fear in his eyes. Killian could see it rising with each silent moment.

He was terrified would not make the first move.

Killian did. He slowly slid the robe off his shoulders and let it fall to the ground in a silky heap. Rem's jaw clenched and he squeezed his eyes shut, turning his head away.

"You cannot make love to me if you do not look at me," Killian told him softly.

Rem did not say anything, just went very still, as if any movement could make him snap and lose control. Killian approached him slowly. Coming close, the prince placed his palm on the Consort's chest, feeling the ridges of his magix. Heat flared beneath his touch and Rem shivered.

It wasn't like him to lack this much control, or even show this much emotion.

Killian leaned in and kissed the skin on Rem's chest. One moment they were standing by the door, the next they were falling into the bed, with his body on top of Killian's, lips at his throat, hunger clearly evident, straining against the leather of his pants.

Killian could see a faint black smoke that seemed to solidify into Rem's body. Stunned, Killian left himself open to Rem's merciless lips. He was eager and passionate. Killian couldn't keep up with his excitement. It was overwhelming, but not in a bad way.

Small moans left Killian's lips as Rem hands traveled along his body over the thin lace fabric. Rem's eyes fluttered and in them Killian saw swirls of color. There was something in him that was waking up.

No.

Not something.

Someone.

His beast was there, right beneath the surface. There with every touch, every kiss, every heated breath that left their lips.

Though Rem seemed engrossed in their intimacy, Killian was connected to him and could feel the anxiety in his thoughts. Fear kept him from touching Killian any more than he was. He was trying to make Killian believe that he was letting go, but Killian wasn't oblivious. Rem couldn't hide from him anymore.

Killian cupped his cheek in his palm, watching as Rem leaned in to kiss the inside of his wrist softly. He hovered above the prince, but careful not to let him feel any of his weight.

"You are holding back still."

Rem's jaw clenched angrily as he looked away from Killian. The prince jerked his face back to his, not letting him avoid his gaze.

"Let go," Killian told him.

"He will hurt you. I can feel it."

"He will not. You will not. You love me just as I love you, but you have to let him love me too. Let him love me the way you do. Let him go. Let yourself go."

Rem shook his head.

"I cannot," he protested. "He will bleed you."

"If he hurts me, I will scream and my guards will come just as you instructed."

Rem looked so torn it was heartbreaking.

"He may kill you before the guards get here. They may not reach you in time," his voice was soft and far away. He was staring at Killian but not really seeing him.

No. He saw Tara.

Killian gripped his face tightly. "You will not let that happen. Trust me Rem."

"You do not understand what he is capable of!"

"Trust me, Rem."

Rem was silent, internally fighting a battle before finally caving in and pressing his lips to Killian's. When he pulled away, his forehead still pressed against the prince's, he whispered. "You must scream at the slightest hint of pain."

Killian wanted to laugh but he agreed anyway.

Rem fell upon him, starved. His fingers dug into Killian's hips while his knees nudged the prince's legs apart. He fell between them and this time let Killian feel every pound of him. He was heavy but it was a comfortable weight, especially with the way he pushed his lower body down.

His lips gave Killian no room to protest--not that he ever would--completely devouring Killian. The prince gasped in short breaths as Rem's assault continued. He pressed Killian harder against the bed making it uncomfortable for his wings. Killian slowly pulled them back inside his body.

Rem's hand gripped the back of Killian's head, digging his fingers into the prince's hair and yanking his head back, leaving his neck exposed. Rem dove for it, sucking in the skin harshly causing Killian's breath to catch in his throat.

That is when the tingling sensation began.

It had become so familiar that Killian welcomed it. He wanted the feeling to overwhelm him to the point of delirium.

"More, Rem. More," Killian pleaded, rocking his hips up against him to create that delicious friction he was so desperate for. He wanted Rem's skin on his.

Rem dipped his head between Killian's legs, kissing his inner left thigh. He left a blazing trail in his wake as he made his way down the prince's raised leg until he reached Killian's cuffed ankle. With a pure male smile, he slowly pulled down the lace that covered his leg until it was bare. Repeating the motion with the other leg, Killian watched him breathlessly.

His lips rushed to meet Killian but in that forward motion, he stealthily tucked his hand between Killian's legs, sliding his fingers underneath the strip of his thong. Killian moaned against his mouth as his finger brushed his already soaked entrance.

Rem teased him, sucking on his lip, biting it, brushing his finger against that intimate part of him. Killian couldn't control the noises coming from his mouth, the things his body craved. He didn't understand any of it, but he knew he wanted more.

"I am sorry," Rem said breathlessly.

"For what?" Killian panted.

"I wanted to take this slow, to give you much pleasure at your pace, but it is difficult to hold myself back. I cannot give you a slow lovemaking. I have to take you hard and fast. I did not want your first time to be this way..." he struggled for a moment, a shudder running through his body as he slowly brought his fingers to his lips, coated with Killian's slick. He stuck the fingers his mouth and closed his eyes to savor the taste. The marks of his magix began to glow. Just like that time before, his skin swirled with every color imaginable and his magix heated like lava beneath the surface of a volcano. He was a sight to behold. When he opened his eyes again, they were glowing just like his skin.

"I cannot hold back," he finished.

"Let go," Killian whispered pulling his face back.

He kissed the prince passionately, massaging his tongue with his own, forcing the prince's mouth wider to invade it more. When he pulled back there was a still a thin string of saliva connecting them

Killian was dazed.

His eyes followed Rem as he backed off the bed, their gazes connected. Killian was mesmerized by the swirling colors under his skin. It was like they were telling a story, hypnotizing him.

When Rem slid off his clothes, exposing more of those gyrating colors, it was even harder to look away. Killian didn't want to close his eyes to blink. He watched every muscle roll, coil, and flex.

Rem was beautiful.

Beyond beautiful.

And he was Killian's...for now.

Once fully nude, Rem crawled back over Killian, fitting himself between his legs. He stared down at the thong for a while. He cocked his head at it as if he didn't understand what it was. With two elegant fingers, he pinched the fabric, then let it slip back against Killian's skin. The prince drew in a sharp breath.

Rem's face scrunched in confusion.

The confusion alerted Killian that it was not Rem who did not understand the garment, but his beast. His beast was starting to gain more control.

With a snarl of annoyance, Rem tore the thong in half, yanking it off and tossing it somewhere behind him. Killian blushed under his predatory stare.

His hand began to glide up Killian's stomach, eyeing the patches of lace that covered his torso. He ripped it apart and tossed it away until Killian was bare to him.

The prince shivered in anticipation.

"Rem," Killian called him.

His head jerked up. He blinked slowly and an awareness surfaced. It was really Rem again.

His face hovered over the prince's, while he held himself above him. His hips pressed against Killian's where he could feel the stiffness of his Consort against him. Skin to skin.

Finally.

Killian rolled his hips, urging Rem to do the same. The friction felt wonderful. He kissed Killian again, catching the movement and mimicking it. Little whimpers escaped Killian's lips.

"Rem, Rem, Rem," he chanted, digging his fingers into Rem's muscled back. The male's magix burned against his skin.

Rem's rhythm became more frantic, wilder, and untamed.

Though it felt wonderful, Killian could tell Rem was losing himself. His hands were rough on the prince's skin and his grip was bruising.

A wave of slick gushed out of Killian, drenching their lower halves.

It drove Rem crazy. He normally didn't make a sound in the throes of passion, but there was a low grumble in his chest. He was panting with his eyes squeezed shut.

Killian touched his face gently with one hand while the other grabbed a fistful of his muscular butt cheek, squeezing him closer.

The moment he did it, Rem's eyes flew open. One eye was black, but the other...was a bright, bright orange. Killian wanted to be startled but he couldn't say that he was. Rem's expression grew tortured again.

One hand shot out, gripping the gold-plated headboard, the other squeezed the sheets in a tight fist. His death grip wrinkled the fine silk.

"He is fighting me. I cannot--" Rem strained, his mismatched eyes wide and wild. His body trembled viciously. Fabric tore under his grip, just beside Killian's head.

"Shh, it is okay. I trust you, Rem."

Killian wrapped his arms around Rem's neck pulling himself up to kiss him. If Rem started thinking about it, he'd panic and retreat. If Killian wanted him to stay, he needed Rem to get him pregnant. He needed to go all the way.

"I trust you," Killian whispered against his soft plush lips.

Rem hesitated but eventually buried his hand between them, positioning himself. Killian's heart thudded against his chest wildly. Slick oozed out of him in anticipation. Then Rem was there, warm and smooth, lightly brushing against Killian's entrance.

Rem was slow, careful, gentle, as he pushed the round tip of his shaft inside the prince.

Killian's fingers scratched down his back and his teeth clenched.

It felt strange, but it was not bad. There was no pain, just pressure. As Rem pushed himself deeper, Killian felt a little discomfort. When the last bit of him was sheathed inside, Killian gasped. Biting his lip, he tried not to cry out. He felt full and stretched to the point of bursting.

If Rem knew it hurt, he would stop.

It doesn't hurt that bad, Killian.

Killian kept repeating that in his head until the mantra distracted him enough from the pain. Rem stayed still inside him, letting him adjust while trying to keep himself under control. The bed frame groaned under his impressive strength. A sharp hiss left Killian's lips as Rem's nails became claws, digging into Killian's sensitive skin and drawing rivulets of blood. His fingers were trembling.

"Killian," his voice was strangled.

"I am fine," Killian whispered. "I trust you."

He exhaled then pulled out nearly all the way. The loss was dramatic.

Then he pushed back in. The dance began of his steady push and pull. Killian kissed him furiously, raking his fingers through his hair, tugging at any part of him that he could reach. Rem had retracted his wings a little while ago, but Killian could feel the cartilage under his skin, moving and quivering.

Rem was starting to lose himself in the motion. His hips rolled faster and harder than before. His grunts became louder and his skin grew brighter.

His hands bruised Killian's waist and his arms but the prince didn't care. He was so full of him that nothing else mattered. He felt so amazing. The trembling in his limbs, the heavy weight of his body on his, it was all so incredible.

Knowing it was Rem that he was connected to, made it pleasurable for the prince.

"More," Killian begged. "Please Rem!"

His grinding became erratic and more desperate.

Rem's expression changed. He was fighting again. His jaw clenched and his teeth were bared. His orange eye was getting brighter and stronger. He was crumbling and it was painful to watch.

Rem's shaking grew worse. A lone tear spilled from his black eye.

"He is coming. I cannot stop it. I cannot stop him."

"Rem, it is okay."

Rem growled and it was a sound not native to Incubi. His breathing grew more ragged. His hand held Killian's hip tightly. When he squeezed, Killian could feel his bones protesting. If Rem squeezed him any harder, he was going to shatter them.

"Rem," Killian gasped in pain.

Another tear fell from his black eye and he was shaking his head. "I cannot. I cannot. I am sorry."

"You can."

He wasn't listening, he was shaking his head. His hand contracted, claws tearing open another wound in Killian's flesh. Biting his lip, Killian fought to remain calm and reassuring.

"It is alright. You are okay," Killian told him, stroking his cheek, brushing away a tear.

Though he was protesting, his body was still moving. Killian cried out when he reached a certain spot in him that made him see stars.

"It feels good Rem. So good, I promise."

"I am hurting you," he choked.

"I am fine."

The orange bled into the other eye. The shaking in his frame became so bad, the whole bed trembled until suddenly, it stopped, and Killian was staring up into two bright orange eyes. His head tilted to one side as he examined the prince.

Rem was no longer there.

"Hello," Killian said softly, cupping his cheek.

His hand darted out, snatching Killian's wrist painfully. He stared at it. Killian kept very still, not sure if any sudden movements might have a negative effect.

But the prince was surprised when he kissed his wrist instead.

His eyes met Killian's.

"It is okay," the prince told him. "I am yours."

The beast grunted, leaning down to kiss him, but it was too aggressive. He forced Killian's mouth open until the prince's jaw started to ache in objection.

Killian pounded his free hand against his arm. He darted back and growled again, baring his teeth in Killian's face.

Killian shook his head at him.

"Too rough," the prince said, not really sure if he understood.

He frowned at the prince, then did it again. Killian repeated the motion until he backed away again. A hiss escaped his lips this time expressing his frustration at Killian's fussing.

The prince brought his face up and began a soft and gentle kiss. When he pushed to make it deeper, Killian pulled away. Then he started up again. It took a while, but the beast eventually started to understand.

He could be taught.

When he started thrusting again, Killian couldn't control him. He would not listen to the prince's protests and only pushed harder and faster.

"You are hurting me," Killian tried to tell him, but the beast just growled at him, snapping his teeth in Killian's face. He moved even faster, slamming himself inside. Killian could feel his body rejecting the movement.

It hurt.

It really hurt.

"Rem! It hurts! Rem!"

But the beast was not Rem. Rem could not help him.

"Please...listen to me," Killian begged, trying to capture the beast's gaze. He growled harshly.

"Tara," Killian whispered. "Remember Tara? If you keep doing this, I will go away like Tara. Tara is gone because it hurt."

The beast growled louder.

His hands wrapped around the prince's hips and his fingers dug into Killian skin so deeply he knew he was going to have some massive bruises.

"Tara," Killian repeated.

The beast paused, unsure.

Then he cried.

Those orange eyes leaked precious tears that dripped onto Killian's face, and soft whimpers left his mouth as he cried.

"Shh, it is alright. Everything is okay," Killian cooed, bringing the beast's face into his neck and hugging him close. "I am here now. Just be gentle."

Once he stopped crying, Killian urged him on again with his hips, forcing him back inside. The beast pumped himself aggressively but not as unbearably as before.

Soon they reached the height of their passion, and Killian released his *Haise*.

The beast roared, exploding inside him. Killian could feel liquid heat filling him up, forcing an explosion from his own body as well. All of that pent-up lust had him drunk as he devoured every last bit.

The orange bled from Rem's eyes and the glowing of his body dimmed. He breathed heavily.

Killian was so exhausted and entranced by the feeding, he felt like he was floating. It took him a few tries, but he managed to turn Rem's face to his. "I told you it would be okay."

"Killian," Rem breathed in relief.

The prince smiled lazily at him.

"He can be taught."

Chapter 12

Killian didn't remember falling. Rem was awake, radiating heat like the sun. Killian's cheek pressed against Rem's chest as the prince laid along his body.

It was comfortable.

Though the comfort was short lived once the prince shifted. A sharp pain shot up his back forcing a loud gasp from his lips and a throbbing in his hips.

"You will be sore for a little while," Rem murmured softly in his deep baritone.

Killian groaned at the discomfort when he tried to move again but pushed past it anyway.

"How long have I been asleep?"

"Only a few horas."

Killian peeked up at him, trying to read his mood, but his expression was as blank as ever.

"How do you feel?" he asked Rem.

"Is that not a question I should be asking you instead?" he countered.

"But I asked first."

Rem remained silent for a while before he sighed.

"I do not know what I am feeling. Relieved, I suppose. But worried. Anxious even."

"But why? Everything went so well--"

Rem snorted uncharacteristically.

Killian raised a brow. "What?"

"You have not seen your body. You are not well at all," his voice was cold...withdrawn. Killian didn't understand his mood. He was alive, which means it went well. Rem didn't kill him. They succeeded. What could he possibly mean?

Killian noticed that he was staring up at the ceiling and not at him. He followed Rem's gaze and saw the huge mirror hanging up above. He admired Rem's gorgeous black hair splayed along the sheets, and how his attractive, angular face glistened under the sun's powerful rays. He saw the sharp contrast of his lavender skin against Rem's total blackness. And then he saw scratches.

Huge, hideous, bloody gashes. Bruises formed around them, discolored and vicious looking, littering his skin. Splotches in angry circles or clear imprints of large hands.

Rem's hands. His claws.

Killian tried to lift his right leg to examine a huge scrape on his thigh but a sharp, agonizing pain shot through him, causing him to yelp. It was excruciating in that initial movement, before becoming a less intense but still painful throb.

"Your right hip was dislocated, and your tailbone bruised. I snapped your leg back in place, but it will hurt for a while. You will not be able to walk for some time."

The bruises, Killian expected, but not the scratches. He knew that this wasn't going to be easy and that there would be some complications, but he would deal with the consequences. The injuries were a bit more severe than he first anticipated, but it was nothing too unbearable.

Killian was amazed he didn't feel it happening. The pain should have been unbelievable. He guessed there were other pains that were more intense at the time. If he knew anything about Rem, he knew his Consort would not forgive himself for this.

"I am alive," Killian reminded him.

Rem's expression hardened.

"Barely."

Killian dug his fingers into his chest, making him tense.

"I am alive. I am fine. Bruises mean nothing. Scratches are nothing. A little soreness is nothing. All of this is nothing because I am alive and well."

That was not the response he wanted to hear.

"You know what else is alive? The baby that will soon grow in my stomach," the prince pushed.

"It is unlikely that you are pregnant after one time."

"It only takes one time for it happen."

"You are naive."

Killian rolled his eyes and slid away from Rem.

His teeth clenched as he fought not to make a sound of pain. It was difficult, but he managed. Rem sighed before rolling on his side and grabbing Killian's arm. His hand was piping hot. Killian winced from his touch. His magix flared, igniting the prince's entire body.

Then suddenly...the pain was gone. Well, for the most part. The scratches still remained.

He glanced at his arms and body. All the bruises had disappeared. He was free of most of his injuries. Killian whirled on him in disbelief. He had not known magix extended to healing.

"I can heal minor things. For the open wounds that are bleeding, I am unable to do much."

"If you could heal me, why didn't you do so immediately?" Killian demanded.

"Because I wanted you to see that being with me is dangerous. I wanted you to know the full extent of the damage my beast can cause. You are alive, yes, but for how long?"

"Your job is not done Rem. We still have the rest of today and four days to follow. And every moment of each day, you are to fill me with your seed until I am round with the heir to the throne. You must do it again and again."

Rem's expression was defiant. It reminded Killian of Zev.

Those two had gotten closer than he realized.

Killian leaned over and kissed Rem's chin, sliding his way up to his lips. Climbing above him with a daintiness he had not known he could master, Killian settled on his hips. Rem acted as if he was unaffected by the action, but his body betrayed him. Killian could feel him thicken underneath him.

"Again and again," Killian whispered in his ear.

He shivered.

Killian no longer felt sore and was able to maneuver Rem inside him without any pain. There was discomfort at first, and pressure, but little pain. He slid inside easily.

Rem shut his eyes.

"Rem...look at me," Killian commanded breathlessly.

He didn't open his eyes.

"Rem," the prince said more clearly.

His eyes snapped open, worried.

"He will take over and I am unable to fight."

Killian smiled at him.

"I do not think he will be a problem. I think he is a little worn out and very sated. This time, it is just you and me."

Killian brushed Rem's cheek with the back of his hand before falling back so Rem could mount him. Rem took his time, planting tiny kisses along Killian's spine. The prince moaned, arching his back before his Consort slowly thrust inside.

"So good, Rem. Need this. Need you," the prince groaned.

Rem took his time pleasuring Killian until they both reached their climax. Rem twisted Killian above him again, tucking him into his chest.

Killian snuggled close, breathing heavily, with a thin sheen of sweat coating his body.

"How do you feel?" the prince asked Rem again.

"Happy," he replied.

Killian grinned, kissing his chest.

"We should bathe and eat. It will not be comfortable sleeping like this or sanitary," Rem said quietly.

"Wait. I want to stay like this for a little bit, make sure your seed has a chance to find the way."

Rem laughed.

Killian was amazed to hear it. It was deep and smooth, just like his voice. It made Killian's lower half tingle. If he weren't so exhausted, he'd try for another round.

"It should be settled enough," he said after a while.

Killian giggled and Rem carried him to the private bathroom where they cleaned and consummated again.

The bathroom was large but not nearly as large as the communal bath they were accustomed to using. The ceilings towered above their heads in regal arches of concave white marble with accents of gilded bronze foliage. There was a huge bath in the center with water spouts just a little further in.

Rem lowered himself into the bath with Killian in his arms, settling the prince comfortably in his lap. It was nice to just soak and relax.

Killian nuzzled his face into Rem's neck, inhaling his scent that only seemed to increase with the steam radiating from the water.

"If you get me pregnant, you have an obligation to stay and be King Consort, but if you do not, will you leave me anyway?" Killian asked him softly, knowing all too well that he was ruining the bliss of their post love making glow.

"I cannot leave officially unless dismissed by you."

"I would never make you stay if I knew it meant you would be unhappy for the rest of your life. I care too much for you to let that happen."

"If I stay, you will be harmed."

"Liar," Killian hissed. "We proved three times now that you are no danger to my life. Your beast is no threat to me."

Rem's blank expression irritated him.

"I will always be a danger to you. Or have you forgotten your bruises and dislocated hip so soon?" His voice was hard despite the lack of anger in his features.

He was so stubborn, it was infuriating.

Killian grabbed his face aggressively. "Well then, we will keep making love until it is absolute that I am with your child."

"You will not know if you are pregnant or who will be the father of your first born until after you have lain with all five Consorts. You will not know if it is my child until then."

"Then you are stuck here until we figure it out," Killian growled, shoving his lips against Rem's.

Killian was still inexperienced with kissing and only did what his body thought he should do. Imitating his Consorts' in the act only made things painfully awkward. He didn't know if he was kissing well but it must not have been terrible because Rem couldn't resist afterwards.

The hot water made Killian's body more pliant and he was able to go another round. It was quick and exhausting. After the bath, Rem carried Killian to the freshly made bed. Someone must have come in while they were in the bath.

There were even two plates of food waiting for them on the nightstand. Rem fed Killian his food as the prince's eyes fought to stay open.

"Eat Killian or you will grow too weak. Weak bodies cannot bear children nor can they perform," Rem said quietly.

Killian's eyes flew open immediately and he rushed to stuff the food down his throat on his own.

Rem chuckled.

Killian glanced at him quickly to see even a glimpse of his smile again, but his face was so quick to fall back into that expressionless mask. It made Killian a little sad.

When the prince finished his plate, Rem took the dishes and put them off to the side. They would probably be picked up while they were sleeping.

Killian was so tired, his eyelids felt like lead.

Rem pulled his body close and wrapped his strong arms around Killian. The prince nuzzled into his throat before drifting off into a blissful sleep.

Killian's dreams were filled with strange mirages. They felt like memories but there was no way they could be real. These people in these scenes were some Killian had never seen before. They felt familiar but he knew it was something he had not lived through. Even the settings were some he had not even known existed. Killian did not travel outside the palace walls, there was no way he knew this small town full of tiny brown houses and quiet little shops.

There was a lake with a large birch tree that stood tall, at the tip of the water's edge. There was a little boy, with black curls and coal black skin. A grin split his cherub face. His laugh was like chiming bells, so filled with happiness.

Then there was a female.

She was cute, small and angelic. Her chocolate brown eyes were bright and full of innocence. Her dark brown hair fell down to her waist in wild curls. Her skin was a honied caramel color and wings an even darker brown.

Killian saw her smile, laugh, frown, cry, scream, sing, dance, breathe. He saw everything that she was, over and over again. Such vivid images and a strong undying desire for this female.

Who was she?

Who was that boy?

It was almost as if these emotions, these people, these memories were someone else's. But who?

And why was he seeing them?

Killian opened his eyes, blinking to clear his blurry vision. Once his sight finally focused, he found himself staring into bright orange eyes.

He gasped, flinching back at first.

The eyes didn't blink, just stared.

The beast's head was still planted firmly on the pillow, one arm tucked under it, the other around Killian's waist in a tight, possessive manner.

"Hello there," Killian whispered.

The beast remained quiet, just stared at him. He looked sort of curious, like he was trying to understand the greeting.

Killian scooched a little closer, placing a hand gently on his cheek.

The prince's thumb smoothed his sharp cheekbones slowly and gently. Killian was hoping the softer he was with Rem's beast, the gentler he'd be. It might be pointless, but it was a start. Killian wanted to understand him and wanted the beast to understand Killian.

"Can you understand me?" he asked.

He didn't answer which meant no.

"Do you have a name?" he continued, though it was unlikely the beast would answer. If he even could.

He did not answer.

"I will call you Beast until I can come up with something better."

Beast just blinked at Killian, before his eyes traveled lower. He was staring at Killian's stomach. His hand slid from around his waist to the front of his stomach. He rubbed it in little circles.

"I want you to put a baby there," Killian told him gently.

Beast looked back up at him.

A low grunt rumbled from his chest.

Killian smiled, pressing his hand over Beast's, watching him continue his circular designs. It was as if he were entranced.

Killian thought that he would not try to force intimacy on him, but he was wrong. Once Beast grew bored of drawing circles, he twisted above Killian, shoving the prince's legs around his waist and thrust his hips forward. It was like he was trying to stab Killian with his member.

"Whoa, easy! Gentle!" Killian reminded him.

He didn't care for the prince's words and didn't understand them. He just kept thrusting, but Killian noticed that he was considerably less aggressive with his treatment. Before, he bruised him from the moment he first touched him but now, Beast left less marks on Killian's skin.

Killian guided him inside and tried to control the pace, but Beast was not patient and took control almost right away. After a while, Killian gave up and just let him have his way as long as it wasn't too painful. When he finished, Rem resurfaced.

Immediately Rem began to inspect his body, making sure that Killian wasn't hurt anywhere.

"I am fine," the prince reassured him. Rem didn't believe him, especially since Killian was sporting a few bruises. They were nowhere near the severity of last time. "He was much calmer this time around."

"Calmer?" Rem questioned incredulously.

Killian nodded and smiled.

"He did not even try to force himself on me right away. He was very curious and kind of fascinated with my stomach."

"It is our desire to impregnate you that most likely inspired the fascination. It is our most basic and primal instinct."

"Hmm," Killian hummed before lying on Rem's chest.

It was a little late in the afternoon and they still hadn't gotten out of bed. He guessed they weren't really supposed to.

Four more days with Rem.

He had to make it count.

He had to get pregnant.

He wouldn't lose Rem. Not now.

Not ever.

Chapter
13

Rem was still asleep, with one muscled arm folded behind his head as he faced the opposite direction from Killian. His other hand was placed gently on his sculpted abdomen that peeked from beneath the thick red comforter.

With a wicked grin, Killian shimmied underneath the blanket until he got in between Rem's legs. Thankfully one was bent at a slight angle, allowing him access to that which lay nestled on his thigh. Killian was happy he was still asleep. He wanted to use this opportunity to practice.

The skin was very soft between Rem's legs and dark like the rest of him. Killian cupped the heavy ball of darkness with little tiny wrinkles. He skimmed over the skin gently. Rem didn't stir.

His exploration continued up to the thickness that seemed much smaller now than when Rem was awake. It was very soft and kind of squishy. He squeezed the appendage, unable to help himself.

Rem shifted a little, which made Killian freeze, hoping that he didn't wake.

Killian counted on the fact that Rem was worn out from their previous activities, forcing him into a deeper sleep than normal.

When Killian was sure he was deep in slumber again, he continued his assault, this time with his tongue. Tentatively, he licked the length of him, cradling the softness in his hands. He licked again, with more pressure this time. He was working his way up to taking him into his mouth. When Killian finally gained enough courage to swallow the tip, he reminded himself to cover his fangs. That's what had turned Rem off last time.

Killian sucked on the head of Rem's shaft, hollowing his cheeks, making a conscious effort not to brush his teeth against him. The harder he sucked, the more Rem moved. He groaned quietly, shifting his hips a little, but still asleep.

The more Killian practiced, the easier it became. Rem's breath grew labored and he shifted his hips, unconsciously moving them toward the prince's mouth with slight thrusts.

Killian knew he had him when a hand shot into his hair, tugging at his scalp with a tiny sting.

The prince's jaw started to ache, but he fought through it. He couldn't stop now, he had to make Rem finish. Killian put all his attention into the task until he was suddenly being yanked from under the blankets, thrown on his back and stuffed with Rem's member. His hips snapped forward as his narrowed eyes bore into Killian's.

The moment he was sheathed inside, he released his hot cream. Killian's back arched at the feeling. Coming down from the incredible high, the prince blinked up at Rem guiltily.

"Good Morning?" he tried.

Rem's eyes narrowed even more.

"I was practicing!" Killian explained.

Rem groaned, rolling his eyes and collapsing onto him.

"Practice on the conscious," he muttered.

"If you were awake while I was doing it, I would be too nervous and mess up...Did I get better?" Killian asked hesitantly.

"I do not know. I was unconscious for most of it," he countered.

Killian grumbled in annoyance.

"There is no need to rush with this Killian. You have time to learn, enjoy your innocence while you can. Once you know too much you will wish you had remained ignorant."

"I do not want to be innocent anymore," Killian pouted, sounding like a petulant child.

Rem ignored him.

There was a knock on the door signifying that their food had arrived. Rem shifted, pulling out of Killian who gasped at the loss.

Killian could feel Rem's essence slide out of him. He lifted his hips in hopes of pushing it back in. Rem took one look at him and rolled his eyes with a slight shake of his head.

Killian just wanted to be sure.

Rem walked over to Killian and cupped his cheeks in his palms. His expression was soft but serious. "It will happen if it is meant and you must believe that. If it does not happen, that is all the more reason I should leave. It is an indicator that I will be a danger to you. You do not need to force it. Let the fates decide."

Killian stared up at his handsome face.

Then something flashed in his vision. It was the small boy from his dreams who seemed familiar, yet, Killian knew he had never seen him before.

Who was he? And why did Killian keep seeing him?

Rem's brow furrowed in concern. "Killian? What is wrong?"

Killian tried to shake his head to reassure him that there was nothing wrong but he could barely manage the movement.

There were more images of that boy, crying by the lake at the foot of the birch tree. The same boy who heard voices from the water, coaxing him to enter the dark, chilly depths. He could feel the boy's fear coursing through his veins, fighting against the urge to succumb to demands of the lake.

Killian witnessed a black form emerge from the water and climb toward the boy who was too frozen in fright to move an inch.

It was like a nightmare playing behind his eyes.

Killian wanted to wrap his arms around the small child and protect him, but he could not.

"Killian!" Rem shouted.

Killian jumped and the images faded.

"What happened? You were unresponsive for forty ticks," Rem demanded, worry clouding in his eyes.

"Just remembered a bad...dream," he answered softly, still trying to understand what he had just witnessed.

It hadn't felt like a dream. It felt real. Like it already happened...or it was going to happen.

Killian just wanted to know who that little boy was. He would be a fool not to think he resembled Rem, but he couldn't be too sure. The aura was completely different.

"Tell me about it," Rem insisted, kneeling down until they were eye level, but Killian didn't want to look in his eyes. He was afraid it might happen again.

"I keep seeing a little boy...with skin as dark as yours. And he's playing near a lake by a tall birch tree that sits at the edge of the lake and he kept hearing these voices coming from the waters. He was so scared...I just...I wanted to help him but I couldn't. Then something came out of the water. The little boy was so stiff with fear, he couldn't even move."

Rem's thumb swiped under Killian's eye. He hadn't even realized he was crying.

"I want to know who he is," Killian sobbed.

"Me," Rem said softly.

Killian's head snapped up at him.

"You?"

Rem nodded.

"I am not sure why you are seeing my memories of my childhood but I am certain it is related to your *Haise*. In my village, there were pods of Sirens that lived in our lakes. The governing Incubi always warned us from going near the lakes, but I was a rebellious child and I did so anyway. Any chance they could, the Sirens would try to lure children from their homes into the lake where they would drown them and steal their voices. As you are already aware, the more voices a Siren steals, the more beautiful their song becomes and they rise in status. I did not believe such stories when I was a child and found myself in a situation that could have been fatal. But I was saved...by Tara."

The female he kept seeing...could that have been Tara?

It made sense.

But why was he getting flashes of Rem's past and how? If it was due to the connections they made when he fed on him, how come it hadn't happened with the others. Killian had connected with them as well.

Maybe it was related to his being with Rem now that triggered them?

"It may be best if we contact someone about this," Rem started.

"If we contact anyone, it will stop the ceremony."

"Then so be it, your health and safety comes first."

"No! I am not going to lose my chance. I will tell someone when the Ranking Ceremony is over."

"Killian--"

"No!"

"You are being stubborn."

"I do not care! I am not going to shorten our time together, especially if it is to be our last. I refuse. Do not make me," Killian pleaded.

"I cannot make you do anything. You are Heir, I am but a Consort."

"I can make you stay," Killian told him.

His jaw clenched.

"You can," he conceded.

Killian sighed. "But I will not, if you truly do not want to be here."

"Want is not the issue," Rem said curtly.

It was hard to believe that he wanted to be there, or that he had feelings for Killian when he was constantly searching for reasons to leave. He seemed dead set on them being apart, even though he said it was the opposite of what he wanted.

What did he want?

Killian couldn't figure it out, not for the life of him.

Was it because of Tara? Was there a part of him that would not let her go? That did not want Killian to replace her in his heart? That did not want to love Killian the way he loved her? Was Tara the cause of it all?

No Killian!

Being jealous of someone who was dead would lead to nothing but unnecessary grief and anger. He'd end up distrusting Rem for no reason.

"Rem..." Killian started, not looking at him but the determination burned in his core.

Killian tilted his head back to stare directly into those pitch black eyes.

"I love you."

Rem was caught off guard, and something about that satisfied Killian. Unsettling Rem was no small feat, since he was always calm and collected. Sure, he was showing a lot more emotion than before, but there was still so much of him hidden away. It was still impossible to get past his walls.

Then Killian saw the patronizing gleam in his eyes. Rem opened his mouth to lecture him, to tell Killian that he didn't know what love was, that he was being too naive.

Such an overused word: naive.

Who cared if he was naive?

It didn't change the fact that he loved Rem.

"I love you," Killian repeated, cutting him off as he took a breath to speak.

"Killian, you do not--"

"Do not tell me I do not know what I am feeling. Do not tell me I do not know what love is, that I am too young. I know I do not know what it is, but I feel this."

Killian grabbed his hand and placed it over his chest where Rem could surely feel the prince's heart beat crazily within his frame. How wildly it sped the moment their skin touched. "I do not know what this is, but do not tell me that it is nothing because to me, this is love. If we are apart, it will not just hurt mentally, but it will cause me physical pain. Being away from you will hurt me in so many ways, I am not even sure you will be able to call me a person after that. If you leave, I will be but a shell. I do not want that Rem. You have to believe that I do not want to lose you, not for a night, not for a second. I love you and I just want to know if you love me too."

Rem stared at Killian seriously. He didn't blink, but the prince could see he was processing his words seriously. He wasn't brushing them off this time.

He brushed Killian's hair back.

"I do. I love you too, Killian. Much more than I should. Much more than is safe for you, and it is because I love you that I must find the strength to let you go. It is what is best for you, even if I want nothing more than to stay by your side."

"Then stay by me. Forever." Killian crawled to his knees and wrapped his arms around Rem's neck.

Rem tipped his head back and stared at the ceiling.

Killian leaned in to kiss his exposed throat.

"Stay by me," the prince pleaded.

"We will see," he concluded.

Killian sighed.

The rest of the day flew by. Killian jumped Rem any chance he could, thoroughly exhausting him. Beast came out only a couple times but was easily sated and pushed deep inside Rem. Killian was completely stuffed but fed his *Haise* any chance that he got, taking turns feeding on Rem and Beast.

On the third day, it was the same. Though he did notice that Beast seemed a little restless. He was being a little more aggressive. Killian was worried but it never got to the point of injury like the first night.

On the fourth day, Killian really started to worry. Beast was pushing Rem aside more often and being painfully rough with their intimacy.

On the fifth day, Beast attacked Killian like a wild animal.

"Beast, stop! It hurts! It hurts!" Killian punched at the Beast's thrusting form but he was relentless. Killian knew his right leg was broken and he could feel the bones in his hips starting to shift. He was afraid Beast was going to dislocate it again.

"Beast! Stop it!" Killian shoved at his shoulder but he only glared with fiery orange eyes blazing and a loud snarl escaped his lips. Killian scratched his cheek.

It was a poor move on his part.

Beast darted forward, sinking his teeth into Killian's shoulder.

A blood curdling scream tore from Killian's throat.

The guards rushed into the room. It took twelve of them to get Beast off of him and even then they struggled.

Killian called out to them through his tears. "Do not let him leave. He is not to leave this palace and he is to be unharmed. That is a King's Order!"

The head guard looked at Killian incredulously, but gave a nod in compliance. Beast snarled, fighting the whole way out.

Killian sobbed into the sheets of the bed. Lorn came into the room with a first aid kit and tended to his wounds.

"Do not let anyone hurt him Lorn. He is not himself, he did not mean to hurt me."

"I understand, Your Highness. I will not let anything happen to him. I know how those with magix can lose control."

"Do not let my Father know. Tell the guards, this is to remain between us."

Lorn nodded.

She set his broken leg. "I'll bring Gestina in to heal your leg and shoulder."

Killian nodded.

When she left, the prince did not move from his spot on the bed.

He hoped it was enough time. It was well into the night, early in the morning, almost the full five days. Zev would be there in the morning. Killian just hoped it was enough to get Rem's seed planted inside him. He needed him to stay, now more than ever.

He was never going to forgive himself for this.

Killian cried harder realizing just how terrible this turn of events had become.

There was no changing things now. Once the ceremony was over, the damage he'd have to fix would be tremendous. Rem would never trust himself alone with the prince again. If Killian didn't get pregnant by him, he'd have to force him to stay. It would be the only way.

Damn it!

Even if he did force him, their relationship would be shattered.

Why did this have to happen?

Why now?

Killian tried to wipe his tears away, but they just kept coming.

Lorn returned with Gestina. He appreciated them acting as if they could not see the rivers falling from his eyes. They did not ask questions, they just did their job and healed him.

Killian had to keep this from the King.

If he found out, Rem was as good as dead.

Chapter
14

Sleep had escaped Killian. He lay awake for horas staring at his reflection in the mirror hanging from above. Tears made a steady stream down the sides of his face, pooling into his ears.

The memory of Rem being forced away played over and over again in his mind. His vicious snarls still rang in his eardrums. Even though his body was healed, Killian still felt the phantom ache in his shoulder where Beast had gnawed into his flesh. Blood still stained the sheets.

Rem.

Killian's face grew hot as a new wave of tears poured out of his eyes. He had to get himself together. It wouldn't be fair to Zev to receive him like this. But he just couldn't stop crying.

Were all Ranking Ceremonies like this? Was he supposed to feel defeated and hopeless?

He must have done something wrong.

He must have.

Beast's restlessness must have been his doing. Was it because he was not skilled enough to satisfy him completely? He was trying his best! He just didn't know how. He didn't know how to pleasure him or what he was doing and no one would tell him if he was doing it wrong.

Ethel came into the room without knocking, a cart in tow. Her face crumbled when she saw the prince's tears. Killian couldn't even try to contain them. He just looked at her, feeling his insides shatter.

She sat on the bed beside him. He noticed her eyes flick over to the blood on the sheets. She hid her surprise well but Killian knew it horrified her.

"There now, Killian. It will be alright. You will find your happiness." She brushed the tears from his cheeks.

Finally the flow began to slow until he could no longer feel the wetness on his cheeks, just the stiff dryness of the stains.

She didn't know what had occured, did she? Was Lorn able to keep her word?

"Now let's get you cleaned up," Ethel said.

She helped him out of bed and into the bath, quickly and efficiently washing him until he was fresh for Zev. As she was dressing him in more lace complications, she handed him a folded note.

"From Lorn," she said, then continued helping him into his ensemble.

Killian opened the note quickly.

It read:

My Prince,

Your Consort is safe in the confinement of his room with guards posted around his room. The King is unaware as he is busy with preparations for the Ball. Everything is under control. Be at ease.

Lorn

Killian breathed a sigh of relief before disposing of the note. Now that he knew Rem was safe, he could push the issue to the back of his mind and fully focus on the task at hand.

Though he wanted to be pregnant with Rem's child, he was not going to disrespect his other Consorts by not giving them the same attention and passion. He would show them all his desire to be filled, because after all, it mattered not who the father was, as long as he was with child. His other Consorts' chances would not be slighted.

Ethel bowed before leaving him.

And then...Zev opened the doors.

He closed them quietly behind him and stared at the prince with a cocky smirk. His hair was unbound, dark blue locks waving around him, shocking the eyes with bright, erratic streaks of white. His full pouty lips beckoned Killian forward. His torso was bare, showing rippling abs sinking into low hanging dark silk pants.

His bright blue eyes were dilated, raking over the prince's frame with a predatory gleam.

"Zev," Killian breathed stepping toward him.

Zev was in front of him in an instant, gripping his waist tightly. He dipped down to kiss Killian, but only on the cheek.

"How are you?" he asked.

The Consorts

The question caught the prince off guard. The way Zev stared at him before did not match the question at all but now, his expression held nothing but concern. Killian fought not to cry but the tears welled up anyway.

"Oh Killian," Zev pulled him into his arms for a bone crushing hug. Killian didn't mind it though, he clung to his warmth and support, staining his skin with his tears.

"Make me forget," Killian hiccupped.

Zev pulled back to look at him solemnly, then a slow grin blossomed on his face.

"As you wish, My Prince."

Zev's lips were on his immediately, coaxing them with soft motions, as if luring a small child out from hiding. They kissed through his tears and through his pain.

The Consort led Killian over to the bed, gently laying him down on the soft sheets, freshly changed and free of blood. Killian would have to thank Ethel for that when he was less occupied.

Zev fell between the prince's legs, deepening their kiss. It was a smooth transition, from the slight nudge of his knee widening Killian's thighs, to the gentle weight of Zev's body on his. His warmth spread, heating Killian's inner core.

"Zev," Killian gasped when the male's lips released his own, traveling down his neck. He was relentless in his passion, evoking the maddening tingles in Killian's lower half.

The prince's fingers tangled in his silky waves, scraping gently against his scalp.

The Consort's breath was hot on his skin, burning a fire within him that he had absolutely no hope of putting out. He didn't want to. He wanted it to rage on.

"Killian," Zev whispered, his tongue lightly brushing along the rim of Killian's ear. His breath hitched at the wetness. "I've held myself back this whole time."

Zev's hips snapped forward making Killian yelp. Slick spurted out of him, wetting the thin lace of his thong.

"I'm going to devour you," he promised hotly.

A soft moan left Killian's lips. He could feel him, prominent and straining in the silk of his pants. Killian knew what that part of him looked like. He knew what that part of him felt like. But now Killian knew what that part of him could do.

Killian had never been so eager in his life. He wanted him to plunge inside him, mold his body to his. Killian wanted to know what he felt like. Killian wanted to be connected.

"Zev, I want you," Killian begged in a soft voice. He gasped as Zev rubbed himself between his legs.

"I am going to enjoy this very much, My Prince."

His hands slid along the sides of Killian's body over the lace, until they stopped at a satin bow that sat messily at the base of his collarbone.

Killian watched as his fingers playfully tussled the ends. His bright blue eyes flickered up to Killian's face with a devilish expression. He tugged the bow apart, slowly peeled it away to reveal the prince's naked chest.

Killian's heart was beating furiously, his breathing erratic. He was desperate for him.

"The look on your face, Killian. It should be forbidden."

"It was...for twenty-three years," Killian commented, panting heavily as Zev lowered his lips to the skin of his chest. When his tongue flicked over the prince's nipple a small squeal left his lips. It was strange, the sensation on such a sensitive part of him but it felt good.

Like a carefully wrapped gift, Zev gingerly removed the lacey outfit Killian wore, with a tantalizing slowness.

Bare to him, Killian felt shy. Zev had seen him naked before, he was aware, but Killian had not been entirely conscious during it. He couldn't even remember the encounter. It felt like this was their first time.

Killian's knees snapped closed, covering his most intimate area. His hands flew to his face. The embarrassment was a little overwhelming. Killian's cheeks blossomed with heat.

Zev chuckled deeply.

"You don't need to hide from me Killian."

He tugged Killian's legs apart as he spoke.

The prince watched Zev take him in with a satisfied grin on his face. He saw what he wanted and knew he was going to get it. There was pure confidence in that look.

He slid back and slowly peeled down his silk pants. Killian watched him spring free from his confinements and blushed even deeper.

He crawled back between the prince's legs, bringing his grinning face inches from Killian's. The prince giggled at him, averting his eyes again.

"There's a certain part of me that's very happy to see you," Zev teased, pushing their bare skin together causing another gasp to escape Killian. The prince laughed again, wrapping his arms around Zev's neck and his legs around his waist. "I see now that you've lost your purity, you've become a bit bold have you?"

Killian rolled his hips upward as he had before with Rem.

"Very bold," Zev commented.

He grabbed Killian's hand and brought it down in between their bodies. "It's been a while since you've felt me. I've missed your touch."

Killian's fingers wrapped around the silkiness of his length. It was thick, just as he remembered. Thicker than Rem but not longer. Would it hurt more than Rem?

"I'll be gentle. I promise," Zev swore. He reached down and lightly prodded Killian's soaked entrance. The prince writhed under his touches, moaning loudly, hands flying off of Zev's member and back around his neck. Each stroke was stimulating, bringing on that full-blown burning in his groin.

"I need you, Zev." Killian squeezed him tighter as the male finally pushed a digit inside him. Killian was already so wet that he slid right in, his walls clenching around him, coaxing him deeper.

"So eager," he laughed.

Killian beckoned him on with more vigorous motions in his hips.

Zev added a second finger beside the first. The initial discomfort startled Killian for a second but he was able to get past it quickly. Zev made scissoring motions with his fingers. Killian cried out in pleasure.

"Good! Oh so good! Mmmf!" Killian moaned clutching onto his shoulders. The prince's fingers dug into his skin. Killian could feel nothing but overwhelming pleasure.

"Look at that face Killian," Zev whispered.

The prince looked up past Zev's face to the mirror on the ceiling. He could see his flushed cheeks and sweaty face. He could see how his bright red eyes had darkened considerably, half covered by his hooded lids. His lips were swollen and parted.

Killian looked...well...highly inappropriate, but it was okay.

Everything was okay now because he had Zev.

He favored Rem. He knew he did. Everyone knew he did, but that didn't mean that he didn't have strong feelings for his other Consorts. Zev was special. He was handsome, stubborn, arrogant, and passionate.

Killian could say with all honesty that he loved him.

He loved Zev.

He loved him even more the second Zev slid himself inside him.

Gods above it hurt.

At first, the sharp pain made Killian rethink everything. He became unsure, scared.

"Zev?" Killian hissed in pain, expression panic stricken. The prince looked down at their conjoining bodies and saw Zev slowly sliding all of that thickness inside him. Inch by inch, he disappeared from view, deep within Killian's body.

"It hurts!" Killian cried hitting his shoulder.

"I know, just give me a second," Zev panted softly.

He kissed Killian's neck sweetly, but turned his attention downward as he focused solely on the act of entering him.

Once he was fully inside, he stayed still. Tears were already streaming down Killian's cheeks. His teeth were clenched in pain.

Killian had decided that Zev's being thicker had made his entrance into his body more painful than Rem who had been longer. Much more painful.

Zev did not notice that Killian was crying until he finally looked up at his face.

"I'm sorry, Killian. Is it too much? Do you want me to pull out?"

Killian shook his head, gritting his teeth. He would get through this because if he didn't, it meant he could never be with Zev this way.

"If I start moving, it may feel better."

Killian nodded silently, giving permission.

Zev pulled out a little making the prince gasp. Then he pushed back in. Killian cried out. The Consort started slow with his motions until the sharper pains became dull aches. It was bearable. It took awhile before it started to feel good.

He watched the curve of Zev's blue back bowing and arching from the mirror as he worked inside him. His dark waves were splayed out around them. Killian's own hair was bound in a long braid out of the way.

The prince's legs, slender in comparison to Zev's, wrapped tightly around his waist, heels digging into his back.

Then, just as Rem had before, Zev reached something in him that had him sobbing in pleasure. What was that?

What was that?

It felt so good.

"More, more Zev!"

Zev pumped his hips faster. Killian could hear the sounds of sticky skin slapping against each other. He clenched around the heavy thickness of Zev making his Consort groan in euphoria.

He shifted Killian around, carefully holding his hips so the prince didn't slip away from him as he sat Killian on top. The new angle made Zev reach even deeper in Killian. The prince choked on a gasp. Zev grinned up at him, mischief in those bright blue eyes.

This was a position Killian was unfamiliar with. He felt vulnerable and exposed on top of him. He couldn't even look at his face without his own flaming.

"Don't be embarrassed. You are in control now," Zev said with a happy grin.

"I-I do not know what to do."

"Yes you do."

Zev shifted his hips up. Killian yipped.

Then Zev slowly lowered them.

"Now you," he said.

Bracing his hands on Zev's chest, Killian squeezed his pectorals before raising his hips up then down. Killian controlled the pace now, how deep he went and how fast.

"You're a natural," Zev commented as Killian gathered his own rhythm.

"Does that mean I am doing a good job?" Killian asked.

Zev grunted again, "Yes, Killian. A very good job."

Killian beamed at him, moving his hips more eagerly. Zev's eyes screwed shut and his hands gripping the prince even tighter. Though the fast pace was pleasurable for them both, it was much too physically demanding for Killian to keep it up for long. He slowed down, his legs and hips aching.

"Tired?"

Killian nodded, "A little."

Zev flipped them back over until they lay side by side. He raised one of Killian's legs up by the back of his thigh and started to thrust slowly. Killian watched them from the large mirror on the wall.

Why were there so many mirrors in here?

Zev buried his face in Killian's neck. The prince could feel the tip of his tongue brush along his skin. The feeling had his toes curling.

"I am going to explode," Killian told him as the pressure continued to build within him.

"A little longer," he said.

His hips were moving so fast they were losing their perfect rhythm.

"Zev!" Killian screamed, reaching behind him to grab any part of Zev that he could reach. His Consort's ragged breaths were right in his ear.

When he gave a loud shout, Killian felt warm liquid spurt inside him. Unknowingly, he clenched around him even tighter and Killian's own release.

They sagged against one another, breathing heavily.

"That was fun," Killian panted.

"Fun is putting it lightly," Zev replied with a laugh.

The movement did things to his body. He clutched Zev tighter.

"Oh, sorry," Zev said before pulling out of him.

Killian sighed at the loss.

"Now that I have officially had my go, tell me what happened with Rem. Why were you crying?" he asked.

Killian took a deep breath before explaining everything that had happened. From Rem's concerns about Beast, to the dreams, all the way up to Beast's restlessness leading to his loss of control.

"I have him being detained in his room with twenty four hora surveillance to make sure he does not leave and that he is not punished."

"Damnit Rem," Zev hissed. His eyes stared straight ahead but there was a deadly glint in them. One that scared Killian. He turned to the prince suddenly, hugging him close to his muscular chest, warm and slightly sweaty from their previous activities yet comforting. "We will get through this. I won't let him leave."

"But this is going to set our relationship back, is it not?"

Zev didn't say anything, but Killian could feel the sudden tenseness in his frame. It was going to set them back by a lot. Rem was already skeptical but now he was going to be dead set on leaving. If Killian wasn't pregnant with his child, he'd have no choice but to let Rem go.

Zev held Killian until exhaustion finally swept over them, pulling them into a quiet slumber.

At least...that was what he had hoped.

Killian's dreams were vivid, with dark but crisp colors and images. He saw Rem as a child again, but this time, he held the hand of another small child. It was a little boy with light blue skin and dark maroon waves, with white streaks.

Was that Zev?

But Zev's hair was blue?

Though it wasn't uncommon for a child's hair to drastically change color as they grew older. Killian was certain that was Zev. But...

Zev and Rem hadn't known each other as children...right? How could this be? Was his subconscious creating these images?

Killian watched the children run, fast and hard, listening to the pitter-patter of their feet against the frostbitten grass. Tall trees loomed over them as they ran. It was a desperate run, one that signified a chase.

What were they running from?

The shadows began to move and shift, slithering along the surface of the dark forest they seemed to be running through. They were malevolent and terrifying.

Killian's heart sped wildly as he saw the shadows gaining on the small children.

Young Zev turned slightly as one shadow latched onto his leg, yanking him back. Zev screamed high and piteous, absolutely terrified. The shadows tore him back, pulling him along the rough ground, so fast that Rem's little feet couldn't keep up. But he ran, as fast and as hard as he could with tears in his big black eyes. His hand reached out, almost grasping Zev's.

The shadows dragged Zev into that same lake he saw in Rem's memories. Before Zev was fully submerged in the black depths, Rem leapt forward to grab his hand. And yet, he did not make it and Zev was pulled under. Rem screamed.

Killian screamed with him.

His eyes flew open, his throat choking on the shriek. Zev was up and alert immediately, rolling over to cradle him close.

Killian clung to him, touching him everywhere to make sure he was really there, to make sure that he was safe. That the shadows didn't get him.

"You are alive. You are alive," Killian sobbed over and over again.

"Of course I'm alive. I will never leave you. It was just a bad dream, Killian. Everything is okay, I promise."

Killian heard him but could not process his words. He just hugged him, so thankful that he was okay, that he was safe.

"I thought I lost you," Killian hiccuped.

"You didn't. I'm right here, okay love? Right here beside you."

Zev stroked his hair, whispering reassurances over and over again until he calmed down, leading to yet another intimate session. Zev called it "making love."

This time, Zev took it really slow, making sure to teach Killian many things. He taught him several terms, made him watch himself in the mirrors. He watched the deep arch in his back, the curves of his bottom, the thickness of Zev's shaft entering his hole. He watched himself produce slick and even tasted it. Though to him, it did not taste very good, too sweet. Zev loved it.

He helped Killian put words to the sensations he was feeling. He told him why he was feeling that way and how to make it last longer.

He was slow and compassionate, gentle and tender with his touches. He explored every inch of his body and Killian his. It was a wonderful experience, and an even better distraction.

All day and all night were filled with new discoveries. While the day was spent creating happy memories, Killian could not shake that ominous dream.

He was not sure if it was a memory or a premonition. All he knew was that it couldn't be good.

The second day with Zev, Killian awoke lying completely on Zev's chest. Killian couldn't say that his waking was entirely natural as he felt a gentle probing in his backside that disrupted his sleep.

At first, Killian's eyes fluttered open slowly, still heavy with sleep, until something pushed inside him making him groan. He heard a deep chuckle in response.

Zev was looking at Killian with a naughty smirk, one arm resting behind his head while the other was buried underneath the covers, finger pushing into his entrance achingly slow. He was knuckle deep in him, before he gently pulled out. Then in again.

Killian was a moaning mess first thing in the morning.

Zev picked up the pace, adding a second finger. The prince's breath came out in hot pants, his eyes screwed shut. That intense pressure began to build, the one that led to an explosive finish.

"So wet," Zev commented, pulling out his fingers and inspecting the amount of slick that had caught on them.

Before Killian could protest, he replaced them with something bigger.

Killian exploded the moment Zev entered him.

It didn't take long for him to follow. He didn't need much stimulation either. It was as if the simple act of watching Killian be pleasured was enough for him.

Killian sighed, slumping against him as they finished.

"Good Morning," Zev sang happily.

Killian rolled his eyes, but smiled anyway, leaning up to kiss his chin.

"Good Morning."

He stuck his face in Zev's neck, breathing in his scent. It was sweet but not overbearing. It made him feel comfortable.

Safe.

"Come on, let's get cleaned up and some food in our systems. We're going to need the energy," he grinned at the end causing the prince to laugh.

He rolled off of him and headed to the bathroom. Zev was right on his heels. Killian noticed that the ache in his hips was starting to dim and he was getting used to the feeling of intercourse. It was nice to know that it wouldn't always hurt.

When they were dressed in robes, Zev dished out breakfast. Sitting at a small table at the end of the bed, they ate their meal.

"I want to know more about you," Killian said.

"Well what do you want to know?" he asked.

"How old are you?"

Zev snorted, "Aren't you supposed to know that already? Wasn't it in my file or something?"

Killian pouted, "Yes, but certain things were omitted. My father wanted me to ask you myself."

"Sounds like the King," Zev laughed, then he answered, "Twenty six."

He was only three years older, but the difference in experience made it seem like more. Then again, he was a bit immature at times and liked to throw tantrums, so Killian guessed it wasn't too impossible to believe.

"You are young," Killian commented.

"Older than you though," he grinned.

Killian rolled his eyes.

"Tell me about your home, your family, your childhood."

Zev pursed his lips before staring off thoughtfully. Killian waited patiently as he thought of what to start with first.

"Well I'm from Tarr, as you already know. I come from a pretty comfortable family. My father is a Warrior for the local Guard, my mother is a Healer. I have a younger sister named Natasha who is still in school. When I was young, I trained with my father a lot. I wanted to follow in his footsteps, become a law enforcer like him, then eventually become a Royal Warrior," he stopped to wink at Killian. "At seventeen, I was engaged to a Succubus named Poppy. She came from a pretty wealthy family. Our parents arranged it. At first I was a little disappointed about losing my choice in the matter, but then I got over it. Our parents wanted us to get married early, so the wedding was planned a couple months after our engagement. It was the day before the wedding that I found out she was pregnant. We weren't allowed to be alone with each other so it couldn't have been mine. Come to find out, she was having an affair with one her servants, so our wedding was called off. I can't say I was too torn up over it."

He stopped for a moment, laughed quietly, then shook his head.

His eyes sparkled as he looked at the prince, bright and happy.

"Then I saw this beautiful Incubus on the Orb. The King was making an announcement about some peace treaty. I can't say I was paying attention though. My eyes were on that Incubus. He had this gorgeous maroon hair that fell to his waist in waves. His body was slender but muscular. His eyes were like bright red jewels. He had small, dainty features but you could just tell he was not someone to mess with. He was alluring, graceful, commanding, and everything I wanted in a partner. I was infatuated immediately."

Killian blushed with every word.

"You are exaggerating," he mumbled, shoving a piece of bread into his mouth.

"Of course not. I'm serious. That's why I entered the drawing for your Consorts. It was my only chance to get close to you and by some miracle, not only was I chosen to be one of the twenty-five Potentials but you picked me as your Consort. Second Ranked at that. I'm a happy Incubus, I can tell you that."

Zev beamed at him.

Killian leaned over and kissed him softly.

"I am happy I chose you too."

His smile widened. In that smile, Killian saw that little boy again. The smile dropped from his face as he stared at Zev.

Zev's brows furrowed at his expression, "What's wrong?"

"Did you know Rem as a child?"

Zev looked caught off guard, then really uncomfortable.

"Uh...yeah, kind of."

Killian's brows crunched.

"What do you mean by 'kind of?'"

Zev rubbed the back of his neck and looked away a little nervously.

"I know you're probably going to get mad, but I really don't think I should tell you. It's something you have to ask Rem. It wouldn't be right for me to share. All I can say is that my father would sometimes take me to Tenebris for patrols. I met him a few times when we patrolled his village."

Killian gave him a dirty look.

Asking Rem would not only leave him with his original questions unanswered, but more questions and a whole lot of frustration. He couldn't force Zev to tell him though, it wouldn't be fair to put him in that position.

Killian sighed. "It's fine."

Zev looked at him suspiciously.

"You're not mad?" he asked, a little incredulous and a lot skeptical.

Killian shook his head.

"No point. It is what it is," Killian resigned.

Zev didn't push it, instead they finished their meals and started on their next round of lovemaking. This time, they did things a little differently. Killian laid out on the bed and watched as Zev rummaged around in the armoire that Killian hadn't noticed even existed in the room. He came back with something red and black in his hands.

When he got to the edge of the bed, he grinned.

"What is that?" Killian asked him, jerking his chin at the satin and lace garment he held.

"It's called lingerie. You were wearing it before."

"Lingerie?" Killian repeated.

Zev grabbed his ankle and tugged him down to the edge of the bed. He slid one long black satin sock with lacy red trimming up Killian's leg, then did the same with the other. Then he slid a lacy black thong up Killian's thighs, tucking him into the soft satin pouch. He then clasped a red garter belt around the prince's waist, hooking them to the tops of Killian's socks that reached high up his thighs.

Zev stepped back and admired him. His light blue eyes darkened considerably.

Killian recognized that look.

"I thought we were going to make love?" Killian asked a little confused.

"Oh, we are," Zev replied.

The prince's brows furrowed even further. He glanced down at his outfit.

"Then why did you put clothes on me if you were just going to take them off?"

Zev smiled.

"We're not going to take them off. You're going to wear them while we do it."

"I do not understand, what is the point?"

"Killian, you wear it to turn your partner on, in this case at least. Not all lingerie is meant for that."

"Turn on?"

"Arouse," he clarified.

"Oh," Killian breathed. Then he glanced up at Zev from under his lashes, "Are you turned on?"

Zev made a sound low in his throat.

Killian watched as his member quickly started to thicken up, raising to attention.

"Answer your question?" he said lowly.

Killian grinned at him.

"Now, I want you to listen to my instructions, okay? I know something you can do to drive Incubi wild with desire for you."

Killian gave him all his attention.

"Lean back on the bed and open your legs."

He did as he was told, sinking into the soft sheets and relaxing against the bed. Slowly, he bent his knees and widened his thighs, exposing his lace covered privates.

"Now stick your middle and your ring fingers in your mouth. Suck on them slowly until they are nice and wet."

He did, rolling his tongue around his digits. He could feel himself getting excited. When his fingers were soaked with saliva, he pulled them out of his mouth.

"Good. Now reach under you..." Zev said, kneeling on the edge of the bed. Killian followed his instructions. The Consort guided his hand behind him and underneath his butt. Gently, tugging the thong to the side, revealing his hole, Zev pushed his fingers inside. "Now, I want you to push in and out slowly."

Killian gasped at the feeling. It wasn't just the sensation of something entering him but the additional warm wet feeling that accompanied. He could feel his wet channel squeezing his fingers, slick and squishy. He could feel the rippled resistance as he tugged his fingers out, as if his body would not allow him to retreat.

Zev watched him with hooded eyes. Killian watched him right back, never taking his eyes off of him.

"That's right Killian, don't break eye contact," Zev said huskily. Killian could see his member twitching in excitement, almost painfully stiff. Zev stroked it slowly.

The entire voyeuristic feel was exhilarating. The prince didn't want to stop but he could feel his climax coming. His breathing was irregular and the motion of his fingers increased in speed.

"Zev," Killian breathed, letting him know he was close. "Yes! Yes! Mmff!"

"Stop," Zev commanded.

Killian pulled his fingers out with a wet pop, whimpering at the loss.

Zev crawled between his legs, hooking his legs around his shoulders. He grinned at the prince before diving his head down. Very lightly, Killian felt his tongue circle his entrance.

Then viciously, Zev attacked his entrance with his mouth, sucking, licking, lapping like an animal. His tongue pushed past the barrier of Killian's hole and pierced him repeatedly with fast and quick jabs. Killian moaned over and over again, until his voice caught in his throat and slick exploded out of him, soaking Zev's face and his thong.

Zev backed up slightly, his face glistening with fluids. He closed his eyes and licked the fluid off his lips. Killian was completely mesmerized.

"That will never get old," he said after a while.

After Killian caught his breath, he glanced down and noticed that Zev had climaxed all over his stomach.

That had been enough for him?

The rest of their time together was spent like that. Bringing each other, over and over again until they were exhausted. When the time came for him to leave, Killian was reluctant to let him go. The prince hugged him, kissing him passionately.

As usual, his cocky smirk was in place. He winked at Killian before disappearing behind the door.

Ethel and Lisa came in immediately. He was already showered and clean leaving them to dress him in a red satin lingerie ensemble.

The bed sheets were changed and breakfast was brought in. Killian waited, perched on the bed, patiently. Only a few moments later did the door finally creep open. The prince saw his tail first, bright red, waving slightly, as if leading the way, before his entire body emerged.

Caspian.

He was as handsome as ever, just in his red satin pants, a nice contrast against his bare gold skin. He was in fantastic shape with defined muscles but still sleek and lean. Caspian was graceful. He moved like liquid, his eyes such a bright glowing yellow, narrowed and feline. His lips were elegant curves on his face. His nose was long and straight framed by his high, prominent cheekbones. His burgundy horns curved around his temples as his fiery red and orange hair waved around him. His bangs flopped over his red brows and his dimples puckered in his cheeks.

"Caspian," Killian greeted.

"Killian...you look delectable," he said smoothly.

Caspian gathered the prince in his arms. Killian was completely dwarfed by him. He was so tall, and much bigger than the prince was.

"So I finally get you all to myself. And for three whole days."

Killian smiled at him.

"I'm so beside myself with joy, I don't know what to do next," a slow calculated grin spread across Caspian's face. One that said he knew exactly what to do.

He tangled his tail with Killian's.

"Let's start with this."

He tugged the robe off of Killian's shoulders and revealed his outfit. With a low whistle, he stepped back to appreciate the view.

"Did you get all dressed up for me?" he laughed.

Killian nodded, stepping toward him and wrapping his arms around his waist. He leaned up on his tip toes and kissed his chest. It was as far as Killian could reach with the height difference. Caspian remedied that by leaning down and pressing his lips to Killian's. The prince wrapped his arms around his neck, curling his fingers in his silky hair.

Caspian responded by lifting him up, forcing the prince to wrap his legs around his waist, and led them over to the bed.

Making love to Caspian was a different experience than with Rem or Zev. With them, it was all seriousness. With Caspian, Killian found himself giggling at the things he did. He would laugh with him, make faces at him, tickle him, and it became so much more than consummation. It became a connection. A bond.

Killian found out Caspian loved necking him. He had little bruises all over his neck because of it. He also found that he liked watching Caspian's body move in the mirror. He was so fluid and agile. His back rolled like waves in water, each movement flowing into the other. His muscles were supple, and the bow and arch of his back was fluent. He moved like he had more muscles in his body than normal.

With the moon still high in the sky, they had fallen asleep. Killian woke before Caspian.

There was a faint whimpering in the darkness. Killian blinked his eyes open, trying to find where the sound was coming from.

There was a lump under the sheets. Killian pulled them back and found Caspian curled around his waist, quivering. His eyes were closed, but his expression was distressed. He was whimpering, writhing in his sleep.

"Caspian?" Killian called to him.

He didn't wake, but his whimpers grew louder. The writhing intensified.

"Caspian!" Killian shook his shoulder, but there was no response.

The prince grew desperate when he saw the tears leaking from Caspian's closed eyes.

"Caspian, wake up!" Killian patted his cheek a little roughly.

Caspian's eyes snapped open, pupils completely dilated until almost no yellow showed. He hissed, before realizing it was only Killian.

"I'm sorry," he said quietly, rushing to wipe away his tears.

"It is okay," Killian said to him. He stroked his Consort's cheek. "Do you want to talk about it?"

Caspian was quiet. He had a faraway look in his eyes.

"You do not have to," Killian reassured him.

Caspian hugged him tightly, burying his face in the prince's stomach.

"I don't want to go back," Killian heard him mumble.

The prince hugged him tightly, massaging his scalp.

"You do not ever have to go back. You are mine. Forever. This is your home now."

Caspian's shoulders shook.

Killian knew Caspian came from Faltaire and it was pretty brutal there. They were constantly struck with civil disputes, poverty, and so much violence. It was a hard life, he could only imagine what Caspian had to go through.

When he became King, he would do something about the conditions there. It would be his priority.

Killian stroked Caspian's hair until his shoulder's stilled. He was quiet at first, and then he started to speak in a low, reserved voice.

"I was born to an S-Level Incubus named Jimney. He was a prostitute. I don't know who my Father was, most likely one of his many clients. His Madame, Margot, had him pumped full of drugs most of the time, so he was never really present when I was growing up. Margo hoped I'd turn out to be an S-Level too, as they make the most money and sell for the highest price, but I was not. She was disappointed and abused me as a child. I was forced to do the housekeeping at the brothel and all of the chores. I ran away at age ten and discovered the hard way how cruel the world really was. I almost died of starvation. I was targeted by gangs that frequented the brothel I grew up in. They too were under the impression that I was an S-Level Incubus. When they found out I wasn't, I was beaten. It wasn't until I was thirteen that I found a fight club. I would go there and watch people fight with all kinds of weapons. I think that's when my fascination with archery began. Everyone treated it like it was an inferior art, but I've never felt more powerful than when I was holding a bow."

Killian listened to him carefully, still stroking his hair.

"Eventually, the owner of the fight club found me. He was a Shifter and his name was Kaleb. I thought he was going to kill me, but instead, he took one look at me and said 'You're Jimney's boy, aren't you?' I didn't answer him, just waited for him to force himself on me, only to be disappointed that I wasn't an S-Level then beat me to death. But he surprised me by taking me in. Told me that Jimney was a friend of his. I didn't know my Dad had friends. He was always so drugged, he could barely hold a conversation. But for that I was grateful. Kaleb taught me how to read and write. He taught me about history and the world, different species, everything I needed to know. Most importantly, he taught me how to fight. Of course, he was against me learning archery and also believed that it was an inferior weapon but I was adamant about it, so he taught me. He took me in as his son and raised me, said that he lost his own son in a fight and that I reminded him of him. When I was eighteen, he died. Just when I finally started to feel safe, my haven went up in flames. I became a mercenary, doing odd jobs to keep myself afloat. I still had a lot of targets on my back so I couldn't stay in one place for too long. I mostly slept in forests at high vantage points so no one could sneak up on me. And when I saw the opportunity to escape from that Hell and become a Consort, I took it."

He didn't say anything else after that.

He didn't need to.

Killian just held him, promising that he would be safe now. That Killian wouldn't let anything happen to him. That he was his. Killian told him, over and over again until they fell asleep.

In the morning, Caspian was back to being his humorous self, making Killian smile and laugh. The prince cherished every moment of their time together. Every night, he would have terrors and Killian held him with promises of safety until he fell back asleep.

Three days was much too short a time with him, but Killian was happy that he got to know more about him.

With one last farewell kiss, Killian let him leave and prepared himself for Faust.

Killian was dressed in white satin for Faust.

He watched as Faust politely opened the door and greeted him with a smile. His black eyes sparkled, so stark against the white of his skin and hair. His black horns glinted in the low light and his long white hair was pulled back around his ear and down his back. He wore white satin pants leaving his toned abdomen bare.

"Faust," Killian greeted happily. He made a step to run toward him but the exhaustion of the past few days decided to hit him and he nearly crumbled. Faust was quick, catching him around the waist. His expression was concerned.

"Are you alright?" he asked softly.

"Yes, I'm fine. Just haven't been getting much sleep, as you already know." Killian gave him a reassuring smile. Faust's eyes searched his face for a moment before he finally smiled.

"Indeed, you have been busy."

He tucked a lock of Killian's hair behind his ear. The prince's eyes fluttered closed and before he could blink them open again, Faust's lips were on his. Soft and gentle, just like him.

Killian wrapped his arms around his neck and pressed his body against him. Faust kissed Killian's forehead, then his eyelids, his cheeks, his chin, his nose, then back to his lips. Killian let himself be led to the bed, gliding his hands along Faust's soft skin. His hair smelled like roses and chamomile. It must be all the tea he drinks.

Killian welcomed him between his legs and inside his wet heat.

Making love to Faust was everything he thought it would be. All of the sweetness and passion he dreamed about. Tenderness and compassion shone through with every movement. He held the prince with such care, like he was delicate.

His voice, every sound he made, was musical.

As their first night ended, lying on his chest, just ticks away from slumber, Killian heard Faust whisper, "It seems I have already lost."

The Consorts

The next day, Killian found out more about Faust. He was the head of the education program in Sapientae. His parents had died when he was younger. His mother grew ill first, then his father followed soon after. He was taken in by his grandparents, both of whom were teachers. He plays the violin and almost became a professional musician but felt that his calling was with teaching. He thought about settling down and then there was the call for eligible bachelors for Killian's Consort choosing. Faust thought it was fate. He was a very spiritual believer.

They made passionate love all the way until morning. He was a little tired the next morning but also nervous.

It was the last day of the ceremony and Killian would spend it with Drek.

The last time he had really been with him was that one night in the bath.

Killian just hoped that everything went well. He wanted to get to know him better, since he hadn't really before. He was his Consort now, which meant that they were going to fall in love.

Ethel came in with a huge smile.

"It's the last day, Killian," she gushed as she dressed him for his next Consort. "And the King has been so busy with preparations for the ball!"

Killian tried to match her excitement but the exhaustion was really getting to him. He didn't feel like himself. She seemed to notice a moment later.

"Are you alright, Killian? You're pale."

"Just tired," Killian commented.

Ethel patted his forehead. Her eyes widened as if knowing. She then pulled out a vial from her apron. "Take this. It will help."

Killian tipped the vial back, letting the warm yellow liquid slide down his throat. It was a little bitter but it worked almost instantly, like a boost of energy, and he suddenly didn't feel so terrible.

"Thank you Ethel, I feel much better now."

"It's only a temporary fix, we'll have to get you to a healer once the ceremony is over but it should hold you for your time with your next Consort."

She changed the sheets and disappeared from the room.

Drek came in a moment later with his golden hair pulled back in a high ponytail. He had a faint dusting of stubble along his jaw and intense green eyes. They usually were the same color as his bright green skin, but right now, there was something different. Intense.

Drek was huge, ripped with large muscles, and broad shoulders that tapered down to a narrow waist. He had three small pointed green horns. He was incredibly handsome, especially in his dark green satin pants and bare chest.

"Good Morning, Drek," Killian greeted him with a smile.

He did not reply, just stared at him.

Killian shifted awkwardly on his feet. Should he make the first move or should he wait for Drek to do it? He wasn't sure how to handle the situation. He was a bit more familiar with his other Consorts, Drek was a stranger to him.

Killian stepped closer to him. "Did you...want to have breakfast first?"

Drek raised a brow, but strolled over to the breakfast platter anyway. Killian mentally cursed at himself for being so stiff. He had to get comfortable with Drek since he was going to be his lover. They were supposed to make love all day and night.

He noticed how very agitated Drek seemed. His movements were quick and jerky, his brows were furrowed and his lips were pursed. Killian could remember when he first laid eyes on him. He had this undeniable confidence and dominance. It was the reason why he was in the game so long. It was attractive.

What happened?

"Is something wrong?" Killian asked him, approaching carefully.

Drek's narrowed green eyes flicked up to meet his. There was nothing but coldness.

"Are you angry with me? Have I done something to upset you?"

Drek barked a harsh laugh before getting up in one graceful swoop and lifting Killian off of his feet. Killian's legs wrapped around his waist instinctively. He carried him over to the bed and tossed him on it roughly.

Immediately, he fell upon the prince, lips viciously attacking.

Killian was thrown by his sudden engagement but he was happy that they were finally getting to make love. Though, it didn't feel like making love, it felt like something different. Something harsher.

Drek was most certainly the biggest of Killian's Consorts, but he had known that from the beginning. It was a bit painful to fit him inside, but not unbearable now that he had gotten used to the sensation of being stretched.

When Drek climaxed, their coupling ended.

Killian was disappointed.

They had gone continuously during the day and night, barely stopping for meals, and when they finished, Drek did not cuddle him like his other Consorts had. Instead, he turned on his side so his back was facing Killian and fell asleep.

The distance between them was astounding.

Killian woke up that morning feeling cold, and knowing nothing more about Drek.

When it was time to leave, Killian stopped him.

"You are cross with me. What have I done to upset you so?" he pleaded.

Drek's face became a harsh mask. It wasn't right on his handsome face. It reminded him too much of Zev during his temper tantrums, only worse...more serious.

Drek stepped up close to Killian, leaning down so his face was inches away. Killian got a good look at the those wonderful green eyes of his.

His lips touched Killian's just barely before he whispered, "Do you think you will grow to love me?"

The prince was stunned by his question, gaping up at him.

Drek pulled back and glared down at him.

"Didn't think so," he growled before swiftly storming out of the room.

Chapter 15

When the ceremony was officially over, Killian rushed over to Rem's room.

Technically, he was not allowed to see any of his Consorts for three days but this was a special circumstance.

There were six guards outside his door. They all jumped to attention when they saw the prince, the head of the group, Deryl, looked surprised and a little uneasy at seeing him.

He wore the standard uniform that all the guards and warriors wore; a slim fitted black bodysuit with plated silver along their vitals and tall silver boots. As the captain of this squad, Deryl wore a deep red cloak clasped by two silver pins on his shoulders, holding the emblem of the Innis family: four horns intertwined with vines. He was a handsome incubi and powerful with three red horns and pointed ears, but his features were a little too rugged for Killian's liking. His hair was a light copper and his eyes were bright pink. He had thin lips and his nose was just a tad crooked, no doubt from multiple breaks. And he had adorable dimples, almost as cute as Zev's and Caspian's.

Killian was a sucker for dimples.

"My Prince," he greeted with a bow. "I thought you were not--"

Killian cut him off with a raised hand.

"Speak nothing of this. One word to anyone and I will have your head."

He gulped and nodded quickly. Stepping aside, he let the prince pass. Killian slipped into the room and shut the door quietly. He was still facing the door, his back to the room, taking a couple deep breaths before turning around. Three more guards stood by the window.

No Rem.

"Where is he?" Killian demanded of them.

They looked at him curiously.

"I am right here," a deep voice rumbled from right beside him.

Killian jumped nearly six feet into the air. It was as if Rem materialized beside him. The spot was empty, then suddenly not.

"You scared me," Killian gasped.

Rem frowned.

He looked tired. His thick black hair was wild on his head. There were faint bags under his eyes, slightly swollen.

Killian glanced at the guards.

"Leave us," he commanded. They started to move.

"No! Stay," Rem instructed. They stopped.

Killian glared at him.

"Killian please. It is for your own safety."

"You are not going to hurt me--"

Rem's fist slammed into the wall beside the prince's head, going straight through it. A deep snarl left his lips. The guards looked uneasy, tense and prepared to step in.

"Are you suicidal? Have you forgotten what had occurred ten nights ago?" his voice was mangled with growls, but he knew it was just Rem. His magix did not glow. Beast was nowhere to be found.

Killian ignored his questions. Instead, reaching up to stroke his cheeks. His thumb soothing over his bags.

"You have not been sleeping."

"How could I?"

Killian tried to kiss him but he turned his face away.

So stubborn.

The prince had become accustomed to the torture in Rem's eyes and it saddened him. He didn't want him to suffer, he wanted his Consort to be happy. It may be selfish, wanting him to stay even though he was so adamant about leaving, but Killian knew that he would live his entire life in misery, thinking that he could never love or be loved because of the being that shares his body. Killian would not wish that on anyone. And it wasn't true. He was loved, so loved.

Killian would keep fighting, keep being persistent, and keep loving him until they both drew their last breaths.

"I love you, Rem. And I am never going to stop loving you."

Rem's shoulders sagged. Killian felt him collapse against him.

Over his shoulders, Killian looked at the guards. With a jerk of his chin, he dismissed them. They bowed and silently left the room, though he knew they were going to be right outside just in case.

Killian ran his fingers through his hair, lightly massaging his scalp in silence. It was a very fragile yet important moment for them, sharing each other's warmth and strength, not ruining it with words.

Words were unnecessary.

But alas, the spell was broken when Rem spoke.

"You have to go."

Killian held him tighter in response.

"I will be fine. But you must go," Rem repeated.

He stood taller and Killian stared up at him, searching his eyes for any hint of unbalance. He looked as he normally did; completely void of any emotion but still content.

"You will not try to leave?" Killian asked softly.

"I will stay."

"Your word?"

"I give you my word that I will not try to leave. I will await you."

Killian sighed in relief. He thought this would be harder than it turned out to be. He smiled up at his lover.

Lover.

"I will see you again soon."

The promise charged the air between them. He drew near like a wave to the shore, before crashing down on the prince. Killian twisted his fingers in his hair, arms around his neck, and kissed him with everything that he was.

I love this male so much, he thought.

When they parted, Killian watched as he stepped away and turned to the window, gazing out thoughtfully. Killian felt confident he wasn't going to leave. He nodded to the guards and took his leave.

Ethel was waiting for him in his room. She didn't ask where he had been, but the look in her dark eyes confirmed to him that she knew. He should have been worried, but Killian knew that Lorn would never tell, and Ethel would be on his side.

"The King and Queen await your presence at breakfast."

Killian nodded and let her escort him to the dining room.

His father and mother were seated at the table. Killian took his place opposite of his mother with the King at the head.

Queen Jessa was smiling at him.

"How do you feel, sweetheart?"

"Tired," Killian mumbled.

His father laughed...loudly.

"I'm surprised you can even walk!" he guffawed.

Killian face heated up and his mother gasped.

"Ellis!" she hissed.

"What? I'm just saying!" Father whined. "Remember back during my Ranking Ceremony? You had to get Ethel to escort you around! I sure--"

"ELLIS!"

The King pouted, sinking into his chair like a sulking child rather than the King of Incubi.

The Consorts

Queen Jessa looked like a cross between angry, embarrassed, and exacerbated.

"We hope you enjoyed spending time with your Consorts. Make sure you get a lot of rest over these next few days. Eat up and take it easy. Lorn will be ready for you in three days. You'll be tested for pregnancy then all of your Consorts will take a paternity test."

Killian nodded.

They began eating. Killian sat in silence while his parents talked. They discussed all the preparations for the ball. Color schemes, food, music, and the invite list. Killian listened to them prattle on with little to no interest. Though the ball was for him and about him, he wasn't really comfortable in those types of settings. There were always certain topics to talk about, certain mannerisms to adapt when talking to specific people. The whole thing just seemed so artificial and that wasn't something Killian was comfortable with. He ignored the rest of the conversation.

Then they mentioned his cousins coming. Killian wanted to gag. Those people were absolutely dreadful and he did not want them anywhere near there.

Not at all.

It would be nothing but trouble. It always was when it came to them.

Killian plastered on a fake smile and laughed his way through the conversation. He was surprised that his family hadn't already drawn any conclusions about how terrible his cousins were. Every time they came around, something awful happened. Some type of drama always surrounded them. It was obvious who the culprits were but his parents were blinded by the fact that they were family. Well, family didn't matter when the relatives were evil.

After breakfast, Killian went back to his room to work through some documents that had become his responsibility in the process of becoming ruler.

Lunch came and went, and dinner did the same. Killian spent his time in and out of sleep. When he did manage to stay awake for a period of time, he spent it working.

It was a solitude that he was okay with, but only for the moment.

If he were to stay this way for more than three days then he would go insane. Killian had dealt with solitude for long enough.

The night was rough, plagued with more nightmares about Rem and Zev as children, running from the strange inky blackness. He listened to their screams of terror, the helplessness of not being able to save them no matter how desperately he tried.

Why was he seeing these memories? Why now?

The dreams had been calm towards the end of the ceremony. Was it because he saw Rem earlier? Would it happen every time he was in contact with either of them?

Killian don't want anything else to go wrong. It seems like every time he turned around, something bad happened. He just wanted to be happy with his Consorts...why were there so many obstacles? What else were the fates planning on throwing at them?

Killian sighed, sinking into the bed after another nightmare. The second day ended the same and the third was even worse. All the time that he was supposed to be resting, he did not sleep a wink and anxiety coursed through him. He felt exhausted and edgy.

The blackness of his dreams was starting to haunt him. It was almost as if the being was starting to come to life.

Killian was scared.

When the time came for him to see Lorn, he was restless. She seemed to notice right away.

The prince sat on the soft leather bed staring at the white walls and glimmering medical orbs. There were no places for shadows. He was safe in there. He wanted to be relieved but he couldn't. The anxiety was fierce.

"Are you alright, My Prince? You seem on edge."

Killian nodded at her, but didn't look in her direction.

From that, she knew he wasn't going to talk. She didn't push the matter, but did give him a shot of something that immediately helped him relax.

She then drew his blood, took urine samples, and performed several other physical examinations. It took about three horas until she finally emerged from her work with a very large smile.

"Congratulations! You're pregnant!"

He had better be after fifteen days of sex. Still, he felt his eyes water and his hands floated to his stomach.

"I am pregnant," he whispered.

Though flat, he had a little bud of life growing in there. He was sharing a body with another being. Another living being...

I'm pregnant!

His mother burst into the room with his father and Killian's lovely Consorts. They all took seats except for Queen Jessa. She practically ran to Lorn, grabbing the Succubus's hands and asking, "Is he?"

Lorn smiled.

"Yes, My Queen. He is."

The Queen squealed in excitement, rushing over to her son and pulling him to her chest. Killian let her hug and smother him, blubbering about nonsensical things. She was happy. He let her be. The King was happy too and relief rolled off of him in waves.

Killian let them be excited, but couldn't quite reach their level just yet. Something nagged at him.

Who was the father?

Killian glanced at all of his Consorts and they were staring back.

Rem with his quiet stoic nature, not giving anything away. Zev grinned widely, proud of Killian, dimples puncturing his cheeks and eyes twinkling brightly. Caspian watched him with a small smile but had a mysterious glint in his yellow eyes. Faust smiled kindly, but there was something about it that made Killian think he knew it wasn't his child.

Drek was not smiling.

Drek just stared at him with a blank expression. At least, he was actively trying to keep it blank but Killian could see it in his eyes, ever so slightly. The sadness.

Killian wanted to talk to him but now was not the time. Now, it was time for the paternity tests.

Lorn collected samples from them and they waited as she and her medical team worked. It took quite a long time as there were so many Consorts, but when she did have the results, Killian could tell something was up.

She was staring at the paper in her hands, reading and rereading it intensely. She told her staff to check a few things, leaving everyone in the room waiting in painful suspense.

Who was it?

Was it Rem?

Zev?

Caspian? Faust?

...Drek?

Who?

The King grew impatient.

"Well? Who is it Lorn?" he demanded.

Lorn cleared her throat a little awkwardly.

"It seems we have another rare case," she spoke and a little uneasily. "Excuse me for being cryptic, I wanted to make sure. For us to have two cases here in the span of a couple of weeks is a little unbelievable. It must be a dominant gene in the royal bloodline. It could be possible with the history. Two prior generations of the Innis line have also--"

"Who are the two fathers then?" Queen Jessa asked carefully, cutting off Lorn's rambling.

The Healer cleared her throat to regain her composure.

"Consort Zev Lane," she said.

Killian watched Zev's jaw drop. His eyes were wide as saucers, staring at Lorn until they flickered to Killian with immeasurable joy in his features.

"And Consort Rem Brangwen."

Killian fought hard not to show his relief that might have offended the other Consorts, but he was so happy he could cry.

Rem was a father.

He would stay.

Rem would stay.

Killian vaguely heard his father and mother congratulating the two. He heard Lorn instructing his Consorts on how to treat him, what he should be eating, and what his habits would be like. But Killian couldn't really pay attention. He was still stuck on the news.

Rem and Zev.

They were the fathers of his child.

Finally, one tear escaped.

Then another.

And another.

Until he was full blown sobbing into his hands. Rem was quick, coming to pull him into his arms. Killian wrapped his arms around his waist and hugged him tightly.

He wasn't going anywhere.

He was staying.

And Zev...he came to his other side and held Killian's hand, rubbing soft and soothing circled along the back of it.

He would be with him too.

They would all be one happy family.

Killian pulled away from Rem and looked at his other Consorts and smiled at them through his tears. Killian pushed away to approach them. He took Caspian's hand and Faust's, while looking at Drek.

"Though not by blood, this child is yours as well. This is a celebration for us all. Zev and Rem are not the only fathers here."

Killian looked at each of them meaningfully.

"We are going to have a baby," he whispered.

Faust grinned widely. He reached to hug the prince, pulling him close and whispering how happy he was and how excited he was for them to start their family. Caspian was next, his tail wiggling with excitement.

Killian hugged him close and told him that he knew Caspian would be a terrific father. When it came time to acknowledge Drek, Killian wasn't hesitant. He was sure. Drek looked uncomfortable but Killian took his hand and placed it on his stomach. The prince watched him as he gazed at it curiously then shot Killian an uneasy look.

"I know you will be a great Father too."

Killian smiled at him even though he knew he would not smile back. It was okay. There was nothing that could ruin this moment.

Nothing.

"Your Highness," a servant came rushing in. "Lord Netter and his family has arrived."

Except that.

Killian become an expert at masking his emotions with many years of practice. It was a defensive mechanism that was crucial in royalty. In court, it was imperative to keep his thoughts and opinions to himself. No one was allowed to know what was going on in the ruler's head or else they'd use it against him. Everything was used against him which is why he gave them nothing. If one loses control, they lose everything.

Killian had that control.

He had that skill.

But for some reason, his masked slipped.

He'd say it was the hormones, but he was not so sure they would have kicked in so soon. He had only just become pregnant.

How could he be so careless?

When the servant announced the arrival of his relatives...he frowned.

His Consorts picked up on it immediately, even Drek who was the furthest from him. He watched their eyes narrow.

But even worse than that...his father caught it.

"Are you unhappy with that news?" The King asked him. He watched him with a darkness behind his expression that Killian never wanted to see. Granted, he had seen it multiple times before, but never directed at him.

The King was protective of his brother, Lord Netter. Scarily so.

The frown was so fleeting, quickly replaced with a fake smile of rehearsed joy, but once his father saw it, he wasn't going to let it go.

The King knew the game.

And he'd use it against him.

"What ever gave you that idea, Father? I am overcome with joy at the news."

Killian sounded sincere and so genuine that he almost bought it himself. He had become terrifyingly good at it.

"You're lying," the King said coldly.

"Ellis, what are you fussing about? You're making a big deal of nothing! Why would Killian be upset about that? He loves when they come to visit," his mother piped in.

Killian was a little sad that his own mother didn't know him well enough to know when he was lying. Even his Consorts were able to pick up on it.

King Ellis didn't say anything. He just watched his son.

He wasn't going to let it go.

But he would push it aside for right now.

Damn it.

Killian suddenly felt tired, leaning against Caspian, closing his eyes softly.

"Killian isn't up for visitors. You men take him back to the room and make sure he gets some rest. We'll see you all at dinner," he heard Queen Jessa say.

Caspian scooped him up into his arms and carried the prince away. Killian snuggled closer to his warmth and sighed in relief.

He could put off seeing them. Even if it was just for a few horas.

When they got to the room, Caspian laid Killian on the bed. The prince curled around a pillow and looked at them all. They were standing around the bed quietly.

It was awkward.

Rem and Zev were still watching him carefully. Both of their eyes narrowed in identical suspicion. Faust watched them, picking up on the tension.

"Twice," Zev said finally, breaking the silent stalemate.

He didn't need to elaborate, Killian already knew what he was referring to, but he asked just to prolong the inevitable.

"Twice what?" Killian feigned innocence.

"Don't play coy, Kill. Twice now that you've expressed your distaste for your relatives."

Killian widened his big red eyes in a way that said 'I don't know what you're talking about', still playing the game, seeing how long he could brush it off. He didn't want to talk about this. Not now.

"Drop the act Killian. You're naive with intimacy but smart as hell with everything else. Stop playing innocent and answer the question."

Killian narrowed his eyes and grinned harshly.

"You did not ask a question."

Zev clenched his jaw, eyes like glaciers, slicing him with that glare.

"Why is it that you dislike your visiting family?" Rem asked, finally speaking up.

Killian stayed quiet. That taunting voice whispered to him, seeping from the darkness.

You'll live and you'll die alone.

It reverberated in his head. Always a reminder.

"You will find out soon. That, I promise," he answered bitterly.

"If you don't wish to speak of it, it is alright. We will not force you. Just know that we are here for you and only wish for your happiness. If anything is upsetting you, let us know. You can talk to us...trust us," Faust reassured, sitting on the bed and stroking the prince's hair.

Killian smiled at him, a real one this time.

"Thank you," he said to him.

He returned the smile.

"You should rest. You look exhausted. We'll be here when you wake."

Killian studied him and then turned his attention to his other Consorts. When he was satisfied with all of their approval, he closed his eyes and drifted off to sleep.

A quick nap...was what he hoped for, but the terrors plagued him even then. Rem and Zev were always running, always afraid, always being eaten by the darkness. And he was never able to save them.

Killian awoke screaming.

Rem's face was the first he saw, crunched in concern for him. It was not his face that Killian needed to see for reassurance. He pushed away from Rem, eyes searching for blue ones.

"Zev! Zev!" he screamed frantically. Tears blurred his vision.

He appeared beside Rem with identical concern.

"I'm right here, what is it?" he asked.

Killian threw himself against him, burying his face in his neck, his arms wrapped tightly around it. Killian sobbed against him, his heart beating so fast he thought it would give out.

Why did it keep happening? Why him? Did this mean something? Was he in danger? Please don't let him get hurt. He didn't want to lose him. He just found him.

"Killian, you're hysterical. What's wrong? Why are you so upset?" Zev asked.

"You are alive," Killian whispered.

"Of course I'm alive. Why wouldn't I be?"

Killian shook his head and held him tighter. He didn't want to let him go. If he did, the darkness might get him. In his dreams...it always did.

"It was just a dream. Just a bad dream," he reassured Killian.

"Is it the same dream? From before?" Rem asked the prince.

Killian pulled back to look at him, blinking away the remaining tears that had gathered in his eyes.

"You were having nightmares before, when you were with me during the ceremony. The memories, are they the same?" Rem continued.

Killian nodded, then added, "But this time they are with Zev. And Zev always gets pulled into the darkness. Every time. And I cannot save him. I tried. I tried, but I am useless!"

"Calm down. I'm alright, I'm right here with you."

"What dreams?" Faust asked.

"He has been having nightmares. They are memories from my childhood. I am uncertain why he is seeing them, but it is most likely due to the conjoining of the minds during his *Haise*," Rem explained.

"What are the dreams of?"

"Back in my village, there were pods of Sirens that used to lure children to their lakes. I was attacked by one. Though, in Killian's version of the memory, the Siren is replaced by a dark figure."

Faust looked to Killian for confirmation.

Killian nodded at him.

"Zev is now in the dream and he is the one that gets attacked by the dark figure?" Faust continued.

Killian nodded again.

"What happens exactly?" he asked.

"Zev and Rem are running away, but the shadow grabs Zev and pulls him back into the water. Rem is unable to run fast enough and I cannot do anything. I cannot touch them, I can only watch."

Killian clutched at Zev's shoulder.

Just talking about it sank his gut and he started reliving that horrible moment over again. He desperately grasped at Zev's hand and watching it slip right through his fingers. And hearing those screams.

Killian felt his face crumple as he started to cry again.

"Killian, don't cry. It was just a dream," Zev said.

"If it was just a dream, I would not keep having it over and over again!" Killian screamed, shoving Zev in the chest, but didn't let him stray too far, grabbing Zev's hand in his.

"I am probably overreacting. It just feels so real."

Killian didn't have premonitions. He wasn't that type of Incubus. It was unnerving that he kept having the same nightmare. He couldn't say it was completely because of Rem's memory because there are things that are different. Zev wasn't there in Rem's memory. He wasn't there when Rem was attacked by the Siren, so why was he in his dream? And why wasn't the Siren an actual Siren in the dream? What was that dark shadowy figure? What did it represent and why was it manifesting itself in his dream? Why was it different?

It was making his head hurt.

"Let's go to lunch. You might feel a little better with some food in your stomach."

The sinking feeling in Killian's gut only increased.

Going to lunch would not make him feel better. He was certain that it would make him feel worse considering who was going to be present there.

Killian took a deep breath to calm his nerves.

It would be okay. The sooner he dealt with them, the sooner they would go away. He just had to get through these next few weeks and everything will be okay again.

He could do this.

He would do this.

With his resolve, he got up and made himself presentable. He instructed the others to look their best as well.

In front of his relatives, he must be beautiful, graceful, and powerful. He must be better than them in every way possible.

When his hair and ensemble were perfect, he led them down to the dining hall. Before entering, he masked his expression in a perfect, mild smile. The long mahogany table was filled with five more people than normal.

His relatives.

The King sat at the head of the table, Queen Jessa beside him. His Consort mothers were not present.

At the other end of the table was his uncle, Netter. He was a handsome man, nearly spitting image of King Ellis, just a little older looking. His brown locks were cut short, curving around his sharp chin. His gray eyes were warm and kind, sparkling just like the King's. His skin was a saturated lavender like Killian's. His four pointed horns were prominent on his forehead. He wore red velvet with a silver family crest on his chest.

Beside him was his aunt Kendra. She was lovely with bright red hair like Orion's, curling over her shoulders. She had two white horns that nearly blended in with her pale skin. Her eyes were a darker red. Her lips were a perfect bow. She was almost always smiling. Across from her were his cousins.

Bennett, the oldest, with brown wavy hair pulled back into a short ponytail. His face was handsome enough, inheriting the strong bone structure from Uncle Netter. But his eyes were a weird mix of both his parents, making them an eerie dull, muddied pink. His skin was a pale lavender color and three horns to match.

Next to him was Marza with her black dyed hair piled in elegant curls on her head. Her eyes were the same dark color as her mother, but they didn't quite hold the same sparkle. Maybe because she was evil.

She had small dainty features...like a demon pixie. Her skin was white like her mother as were her horns. She was small compared to her brothers, but made up for it with her horribly snobbish personality.

Last was Filo.

The devil himself.

His hair was a bright red like his mother, a curly mop on his head. He too had dainty features. One glance and he appeared like an angel. His skin was a creamy white and four black horns protruded from his head. He was the only one out of his siblings to receive all four horns and pointed ears. He had the most royal blood in him.

Inheriting his father's gray eyes, and his mother's full bow shaped lips, he was annoyingly beautiful.

It wasn't something he let anyone forget.

As soon as he saw Killian, he smirked.

Killian wanted to grab all his Consorts and run away, but he didn't. Instead, he smiled warmly at them.

"Killian! Look how you've grown!" Lord Netter exclaimed.

He stood, sweeping across the room quickly and pulling Killian into a huge hug, nearly lifting the prince off his feet.

Killian hugged him back before pulling away and giving him a real smile.

Uncle Netter was always so kind to him. So full of warmth and compassion. Aunt Kendra was just the same. How they could create such horrid spawn continued to baffle him. She followed close behind her husband and gave him a tight hug after.

Killian accepted and returned their compliments before taking a seat. He gestured to his Consorts where they should sit. He had Rem and Zev on either side of him. Faust next to Rem and Caspian next to Zev. He was a little worried about Drek who sat the furthest from him...right next to Filo.

Killian tried to catch Drek's gaze but he avoided looking at him. Looking at anyone really. Killian sighed internally. They still had to talk.

Killian tried to avoid having any interactions with his cousins. For a while it actually worked. He only talked to Uncle Netter and his father, but conversation had been misdirected and not in his favor.

"Cousin dearest, you have certainly lucked out. What a lovely assortment you have of genes displayed," Marza commented in a sugary sweet voice that made Killian want to gag.

He fought the urge to sneer at her.

Her eyes raked over Caspian much longer than necessary. To speak of them like they were objects...despicable.

Killian's eye twitched ever so slightly.

"I assure you, they are much more than just a means of reproduction, cousin dearest."

Marza's red stained lips quirked at the corner. Her eyes glinted.

"Of course. I just meant that they certainly look like capable men, our Kingdom will be in great hands. I have every confidence in your heir."

"Thank you," Killian smiled, biting his tongue.

Of course.

"Oh cousin, I saw our sweet Juliet the other day. Can you believe she's engaged? To Uther nonetheless! But I guess that's not surprise right?" Filo piped in, eyes glinting with mischief.

Killian clenched his fist under the table. Rem noticed.

The prince felt Rem's hand slide over his, gently coaxing it out of it's tight fist and intertwining their fingers together.

Killian relaxed.

Juliet was a touchy subject and that bastard knew it.

She was an old friend of Killian's. The only friend he ever had...allowed to have, but of course she was easily manipulated. Filo was not only irresistible in appearance but had a tongue like honey. A few seeds planted and now...she hated Killian.

"I am elated to know she is doing well," Killian responded kindly. "I will have to send her my regards."

"Are you sure that's a good idea?" he asked with an innocent tilt of his head. The look on his face was anything but innocent.

"I am certain that old childish grudges are forgotten now."

"I guess so. Be sure to tell me how it goes."

Killian smiled at him.

"Of course."

You little shit eating bastard.

Killian tried to grin and bear it throughout the rest of the meal, but it grew increasingly difficult. With Marza eyeing Caspian like a piece of meat and Filo sending flirty signals to Drek, Killian was worried. He hated his cousins not just because they had tormented him all of his life. But because they were dead set on isolating him. They wouldn't be satisfied until he was completely alone.

Now that they were here, Killian knew exactly what they were going to do. He knew it was going to happen as soon as Gilra told him that they were coming to visit.

They were going to try to steal his Consorts away from him.

They were going to manipulate them.

And from the looks of things, Filo had found his first victim.

Killian's weakest link.

Drek.

Chapter
16

Killian managed to survive dinner, just barely.

He excused himself early, with the excuse that he was feeling sick. It worked perfectly. His parents grinned knowingly, thinking it was caused by the pregnancy. Killian wasn't lying either, he really did feel ill and it might be because of the pregnancy or it could be bearing the presence of three demons for more than a second.

But with him came his Consorts. They bid everyone farewell and headed back to the bedchamber. Feeling a little dizzy as they approached the doors, Killian swayed, stumbling into Drek. His arms wrapped around Killian's frame tightly, making sure he wouldn't fall or bump into anything.

Killian warmed at his concern. It was clear on his face no matter how hard he was trying to fight it. Drek wasn't a bad person. He cared. He was just upset.

He let Killian go after steadying him, then pushed into the room. Killian watched. Curious.

Maybe he's lonely?

"Are you well?" Rem murmured, placing a hand on his waist.

Killian nodded, letting his Consort guide him into the room.

As Killian walked inside, he happened to glance down the hall. He could see Velma peeking from the side of the corridor. Watching. Smirking.

He hurried to shut the door behind them. His Consorts looked at him startled. Damn it all, he was not letting it happen again. They would not take his Consorts away from him. He was not going to let them get away with tormenting him. He refused.

Forgoing all formalities, Killian looked at each of his Consorts in the eye.

"You all are to stay away from my cousins and from Velma. I do not care if they pull rank. I outrank them all. This is an order from your King. You are not to be alone with them. You are not to engage in conversation unless it is absolutely necessary."

He was met with furrowed brows and confusion.

"I mean it. I swear to the Clouds, if I catch any of them with you, I am not sure what I am going to do."

It wasn't a threat for them, it was a threat for his cousins. If they tried anything, Killian was going to lose it. He didn't care if his father grew angry with him. He didn't care about the consequences. Nothing was worth losing them over.

"Wow, you really don't like them," Caspian commented.

"This is not a joke. This is serious. Stay away from them, come up with any excuse that you can to get away. I do not care what it is, I will cover your story for you. Just please, do not ever let them catch you alone."

"What is it that they have done to you?" Faust asked softly, concern etched into his features.

The dizziness hit him again and he staggered. Zev was the closest, catching him around the waist and scooping him up into his arms. He laid the prince on the bed while the others gathered around.

"I am fine, just a little bit dizzy. Lorn said that as an S level, I would be experiencing morning sickness throughout the duration of my pregnancy. Seven months of illness. I just didn't expect it to happen immediately after consummation," Killian snorted miserably then continued his explanation.

"I had a friend, her name was Juliet. She was the daughter of one of my father's friends. She was a pixie. Cute and shy. She visited the palace a lot and my father encourage our friendship. He wanted ours to be as rich as the one he had with her mother. And it was heading in that direction. We were pretty much inseparable.

But then, my cousins came to stay at the palace for a little while and we were all forced to hang out with each other. It was fine at first, until Filo got bored. Filo has a penchant for stirring up drama for his own amusement. He started putting ideas into her head. He told her that there were a few boys around the palace that really wanted to date her. He told her that she had to start changing her attitude, the things she wore, the way she talked. He basically molded her into female version of himself. And Filo is very...promiscuous. I should have known something was up, but I was very passive back then and did not really get involved in much. Juliet was stunning, it was no surprise that guys lined up to date her, but coming from Filo, I should have been.

Well...there was one guy in particular who she fancied, his name was Uther. Uther was a shifter, handsome and popular. Filo told her that Uther wanted to meet up with her secretly to go on a date. When she snuck out to meet him...he did some awful things to her. Things that I will not mention, but he humiliated her. Word got out and our parents got involved. Uther told everyone that I commanded him to do it, that I enforced my right as Heir. And Juliet believed him. I was punished severely for it which is ridiculous considering I had never even met Uther.

And it was all because of Filo. He persuaded Uther to go along with his plan. And my cousins just laughed. It damaged the relationship my father had with her mother and hurt the alliance between the Pixies and the Incubi," Killian explained.

"How did he persuade Uther?" Zev asked.

Killian laughed bitterly. "He had sex with him."

No one said anything after that. Killian's chest throbbed as he remembered the look of betrayal, disgust, and hate on Juliet's face when she looked at him. And now that he knew more about sex, it all made sense. When he was younger, he didn't understand Filo's behavior. He didn't understand most of the words he used and his ignorance cost him.

"They all laughed and Marza said, 'Freaks like you don't have friends. You'll live and die alone.'"

"That was a long time ago. Surely, they have grown out of their childish ways," Faust tried to amend. Killian shook his head.

"That was only one instance. There have been others and there will be more to come. They have not changed, he has not changed. Only gotten worse. It is as if he feeds off of the chaos and destruction he creates."

Killian glanced over at Drek, then Caspian.

"Marza will target Caspian and Filo...he will go after Drek."

Caspian looked surprised, clearly not having noticed that he caught the attention of Killian's cousin. Drek...was shocked. His lips parted and his green eyes were wide.

"I am not worried too much about Caspian. Marza is not as seductive as she makes herself out to be. Filo on the other hand...he is a monster. Drek is in the most danger."

Drek's shock morphed into a disgusted and frustrated sneer. "What? Do you think I am so weak willed that I can't fight off a pint-sized Incubus? Do you have such little faith in me?"

"Do you think that I am weak for falling prey to their tricks? It is not about strength of will. That does not matter. Filo is ruthless, if he cannot seduce you, he will blackmail you. He will stoop low and stop at nothing to get you to do his bidding. You are not safe Drek."

Through the silence, Killian watched as the information sunk in. They knew now that this was not something to be taken lightly. This was royal treachery at its finest.

"Caspian and Drek, you are to be on guard at all times. Understood?"

Caspian nodded.

Drek...hesitated, still clearly upset, but he knew his duty and took it seriously. He nodded.

"Good," Killian breathed in relief.

Everything would be much better once they left. Killian was looking forward to it.

"You are looking a little pale, Killian," Faust noted, stroking his hair back behind his ear.

Killian took a deep breath. He could feel his skin heating up a little bit and a thin sheen of sweat beginning to coat his skin.

"Nothing to be concerned about. I am fine," he told him.

"Are you well enough to take a bath?" Zev asked.

Killian nodded. "It might even be beneficial to my health."

Zev and Faust helped him out of the bed.

At the far end of the room, his private bathroom waited. It came with his new room. The shower and tub were spacious enough to fit the six of them. There were even six sinks lined up on the counter. Six cupboards and six toilets.

His Consorts all slipped out of their clothes and climbed into the tub of hot water, not at all shy about their nakedness with each other. Killian was nervous.

He was going to be naked with all of them, at the same time.

Killian took a deep breath before shimmying out of his clothes. He let them drop to the ground in a soft puddle and daintily stuck one foot in the hot water. All of them watched him and it wasn't just the water that was making him feel hot. Killian settled in between Caspian and Drek. Well, really he was on Caspian's lap. Caspian pulled him between his long legs and wrapped his hands around his waist. Killian sunk back into his chest and closed his eyes briefly. It was comfortable...and arousing.

He could feel the tingles starting. He squeezed his legs shut, hoping he wouldn't dirty the water with his slick.

Caspian moved his hand, unintentionally brushing Killian's inner thigh and he moaned, parting his lips and squeezing his eyes closed.

He wanted more.

The light conversation that had started, stopped completely.

"Are you okay?" Caspian whispered. His hand brushed Killian's thigh again, this time closer to his groin.

Killian trembled. His breath came out in soft pants.

Seriously? Now of all times?

Killian recognized the symptoms immediately. His *Haise* was here, and it was going to hit him full force.

He knew he should've pushed Caspian away. He knew he should have said something. But this time around, he had come to realize that now that he had lost his virginity, his *Haise* was a thousand times stronger than before and extremely hard to control. He fed recently, which meant he would not be motionless and that made him all the more dangerous. If he could move, he could hurt them.

Killian grabbed Caspian's hand and forced it between his legs. He pushed it against him, rocking his hips.

Rem's eyes widened. He recognized it too.

"Get out of the bath!" he commanded, yanking Killian out of Caspian's arms. "Now! Drek, Caspian, get out of the bath!"

Caspian and Drek quickly scrambled out of the bath with confused expressions. The two watched the rest of them uneasily. Rem set Killian on the opposite side of the tub. Zev and Faust caught on, keeping their distance.

"What's going on?" Caspian asked. He reached to touch Killian.

"Don't touch him!" Zev shouted.

Caspian froze, then stumbled back. Killian's power started to seep out of him and into the water. The three Consorts still seated in the bath cringed as the power attacked them. The prince's body acted on its own, shooting toward Zev. Killian clambered onto his lap, mounted himself on his member and kissed him deeply.

Killian fed from him, reliving every sexual encounter they ever shared. He had plenty of material after the Ranking Ceremony. He moved his hips desperately to push more lust out of his Consort. When Killian had sucked enough out, he left him for his next meal. Zev slumped over.

Faust was next. Killian was there, sucking him deep inside his body, as he threw his head back and moaned. Faust's eyes closed and he slumped over after he was drained.

Rem was ready when it was his turn. Killian was just a little more vicious with him. He clawed at him, furiously pumping his hips on him. Taking what he and Beast eagerly offered. Killian's nails scraped along Rem's arms and his teeth sank into the male's shoulder. Killian lapped at the blood he spilled, mewling when he fed.

Only when he had drained Faust, he fell back into the water. Rem caught him before his head could slip under. It was surprising that he was even able to move.

Zev was sluggish and Faust had completely passed out.

"What the hell...what the hell was that?" Drek exclaimed looking horrified. Caspian expression wasn't far off either.

Rem ignored them, stroking Killian's cheek. "Do you feel better?"

Killian nodded slowly.

Then Rem turned to the two Consorts who had not participated.

"His *Haise*. You two have not experienced it, nor have you made the mental connection yet. I am unsure of what would happen had he fed on you. It is dangerous when not handled properly. I expect that you both will soon be connected with him and after that, expect attacks such as this very frequently. It will increase in number and in power the further along he gets in his pregnancy," Rem explained.

"I don't think I have a problem with him jumping me for sex," Caspian grinned.

"Caspian," Killian mumbled.

He wanted to touch him.

"Not yet Killian, wait until your *Haise* passes. You do not wish to hurt him," Rem murmured.

"No, I don' wanna hurt 'im," he mumbled, words slurring.

He should have felt energized, but he only felt heavy. He was about to pass out, as he usually did whenever his *Haise* struck him. He fought it this time.

"I did not know it was coming," Killian whispered to them apologetically.

"You don't need to worry," Zev murmured, regaining his ability to move again. Even Faust was starting to come to. "It's our job to take care of you."

"Mmm," Killian hummed, nuzzling his face into Rem's chest. "Do not let Drek and Caspian leave," he mumbled.

"They are not going anywhere," Rem promised. Killian's eyes started to droop again.

"Drek, do not leave," he said again.

Rem lifted him out of the bath and dried him off, dressing him in a short satin nightshirt. Zev helped Faust out of the bath too. As everyone headed for the bed, Killian reached out, hand searching for Drek.

"Drek, do not go," he told him. His eyes were nearly closed, but he was desperate in finding Drek. Once he got a grasp on his arm, he tried to turn to him.

"Drek," Killian said again.

"I won't, Killian. I won't," he said finally.

Rem laid Killian on the bed and he called out for Drek again. Killian feared if the male wasn't right beside him, Filo would snatch him away. Drek took the spot next to him, Rem on the other side. Zev next to Rem and Faust on Drek's other side. Caspian was underneath the blankets wrapped around Killian's waist, using his stomach as his pillow. Killian forced Drek to hold his hand.

If he didn't want to, Killian couldn't tell. He made an effort to hold it all night.

The next morning, Killian woke up full of energy. He ate his breakfast quickly and headed straight over to Titus's room to see how Orion was doing while his Consorts were training.

Killian knocked on the door and Titus answered almost immediately. He looked a little tired and worried. His silver hair was a mess on his head and his normally bright white eyes were a little dull. Dark bruises stained the underside of his eyes.

"Are you alright?" Killian asked him.

Titus hesitated, as if he didn't want to answer that honestly. And he chose not to as he nodded his head. Killian gave him a pointed look. He sighed, running his fingers through his hair.

"What is wrong? Where is Orion?" Killian asked, peeking around him to glance into his room. From the looks of it, Orion wasn't in there. Titus's eyes darkened and a mean look crossed his features.

"He's not here. He left...with Lord Pierce."

Killian's face crunched in confusion. "What?"

"Lord Pierce came here about a week ago and demanded that Orion come with him. I cannot refuse the Lord's orders, so I had to let Orion go."

Killian's eyes narrowed.

That spoiled little...

"And you have not seen him since?"

Titus shook his head, then it hung sadly. "Lord Pierce forbid me from seeing him."

Killian growled angrily.

"I will handle this," he told him. "Get some sleep okay?"

Titus nodded, then closed his door. Killian stormed off in the direction of Pierce's room. Without alerting him of his arrival, he threw open his door. And he kind of wished he hadn't.

Pierce and Orion were clearly...occupied.

Fighting the blush that threatened to spread, Killian glared at them.

"Put some clothes on...now."

Orion rushed to cover himself with the blanket. Pierce only glared back at the prince furiously. A drawer from his dresser flew out and hit him square in the chest. He grunted at the impact and Killian raised a brow at him, daring him to disobey again. He grudgingly put on his clothes and tossed a shirt to Orion so he could cover himself.

"You have a lot of nerve, little brother," Killian said once his brother was decent.

Pierce's lip curled.

"Where the hell did you get the idea that you had the right to forbid Titus from seeing Orion?"

"It's my child he carries," Pierce retorted.

"It is Titus's child as well. Or have you forgotten that? Titus was the one who stepped up and took responsibility while you sat there and sulked like a child."

Pierce winced.

"That baby carries royal blood--"

"Royal blood or not, it does not change the fact that it also carries Titus's DNA."

Killian sighed heavily.

"I know this is unexpected and I am sure you are confused and scared, but this is not how you go about it. You cannot force things to go your way, not when you have people who now depend on you. You have to grow up, now faster than before because you are going to be a father. You have to think of others before yourself. You have to do what is best for your child and even Orion. Banning Titus from being a part of their life is not the way to go."

Then he turned to Orion.

"And you need to get it together. You are pregnant. You are going to be a father too, so start acting like it."

Killian looked at them both and frowned.

"I am lifting the ban off Titus. You are to spend equal time with both of them," Killian told Orion. He nodded quickly.

"And you will be staying with Titus in his room. Pierce, I am assigning you a mentor. Someone to teach you that there is more to life than fighting and fucking." Brows raised at the prince's crass word choice, picked up from Zev of course. "You need to know how to care for a pregnant Incubus and you need to start preparing to raise a child."

Pierce clenched his hands into fists but nodded anyway. Killian jerked his chin at Orion. He scrambled off the bed, quickly rushed out of the door, and hopefully back to Titus's room.

When Orion was finally all moved in with Titus, Killian assigned three attendants to them: Mary, Lila, and June. They were to make sure that things went smoothly between the three-way relationship and they were there to assist in Orion's pregnancy.

Due to Killian's own pregnancy, the staff and medical unit would be more focused on taking care of the prince than Orion, but Killian didn't want Orion to be forgotten. He wanted to make sure that the male was being taken care of too and not pushed aside. Being around royals was a pain sometimes to those who weren't. The privileges could be overwhelming.

All three attendants were highly trained and were ordered to focus solely on Orion. That was one less stress to deal with.

Killian could feel a headache coming. He winced, rubbing small circles along his temples. That was how Caspian found him.

"Killian? Are you unwell?" he murmured, kneeling down to Killian's perch on a bench in one of the grand halls.

Killian had been on his way to the study to discuss a few upcoming meetings with his father, but the headache had been too strong and he needed a moment to rest.

"I am fine. Nothing to worry about, just a headache."

Caspian did not look like he bought it for a second. In fact, Killian sure he was ticks away from dragging him off to the infirmary until they suddenly had guests in the hall.

Great.

It was Filo and Marza.

Caspian nodded to them respectfully but kept his mouth shut. Killian simply stared at them.

They stared back, smirks on their faces.

"I see the pregnancy is catching up with you," Filo finally said, breaking the tense and charged silence. Killian raised a brow at him, unamused with his obvious observation.

"At least it means the baby is alive and kicking...we wouldn't want anything to happen to the next heir, now would we?" Filo continued, a devilish glint in those gray eyes of his.

Killian narrowed his eyes.

"Is that a threat, cousin dearest?" Killian said, his voice dropping low and deadly.

The corner of Filo's mouth quirked.

"Clouds no, cousin. I would never."

Caspian hissed, baring his teeth in warning, his body had shifted in front of Killian's ever so slightly and the prince could see the tenseness in his frame that was just itching for a fight.

"Down kitty. You know, cousin dearest, you should really teach your pet some manners," Marza laughed in her nasally voice.

"Watch your tongue when you address my Consort," Killian warned.

Marza shrugged and the two walked off, whispering to each other and laughing, no doubt at his expense.

When they were gone, Caspian relaxed...slightly. His face was scrunched up in distaste and his tail swished about angrily. He glared in the direction they had gone before he turned to Killian, shaking his head.

"I can see now why you dislike them. They are unpleasant. Was it really okay for them to get away with threatening you like that? And our child? They won't actually do anything to you right?" Caspian questioned.

Killian didn't answer him, but that was answer enough.

Caspian swore.

Killian wouldn't put it past them to do something to harm him, but not to the extent of physical harm. They would most likely aim to destroy his relationships and sully his reputation. That was more of their style. Killian didn't think they posed a physical threat, but he didn't like how open Filo was being about it. Normally, he'd be stealthier with his threats and insults, especially with his Consorts around, since he wanted them to turn on him. What was he playing at now?

Killian shook his head, refusing to dwell on it anymore.

Caspian offered his hand and helped Killian up. The King was having another meeting about the incident with the Kappas. Apparently, it was getting worse. He wanted to discuss some things with General Lee, and he wanted Killian to be present for it. Killian would usually be accompanied by Rem; he was Captain of Killian's Consorts. Zev would be next in charge since was Rem's lieutenant, but both were busy with Lorn in preparation for the duration of his pregnancy. Caspian was third in command; the task now fell on him.

Killian filled Caspian in on the way there.

He was quiet, expression serious as they walked inside the study. The King was seated at the head of the table with a bunch of papers spread around him. He looked healthier than when Killian had last seen him in the same position, ill with stress. He looked up at their approach and Killian expected to see his jovial smile, but it was not there. He looked serious. How bad was it?

General Lee sat beside Father at the table. His hair was the color of spun gold, lying in silky waves to his sharp chin. It was almost the same color as Drek's, only a little bit darker, less luminous, but gorgeous, nonetheless. His skin was a pastel orange and eyes were like bright flames. He was a bit older, closer to the King's age and it showed in the miniscule wrinkles by his eyes and mouth.

He wore the same uniform the other soldiers, but instead, his body suit was red with silver plates. His cape was a black velvet, hooded, with silver clasps on his shoulders that showed the family emblem.

When Killian entered the room, he stood, bowing in respect.

"My Prince. I am glad to see you well."

Killian nodded at the greeting before taking his seat. Caspian sat beside him, placing his hand on his knee and giving a light squeeze. It was a way of letting Killian know that if anything was wrong, he'd take him straight to the infirmary.

"How are you feeling, son?" The King asked. His voice was a little off, not at all like he normally was. Killian tried not to focus on it.

"Just a headache and some dizziness. Lorn said it is normal."

His father nodded.

"Congratulations on your pregnancy, My Prince. Long live the heirs."

"Thank you, General Lee."

Caspian rubbed his knee gently. Killian glanced at him, but he wasn't looking at him. His eyes were focused on General Lee. There was a peculiar expression on his face. Not hostile, but not entirely friendly. Killian brushed his tail against Caspian's, drawing his attention. The prince shot him a curious look, but he only gave a little smile, with a twinkle in his eyes.

Weird.

"Now let's make this quick. I have some other business to attend to," King Ellis said with a mild sigh.

"Right," General Lee said, before clearing his throat and looking down at the files he had before him. His face became serious and all business.

"We've been doing some research on the situation regarding the Kappas and the Nymphs. There have actually been quite a few murders that we have finally connected with the dispute. There have been nine Kappa murders in the span of six weeks. Each victim suffered the same fate, their houses ransacked, and their hearts ripped out. Their bodies are always found three days after the murder. I'm sure you are aware of the Nymphs' past when dealing with Kappas."

In the past, Nymphs coveted the hearts of their lovers and ate them. It gave them a power boost. In particular, Kappa hearts were especially powerful. The reason remained unknown, but it was because of that, the Nymphs and Kappas never got along. The Kappas didn't trust the Nymphs, despite signing an agreement that the Nymphs would never do it again. To do so would be against the law. A law that Killian's great great grandfather put into place.

"Well that makes sense, in a way. It explains the reasoning for the disputes between the two, but what it doesn't explain is the deaths. Are the Nymphs behind it?" King Ellis asked General Lee.

"At first glance, it seems so, but after a little digging, I'm not so sure. I have some of the suspected Nymphs in custody, but they all have alibis. Valid alibis. So, for the time being, we have no culprit."

"Any leads?" Killian asked.

"We noticed that some of the files from the Stock house have been stolen. It contained a segment concerning the Kappas' past. The whole section was taken so we can't narrow down what the culprit was specifically looking for."

The Stock house was a government library that held documents pertaining to all records of history, separated by species. It had a log of everyone's past and prognosis of potential futures. Security was incredibly high there. It was alarming to hear that someone broke in. Unless of course, it was an inside job...

Could they have a traitor in their midst?

What was their gain?

Their angle?

"And how do you plan on smoking out the culprit?" his father asked.

"If we find a motive, then we can narrow down a list of suspects. I have our researchers studying the patterns of the house raids of the victims. There may be something there that our initial sweep didn't catch. Their houses weren't ransacked for no reason, there had to have been something the culprit was looking for. With enough research, we may be able to discover what it is."

Father pursed his lips, ruminating over the new information.

"Make sure you keep the information you receive down to only your most trusted. All new information comes to us first. Understood?" Killian told him.

Father and General Lee looked raised a brow.

"Understood?" Killian repeated.

"Yes, My Prince."

"Alright then. Meeting adjourned."

Caspian and Killian left first. On their way back to their room, a wave of dizziness hit the prince again. He stumbled and Caspian caught him.

Damn it. Why was it happening so frequently? This couldn't be normal.

"Killian please. Let's just get you checked out. What if something is wrong?" Caspian begged.

Killian chuckled a little, a bit strained with the pain stabbing at his head. "I did not take you for the worrying type, Caspian. You are always so carefree."

Caspian shot Killian a goofy grin, "I am carefree." Then his smile disappeared, "But I'm worried about you and the baby. You've been experiencing a lot of pain lately. I don't know, it just doesn't sit right with me. Like something is wrong."

"Nothing is wrong. I am fine. Lorn said this would happen."

"Yeah, but--"

"No buts," Killian smiled at him. "Just help me into bed. I need a little nap and I am sure I will be all better afterwards."

Caspian sighed, but did what was asked.

Killian was glad to see that Drek was in the room. He was doing pushups at the foot of the bed. He popped up gracefully when he heard them approach. When he saw the prince in Caspian's arms, alarm clear in his features.

"What's wrong with him?"

"He's not feeling so hot," Caspian told him. Then he paused and felt his forehead. "Scratch that, he's a little too hot. I think he has a fever."

"I am fine," Killian insisted.

"I'll get Lorn," Drek said, rushing and opening the door.

"No!" Killian shouted, throwing his hand out. The door slammed shut and his head throbbed.

"Killian," Caspian sighed, exasperated.

"I am fine, I just need to sleep it off. I swear. If I wake up and I am not better, I will see Lorn but right now, I just want to sleep. Come to bed with me...please?" he asked them.

Caspian looked at Drek who narrowed his eyes then sighed and came toward them. He shrugged off his shirt and climbed into bed. Caspian placed Killian in the center before coming behind him. Closed in between their bodies, Killian felt comfortable. He closed his eyes and let himself succumb to much needed rest. Only like usual, it wasn't so restful.

He opened his eyes and was lying in a tub. A familiar tub, the one in the private bathroom. But it was empty. Eerily empty. He tried to raise his hand to drag himself out of the water, but he couldn't move. As much as Killian tried to squirm, his body did not move. He could do nothing but watch.

But then he noticed something. He was angled in the tub just enough to be able to see into the clear water. His stomach...it was huge.

He was fully pregnant.

How--?

Fear and panic spread within him, making Killian's desperation to move all the more erratic. He laid there, in the water, still as a statue only able to watch. And then...the lights went out and he was shrouded in darkness.

What the hell?

Chills ran up his spine, raising bumps in his flesh.

And then he wasn't alone. He could feel someone behind him, but he was still paralyzed. Not that that mattered considering it was so dark, he wouldn't be able to see them even if he could move.

Who was it?

Who was there?

Soft breath touches the back of his ear. Killian screamed silently, unable to make a sound, choking on his paralysis. Only soft whimpers leaving his lips. And then the whispering started. Incoherent whispers, aggressive and inhuman.

Wake up!

WAKE UP!

Killian could feel hands slithering along his stomach and that was the breaking point. Somehow his scream finally pushed out of his throat.

"Killian!" He heard Caspian shout.

He blinked his eyes open and could see Caspian hovering over him. Drek's face close to his. They were both staring expressions filled with worry.

Killian jumped up, pushing them aside, leaning over the edge of the bed and vomiting onto the ground. Caspian held his hair back while Drek rubbed circles into his back.

"That's it, I'm getting Lorn," Caspian said with finality.

He didn't even have the strength to argue. He just felt so weak. He watched as he left unable to do anything. Drek took the liberty of cleaning him up and his mess.

"I know I'm not your main lover, but can I please be let into the loop? What's going on with you? Why won't you let us just get you help?"

When Killian didn't answer him, he sighed, running his hands through his hair in frustration.

"Just a bad dream," Killian whispered.

Drek looked at him curiously but didn't say anything. Instead, they just waited until Caspian came back with Lorn.

She was quick to get started on checking his vitals and an overall physical exam. Killian felt uncomfortable when she touched his stomach and ended up swatting her hands away. They felt too much like the hands in his dream.

He had to protect his baby.

"My Prince, I mean you no harm. I just need to see if your child is alright."

Killian wrapped his arms around his stomach. "No, do not touch me."

"Killian--" Caspian began.

"No!" he hissed.

Then he took a calming breath and released his stomach. He was behaving irrationally. It was just paranoia from the dream.

"I am just a bit shaken. Please continue."

Lorn nodded then proceeded to press along his stomach. Her eyes scrunched together.

"You shouldn't be showing so soon but you have the smallest of bumps. You might be a little earlier than expected."

"Could that be the reason for all of the headaches and other symptoms?" Caspian asked.

"Most likely. It's not completely surprising. Sometimes it happens."

Caspian and Drek looked relieved.

Rem and Zev took that moment to enter the room. Once they laid eyes on him, they were immediately concerned.

"What's going on?" Zev demanded.

"Killian has a fever and had another nightmare," Drek said filling them in.

"You said he was throwing up as well?" Lorn asked.

Drek nodded.

"Make sure he drinks water regularly and give him some ginger and lemon tea. It should help with the nausea."

"We will make sure he does," Rem confirmed.

With that, Lorn packed up her stuff and left.

"Where is Faust?" Killian asked.

"Reading in the garden."

Killian nodded, then rubbed his stomach.

"You had another nightmare? Was it the same as the one before?" Zev asked.

Killian shook his head.

"No, this one was different. I was in the bathroom in the tub and I could not move, could not speak. Then it got dark and someone started whispering in my ear."

"What were they saying?"

"I could not tell. It was not coherent."

"You're probably hungry. Let's get some food in you," Zev said then sent for some.

Rem sat beside him on the bed and pushed his sweaty hair back from his face. Killian stared up at him feeling a little vulnerable.

"Do not overexert yourself," he murmured.

His eyes slid down to Killian's stomach. He reached out to touch it, then retracted his hand thinking better of it. A part of the prince was glad that he did. He knew Rem wasn't a threat to him, but he couldn't help the irrational fear of people hurting his baby. He didn't want anyone near his stomach.

"It is alright. I understand," he said.

It was like he could read Killian's mind.

Killian leaned against him until the food came. They watched as he ate and made sure that he finished every bite.

"Maybe you should just stay in bed for the rest of the day," Zev suggested.

Killian started to protest but Rem gave him a sharp look. He huffed but gave in and agreed. His Consorts agreed to stay with him to keep him company. Drek went to go fetch Faust, but Killian felt a little uneasy at letting him go alone.

Faust and Drek returned rather quickly though, easing his discomfort. He cuddled in bed with all five lovers. Though he was supposed to be comfortable, he couldn't shake the heavy feeling of foreboding that sat in his gut.

Chapter
17

Killian had been plagued by the same nightmare for a week now.

Over and over again, the paralysis, the bathtub, the indecipherable whispering. All of it, every time he closed his eyes.

He hadn't slept in days. Because of that, the headaches were worse, the dizziness was worse, and the vomiting was worse. Everything had amplified. And his stomach had gotten bigger. Not by much, but enough that he noticed it. Lorn still said not to worry, so he hasn't been...yet.

He didn't tell anyone but his Consorts about his nightmares, ordering them not to say a word to anyone either. If word got out that the heir was losing it, the Kingdom would turn to madness. And he definitely had to keep it from his cousins. They'd do anything to tarnish his name.

Killian wished he knew why he kept having them. And who it was that was whispering. Maybe not even who but what.

A sharp pain shot through his head. He winced, letting out a small whimper. Burying his face in the pillows on the bed, he squeezed the sheets between his fingers, waiting for the pain to pass and hoping it did quickly.

"Killian, what is wrong?" the prince heard Rem's deep voice question softly. His hand fell on the bare skin of his back gently.

Killian couldn't answer him for a moment, the pain was too intense. And then just like that, it faded into a dull throb. He breathed a sigh of relief, then twisted his head to look up at him.

"I am okay," Killian whispered. His voice sounded weak and unconvincing.

Killian heard a growl of frustration. His eyes slid over to Zev where he ran a hand angrily through his hair. His jaw was clenched, and he was baring his teeth viciously.

"I can't take it anymore! Are we really just going to sit here and act like there isn't something seriously wrong with him?" Zev fumed.

Caspian sighed, "Zev, we can't--"

"Look at him! Are we his Consorts or not? How can we just let him suffer? We're supposed to be his protectors damnit!" Zev interrupted.

Each of his shouts pounded into Killian's head like daggers. He moaned in pain.

"Keep your voice down," Rem commanded icily.

Zev was silent but his face twisted into a hideous arrogance that he frequently hid behind. His arms were folded over his chest making his pectorals bulge.

"Zev," the prince croaked softly. He reached out for him weakly.

Zev immediately went to the prince's side.

Killian pushed himself up until he was sitting, facing Zev. His palm rested on Zev's lightly stubbled cheek, and he leaned in closer, sliding his cheek along his jaw, before falling against him. The prince's face in the crook of his neck.

His arms came around Killian immediately.

"I will be alright, okay? It is just the baby," Killian told him.

He snorted.

"You know damn well the baby is at no fault."

"Please, Zev?" Killian begged.

Zev was quiet for a moment before his head tilted back and he stared at the ceiling. Then he brought his face to Killian's neck, planting small kisses there.

"I can't Killian. I'm sorry. I can't just let this go. Something is wrong and what if it ends up hurting the baby? We have to tell someone."

"As much as I dislike it, Killian is right. We cannot reveal this information just yet. The outcome will be worse if it gets into the wrong hands. We must monitor his health and discretely research possible causes for the nightmares. Faust is already looking up what he can in the library about *Haise*. We all must do our own parts, but we must do it in a way that does not expose weakness," Rem said.

"Rem-" Zev began to protest.

"Enough," Rem said with finality.

Killian could feel Zev's heart racing in his chest. He was still clinging to him until his stomach betrayed him, growling loudly.

Rem pulled him away from Zev.

"Let us fill your stomach," Rem said, starting to help the prince out of the bed.

"I think you've got that covered, mate," Caspian laughed, which died off awkwardly as he noticed the unamused glare Rem was shooting him. "Yeah...food...right."

Caspian served up a bowl of soup and some slices of toast. It was hard for Killian to keep things down lately. Rem sat the prince down on one of the lounge chairs and pulled up one of the sliding tables as Caspian placed the food in front of him. Killian tried to eat slowly, but his stomach really wasn't having it. Rem had a bucket on standby in case he threw it all up.

Killian rubbed his stomach with one hand as he took a sip of soup from the shiny silver spoon in his other. It was difficult, but he managed to keep most of the food down.

He gagged just a bit toward the end. Thankfully, that little bit of food gave him some energy. He stood on his own--though his Consorts hovered--and staggered off to the bathroom.

He almost froze when he saw the tub, having flashbacks of the dream. A shudder ran up his spine, but he fought to ignore it and go to the sink. He washed his face for the third time today. He had been sweating like crazy lately.

When he examined himself in the mirror, Killian could see why everyone was worried. He looked horrible. HIs skin was clammy and a sick grayish color, there were heavy bags under his eyes, and his cheeks looked a little sunken in.

He sighed, before heading back to the room. Zev was right, they couldn't just sit here and wait for him to get better. He had to keep up appearances. If he didn't show his face around the palace, his cousins might start up trouble.

Gathering all his strength and willpower, he headed for the main door to the hall.

"Killian, where are you going?" Caspian asked.

"I need to show my face around the palace. I cannot remain bedridden. Being here is part of the reason I am going crazy in the first place."

"Killian, you are still too weak. You were only just able to keep your food down today, let us not push it," Rem said.

"But that is exactly why I should! I finally have a little strength, who knows how long it will last? It will only get worse after this."

Rem's eyes slid over to Drek, he gave him a pointed look.

Drek was quick, stepping in front of the prince and slamming the door shut. He stood before him with his arms crossed, blocking the door. Muscles were bulging and his eyes were serious, daring Killian to challenge his imposing form.

"Step aside, Drek."

Drek looked past him to Rem, then his eyes slid back to Killian. He didn't budge.

"I said step aside," Killian hissed angrily. "That is an order."

Drek's eyes drifted to Rem again before returning to the prince, continuing to disobey. Killian's head snapped back to Rem and he glared at him.

"Have you forgotten that I am your King?"

Rem cocked his head slightly, his stare heavy.

"As Captain of your personal guard, Rank One, and Consort King, I have full authority when it comes to your safety," he replied.

Killian snarled in rage.

Then he felt Drek knock the back of his knees, making him buckle before catching the back of his head and hoisting him into his arms. Killian fought back despite knowing how pointless it was as Drek carried him to the bed.

"Rest," he said.

They've been telling him that for days and it hasn't worked. It wouldn't now either. But hearing his low voice made Killian's eyes droop involuntarily. He was scared. He didn't want to fall asleep.

"The nightmares," Killian whispered.

"We will be right here," Rem said.

His eyes closed.

Like clockwork, he was in the bathroom. Lying in the tub, unable to move. Something seemed different this time around. There was an intense eeriness chilling the air, making it hard to breathe. He glanced down, expecting to see his full, very round stomach, but instead, he couldn't see anything. Nothing but thick opaque redness. A deep red.

Blood.

The whole bath was full of it. Killian tried to scream, to move, to do something. But he couldn't.

The baby.

His baby.

Please be okay. Please.

There was a stillness within him that scared him even more. He couldn't feel the baby. He couldn't see his baby. He expected the lights to go off, like they usually do at this point in the dream. Instead, they stayed on and he noticed something else.

Someone watching him in the corner of the room.

Though he was not sure that someone was correct. It was a figure. Dark and wispy. The edges of it's form faded in and out, indefinite. Male or female, he couldn't tell, but it was definitely a figure. One that was similar to the dark shadow that would snatch young Zev away from Rem. The dark shadow he could never save him from.

The shadow began to edge closer. And then the whispering started. It was loud and incessant, all the while, the shadow lowered, then began crawling forward. It was a slow creep that drove Killian crazy with fear. He still couldn't move.

No.

Stay away!

Closer and closer.

Killian screamed. The blood curdling scream woke him up. His Consorts all jumped up immediately.

"Killian?"

He screamed again, scrambling back against the headboard away from them.

Don't touch me, he thought. Don't touch us.

"Killian, please calm down."

A hand reached toward him and he panicked. He lashed out, scraping the offending appendage with his nails, drawing blood. It splattered against his bare legs.

"Shit!" they swore.

Someone else tried to come near him and he hissed.

"Easy Kill, we're not going to hurt you..." a voice said gently as if trying to appease a wild animal. There was movement again and all his defenses raised.

"Do not approach him," a deep voice commanded. "Give him space."

The Consorts

Killian's body felt hot with panic. He panted, breathing heavily. He was hyperventilating. Sweat began to drip from his temple down to his jaw.

"Killian," someone tried again.

"Stay away from me. Do not touch us!"

There was a wetness between his legs, that grew and grew. He tried to ignore it but the tingling sensation that accompanied it was too intense.

His panting grew erratic and he leaned his head back against the headboard.

"Killian, let us help you."

"Stay away."

He clutched his stomach.

"You are okay," Killian whispered to his unborn child. "I will not let them hurt you. You are safe. I will keep you safe."

"We are no threat to you," a deep voice said softly.

"I have to protect my baby," he insisted.

"And we have to take care of you. Let us."

Killian blinked past his fear and saw the concerned faces of his lovers. Rem was the closest. He offered a hand, letting Killian decide whether or not to take it. He kept a comfortable distance. The prince squirmed, noticing how the sheets were soaked with his slick. How could he be aroused at a time like this?

He looked past Rem and saw Caspian and Zev. Caspian was wrapping Zev's hand. It was Zev he attacked.

"I...do not want to be touched."

Killian stared at Rem, into his dark eyes, wishing there was some way he could convey these feelings to him.

Rem, I don't feel safe.

Killian was almost certain Rem couldn't read his mind, but his eyes narrowed as if he could.

I don't feel safe at all.

One second, Rem's eyes were black. Then another past and they were bright orange. His magix glowing underneath the thin fabric of his black t-shirt.

"Beast," Killian whispered.

Beast leaned forward. Killian watched him with careful and cautious eyes. His eyes were blazing. He brushed his cheek along the prince's, before grazing his jaw and inhaling at his neck.

"Rem-" Zev started but Killian shot him a warning look and gave a very subtle shake of his head. He caught on immediately.

Killian's heart hammered in his chest.

He was pregnant now. If Beast attacked him, his baby was done for.

Killian let out a shaky breath as Beast's nose skimmed his collarbone. He trailed a path down Killian's chest and stopped at his stomach. His breathing grew erratic. He stared at him terrified.

"Ki--" Caspian started but Zev slammed his hand over his mouth. Caspian looked at him like he was crazy.

Zev leaned close to Caspian's ear and it barely looked like he moved his lips but Killian knew he breathed into his ear, "Not a sound."

Beast gripped Killian's hips tightly. The prince whimpered. Beast's eyes darted up toward Killian's face, beginning to bare his teeth but not fully. It was a quick movement, almost like a warning. Then he continued his exploration, smushing his face against Killian's stomach. Getting fed up with the silk tunic Killian wore, he tore it in half. Killian was unable to breathe when he brushed his face against the bare skin of his stomach. A little whine left his throat.

Beast closed his eyes as his cheek pressed into the prince. Then his tongue darted out and licked him. Small little licks almost like a kitten.

Killian didn't trust him. If he moved, Beast might attack. He stayed still. Still as a stone. Beast stopped, then glanced up at Killian, seemingly expectant. Killian didn't know what to do, so he brushed Beast's cheek with shaky fingers. Beast turned his face into Killian's wrist. He sniffed at his vein. His breath was soft, warm.

"H-hello Beast. Are you feeling better?" Killian stammered.

Beast whined again, then licked his wrist. He curled into Killian's lap, burying his face between the prince's legs. With no clothes on, it was a bit awkward. Killian hoped his slick didn't send Beast into a frenzy. He kept licking, right between Killian's legs. But it wasn't sexual, it was like...he was cleaning him. Killian didn't understand it but he didn't challenge it either. He let him. Beast was almost done, when Caspian made a sound. Killian wasn't sure what he did, but the noise was loud enough to draw Beast's attention.

Beast's head snapped over to the two Consorts. His eyes narrowed and a low snarl coming from his curled lips.

Zev may know vaguely that Rem's Beast exists, but he had never seen him before, neither had Caspian. Killian watched the two of them drinking in Beast's appearance and what it looked like when he took over Rem's body.

They both looked scared.

There was a part of Killian that knew that Beast felt something for him. He loved Killian as Rem said. But that meant that he felt something for him. While he had hurt Killian before, his intentions for doing so weren't bad. Beast didn't view Killian as a threat. But Zev and Caspian?

They were the unknown which meant they were threats.

Killian touched Beast's shoulder.

"Beast," Killian said softly.

He turned his blazing eyes on the prince. Killian brushed his cheek softly before leaning his head on his shoulder. His arms came around the male's waist, hugging him, but also keeping him in place. Killian glanced at Zev from the corner of his eye. It was a warning to tread carefully.

Don't move, he mouthed.

Zev stared at Killian, narrowing his eyes slightly in understanding.

Unfortunately, Killian couldn't keep Beast's attention. He was already aware of another threat in the room and it had all of his attention. Like smoke, his disappeared from the prince's arms. And in a black murky puff, he appeared right in front of Zev. Killian had seen Rem use that power once before, in the beginning of the Ranking Ceremony, but it was so fast, he wasn't sure if it actually happened.

It happened alright.

Zev had nerves of steel because he didn't even flinch. He kept still and let Beast examine him. Beast leaned toward him and growled. His face was not friendly. Zev still didn't move, but he met Beast's gaze evenly. He didn't waver. The air was charged between them and Killian found himself holding his breath. Killian was scared, scared for Zev. He didn't want Beast to hurt him.

Instead, Beast leaned into Zev's neck and sniffed him. Zev looked over at Killian, trying to reassure him that he was fine.

Beast's hand ran along Zev's waist, yanking the blue male close until his body slammed against him. Black and blue together. He was still sniffing Zev's neck before he pulled his head back slightly. They stared at each other again. Beast leaned close again, his nose brushing against Zev's full pouty lips. He took a whiff. Then a little lick.

Seeming satisfied, Beast released him. He then turned his attention to Caspian. Now everyone was worried.

"Beast," Killian tried again, desperate to get his attention away from Caspian.

Caspian looked uncomfortable. His hackles raised. He was on high alert, ready to spring into action without a moment of hesitation. Caspian could keep up with Rem in a fight, but Killian wasn't so sure how he would fair against Beast.

Killian could see the raw fear and clear defenses raise in Caspian's face. He didn't bother hiding it, but Killian didn't expect him to. Beast was not deterred by the sound of the prince's voice. He stalked Caspian. When Caspian took a step back, Beast froze. He stared at Caspian's feet, looking confused. He took another step forward and Caspian took one back.

Beast clenched his teeth in frustration.

"Stay still," Zev hissed.

Caspian gulped before grounding his feet and looking uneasy doing it. Beast tried to get close again and was finally able to do so. He leaned close to Caspian's neck and began sniffing him. He took a little bit longer with Caspian than he did with Zev, but he was soon satisfied. Strangely though, he turned to Killian and made a guttural noise. Though the sound seemed unpleasant, it was almost as if he was asking...approval?

Killian stared at Beast confused.

He looked back at Zev and Caspian then to Killian again, making the noise again.

"Yes. They are okay. Not bad," Killian said.

Beast stared as if he hadn't spoken.

Killian nodded slowly. That, he seemed to understand a little better. Killian wanted him away from them though. He opened his arms to Beast. He appeared like smoke in Killian's arms. He was warm when he solidified. He started to whine, pushing his face into Killian's neck and hugging him close. Killian stroked his hair gently.

"Beast?"

He huffed.

"I would like Rem back now."

Beast whimpered loudly.

"Rem," the prince repeated, a little more firm in tone.

Beast whimpered again, more quietly, then suddenly it was Rem. He pulled back and surveyed Killian immediately.

"I am fine. He did not do anything," Killian reassured him.

He sighed in relief. Then he whipped around to Zev and Caspian. Beast had never come out around them, it shocked him.

"He did not harm anyone?" Rem asked sounding stressed.

"No, all he did was sniff and lick us."

Rem looked confused.

"You both as well?" he asked, talking to Caspian and Zev.

They nodded.

"He did not attack?" Rem asked more to himself, disbelieving.

"Would he normally?" Killian asked.

Rem nodded.

"So that thing just comes out at random?" Caspian questioned with frustration.

Killian shot him a frosty glare.

"He is not a thing."

Rem snorted uncharacteristically.

"My apologies," Caspian sneered, rolling his eyes. He was still freaked out. Killian didn't chastise him for it.

"He did something strange though."

"What?" Rem demanded.

"He tried to communicate with me. I could not understand what he was saying but it was almost as if he were trying to get my approval."

"Approval of what?"

"Zev and Caspian. It was after he inspected the two."

"Maybe to see if we were a threat?" Zev suggested.

"It is not that developed. It acts only on instinct, there is no rationality in it," Rem snapped.

"You are wrong, and you know it. We went through this already, he can be taught."

Rem shook his head in annoyance.

"Rem, you know it is true. He even listened to me. I asked him to let you come back and he did. He is rational."

"You asked it?" Rem was the incredulous one this time.

Killian nodded.

"And it listened?"

Killian nodded again.

Rem blew out a breath.

They were all quiet for a while, taking in all of this information. There was one other thing Killian noticed with Beast.

"Has Beast ever fallen for two people at the same time?" Killian asked Rem.

"No."

"I think he has this time," he said, then looked at Zev.

Rem followed his gaze and eyes widening a little.

"I do not think so. I would know."

Killian let it drop but kept it in the back of his mind.

Rem and Zev left in search of Faust and to do more research on Killian's condition while Drek had Consort training, leaving Caspian to babysit him.

Caspian was silent, just lying beside Killian on the bed, playing with a few tendrils of the prince's hair, tail wiggling slowly in the air. They studied each other, drinking each other in.

Caspian had strong features. His cheekbones were prominent and his jaw sharp...strong. His eyes were thin, slanted inward in an elegant slope, tapering at the end, just like a cat. This close, Killian could see in detail those bright yellow eyes. He didn't notice the flecks of gold in them, but they rimmed his iris. His pupils were slivers in that cross shaped way that all Incubi and Succubae were. His curly bangs were slightly ruffled, catching on his thick burgundy horns that curved around themselves.

"You must have been very surprised," Killian said, trying to start a conversation, though it was not something he was supposed to be doing.

Caspian raised a brow.

"Surprised?" he repeated.

"Rem's Beast. You had no knowledge of him. To be thrust into that situation must have given you a shock, no?"

Caspian laughed lightly.

"I think you have forgotten our talk in the trees, those weeks ago. I had been there, remember? When Rem told you his story. Told you of his first wife. I had known of Rem's Beast. I just hadn't experienced it before."

Killian lips popped open in shock. He had forgotten. It just seemed so long ago; the memories were but distant buzzing in his mind. And rightfully so, as he has had much more to ruminate as several events took a turn for the worst.

They laid in silence again. For a while, Killian simply listened to their even breathing, then began his exploration of Caspian's face once again. Brushing his full lips with the pad of his thumb, he savored the feel of their softness. His tongue darted out, sweeping the tip. Killian witnessed the dilation in his pupils. Liking the reaction and wanting more,

Killian leaned forward and placed a soft kiss on his lips, running his fingers gently over his bare chest.

Caspian smiled making his dimples show.

"You should be sleeping," he murmured.

"I cannot," Killian said, pushing himself closer to him. "Not with you so close to me."

"Then maybe I should move away," he countered.

Killian threw his leg over his hip, pressing their pelvises together. While he was wearing a short tunic, Caspian wore nothing.

"Do not dare," Killian growled playfully, staring into his intense eyes. His grin widened and the hand that instinctively grabbed his waist moved down to grope his butt.

"Caspian," Killian moaned when he grabbed a little tighter.

The prince's lips were right up against his, only a millimeter away. Killian could feel the heat of his skin, breathe in the air he exhaled. He could taste him. His eyes drooped as the rush of sensations shot through him. Killian wanted him. He wanted him so badly, it was starting to hurt. Caspian didn't kiss him, and it was absolute torture. His shit eating grin said he knew it too.

"Has no one ever taught you patience, My Prince?" He teased, his scent intoxicating.

Patience be damned. It was this male in his arms that he desired, the one whose flesh he wanted flush against his own, whose body he wanted to be one with. Killian wanted him so deep he'd reach a place undiscovered. He wanted Caspian to look upon him like he was the only thing tethering him to the world. He wanted to be his lifeline.

For so long Killian had dreamed of what this would be like, how it would feel to have someone truly care about him. To have someone want him so badly that every bone in their body ached for him. That they quivered at the sight of him. Them to look upon his naked flesh as if he were a God.

And he wanted to return the favor. Caspian wanted Killian. Maybe not as badly as the others, but he wanted him. He had a purpose.

Screaming his moan, Killian relished in the utter fullness he felt when Caspian sheathed his sword inside him. It was powerful, pleasurable, exhilarating, he couldn't stop himself from unleashing his *Haise*.

Caspian's body stiffened, as Killian's power yanked his mind from his body.

It was fragile in the prince's grasp. Delicate...breakable. Like a newborn, he cradled it against him, feeling the very essence that made up his lover. Killian literally held Caspian's life in his hands.

The ritual bath kept his powers tame and helped him with control.

He should not have released his *Haise* on Caspian when he was this unstable.

Killian could kill him. He could break him. He could shatter him.

Do it, a voice urged. It was like liquid honey, sweet and reasonable. That voice rang in Killian's ears like a symphony.

Shatter him, it urged again.

Killian squeezed Caspian's essence a little tighter, feeling his body jerk and blood trickle down from his nose. Caspian was staring at Killian with vacant eyes, jaw slack, body immobile. No one was home.

Go on...break him.

Break Caspian?

Killian didn't want to do that. He was nearly half broken already. The night terrors he suffered and uncontrollable paranoia were signs enough of that. If Killian broke him, he wouldn't see his smile again, hear his laugh, feel his lips on his, his body in his. He would not be his lover anymore. He would be but a husk.

No.

He would be dead.

But he'll be a part of you. You will drink him in, and he will never leave your side.

Killian caressed Caspian's essence. He could protect him if he was a part of him. No one would ever hurt him again. He would be plagued by no night terrors. He would be happy.

Break him, the voice whispered again, echoing inside Killian with all of the possibilities. All of the beautiful outcomes of just sucking this male into the prince's being. It would be so easy.

But did he want to?

The unease teetered back and forth. The confusion settled over him like a heavy fog, thick and opaque. He couldn't see his way through it. Killian only had the voice leading the way.

Killian? A soft voice echoed in his head. Soft and unsure...frightened.

Caspian.

With that small voice came a whirlwind of fear. Like ice prickling in his veins, stiffening his limbs and clawing at his heart. Caspian was so afraid. Of him. Of what he was contemplating on doing to him.

The whispers started. Those monstrous whispers that he had no hope of understanding. They were angry, very angry. But that rage is what snapped Killian out of it, cleared the fog.

Killian shoved Caspian back into his body, finally regaining control. Caspian panted heavily above the prince, breathing hoarse and ragged as if he had run a marathon...or run for his life. A thin sheen of sweat coated his skin. Killian watched the blood from his nose trickle down onto his lips. He ignored it, concentrating on slowing his rapid heart that even Killian could hear beating like mad.

Tears brimmed in the prince's eyes, his chest felt heavy and his throat constricted.

He almost killed him. He almost killed Caspian.

Oh Gods.

A horrible sob broke free that he tried to stifle, covering his hands over his mouth. He wanted to squeeze, cut off his very oxygen so that he might repent.

Caspian's wide eyes flickered to Killian. They were gentle...concerned. How could he care for him when he just nearly stole his life? Killian was a monster.

Hysterical sobs left Killian lips. He cried so hard he was screaming, digging his nails into his skin until they were slick with blood. He made a messy ruin of his face while Caspian tried desperately to calm him, restrain him. The Consort's hands locked around Killian's wrists, pinning them above him.

Killian's head swam and his chest was so tight that he could barely get a breath in.

"Killian, calm down," Caspian urged. Worry and panic on his face.

Hearing his voice made Killian cry even harder. He could have taken that sweet honied voice away. He would have taken it away.

"Shit!" Caspian swore in anxious frustration then tilted head toward the door screaming for the guards.

Two burst into the room.

"You," Caspian commanded to the first one. "Go get Rem, Zev, and Faust."

The guard sprinted out of the room faster than Killian's eyes could catch. Caspian turned to the second. "And you, go get Drek, Lorn and Ethel."

He disappeared as well.

Caspian turned back to Killian, pain in his eyes.

"Please, Killian, you have to calm down."

He made a move to tug the prince into his arms, but Killian fought him. He couldn't let him hold him, not a monster like him. He almost killed Caspian. His vision dimmed. He couldn't get enough air into his lungs, soon he would be pulled under.

"I--" Killian choked, trying to get the word out, muffled against the skin of Caspian's shoulder where he was pressed to him.

How did one apologize for almost murdering their lover?

How did one apologize for being a sadistic, bloodthirsty monster?

"It's okay, Killian. I knew you wouldn't," Caspian said, knowing what the prince was trying to get out.

Liar.

Killian could feel the stumble in his heart beat. He was afraid, petrified, and he didn't trust Killian not to kill him.

Killian knew Caspian. Much more than the Consort realized. Killian knew that despite all the smiles and the promises, Caspian didn't trust anyone. He'd been a stray for too long. He thought Killian was going to kill him, he knew he would.

Bile burned in Killian's throat. Then the room filled with smoke. Thick black smoke that solidified into three beings.

Rem, Zev, and Faust. They rushed over to them immediately, surveying the damage. It was their faces hovering over him, the last image Killian saw before darkness claimed him.

When Killian awoke, it was to the smell of spices and warmth. Though his limbs were heavy, his eyelids were light. They popped open almost immediately. Too fast and his vision blurred. He tried to sit up immediately, but hands shoved him back down. Warm hands, large and calloused.

Rem.

Killian blinked past the blurriness and gazed up at him. Like the highest peaks in the darkest of shadows, Killian could make out his facial features.

"Rem," Killian breathed.

The Consort didn't say anything, just brushed the prince's hair back from his face softly. Killian tilted his head around to gauge his surroundings. They were still in his bedroom, but it was empty. Only Rem and Killian remained.

"What happened? Where is everyone?" he asked him.

Rem still didn't respond, just continued to stroke his hair.

"Rem?"

"They are dead," he said solemnly.

Killian froze.

"Dead? What do you mean they are dead?" Killian questioned, refusing to believe this preposterous news.

There was no way that anyone was dead.

"You killed them," he said. "You killed them, and I helped."

Killian shot up, but Rem shoved him down again, forcefully this time. His teeth were bared and his skin glowing. Killian was startled as he looked into one bright orange eye and one black one.

"We killed them together. There is no one but us."

Rem reached beside him on the bed and showed him two small gruesome lumps covered in blood. One was black as night and the other pale blue. But Killian couldn't tell what they were from their strange shape and gory covering.

He held them out to Killian and smiled widely. It was off putting with his strange eyes and mania. Killian have never seen Rem smile like that before. But it was that look that made the prince realize what...who he held in his hands.

No.

Please Gods, no, no, no.

Killian reached for them, the small balls of flesh. Then he saw those tiny partially formed eyes.

And he snapped. Something in him just completely shattered. He could see nothing but red. No, not red.

Orange.

A thick orange haze fell over him, blanketed by rage, primal in its glory. It called to the prince with its sweet melody. It was hopeless to fight. Killian could only sit back and let this feeling ride him. When it was gone, he was able to open his eyes, clear. Free of the fog.

Blinking a few times, he stirred, trying to move, noticing how sore his body was. Every joint in him ached in protest. When he tried to sit up, his body was immediately restricted. Glancing down, he noticed the cuffs on his wrists and the belt around his chest. Even his ankles were shackled.

What the--

The prince glanced around. He wasn't in his bed chamber, instead a small white room that mimicked their medical wing but not quite, there was something a little off.

It was alarming to see his father sitting in a chair in the corner. Even more so, seeing Rem sitting in a chair beside him. Both had their eyes closed in an uncomfortable slumber, but the moment Killian jostled his cuffs, they both blinked awake and were at his side.

"Why am I--?" Killian started, gesturing to the restraints.

Both were quiet, looking solemn.

"Father?" Killian prompted when they didn't answer.

"We knew it was a possibility," he started, then stopped.

"A possibility for what?" Killian pushed.

"That with a Beast holder as a Father for your child, the child might also...have a Beast of its own," his father finished.

Killian stared at him blankly, then looked at Rem, someone who remained quiet.

"I do not understand."

Killian also didn't understand how the King knew about Rem's Beast.

"H-how did you...?" Killian stuttered.

"I am not as clueless as you seem to think. I am aware of Rem's magix and I am aware of what the beast in him has done so far."

Killian gaped at him. "And you did not order for his execution?"

"No, because Rem to you is what your mother is to me. As King, you need someone whose very presence will bring about rationality. Someone who will calm your rage and someone who puts you at the paramount of their world. For you, that is Rem. You need him."

Killian let that sink in.

His father knew.

He knew about what happened during the Ranking Ceremony. He knew about Beast losing control. But how? Killian was sure that they did well in keeping it hidden. And that still didn't explain why he was being restrained.

King Ellis seemed to pick up on the unspoken question.

"We think that the child's magix is leaking into you and you now are showing symptoms of having an entity. This is still in the early stages of hypotheses and is not definite, but that it is the only explanation that we can come up with for what happened."

There he goes, talking around the question.

Rem seemed to pick up on Killian's frustration and answered. "You slaughtered two servants, six guards, and one attendant."

The prince's jaw dropped in horror.

And then he noticed their outfits. Killian's father and Rem wore black as if in mourning.

"What?" Killian choked.

"We'll have to find you a replacement attendant as soon as possible," his father said, trying to lean the conversation away from the word 'slaughter.'

A replacement.

Meaning it was one of his attendants.

Oh Gods.

"Who?" Killian whispered.

The King didn't answer him, looking away in despair.

Killian looked to Rem.

"Who?" he repeated.

"Kara."

Kara.

Killian killed Kara.

He'd never see that smile again, sweet and genuine, spreading along that beautiful...kind face, just lightly aged. He'd never hear her laugh as Ethel scolded him or hug him when the pain of being Heir became too much. She will never be his anchor again. Because he killed her.

Oh Gods.

"Killian--" Killian heard Rem start but he held up a hand.

He did not want to hear it.

Killian knew what he was going to say, what he was going to do. Killian didn't deserve comfort right now. He was a monster, through and through. Oh Gods, how was he ever going to look Ethel in the face again?

The King began to delve into an explanation as he stared blankly at his hands, not seeming to really come to terms with what they were capable of.

"We think the Beast awakening is connected to your *Haise* and potentially a lack of feeding. We know that you have been feeding, just not as much as you should be. Especially with your baby--"

"Babies," Killian corrected.

The King and Rem faltered. Identical looks of confusion on their faces.

"What?"

"Babies," Killian said again, his voice just barely above a whisper.

He saw the vision flash into his mind. Rem's outstretched hands and two bloody lumps.

He knew it was right. He was having twins.

"There are two. One with skin like blue summer skies...the other, black as winter night. I am having twins," Killian further explained.

Rem was quick to recover.

"How do you know this?" he demanded.

Killian looked up at him and smiled. He could tell it was a hideous one, full of madness and despair.

"You showed me."

Rem frowned but didn't bother questioning his bizarre answer.

"Unchain me," Killian commanded not wanting to talk any more. The gnawing in his gut increased and he felt nauseous. He would not vomit, but he still felt like it. They did so without hesitation. Killian sat up and swung his feet over to the ledge of the bed. His bare soles touched the cool marble floors, sending an icy shock up his calves. The world around him wobbled as if he were staring at the mirage above the licking embers of a fire, burning so bright his eyes ached. Ignoring it, he stumbled to his feet. Rem was ready to catch him, but the prince glared at him, not wanting to be touched.

Rem understood and backed off. Killian started for the door and then stopped to look at his father.

"I am not suited to be King."

King Ellis approached him before gently stroking Killian's hair back behind his ear, then lightly cupping his cheek with his warm large palm. He had the full force of those gray eyes on him, smoldering intensely. Killian did not feel like he was twenty-three. Instead, he was a little boy stumbling around with shoes too big to fill and a crown that slid to his neck, suffocating him.

"I have not for a second regretted naming you my Heir. And you have proven my decision to keep you there every day so far. It is hard now, my son, but it is how you face it that makes you strong. Let yourself grieve only for a few moments, but keep in mind that this is just a battlefield. You develop a strategy and conquer your enemies. I have no doubt in my mind that you will emerge victorious."

Killian's chest tightened at his words, even more so when he leaned down to kiss his forehead. The way he used to when he was a little boy.

Killian took a deep breath and nodded numbly.

He was right. He didn't have time to get choked up. Lately all he had been doing is staying holed up in his room and letting these things happen. That wasn't him. He was not the type of person to just sit there and let things happen...well in some cases he was. But not anymore.

Killian was Heir.

He will be King.

He needed to start acting like it. And the first thing on his list was finding Caspian. The King left them, and Killian looked at Rem, "Come."

Rem followed wordlessly as Killian made his way down the hall. Though they had not officially connected during his *Haise*, he could still feel him. Like a small string tugging him in one direction and another until he found him in the sparring room with his remaining Consorts.

When he saw Killian, he stood up.

His tail didn't swish in excitement, it stayed limp behind him.

Bad sign.

Killian walked up to him and looked deep into those captivating yellow eyes widened in shock holding a bit of anxiety.

"I am sorry," Killian said to him. "I am sorry for letting myself succumb to such darkness. It is because of my weakness that I nearly took your life--"

"Killian--" he started to interrupt, but Killian held up a hand and continued to speak.

"My weakness is what lead to that unfortunate event. But I make this promise to you. I will get stronger and not let myself falter again. Though you will remain wary I am sure, I just want you to know how deeply sorry I am and that I will not let it happen again."

Caspian opened his mouth and then closed it, then opened it again. Killian thought he would finally speak, but instead, he closed his mouth and nodded. Killian turned to the rest of his men and apologized to them as well.

"I have been wallowing in misery and self-pity for far too long. It is inexcusable. No more. I will be to you the King I am supposed to." He looked at each and every one of his men in the eye, hoping that what they saw was not the defeated male they have become accustomed to in the few weeks they have been here but the male that stood with power and authority when addressing his people.

"Zev and Rem, I want you to continue to research the *Haise* and I also want you to look up anything you can on magix, any mention of Beasts are vital. We must learn all that we can. Faust, you will be assigned to researching what you can on the feud between Kappas and Nymphs."

They nodded.

Killian turned to Drek and Caspian.

"You two will come with me. It is time I fulfill my duties which I should have been doing all along."

He turned on his heel and began to walk out the door, but a voice stopped him.

"Killian!"

Killian paused and turned around to look at them all.

Caspian's expression was pained.

"You have been through a lot, maybe you should just rest," he said.

Killian smiled at him sweetly.

"I have rested enough."

Even he could tell what a terrible lie that was. Still, Killian continued on his path, expecting the two to follow. He was satisfied when footsteps sounded behind him, echoing in the halls, clicking against the marble floors. His bare soles still cold, it felt like he was walking along the ice in a frozen wasteland. In his head, Killian was a mess of emotions, desperately wanting to blame it on the pregnancy but knowing that this was all him. There was nothing to blame except his lack of control over himself and those around him. How could it have gotten so bad so fast?

Killian had been so lonely before that it literally ate him up inside, creating a husk of a male. It destroyed him, slowly and painfully, but now? Now that he was surrounded by many and every waking moment they are there...he couldn't tell if he was still alone, or if he simply was not ready. Maybe he thought he was ready for companionship when in reality, he was not ripe enough yet. Could it be that he preferred the loneliness over this? Or is this just a whole new level of loneliness?

Killian's hand splayed over his stomach.

He had two beings growing inside of him. There were three of them and he still felt this way. What is wrong with him?

Killian sighed in defeat before opening the large doors to the *Haise* chamber. Caspian and Drek looked around warily, taking note of the large bed--which he now knew the purpose it held--and the small pool of bright blue waters before it.

Closing the door behind them, Killian commanded their attention.

"Remove your clothing."

Killian was slipping his own robe off before stepping into the pool. The familiar charge of power ran through him, raising the small bumps on his flesh, sending every hair to attention. Killian groaned, rolling his neck. Before he could completely submerge himself in the water, he looked at his two men.

"When you come into the water, do not touch me. Stay as far away from me as you can. Let me come to you. And when I do, you will open your mind to me. Do not hold any part of yourself back. It will feel strange, but I need you to bear it."

They didn't say anything, but Killian didn't move until they made some inkling of understanding. Drek finally nodded his head, looking a bit uncomfortable. Killian took a deep breath and sank into the water. His body instantly going numb as the smell of nutmeg swept up into his nose, completely overtaking his senses. The prince sighed. He'd have more control this time, since he was not starving.

He stared at them with a slight shift of his head, signifying that they too were to enter the bath. They were hesitant at first, so he coaxed them with a small push in his direction. Drek was the first to step in the water and as soon as his foot touched it, he went stiff. His breathing became labored and Killian saw his hair rise on his skin. With clenched teeth, he fought through it and sat in the furthest corner from him.

Caspian gulped before following suit. As the might of Killian's power hit him, his tail went ramrod straight and his back bowed, just like a frightened cat. And Killian was proud of him when he pushed forward and sat next to Drek in the water. They looked at each other then at the prince.

Killian held both of their gazes, his power building in him, filling him up like water in a bath. It expanded, stretching his inner core.

The Consorts

Caspian was first. Killian already had a slight connection with him and his power sought it out. He urged every tender moment they shared. Every kiss and touch. He pushed it to the forefront of both of their minds. Caspian's eyes dilated as he held his gaze. His body reacting as if he could feel Killian's phantom fingers, caressing his length.

His frame trembled slightly and that's when Killian struck. He sent his power slamming into him as he crawled forward, sucking him deep inside him, pulling his entire essence into Killian's being. Caspian was so afraid. Though his body went slack in the prince's arms, his consciousness was trembling viciously. In his head, Killian saw him. But not the strong male he had the honor of knowing. A child.

With big innocent yellow eyes, that surely took up most of his face framed with bright red lashes, slightly shiny with fresh tears. His hair a curly mess down to his tiny shoulders, and red tail wrapped tightly around his huddled form. He stared up at Killian with his full baby lips parted, button nose flared, ears twitching.

The prince crouched before him.

Caspian scooted further away into the corner of darkness that they resided in. His adorable young body shaking like a leaf.

Opening his arms to him, Killian sent waves of comfort and safety to him.

"It's okay," the prince cooed. "I won't hurt you. I'll make sure you are never hurt again. Not by me or anyone else. You are safe."

A tear escaped his widened eyes. Killian didn't dare make a move toward him.

No. Caspian must come to him.

When he realized this decision was his and his alone, Killian saw the tentative curiosity. The prince could see his uncertainty, wondering if he could be trusted. Sniffing in Killian's direction, Caspian finally inched closer. Just a little bit. Killian waited patiently. There was no rush.

"No...hurt?" The soft cherub voice asked hesitantly.

Killian smiled at him.

"No sweetheart. Not anymore."

Caspian's tail twitched before he finally crawled toward Killian and with each inch he gained, the brighter their surroundings became.

Finally, Caspian scrambled into Killian's lap, his tiny, too thin arms wrapping around his neck. He could feel Caspian's cool nose touch the skin where his neck met shoulder. His legs wrapping around the prince's waist. He gently stroked Caspian's hair, softer than clouds. And in his mind Killian could see.

Faces flashing past, angry snarls. The prince could feel his pain as he was struck over and over again. The gnawing hunger that threatened to tear him apart from the inside. The sadness overwhelmed Killian as young Caspian shook a small Incubus male with fiery red locks identical to his own, pleading for him to wake up. Killian could feel the smooth wood of the bow and the rigid straightness of the arrow as he took up archery for the first time.

Happiness cradled Killian when the image of a huge burly male with dark mocha skin and dark brown eyes smiled at Caspian in approval. When this male ruffled his hair and Caspian pretended that it bothered him, swatting the hand away when inside he was practically beaming with pride.

Killian could see a small orange and white tabby cat, curled up in Caspian's lap as he lazily stroked their fur. Then the crippling agony when the cat lay in a pile of blood with seven predators leering around him.

Killian could feel every part that made Caspian who he was. And then Killian pushed the lust forward. He saw himself in Caspian's eyes. Practically glowing with saturated lavender skin, smooth and unblemished. Wavy maroon locks always styled perfectly, framing high cheekbones, sensuous lips, and bright red eyes with long lashes. The way he moved was graceful, elegant...powerful. Though mild in emotions, there was a purity shining under his skin, an innocence in those wide red eyes and with every blush on his cheeks.

In his eyes, Killian was stunning.

Even more so when he was panting underneath him, his legs hooked over Caspian's arms in the crease of his elbows, his teeth gnawing on his bottom lip, his arched back, and loud sensual moans leaving his lips. It drove him crazy.

Killian fed on it. All of it, he took it all inside of him sating that thirst, that hunger. He slammed his lips onto Caspian's, pushing him back inside of his body and as soon as he did, the Consort was on him. Shoving his hips up trying to impale Killian with the stiff length of him. Killian pulled away, just out of reach. Caspian convulsed before slumping over to the side.

Killian took a deep breath before setting his gaze on Drek. The Consort met his gaze levelly, not a hint of fear. It was a challenge, daring Killian. The prince slid on his lap, placing his hands on the male's shoulders, staring deep into those bright evergreen eyes. Drek stared right back. With the tip of his index finger, Killian gently brushed the length of his stubbled jaw. His golden hair unbound around him, straight and silky.

Killian tilted his head slightly before pushing his power into Drek, summoning all of their built up lust. They had only been intimate with each other a couple of times, but their desires for each other had grown significantly.

Sucking him in, Drek's body went slack and Killian was immediately transported into a hospital room. White and sterile with a steady beeping. Drek sat at the edge of the hospital bed, watching intently as someone slept.

An Incubus with short gray curls and pale blue skin. The Incubus was wrapped in so many medical vines, Killian couldn't even tell where his injuries lie. Drek held the small, boney hand in his, clutching it like a lifeline. It was then that Killian noticed a bright red ribbon tied around the patient's wrist, a burst of color amidst the pallidness. There was silence in the room except for the steady hum of magic contained in an orb that sustained the unfamiliar male's life.

The Consorts

Killian noticed that Drek looked younger, no older than twenty years. His golden mane much longer than he had ever seen it and no stubble on his jaw. His youthful appearance distracted Killian from the entering of an Incubus and Succubus. One with skin a clear blue that clearly resembled the patient and the other with curly gray locks.

His parents.

"Drek, it's time," the Succubus said softly, her voice choked up as if she would break out into tears at any moment. The Incubus rubbed her shoulders gently.

Drek's own eyes filled with tears, but he gave a curt nod before placing a chaste kiss to the patient's forehead and then backed away. A Healer came in at that time and surveyed the grim faces around him. His own crinkled with sadness before the cool calmness that all Healer's had overcame him. He nodded at the parents before he started messing with the glowing vines.

Unwrapping them.

The magic in the orb went crazy, sparking like mad until finally it dulled. The Succubus howled in sorrow, sobbing into the chest of the Incubus who also had tears streaming down his cheeks. Killian looked over to Drek who was crying silently. Teeth bared, jaw clenched, and hands in fists. He stormed out of the room and the scene faded into another.

Training as a young boy. Covered in blood and bruises, Killian watched as Warriors twice his size struck him again and again. Some taunting him, laughing as he spit up blood. But there was a rage in him that was unmatched, burning in those green eyes.

He was a lion in disguise.

The prince watched on as he endured bullying in the ring and in the locker rooms. How the older Incubi would shove him, hide his clothes, sabotage him. Killian saw how he endured it all with clenched teeth. He watched how when Drek sat at the dinner table with his mother and father, covered in bruises and scrapes, the silence tore at him. Killian watched his father strike him, calling him weak and an embarrassment. He watched Drek's mother ignore him as he lay bloodied and broken afterward.

Killian watched as he grew older and the anger and aggression grew. He watched him mature with thicker skin. Confidence that should have been beaten out of him oozing from his every pore. He watched over time, people began to take notice. They watched Drek's body fill out with powerful muscles, they watched as his rank increased amongst the Warriors. They watched as he became a male to be desired. Those who tormented him now kissed the ground he walked on.

He never forgot any of their faces.

Then that Incubus appeared, the one that lay in the hospital bed. He was smiling, eyes the color of pure silver, gleaming with happiness, but a quiet kindness to him that Drek adored. Killian watched some of the fire in Drek dim when he was around.

It was love, but not of the romantic kind.

No, it was a friendship. A bond so deep, Drek swore with every fiber of his being that he would cherish it, protect it with everything he had. They did everything together, went everywhere together. They became brothers in a sense.

Then...some of the Warriors who were jealous of Drek's success went after the one thing that would hit Drek the hardest. His friend. They beat him within an inch of his life, putting him in a coma. He was under for four years until his parents couldn't take it anymore and decided to pull the plug. Drek blaming himself the whole time. An image of Drek clutching that red ribbon his friend always wore in his hands and sobbing flashed in his mind.

Killian saw himself next, from that first day at the ceremony. Regal and divine, trailing behind his father. Drek noticed the innocence, the same kindness that his friend had. And when he met those exquisite red eyes and saw the blush color those already rosy cheeks, he knew. He knew that he needed him. He knew that this Incubus, this Prince, would be his next lifeline. Would be the reason he got up in the morning, his reason to keep fighting. He knew that Prince Killian Innis would be his new best friend.

And then he saw him slowly drift away. He saw the Incubus find comfort in the others, looking at everyone but him. He saw that small tether to life pull taut. When he heard him offer the last proposal to Orion, that tether snapped.

He was not wanted. He was not needed. He was nothing.

He heard every word exchanged between the two Incubi, the anger, the sorrow.

And when Killian came in that one day, asking Drek to be his official Consort, the rage and self-loathing ate at him.

Drek kept thinking to himself: Why aren't I good enough?

He wanted to be angry at Killian, he was trying so hard. And the day that Drek asked him--no--begged to tell Killian why he was so upset with him, the self-loathing only grew.

Then he began to believe that the Gods did not want him to be with the prince, that Drek would only destroy him as he did his best friend. So he tried to keep his distance, even though every part of him was so painfully aware of everything Killian did.

When Killian finally lost it, it killed him inside. Drek convinced himself that it was his fault, that he was cursed and that he would be better off without him. He was preparing himself to leave, to work up the courage to let Killian go. And then the prince called out to him, begged him to stay by his side.

Drek had crumbled.

Killian had not realize any of this. He had not noticed how Drek suffered. He kept it all hidden so well. Killian had known something was wrong, but never to this extent. He had known nothing about Drek...until now.

Killian tugged on Drek's desires for him and it hit him like a wave. The prince's body vibrated with it as he drank it all in before shoving Drek back into his body with a kiss.

He shivered.

And as the others had tried to ravish Killian right after being put back, Drek did not. He simply stared at the prince, with hooded eyes and gently brushed his hair behind his ear, fingers caressing the pointed rim of it.

Killian shuddered, eyes fluttering closed before opening again.

"I apologize," Killian whispered over the heavy silence. "I-I did not know."

Drek didn't say anything, just averted his eyes.

The prince's expression turned insistent. "You have to know that none of this is your fault. I just struggle with--"

"You are not weak," he snapped, his deep voice hoarse.

Later, when Caspian was able to move again, they got out of the pool, dried themselves off and dressed in fresh clothes. None of them spoke the entire way back to the room, but every once in a while their hands would brush and an electric shock ran through them.

It was different this time.

Bonds had formed and they were stronger than ever. And for once, Killian finally thought that things would be alright.

Chapter 18

Killian had strange dreams the past few nights.

Surprisingly, they weren't nightmares. It was different from his usual, allowing him to feel well rested and rejuvenated when he awoke. It had been so long since he felt this way, it was a bit suspicious. He couldn't trust that things were beginning to work out, as pessimistic as that may sound.

What was even stranger was that in his dreams, he could see them. The both of them, skin shining bright enough it was almost glowing.

Drek's like polished emeralds.

Caspian's like the finest gold.

Both welcoming Killian into their arms. Though he had not had dreams like these with the other's he was not very surprised by it. What held his interest was the thin strings of light that attached them together. From Killian's navel, they burst out, like glittering threads, glowing just as bright as their skin, latching onto a path directly to their chests. The three were connected.

It couldn't have been the *Haise* causing this, as he had never experienced it with Rem, Zev, or Faust and they were the first to share it with him.

Each time he woke, he wondered if they felt it too. Killian wanted to ask, but could never find a moment to bring it up. There was too much going on with the attacks on the Kappas, the upcoming Ball, his cousins creating mischief, his pregnancy, his baby's magix, and his temporary loss of sanity. But on the bright side, his relationship with Drek had been mended. The male was back to being his old cocky self. He and Caspian had a little bond that kept them glued to each other's sides...for the most part at least.

Caspian approached Killian earlier, pulling him to the side where they could speak in private.

Killian knew from his expression that something was wrong, but he was trying hard not to show how big of a deal it was. "What is it?" Killian asked him.

"I thought you should know that Lord Filo has been approaching Drek a lot lately. I saw them talking a few times. I wasn't sure if Drek said anything about it."

Killian frowned.

No. He hadn't.

"Don't be mad at him," Caspian said quickly. "I don't think he is trying to be deceitful or anything. I honestly didn't expect him to tell you. It's just strange, when I asked him about it; he completely denied it. It seemed like…" Caspian trailed off looking unsure.

"What?" Killian prompted.

"It seemed like he genuinely didn't know what I was talking about. If I hadn't seen him with my own eyes, I would have taken his word for it, without a doubt."

It was dangerously suspicious. Now, with all of his Consorts gone, busy with their duties, Drek was assigned to stay by Killian's side in their room. He watched him from the corner of his eye, drinking the tea that was freshly prepared. He was sitting beside him on the lounge chair, looking over some documents the King had given him earlier intently.

"Drek?"

He glanced up at the prince after taking a few ticks to finish whatever sentence he was on. His bright green eyes were alert and attentive. Killian studied his face before asking, "Has Filo been approaching you?"

Drek frowned looking slightly confused.

"No, not aside from that encounter I told you about before."

"Are you sure?" Killian pushed.

Drek's frown deepened. "Yes, I'm sure, why?"

"I was informed that he has been approaching you and that you've been having conversations with him." the prince was careful with his tone, so it didn't sound like he was accusing the Consort of anything. Just asking him, trusting him.

"Like I said, the last time I spoke to him was when I told you. I would remember if there had been any other times. I've been avoiding him, just as you instructed."

Killian tried to read every inch of his face and his body language, picking up on every twitch of his muscles. But it all seemed genuine. Like he honestly didn't know what Killian was talking about. Had Caspian been mistaken?

He doubted it. Especially since he too mentioned Drek's strange honesty about not knowing. Killian had a bad feeling about this.

Drek was watching him, confusion still apparent. The prince smiled at him and waved it off, "Don't worry about it, I'm probably just being overprotective."

Drek didn't looked convinced with that answer but Killian ignored him and continued to eat. He took that as his cue to continue reading the documents. His eyes were scanning over them intensely, brow furrowed. He flipped back and forth between a few more papers before whispering, "Only six."

The Consorts

Killian placed his tea down next to his empty plate and scooched closer to Drek on the lounge chair, wrapping his arms around his bulging green bicep and leaning his head on the male's shoulder, peering down at the papers with him.

"What are you looking at?" Killian asked him.

"Applications for your personal Guard."

The prince frowned.

"You are my personal Guard and the rest of my Consorts."

Drek smirked, pupils sliding to the corner of his eye to glance at him.

"Crown Prince and you don't even know that you have your own army," he chuckled.

His head popped up at this.

"Army?"

"Lord Pierce will take over as GA or General of the Royal Army, but as for the Crown Prince, a separate army is constructed. Rem, Rank One is the General of us all. Zev, Rank Two, is his Lieutenant. Caspian his Third and so on. But each of your Consorts are Generals of their own factions. These factions consist of our soldiers. I have to choose who will be a part of my faction. All of the others are doing the same. Well, except Rem seeing as his faction is the remaining Consorts. But each faction has a certain area to cover. Zev and his faction cover combat, any stealth or spy work is his jurisdiction. Caspian's is aerial combat. All combat in higher ground or in the air is his job. Faust's is our intelligence faction. And I am in charge of ground combat. Foot soldiers and such. Keeping that criteria in mind we have to choose our warriors," Drek explained.

"But I thought I was going to inherit my father's?"

"If you took the King's, who would protect him and your Consort mothers once you take the throne and they leave the palace?"

"That makes sense."

Drek smiled then turned his attention back to the forms. Killian gazed at the pictures with him, scanning their background details.

"It's just a little annoying that out of twenty applicants, only six have any real training." Frustration seemed to leak into his voice. Killian stroked his arm softly, placing a gentle kiss to his stubbled jaw. Drek stopped, lowering the papers in his hand before turning to the prince and kissing him on the lips. Killian's hands flew to his jaw, lightly gripping it as their kiss intensified. His arm came around, trapping the prince against the back of the chair, pinning him down with his massive body. Killian moaned a little as Drek fell between his legs.

Drek and Killian... hadn't done anything intimate since the time of the Ranking Ceremony despite the immense desire to.

Everything now seemed...brand new. Like this was the first time. And he supposed it was considering how very...cold their last coupling was.

Drek's body was hard, roped with thick bulging muscles, much bigger than Killian's other lovers. Bigger than he was used to. He couldn't stop touching them, caressing them, admiring them. Him. He was gorgeous. This was a male who deserved to be worshipped. It made Killian wonder...about his friend. The one who died for him.

Had he realized this? Had he known what kind of male Drek was? How did he see him? How did he treat him? Had he known that Drek was too precious to let go? Did he know how special he was? Just as Drek prepared to enter Killian, the prince cupped his cheek.

"What was his name?"

Drek paused, looking confused.

"What?" he asked a little breathlessly.

"Your friend. The one with curly gray hair...what was his name?"

The skin around his eyes pulled tight as his expression hardened. He pulled away from the prince. Killian waited patiently for an answer.

"Marsh...Marsh Landal."

Marsh.

Killian could see that smiling face in his mind again.

"Would he have...liked me?" he asked.

Drek didn't look at him, but he laughed once, then smiled to himself softly.

"He...would have loved you. Probably would have stole you from me." Drek looked at Killian then, eyes glistening with unshed tears. "And you would have loved him too."

After a brief silence, Drek cleared his throat and then stood.

"I have to go turn these in. Zev and Rem should be back soon." And with that he gathered his papers and left.

Killian looked down and his soiled bottoms and sighed. Maybe he should have asked him after they had sex.

Groaning, Killian peeled off his soiled bottoms until only wore a thin silk top that barely covered his lower parts. Grabbing a towel from the closet, he laid it out on the bed before climbing on top of it. He could take care of this himself. Of course, he just lost out on a feeding but there would be other opportunities for that tonight. Right now, if he didn't find any release, he was going to explode and not in a good way.

Spreading out on the towels splayed against the silk of the sheets, he splayed his legs and reached down with shaky hands to gently touch the bare skin between his legs. His member was stiff and sensitive. Killian found himself lightly stroking it as he would with one of his Consorts. The sensation was incredible.

He groaned a little, when his hand tightened and his grip became a little more intentional. He felt around the length, licking his lips as he imagined his Consorts touching him. Licking him.

His hips rolled off the bed and slick filled his entrance. The tip of his tongue swiped at his bottom lip as he squeezed his length, rubbing a steady rhythm.

"More," he whispered lightly, not speaking to anyone in particular.

His legs spread even wider as his back arched off the bed. With one hand stroking his length, the other snaked up his stomach, underneath the shirt, until he reached his budding nipples. His Consorts could get enough of them and when they touched them, licked them, bit them, sucked on them, it felt wonderful. When Killian did it, it only hurt. What were they doing different? Was it because it was them? Or was he just not doing it right?

He tried to brush over them softly the way Faust and Caspian always did. It ached a little but did nothing to soothe his overheating body. He pinched them the way Zev did, flinching when the pain struck him. Flicking them hurt even worse, which meant he wasn't doing it the way Drek would. Biting them was out of question. Killian couldn't reach them with his mouth like Rem could.

Now they hurt, sore hardened peaks. Killian groaned again loudly, half in frustration, the other half in pleasure. He shoved his hands lower and felt around his wet hole, stroking it the way his lovers would. Gods above it felt amazing.

Soft moans escaped his lips when he pressed against the puckered flesh. His fingers were soaked but he didn't care. He just needed to reach that sweet release. He tried to push a finger in, but the position was making it too difficult to reach. A hiss of aggravation left him and he ripped his shirt off then pushed himself on all fours, burying his shoulders and face into the pillows as he reached behind him to his raised bottom and spread legs, pushing his fingers inside.

Goodness it felt fantastic, but it was still lacking.

The burning, the clenching, the lust continued to build until it was damn near unbearable. Yet no matter how hard he tried, he couldn't get release. Tears started to burn in his eyes as he clenched his teeth and shoved his fingers in deeper and faster. Trying so hard to climax.

"Damn it!" Killian hissed.

It wasn't enough. Why wasn't it enough?

The door opened and voices flooded into the room.

"I'm worried about Faust. He's still being distant and I heard him throwing up earlier. Caspian said he was still getting those headaches."

"We cannot push if it is unwelcome--"

The voices stopped abruptly. Killian watched as Zev and Rem stared at him with open mouths and shocked expressions. Well, Zev looked shocked. Rem's face was as unreadable as always. Killian sobbed with exasperation.

"I cannot make it go away," he cried to them.

They didn't say anything, didn't move a muscle.

"Help me!" the prince growled, a tear finally escaping.

Rem was the first to move, quickly appearing beside him on the bed. He grabbed Killian's hips and turned him over, pulling him onto his lap, and placing his lips on the prince's. Killian kissed him with everything he had, like he was starving. And he supposed he was. The prince's hands flew into his hair, gripping it firmly at the roots, tugging him closer until lips were smashed together painfully.

"Please, please, please," Killian begged between kisses.

His breath was hot, blowing on Rem's skin, but Killian knew he liked it.

Then Zev was there, dipping between his legs, taking his member into his mouth in one huge swoop. Killian choked into Rem's mouth but the dark male only plunged his tongue in deeper. Zev released Killian with a wet 'pop' before kissing his way lower, a place he knew he loved. Eager whimpers left Killian's lips and his hips kept jerking forward. Zev held his hips down but placed his legs over his shoulders while he feasted. So good, it felt so good. But Killian wanted more.

Rem kissed his way down the prince's neck, sucking on his skin and leaving bruises in his wake. When he reached Killian nipples, he gently tugged on them with his teeth. The prince cried out, digging his nails into his shoulders, tossing his head back and screwing his eyes shut.

Yes.

Yes!

This was exactly what he needed.

Make him moan.

Make him beg.

Gods he needed this.

He needed them.

"More," Killian whispered.

Zev pulled up for air, face glistening with Killian's fluids.

His eyes met Rem's and then he licked his lips slowly. They shared that look for a moment longer before those blue eyes slid to Killian. His chest was heaving but Killian didn't care. He met that gaze. Zev leaned forward and kissed him, letting him taste the sickly sweetness of his essence on his lips. Letting him taste his slick.

When his lips were shining with it too, Killian pulled away and tipped his head back, kissing Rem so he too could have a taste. Rem groaned low and deep in his chest. His magix flared and his skin began to glow. Killian leaned back against his chest, still breathing heavy, his head resting in the crook of his neck. Killian fixed his attention on Zev before lifting his hips in an eager offering.

"More."

Zev's expression was purely predatory as he took Killian in. Rem nibbled on his neck while Zev lifted the prince's hips and positioned himself at his entrance. Killian hadn't even noticed that both he and Rem were nude. He didn't remember them taking off their clothing and he didn't care. They were naked and that was the only thing that mattered.

When Zev finally pushed inside, a high pitched squeal of pleasure left Killian. Rem stole the sound from his mouth as he rushed to kiss him, pushing his tongue inside, swiping the roof of his mouth. Zev started a slow thrust. Rem had leaned them back against the headboard giving Zev a place to brace his weight. And though there was an abundance of sensations clawing at him from all angles, he wanted to feel more.

Reaching behind himself, the prince searched for Rem's member and gripped it in his hand. Rem moaned at the contact, even more so when he began stroking it to the rhythm of Zev's thrusts. Zev was grunting in time with them. Killian tried to touch his cheek with his free hand but it wouldn't move from being lodged in Rem's hair.

Rem's tongue caressed Killian's and it only made the burning in him increase. He released Rem from his grasp and placed a hand on Zev's chest in a command to stop. He pulled out immediately and Killian whimpered at the loss. The prince pushed Zev down on his back, bracing a knee on either side of his hips and wiggling it in front of Rem as an offering. It didn't take much for Rem to fill Zev's place while Killian planted his lips onto his second ranked. Zev responded with just as much fervor, raising his hips as Killian reached down to stroke him.

Rem was lovely, rolling his hips against him, thrusting in a fluid motion. Killian groaned against Zev, snapping his hips back to meet every thrust.

And yet, despite it all, it wasn't enough.

Faster.

Harder.

Deeper.

Rougher.

No matter what, Killian still couldn't reach that peak. He was feeding from them both freely, drinking them in heavily until he thought he might burst and yet...no release.

They continued to switch positions and Killian continued to switch between partners. While they found release several times, Killian had yet to climax once. And it was starting to hurt. His entrance clenched and unclenched as if were screaming. It too was begging to be freed from this insatiable lust. Their bodies were slick with sweat and other fluids. All of them were breathing heavily, trying to slow their racing hearts and catch their breath. Tears stung Killian's eyes yet again.

"It is still not enough. I need more," he told them.

"I do not know how much more we can give you," Rem admitted.

But they tried again and again until all three were exhausted and the fire within Killian died when his final embers of energy ran out.

Before they could succumb to total slumber, the group managed to wrangle themselves out of the bed, detangling themselves from the sweaty rumpled sheets to call for servants to change them. They took a bath together, washing each other with a brisk efficiency that gave Killian's *Haise* no room to appear again.

After practically begging Rem, the dark Incubus allowed Killian to go for a walk around the wing as long as his two Succubae guards remained with him while he and Zev went over some important documents about their factions.

The prince moved slow down the hall, still feeling exhausted but needing to stretch his legs, he was happy to get out of the room. Nearing a corner, he heard voices.

Killian paused, then slowly crept closer to the corner to eavesdrop.

"Has he caught on?" a voice whispered.

That was Marza.

"No, of course not, he's an idiot."

And that was Filo.

"You're doing it too much, he's going to pick up on it eventually, then he'll know it was you," Marza warned.

No doubt they were talking about Killian...

Filo snorted, "Hardly. And even if he did find out it was me, he's not going to do anything about it. He's too much of a sniveling little welp."

There was a bit of mumbled whispers that Killian couldn't hope to decipher. When he realized he wasn't going to get any more details, he stepped out.

"I hope you are not talking about me," he said.

Marza glared, but Filo only smiled. Not answering right away he sashayed toward the prince. Then he leaned close to his ear, until he could nearly feel those bow shaped lips slide against his skin.

"Wouldn't dream of it, cousin dearest."

He continued down the hall and Marza followed right after him, glaring at Killian the whole time. Killian started toward them long after they disappeared. He was behind the nightmares...Killian just knew it. But how? He had no other abilities than telekinesis, as all Incubi and Succubae do. Killian knew it though. He knew he was up to something. He'd have to stay sharp if he didn't want to fall prey to another one of Filo's schemes. No. Not when he had his babies on the line, and his men.

Killian turned down a series of halls until he reached a room he wasn't necessarily searching for, but was happy he stumbled across. Killian knocked on it twice before it opened. Titus was already smiling before he saw him. When he realized who it was, he bowed. "My Prince."

His silver hair was tied up neatly in a low ponytail. His white eyes were bright again, and he looked well rested. Much different from the last time Killian saw him.

"Titus, you look well. May I come in?"

"Yes, of course," he replied, then stepped aside to let the prince in.

Orion was sitting up in bed with a thin white robe on, his hands splayed on his slightly raised stomach. His red curls were a mess on his head and his bronze skin seemed even brighter. He was smiling when he looked up at Killian. Bowing his head he greeted him, "My Prince."

Titus crawled across the bed and kissed Orion on the cheek, then his belly. Orion blushed and giggled.

Killian sat on his other side.

"How are you feeling?"

"Aside from the constant morning sickness, I feel great." He looked over at Titus before adding, "Happy."

"And how have the visits been with my brother?"

Orion frowned slightly before quickly hiding it with a fake smile. He wasn't nearly as skilled as he might have hoped, which made it very easy to spot the insincerity.

"It's been great," he said.

Killian gave him a dry look, "Honesty."

Orion's frown returned.

"Cold," he said sadly. "Very cold."

Killian sighed, running his fingers through his hair.

"Give him time. He is a sweet and caring boy, but he is still a boy. Only seventeen. And at that age, he is prone to tantrums. Being forced into manhood is a great shock."

Orion nodded, "I just hope we can all be happy. We can be one big family." The prince brushed a stray curl behind his ear and gently cupped his warm cheek.

"We will be," Killian promised.

Dropping his hand, he looked over to Titus. "You will be assigned to my personal guard, it will give you a reason to remain in the castle without any suspicion. You will work under Drek."

Titus gave a sharp nod.

Then he turned to Orion. "Your sister, you said she was well versed in swordsmanship?"

Orion nodded.

"Has she had formal training?"

"Only the best. Both of us did," he replied.

"Alright, that was all I needed. Be well." he made his exit and headed to the library, but not before sending one of the servants to go fetch Lisa and have her meet him there.

Of course she was already there before he arrived, fixing her glasses with her parchment in hand.

"You sent for me?" she asked after a curtsy. It was so strange for her to be so obedient. Killian was used to being yelled at by her for his 'un-princely' behavior.

"Yes, please send for Jo Warris from Rhettick. She is to be assigned to my personal guard after inspection from Drek. Also have a fund set up for the Warris family."

Lisa didn't ask any questions, just nodded with a "Yes, Your Highness."

When she left, Killian went rummaging through the books in the library, looking for anything on magix. He shouldn't have been surprised when he found Faust, surrounded by tall stacks of books, sitting in a small corner in the back of the aisles. He didn't notice Killian was there, seeming engrossed completely.

Killian watched him as he took a sip from his tea. As soon as his throat bobbed, swallowing the liquid, he saw his eyes unfocus. Then suddenly, he was back to normal. Killian glanced at the cup, trying to see what was inside but couldn't with this distance.

He was drinking tea, right?

Killian drifted closer.

"Going for a stroll?" Faust asked without looking up from his book. Killian should've known he'd pick up on his presence. He was almost as good as Rem with that.

Killian stepped out from behind the shelves and stood before him, then kneeled. Killian glanced at his cup swiftly. It was a brown liquid...that looked like tea and was steaming like tea...but.

"What are you drinking?"

"Black Tea," he answered, still not looking up from his book.

Killian brushed his fingertips over Faust's long legs, clad in tan cotton pants tucked into high brown boots. His exploration continued up his chest, covered with a loose cream tunic unlaced at the neck exposing his impossibly white skin on his muscled chest. Killian caressed his neck all the way up to his jaw until those pitch black eyes were staring directly at him. Killian met his gaze.

"I know what you are doing," he said simply. He lowered the book in his hand and touched the prince's hand that was still resting on his face. "I am fine."

"You do not look fine. Zev said you have been throwing up."

Faust looked a little guilty then. "I will admit, my stomach has not been so kind to me lately, but I feel fine, truly. I am taking precautions in the event that I am catching a cold. And it warms me that you all care so much, especially you, Killian. But I promise you that it is nothing to worry about, nothing that I cannot handle on my own. I wish not to worry you or anyone else, not when there is so much more that needs your immediate attention."

Killian frowned. "You will tell me if it grows worse?" he asked.

Faust nodded.

"Promise me," he commanded.

Faust smiled softly, "I promise."

Letting out a breath, Killian leaned forward and kissed him lightly, then sat back. Looking at all the books surrounding them, he noticed that they were all related to Nymph and Kappa history.

"Have you found anything out?" I asked.

Faust nodded absently, looking down at a few notes he had written with a frown before darting his gaze back to the text in front of him. "Quite a few centuries ago, there was a legend about altering genetics. As you well know, the percentage of power one is allotted is very loosely based off of familial genetics. Despite having two parents with high levels of power, their offspring could have very low levels of power. Back then, the Nymphs had discovered that they could increase power levels by eating the hearts of Kappas. But not just any Kappas. They had to show signs of having a specific gene. And a sign of them having that gene was if they were hemophilic. If a Nymph ate the heart of a hemophilic Kappa then their power level would increase to match an Incubus. Of course, with that revelation came the ban on the act so as to keep Incubi and Succubae at the top of the food chain. Thus making genetic alterations in that manner, illegal. Punishable by death."

"So you think the Nymphs are starting up the practice again?"

Faust pursed his lips then said, "It is a strong possibility, but I am too unsure to make that definite conclusion. I am trying to figure out if that practice is limited only to Nymphs or if it can affect other species as well. If it can, then we have a much bigger problem on our hands."

It would seem so. Killian squeezed Faust's knee.

"If you find anything else out about it let me know," Killian told him standing.

"Of course."

"And if your symptoms persist or get worse, you will tell me as well."

Faust chuckled but agreed.

Killian left him to it. But not before glancing at him one more time. He looked so tired and worn out. Killian really hoped he was right and that there is nothing to worry about. He'd keep an eye on him. Just one more thing to add on his plate.

The next few weeks were hard.

After a checkup with Lorn in regards to the whole issue Killian was having with release, they had come to the conclusion that it was because he wasn't feeding as frequently as he should be. And with that came the instruction to feed off two of his Consorts twice a day. Of course, his Consorts had no qualms with that.

Faust, on the other hand, had to be left out of the equation. He still wasn't feeling well, and it wasn't helping that he was nearly working himself to death. Killian tried to get him to go to the medical wing but he's dodged every attempt. He even tried to send doctors to him but he dodged them as well. It was as worrying as it was infuriating.

And he still wasn't any closer to figuring out if the practice of eating Kappa hearts could increase the power level of creatures other than Nymphs.

Orion's sister arrived and she was the spitting image of him. Just in a smaller, feminine package. Their personalities were completely different. While Orion was very mild mannered and shy, Jo was incredibly outgoing and excited. She was like a ball of energy. Drek took a liking to her immediately and accepted her into his ranks along with Titus.

Orion was going through his pregnancy without a hitch. His morning sickness was much milder than Killian's. And his baby was growing at a healthy rate. He genuinely seemed happy. Which was good, it made Killian happy.

As for his own pregnancy, Killian was starting to show...a lot. There was no doubt that he was carrying twins. His stomach had swelled, protruding at least four inches more than normal. The extra weight was hard to deal with and Ethel had to make a completely new wardrobe for him.

Speaking of Ethel, facing her after what he did to Kara...was hard. As soon as he saw her, he started sobbing, begging her for forgiveness. Kara was like a little sister to her. She was family to them both. And he killed her.

"Hush child, it's all right. I do not blame you," she had said to him, pulling him into her arms and stroking his hair like she used to when he was young.

And after that, his emotions were a wreck.

His Consorts had been walking around on eggshells because they weren't sure what would set Killian off.

Sleeping sucked.

He had to pee so much, there was never enough time for him to actually close his eyes. And the vomiting only got worse.

"How are you feeling?" Drek whispered, voice husky from sleep. He brushed Killian's hair back from his sweaty forehead.

Killian groaned, feeling nausea twist in his gut. He rubbed small circles over his stomach hoping to soothe it but to no avail.

"Bucket," Killian rasped, then threw up right when Zev handed it to him.

Caspian was there with a warm and wet cloth, wiping his mouth while Drek disposed of the bucket.

"I wonder why Orion isn't getting it this bad?" Caspian wondered aloud.

"Orion is not having twins," Killian said.

"Hearing that still blows my mind. But it definitely explains why your stomach is so much bigger than his."

Killian hissed at him.

Caspian raised his hands in surrender.

"Are you hungry?" Drek asked Killian when he came back, sitting on the bed.

"I do not think I can keep anything down right now."

"And what about your other hungers?"

"I am fine on that end too."

Drek and Caspian had done a good job in keeping him sated in that department.

"Help me get dressed? I have a meeting with my parents."

Drek pulled one of his arms around his neck and placed his arm around Killian's waist, helping him slide to the edge of the bed then supporting his weight as he stood. Caspian was already grabbing him some clothes, helping him slide his feet through the holes of his undergarments. Then helped him into the loose fitting pants and stretchy thin sleeveless top. Drek braided his hair and put a crown on his head.

Killian stopped into the bathroom to freshen up before taking his leave. Caspian offered his arm to lean on as they walked. Drek stayed close to his other side.

The King and Queen were in the tea room, sitting around a white circular table with white high back chairs, decorated with floral design. Plants of all types sprouted around the room and the ceiling was completely made of glass, allowing the sun to shine through.

Caspian helped Killian into a chair across from his parents then joined Drek as they stood by the door, taking up Guard duty, despite there being six other Guards around them. Queen Jessa was smiling at him.

"Killian my sweet, how are you feeling?" she asked sweetly. Her red eyes glistening with happiness. The look on her face was pure joy.

"Absolutely sick to my stomach. I do not know how you did it," Killian complained with a sigh.

"I would say it gets better but...you are going to be experiencing it all throughout your pregnancy so it's unlikely that it will get better."

Killian sighed again.

"Just think of the life you are bringing into this world! It's a wonderful thing. Once you hold them in your arms, hear their little cries..." his mother started to trail off getting a glassy look in her eyes. Then her eyes began to water and next thing you know, she was sobbing. Happy tears thankfully.

"Oh I can remember the moment you opened your eyes, staring at me so preciously. The way you held onto my finger as tight as you could. Your chubby little cheeks and tiny baby feet!"

She was off in her own world. Father was smiling at her fondly. Then he looked to Killian.

"I remember when you took one look at me and started wailing. I was offended," Father said with a laugh.

"Hun, you were blubbering all over the poor child, anybody would start wailing if they had snot dripping all over them," Mother tsked.

Killian laughed a little.

"He's probably going to cry all over your children too once they are born. Best to keep your distance," his mother joked.

Father pouted. "I'll just do it when everyone is asleep."

"Father, that is creepy," Killian chuckled.

Father only grinned.

"Have some tea, it was a gift from your cousins," Mother said, gesturing to the steaming teapot. Just the thought of it made him nauseous, regardless that it was from those demons.

"No thank you. My stomach is already in disagreement with me, I don't want to aggravate it any more."

Killian watched his mother carefully as she took a sip, seeing if her eyes unfocused like Faust's had. But they didn't. She behaved normally. Killian glanced at her cup and saw the liquid; green. Hm...different. Maybe it was a different tea or maybe it wasn't the tea at all and he was overanalyzing things? Or it could be entirely different reason that he just wasn't picking up on it.

The rest of the visit was spent pleasantly reminiscing until they began to lecture the prince on his use of his powers. Being pregnant made his use of his powers unpredictable and unstable which could have negative effects on the womb. They both warned to stop using his powers completely until he had given birth.

"I will try," Killian said.

"Trying isn't good enough, Killian. Not with twins," his mother said softly.

Killian winced, then nodded. His father jerked his chin in the direction behind him. Immediately, two tall beings flanked Killian's chair. Hands clasped behind them with blank expressions on their faces.

Caspian and Drek.

"Make sure he doesn't use his powers. It's dangerous for him and for the twins," the King told them.

They gave a sharp nod. Not sure how they were going to stop Killian, it was something that only he could control, but he supposed they could serve as a reminder of the dangers any time that he lost control. He guessed that meant he would have to stay away from his brother. Just the thought of that made him sad. Stay away from his baby brother? His little Pierce?

Killian couldn't.

Control your anger, Killian. It shouldn't be that hard and this should not be that big of a deal. Get over it.

Killian took a deep breath, filling his lungs until his chest was tight before releasing it. Drek offered a hand and he took it gratefully. Drek grabbed his waist, supporting most of Killian's weight. He sagged against him once he got to his feet. Drek kissed his temple before all three of them bowed to Killian's parents then left.

"I have been using them a lot," Killian said to them as they walked in silence.

"We won't let you use them anymore," Caspian promised.

"How are you going to do that?"

"You only use them when you're upset. And we have a secret weapon for that."

Killian's brows furrowed.

"What weapon?"

"Rem," they said in unison.

Killian rolled his eyes.

"Sometimes Rem might be the cause of the frustration," he muttered.

They both snorted, covering their laughter.

Killian frowned.

"What?"

"You couldn't be mad at Rem even if you tried," Caspian laughed.

Killian pouted.

"That is not true! He has infuriated me plenty of times!" he shouted in protest.

Caspian and Drek shared a look before bursting out in full blown laughter.

"Yeah right," Caspian chuckled.

They laughed at him the entire way back to the room. And speak of the devil, Rem was there. Sitting on the bed, looking through a pile of papers. His hair was unbound and wild around his broad shoulders. He was dressed in a white tunic with the top laces undone and black pants that looked absolutely delectable against his onyx skin.

Killian rushed to him, pressing his lips to his Consort's, brushing aside his papers so he could slide into his lap. Killian hands tangled into Rem's hair and his shoulders raised with the tenderness of the kiss.

Rem's hands slid to Killian's hips to make sure he didn't fall, then pulled back to stare at him. He had the very faint smile on his lips. The kind that you really had to search for, as there was a very tiny uptilt to the corners of his mouth.

Caspian and Drek were laughing even louder behind him.

"Point proven," Caspian mused.

Rem didn't bother to acknowledge it. He was too busy focusing on Killian. His gaze slid from his eyes down to his stomach. Then the hands that wrapped around his hips now traveled to his swollen stomach. Rem caressed it softly...gently. That faint smile still there.

Killian swore he saw a flash of orange in those eyes amongst the many colors that made up those black depths.

Beast.

Not pushing forward but always there. Always watching.

It had him thinking...Beast should get used to all his Consorts, not just Caspian and Zev. In the occasion that he came out when they were around. And Killian needed to know...was there a way to summon Beast? Or did he only come out when he wanted?

Killian cupped Rem's cheek in his hand, but the Consort didn't tear his eyes away from the prince's stomach.

Turning to his two other Consorts, he called out to them, "Where are Faust and Zev?"

"Faust is in the library and Zev is in the sparring room," Drek replied.

"Go get them."

Drek nodded and disappeared.

Caspian took a seat on one of the lounge couches.

Killian turned back to Rem. He was staring at him, suspicious.

Very suspicious.

Killian kissed him again, pushing himself closer to him. Molding as much of his body as he could to his and wrapping his arms around his neck. Caspian whistled from behind them.

"Yay, a free show!"

Killian wanted to laugh but his mouth was preoccupied. He only stopped to break their kiss when the door opened again.

Zev was first to walk in. His hair tied up in a messy ponytail and his chest bare. His blue skin glistened with sweat from a fresh work out and his muscular legs looked incredible in those navy blue leathers tucked into tall silver boots.

Faust followed him and Killian jumped up in concern. He looked sleep deprived and sick. His white skin was gray, his hair was messy with white strands everywhere, nothing like it usual smooth and silky state. There were dark bags under his eyes and his lips were thinned. He was dressed in a loose white tunic and gray cotton pants with black leather boots.

"Faust," Killian cried, rushing to him. He reached to touch his face but he stepped away from him.

"I'm fine," he said softly.

"You are not fine! Please! Why will you not let a Healer look at you?"

"Sweetling,"he started gently, "I promised you that I would tell you if it got worse, it has not. I actually feel a little bit better than before. I just missed some sleep. That's all. I'll take a nap later."

"Promise?"

"Promise."

Killian tried to step toward him again and this time Faust let him. The prince reached up to stroke his face before kissing him on his dry lips. Stepping back, he looked at all of his Consorts. Drek closed the door and they stood in silence. They were waiting for Killian to say something. He cleared his throat.

"There is something all of you should know. Some of you already know but I thought it best if everyone were aware as to prevent any accidents from occurring. As you all know, Rem has magix. With magix he has another being inside him...a Beast. And now, our child has one. And as I carry our child, their Beast is within me as well. While our child's Beast is still underdeveloped, Rem's is not. And he is learning how to interact with others. He is developing."

Rem stood quickly.

"I do not like where you are going with this," he said lowly.

Killian ignored him.

"Beast needs more interaction with people, especially ones he should grow to trust in order to learn more. To understand."

"Killian, whatever it is that you are thinking--"

"I think you should all at least get to meet him. But I warn you, do not move and do not make a sound. He will want to assess you, let him."

"Killian do not--"

Killian turned to Rem and stared deep into his eyes, calling with his mind as well as his voice.

"Beast?"

Rem's face twisted.

"Killian do not do--"

"Beast, I would like to see you."

Rem's skin began to glow and the orange quickly bled into his eyes. His magix shining brightly through his tunic.

Killian didn't think it would work, just calling out to him, but he supposed he was very attuned to him. Beast cocked his head to the side, staring at the prince. His chest rumbled lowly.

"Hello Beast," Killian greeted then slowly and carefully approached him. He touched his cheek softly, rubbing his thumb back and forth. Beast's tongue darted out and licked

Killian's palm. It tickled. Killian laughed a little. Beast's eyes narrowed, his head tilting more before he licked him again. Killian laughed again. He grumbled a sound. Stepping close to him, Killian smiled.

Pointing to his lips with a single finger Killian said, "Kiss?"

He looked at Killian's lips then his eyes then back to his lips again. His head darted out fast and his mouth slanted over Killian's roughly. The prince squeezed his shoulders when he became too aggressive, digging his fingers into his skin. He pulled back and growled. Killian glared at him.

"Too rough. We talked about this. Rough is bad. No being rough."

Beast made a series of noises, growls and whines.

Killian shook his head. "No."

Beast pushed his face in Killian's hand like a pet craving affection. He rubbed his cheek all over his palm, whining. Killian pulled his head to his neck, forcing him to bend and stroked his hair.

"It is alright. I forgive you."

Killian pushed him back a little and looked at him as he straightened. Then he pointed to his lips again, "Kiss?"

Beast hesitated this time but descended. Still aggressive but much less. Killian pulled back, smiled and nodded. He practically preened at the praise. The prince was very aware of the Consorts behind them watching their every move and Killian was grateful that Beast's attention was wrapped up on him that he hadn't noticed them yet, but he would.

"Zev," Killian said, not looking away from Beast.

Zev was slow and quiet as he stepped into Beast's field of vision.

Beast's head snapped in his direction immediately. He shoved the prince behind him and Killian stumbled, catching himself on his back.

Zev didn't panic, just stared Beast down.

Beast growled.

Zev tilted his neck and Beast stopped, curiosity all over his face. Before he stepped close to Zev and gave a sniff. He seemed to recognize him then and stepped even closer, wrapping an arm around his waist. Zev grunted as he slammed against Beast but other than that, stayed silent, still offering his neck.

Beast sniffed his neck before running his nose along the skin. His nose skimmed Zev's jaw before he stared him directly in the eyes. Their faces were so close.

Beast leaned in until his lips were mere millimeters from Zev's. He paused. Then his tongue slipped out of his mouth and he slowly ran it across Zev's. Beast's hand caressed Zev's waist before he did it again. This time, Zev's lips parted, eyes drooping. When Beast went in for a third time, Zev's own tongue met his.

Killian didn't bother to hide his gasp of shock.

Beast's eyes darted over to him, but then back to Zev.

When he leaned in again, Killian thought he was going to kiss Zev, but instead, he ducked his head and planted his mouth on Zev's neck. He could hear him sucking on the skin for a moment before Zev winced.

"Ow!"

Beast was biting him.

"Beast!" Killian said sharply. "Stop it now!"

Beast released Zev, leaving a large bruise in the shape of teeth on his neck before growling at Killian. The prince kept his face stern, placing his hands on his hips, then shook his head. Beast understood that. He gave Zev one last lick before releasing him.

"Caspian," Killian said.

He heard him gulp but stepped up to Beast.

"You better not bite me cuz I'll bite back," Caspian hissed.

Beast snarled in his face and Caspian immediately shut up. Beast took a whiff of Caspian and grunted. Already satisfied with knowing who Caspian is, he dismissed him.

"Faust," Killian said.

Faust was slow to approach and Beast immediately raised on his haunches, snarling viciously. Faust tilted his neck like Zev had done, but Beast did not move closer. He was still growling.

"Beast," Killian said, touching his back.

Beast looked at him.

He walked past him to Faust and gave Faust a quick kiss.

Well...tried to at least. Beast yanked him back before he could.

"Beast," Killian warned sharply.

Beast stopped growling. He pulled his arm free then approached Faust again...this time, successfully giving him a kiss.

Killian looked to Beast as he did it, to show him that Faust was okay. Beast was looking on curiously. Then his eyes flashed, black trying to fight it's way back.

"Rem, no!" Killian commanded.

The flickering stopped. The prince breathed a sigh of relief. He focused on Beast and jerked his head toward Faust. Beast started sniffing him then licking his face. But this was different from the way he licked Zev. While that was all sexual tension, this was different. Like he was trying to clean wounds or something.

It worried him.

Faust let him do as he pleased before Killian finally called him off.

"Drek," Killian said finally.

Drek stepped forward. Tall and imposing.

Drek didn't mean to be intimidating, he just was. It was in his broad shoulders, towering frame, and rippling muscles, but it completely set Beast off. Beast lunged for him in an attack.

"Beast!" Killian screamed but he wasn't listening.

"Beast stop it!" He pleaded. His other Consorts made a move to step in but Killian jumped in ahead of them. Beast was too busy snarling trying to rip out Drek's throat with his teeth. Drek was having a very difficult time fending him off.

"Beast!" Killian screamed with every ounce of his being.

Beast's body jerked.

"Stop!"

Beast's movements halted.

"Get up."

Beast rose to his feet and off of Drek who rolled over coughing, rubbing his neck.

"Come here."

Beast walked over to him, sluggishly.

"Bring Rem back now."

Immediately, the orange faded from his eyes and black replaced it. Rem choked on a gasp, chest heaving. Then he spun on the prince quickly, glaring.

"Are you mad?" Rem screamed in rage.

Killian trembled in fear. He had never yelled at him like that before.

"How could you have done something so irresponsible? You put everyone here at risk!"

"Rem--"

"Did you not think of the consequences? He could have killed--"

"Rem!"

Rem stopped yelling.

"I thought they should meet him when planned instead of unexpectedly. I did not know he would attack Drek," Killian told him, his tone apologetic.

"Yes, but I did! And I was trying to warn you but you shut me out!"

Killian frowned guiltily. "I was not thinking properly."

"And that is precisely the problem. You do not think, you act."

Rem growled in frustration before disappearing in a huff of smoke.

Tears pricked Killian's eyes and he tried not to let them fall but they did anyway. His shoulders shook as he started to sob. Warm arms came around him.

"It's okay, Kill. You know how he gets. He's just trying to keep you safe. Give him some time," Caspian said softly in his ear.

"He is always mad at me. I keep messing up. I mess everything up!"

"No you don't. Why don't you lay down? All this excitement can't be good for you or the twins."

He led Killian to the bed and Killian watched through blurry eyes as Drek got to his feet, still rubbing his throat.

"Why am I always the one getting the shitty deal?" Drek groaned.

"Maybe Beast felt threatened by your size? You are considerably larger than the rest of us," Faust suggested.

Drek rolled his eyes.

Faust came to lay next to Killian on his other side, wiping away his tears while Caspian cradled him from behind.

"In due time, everything will be fine, sweetling," he whispered.

Though his words were meant to be reassuring, Killian had the feeling it would not be that simple.

Chapter
19

It was sometime in the evening when the prince awoke again. The dimming lights dancing on the lower edges of the room, seeping in from the partially opened curtains. Though autumn was fast approaching, he could still feel the summer heat fighting to hang on, hugging the room with it's warm embrace, almost smothering. The two bodies wrapped around him weren't helping.

Their warmth left his body soaked with sweat, leashing their skin together under the cover of the thin red sheets on the bed. The steady breath on his neck was evenly paced but fast enough to alert him of the person's consciousness. The breath on his face, warm and sweet was slower, deeper. Fast asleep.

White locks of hair had plastered itself onto Killian's face, smelling of herbal tea and honeysuckles. Wet with sweat but soft as silk. A long, lean muscled arm loosely wrapped around his waist and a tail twisted with his own. Killian took in the sight of one sleeping lover.

Faust.

In such a deep slumber, he did not stir when Killian sat up in bed. Not even when he slid his arm from his waist. He was so far gone, he probably wouldn't wake up no matter how much noise they made. It was perfect. Staring at the heavy bags under his eyes, the thinness in his lips, the absolute exhaustion on his face even as he rested, Killian made a decision.

"Caspian," he whispered.

Caspian rose behind him, sitting up in bed, placing a hand on his shoulder and his lips to his neck.

"Go get a Healer. And Drek."

Without another word, Caspian was out the door, silent as a cat.

Killian waited patiently, his eyes never leaving Faust, until Caspian returned with Gestina and Drek. Caspian was murmuring to her quietly, explaining Fausts' symptoms.

She approached with her medical bag, dark brown leather, worn with age. It was heavy looking, stuffed to its fullest capacity until the fabric stretched and protruded in odd angles. It even had that sterile smell that seemed to fill the air in the medical wing.

"Caspian, Drek, hold him down. I do not want him escaping this time or using that pretty tongue of his to charm his way out."

Each Consort took an arm and Faust stirred slightly. Gestina began her check up, doing a physical examination, then a magical one. It was only when she drew blood, that Faust woke up. He was calm as he took in his surroundings. Then he looked at Killian and sighed in resignation. Gestina finished her tests and went back to the medical wing with her gathered data to come up with a conclusion.

As she left, Faust spoke in a soft gentle voice.

"You do not have to restrain me, I will not go anywhere."

Killian shook his head at Drek and Caspian, commanding them to keep him held down. Faust took a deep breath and laid there patiently. He didn't fuss, didn't argue, didn't do anything. Just laid there. When Gestina finally came back, her expression was blank.

"Well?" Killian said.

"He is...fine. Better than fine actually. He is incredibly healthy. He passed every test with flying colors. There is nothing wrong with him."

Killian hissed at her. "Look at him. He is not fine!"

"I could not find anything wrong with his health. Perhaps it is lack of rest causing his symptoms, but there is nothing else. Not even a common cold."

Killian snarled at her.

Drek dismissed her before Killian could give her a piece of his mind, then released Faust. Caspian did the same.

"I know that you are worried and it makes me happy that you feel concerned about my well being, but I would not lie to you, my dear Killian. I am fine. I do not feel sick. I do not know why I look the way I do, perhaps it is due to fatigue. And if that is the case, then I will make sure to get more rest so as not to worry you, but believe me, I am fine."

Killian heard him but was unsatisfied. There was no way he was fine. It didn't make sense, none of it was making any sense. He was sick.

Faust sat up, then brushed the prince's hair behind his ear. Faust's skin was warm caressing his cheek.

"Are you satisfied now?" he asked him softly, honestly.

No.

"Yes," Killian whispered.

Faust leaned in and kissed Killian with those dry thin lips. Lips that were not as they had been during the Ranking Ceremony. Lips that were no longer soft, full, passionate...alive.

He must be going crazy.

"I must have been mistaken," he told Faust.

"I do not look well. I understand."

They sat in silence before there was a knock on the door. Killian pulled the sheet up to cover any bare skin before nodding for someone to let them in. Drek called out to them allowing them to enter. It was Ian.

"Brother," Killian whispered with a quiet happiness.

"Hey Kill, I wanted to see you before I left."

"Left?" the prince asked with a furrowed brow.

His younger brother rubbed the back of his neck sheepishly. "Yeah, Gilra and I are going to visit a few people in Aideren. We'll be back soon, it's just...I know how you feel about our cousins and I thought that maybe this would help?"

Killian's brows crunched in confusion.

"How would your leaving help?"

"I sort of told Father that you suggested that they have a little fun and explore the further regions since they've been stuck in the palace this whole time and rarely leave Kerbis in general. And since you've been sick there is no telling when we will actually have the Ball. So..."

Killian smiled at his brother sweetly. He was so considerate.

"Thank you Ian."

Ian smiled back at him, then came forward to give him a hug.

"I'll be back in a few weeks. Feel better."

Killian nodded and watched him leave. When he did, a weight lifted off the prince's shoulders. He wouldn't have to see them for a few weeks. That was wonderful news.

He got out of bed and put on some real clothes. Loose red satin pants, with a gold vest and soft gold flats covered his body. It was comfortable enough for him to maneuver in and didn't make him feel too self conscious with his stomach.

"I am going to the lounge," he told his Consorts.

The lounge was for the private use of the Heir and his Consorts. No one would disturb them when they were in there unless it was an emergency. It wasn't a far walk, just a couple of halls away, but it took Killian a bit since he had to walk slowly. Didn't help that his stomach was cramping. He rubbed it through his tunic and hummed a soothing tune. Reaching the large oak door he raised his hand to the gold knob. And just as he was about to push it open, a voice floated down the hall to his ears.

It was angry...seething.

"How dare he! How dare he?" The voice was furious, sounding a bit deranged. Full of hate and bitterness. It raised bumps on his skin and had his heart hammering in his chest.

"Calm down brother," another voice tried to soothe.

"I'm going to break him. I'm going to shatter him into pieces! Just wait for it," the voice promised. "That's a promise."

Killian waited to hear more but the voices stopped and the steps trailed further away.

His heart was still pounding, breathing ragged but he could barely hear it over the pounding in his ears. That voice...Something about it was different, something about it was...wrong. Killian couldn't put a word to it, but the feeling it gave him...It was as if hearing the sound had flipped a switch in him and turned him into this quivering mess. The sound was demonic.

It was Filo, no doubt.

But it sounded...scary. Like a monster. It didn't sound like him.

Killian may dislike Filo but he did not fear him. He was nothing...no one to fear. Killian was stronger, more powerful. He was better in every way imaginable. And he was Heir. He had nothing to fear.

The prince took a deep shaky breath before pushing open the door finally, trying to clear his mind and rid his head of that frightening voice. Squeezing his eyes shut, he kept taking deep breaths until his breathing was somewhat normal. When he was able to gather himself, he opened his eyes again, taking in the large room before him.

It was huge with gold doric pillars lining the perimeter. In the far center along the wall was a long red velvet couch with plush pillows and gold gilding along the intricate floral armrests and legs. Sheer curtains draped around them with a black rope hanging from above, allowing one to close the curtains around the entire couch.

Off to the side were a few entertainment devices and a lounge area surrounding them. And the other side led off down a hall that Killian could not see where it led. Then near that was some more chairs and loveseats in the same fashion as the long couch with some towering bookshelves filled to the brim with books.

The chandeliers were incredible and the large bay windows allowed for the moonlight to shine in. There was even a balcony that overlooked a private garden with tall hedges so no one could see inside. This place had complete privacy.

Next to the balcony door was a large wooden armoire with gilded bronze and gold in lovely designs. Each door bore a full length mirror. Killian opened one of them, peering inside and seeing a bunch of clothes in his current size.

He smiled before closing the doors and wandering onto the balcony. The cool air was crisp and felt wonderful on his skin. The temperature had dropped considerably within the hora, no longer stuffy with that lasting summer haze. Instead, he could almost taste the falling leaves and autumn wind.

And within the walls of the garden hedges, he felt protected. Safe.

I'm going to break him.

The voice struck him like a knife to the chest. His stomach dropped and his breath quickened again into a wild pant.

I'm going to shatter him to pieces!

Go away. Go away.

Break him.

Stop!

Shatter him.

Stop it!

Killian gripped the sides of his head as if he could strangle the voice in his head. As if he could rid himself of it all and never let it reach him. Never let it touch him. And then the whispering started.

"Stop it! Stop it!" Killian screamed, shaking his head, crumbling to his knees. But as the whispering grew in volume, so did his voice.

That horrible voice.

Scary. Horrifying.

"Get out of my head! Get out!"

His vision started to blur and the panic increased. If he blacked out, he'd see that shadow again. He knew he would.

Please. Don't let him blackout. Please. Please. Please.

"Killian?"

His head snapped up at the voice. It was different from the one in his head. It broke through the haze of it all, sounding concerned but flat. That familiar monotone.

"Rem," Killian choked, looking up at his Consort who was standing in the doorway behind him. He was quick to scoop the prince in his arms, worry in those eyes even when he was supposed to be angry at him.

"What is wrong? Why were you screaming?"

"The voices," he whispered so quietly as if they would hear him and come back.

"Voices?"

Killian nodded before tucking his face in Rem's neck.

"What are the voices saying?" he asked.

Killian shook his head, not wanting to bring them back. He didn't want to hear the whispering and he didn't want to hear Filo. No...not Filo...that monster. He just wanted it all to stop. All of it was just too much.

Killian's fingers dug into Rem's biceps as his chest started to heave.

"Be calm, you are safe. You are safe Killian. I am right here and I will not let anything hurt you. You know that I am right here beside you and I always will be. There is nothing to fear," Rem murmured, lifting him into his arms.

Killian could feel him moving but he didn't dare raise his head from his neck, only squeezed Rem tighter until his muscles ached in protest, trembling from the strain. He finally stopped and the bottoms of the prince's feet brushed the soft velvet of the long couch.

Rem didn't stop his soft reassurances and hearing his voice calmed Killian down considerably. When his breathing finally regulated, Killian rested his head against his chest and listened to his and Beast's heartbeats. Loud and thundering, strong and unyielding.

"How do you feel?" he asked.

"Better," Killian whispered.

His hands drew circles on Killian's back...it felt nice. Until a familiar sensation curdled in Killian's stomach. He shoved Rem away and rushed off of his lap, trying to get further away but not making it as vomit bubbled up his throat and stained his clothes. Killian's throat burned as it pushed it out, and that rancid taste welded itself to his tongue. The smell was foul and only incited more nausea.

He could feel it roiling in his gut, pushing up again but he was rushed into a small bathroom before it could happen. Rem held his hair as he emptied what was left in his stomach into the toilet. As Killian finished, he helped peel off his dirty clothes, wash his mouth and a bit of his throat until he was clean once again.

Rem brought the nude Prince back into the room to the armoire, pulling out a sheer purple robe with lace trimming. He pulled it over and around Killian, fastened the belt, then brought him back to the couch, sitting the prince on his lap. They sat there in silence for a while, Killian curled up against Rem with his knees drawn up, sucking the warmth from his impressive body, feeling the imprints of his magix in his shoulder.

"You should be angry with me," Killian said finally breaking the silence.

Rem didn't reply.

"I apologize for not listening to you and forcing something against your will. I never wanted to be the person to do that. I just...wanted to help. I wanted to make sure that nothing bad happened again."

Rem was still quiet, but Killian didn't push for him to answer. He had done enough forcing.

Then finally, Rem said, "I understand why you did it. Your reasoning...makes sense. I am just worried about the unpredictable and I do not wish to endanger anyone any more than I already have. You may not view me as dangerous...but I am. And it worries me when you forget that."

"I know what you are capable of, Rem."

"No Killian...you do not. You have seen nothing of my power. You have not seen me in battle, you have not seen me succumb to my Beast. He may appear...yes, but it is different when I let him take control."

Let him?

"I do not understand," Killian admitted.

Rem has always fought Beast, suppressed him. Why would he let him take over? Killian simply could not imagine it.

"Have you not wondered why those with magix are not deployed for battle? Why there are none on the Royal or Astorian Army? Why we are not Warriors?"

The prince had assumed it was because of how rare they were.

"If one of us were to fight in battle, we would annihilate the opposing forces as well as our own. It only takes one of us to bring about that devastation. The risk if far too great and that is why is has not been risked. That is why we are kept in a remote community."

"It does not seem right."

"It is the only option. We are far too dangerous for mercy."

"Will I ever...see you in battle?" Killian asked softly, hesitantly.

"I hope not."

Killian stared at him for a while, studying his dark features, so calm and collected, revealing absolutely nothing.

It still confused him though. Why would the King let someone so dangerous enter to be his Consort? Even after Rem lost control so many times? And not to mention Jax slipped through the cracks.

"I want to visit your village," Killian said finally.

"No."

"Rem--"

"I say this with your safety in mind. There are children with magix who do not have the slightest control of their Beasts. If you are not raised knowing how to deal with it, you will end up as your attendant did when you lost control."

Killian flinched.

Rem's hand fell to his stomach.

"I will have to teach our children control so they are not dangerous to be around."

Killian covered Rem's hand with his own before sinking back into his chest, letting the sensation of Rem's hand caressing him overtake his mind.

Inhale. Exhale. Inhale. Exhale.

"You need to feed," Rem said softly.

"Mm."

Rem brushed Killian's hair from his neck and planted small kisses to his exposed skin. Killian squirmed on his lap, letting his lips part and eyes close. Rem's lips were soft, like little butterflies or fresh rose petals and smooth.

Killian's thighs spread a little, encouraging Rem's hands to reach between them and underneath his robe until he brushed his sensitive skin and brought about his slick. Just the thought actually had him wet. Searching for Rem's hand, Killian dragged his fingertips over Rem's knuckles before grasping his entire hand, pulling it down between his legs.

"Touch me here," Killian moaned.

Rem's hand grabbed his privates giving it a little squeeze before retracting it and dragging them up his thigh to stroke his inner knee.

"No," he said and Killian could hear a very faint hint of amusement.

He smiled.

"That's an order."

Rem's lips brushed Killian's ear.

"I do not feel like taking orders."

His low baritone had his body trembling. The sound rumbled his chest and had Killian's breath catching in his throat.

"You are disobeying your King," Killian breathed as Rem's hand dipped a little lower but not quite where he wanted it to be.

"You are not King yet, Killian."

He snorted. "I am to you."

"If that is the case, then I suppose I must comply."

"Damn right," he said cheekily.

Rem's hand found their way back between his legs and he wasted no time probing his entrance. Soft whimpers left Killian's throat as he fingered him with slow precision. The sounds were kind of embarrassing and Killian found himself blushing, wishing that Rem would just kiss him to smother the noise. But Rem liked hearing him moan. He once said that it was the most beautiful sound he had ever heard. And the thought of that made it even worse, his moans growing louder with each passing moment.

"No more teasing," Killian begged.

Rem pulled his fingers from inside him, bringing them up to his lips coated with his slick. His pink tongue darted out and licked his black fingertip. He groaned.

His own hands were shaking like crazy. Killian slid off his lap and reached over to free Rem from his pants. His member smacked against his muscled abdomen stiff and hard it was practically begging to be buried inside the prince.

Killian climbed back onto his lap and lined Rem up with his entrance. Rem let Killian do all the work, watching him with dark hooded eyes as he lowered himself onto his Consort.

Killian had gotten him about halfway in before the door opened.

Zev strolled in glistening with water. His wet hair was tied in a ponytail and his leather pants hung low on his hips showing all of that deliciously muscled blue skin. Killian thought he could even see the faint dusting of navy pubic hair peeking out from the waistband of his pants. His mouth watered.

Zev took one look at them before a slow smirk spread across his pouty lips. He sauntered over to the couch, before sitting right beside them. Killian choked on a moan as he slid all of Rem inside him, savoring the tugging pressure and light burn as he bottomed out.

"Zev," Killian breathed, trying to turn his head to him.

"Do not look upon him when it is I who is impaling you," Rem grunted, snapping his hips up. Killian yelped, clinging to him.

Zev's smirk widened.

Rem began thrusting and Killian could feel Zev leaning toward them. His breath hot on the prince's neck, close enough that he could smell his husky scent, feel his body warmth. Killian tilted his head but Rem gripped his jaw.

"No looking."

Killian whimpered and Rem pushed faster. His mouth was hanging open, drool slipping over his lips and down his chin. Then Zev's tongue swiped up his neck. His eyes fluttered. So good.

"You are not feeding, Killian," Rem whispered.

Killian tried to reach for his *Haise* and it should have been easy, but he was too distracted by the two males touching him.

Killian wanted to see Zev. He wanted to watch those teal eyes darkened with lust. Killian wanted to watch his eyes droop in pleasure. He wanted to see it all.

His hand reached out for Zev, making contact with his rippled abs, down to his leather covered groin where Killian could feel him hard and ready.

"Damn it Rem!" Killian squealed when he reached a particular spot inside him.

"What a dirty mouth," Zev whispered right into his ear. Then he said a little bit louder to Rem, "Do you hear this naughty Prince?"

"I do," Rem rumbled.

"That is...King...to you," Killian panted.

"Enough. You're not allowed to talk," Zev commanded, covering Killian's mouth with his hand.

Despite Rem's orders, Killian looked at him. Zev looked as dangerously handsome as ever. His eyes had darkened considerably, his lips were curved in a sadistic grin, and his face glowed with excitement.

But his eyes were not fixed on Killian. They were completely focused on Rem.

Rem met his gaze with just as much fervor. They stared at each other intensely as Rem filled Killian over and over again. The look between them was so hot and steamy, Killian was so aroused by it. Even more when Zev leaned in closer. They were so close that they breathed in each other's breath. Panting raggedly. Zev's eyelids lowered as did Rem's.

It was so passionate, so intense. Killian nearly lost it.

Then completely lost it when Zev tilted his head, eyes fluttering shut...and Rem's lips met his.

Rem was kissing Zev.

Voluntarily.

Killian watched his expert dark lips move over Zev's blue ones, slow and precise. Zev's chest was heaving as he palmed his own erection, simultaneously caressing Killian's.

Rem kissed Zev differently than Killian. He was very calm, collected. There was no untamed passion fighting to take over him. He was very much in control. But that didn't matter to Zev. Killian didn't even think he noticed.

When they finally broke apart, just a string of saliva breaking between them, they stared at each other. Then eerily turned to Killian at the same time. Zev was smirking at him, eyes mischievous. Even Rem's lip twitched.

"Did you enjoy the show, love?" Zev asked with a deep rumble, his eyes twinkling in amusement.

Killian must've been a sight. His body shaking, eyes wide, lips parted...swollen, eager to see more. Zev chuckled before leaning toward Rem again. Rem's tongue dipped past those full black lips and licked a small path across Zev's blue ones. That was Killian's undoing.

His climax hit hard and fast.

The shock of what he had just witnessed made the experience that much more powerful, his body trembled uncontrollably as the feeling ran through him. Slick wetness gushed out of his nether regions and the highest pitched moan left his quivering lips.

And he fed. He fed from them both for all that they could give him. Rem was fine, seeing as he had Beast and the endless supply of lust inside him. Zev on the other hand was a little light headed and dizzy. His head was tilted back on the couch and his eyes squeezed shut.

His body went nearly slack with the relief, still twitching occasionally with the aftershocks of his release.

"Full?" Rem murmured to him, brushing his lips along Killian's ear.

"Mm," he moaned softly, unable to form coherent phrases. His body--and mind for that matter--still a mess.

Zev groaned quietly, before blinking and sitting back up, his eyes still squinting with effort.

"Now that I am no longer distracted, I came here with a reason. I found some information on Beast. It could potentially help us in understanding him."

Rem tensed beneath Killian. The prince stroked his thigh in a reassuring, calming gesture.

"After going through some files," Zev continued. "I found a few Confidential ones. Thankfully with my new status as a Consort, I have access to them. They are all in the old language which I studied in my younger years, but it was still a bit difficult to translate. Even so, there were a couple of things that caught my attention. First, if an S-Level Incubus breeds with a Beast holder, their child will always hold a Beast and be an S-Level Incubus. So with that, I gathered that at least one of our kids will be male."

"Guess we should start picking out names," Killian mumbled.

Rem's hand found Killian's and gave it a squeeze. He squeezed back.

"Another thing I found out, which is particularly important is that if the Beast and Beast holder are connected in mind and body, the Beast holder will have access to several latent abilities. One of which includes compulsion. Of course, as we know already, some abilities appear even without that connection. Rem has demonstrated that. But I thought that compulsion in particular was interesting. Can you use compulsion?" Zev turned his attention to Rem.

"No," he said simply.

"See, that's what I thought. But I think that Killian can."

His eyes widened in surprise. "Me?"

"Why have you come to this conclusion?" Rem questioned.

"I noticed a few things the last time that Beast came out. Rem, you said that when you tried to resurface, when you sensed that Drek was in danger, that Killian shut you out. How was Killian able to do that? He does not have any sort of power that would allow him."

"That is not enough to sway me," Rem said gently.

"I figured. That wasn't it though. When Beast lost control, Killian ordered him to stop and to bring you back. At first glance, I would've have thought anything of it, but it was the way Killian ordered him and the way Beast reacted. He went slack immediately at the command and each movement afterwards was very sluggish, as if he were some sort of zombie. I think Killian compelled him."

Rem looked skeptical but Killian thought about it and it made a little bit of sense. That time had felt different.

"This information is not in any of our records back home. Why is it that you have found it here?" Rem questioned, voice dropping dangerously with underlying aggression.

"Well it was confidential files, so maybe to keep the information out of the wrong hands?" Zev suggested, sensing Rem's budding anger.

"What of the hands that are cursed? Are we not worthy of knowing our own genetics? Of understanding our burdens?"

"I do not know, Rem. But I do suspect the King knows and that is the reason he has allowed you to mate with Killian and be his Consort. He knew Killian would be able to control Beast."

Rem was seething.

"Maybe it was for your protection? Had this information gotten out, your village would have been raided and most likely those with Beasts would be forced to use their powers. Think of the children and how it would affect them."

Rem was quiet and did not reply, but he was not as angry as before.

Suddenly, Zev said, "Do you trust me?"

Killian frowned.

"Of course," he replied.

"Rem?" Zev asked.

"Yes."

"Good, because I want to let Beast out and see if I am right."

Rem growled, "Absolutely not."

"Rem, you and I both know that out of everyone, Beast will not harm Killian and I."

Rem didn't budge.

"Rem...do you trust me?" Zev repeated.

"I am beginning to believe that it is I that you do not trust."

"Rem!" Killian gasped. "Of course we trust you!"

Rem's jaw ticked. "I find that difficult to believe when every time I disagree with something regarding my beast, you never heed my warning. And then something always goes wrong. I have hurt you several times already Killian. I do not want to risk another."

"I am here to protect him," Zev said.

Rem laughed without amusement. "You cannot rival my beast."

"Rem--" Zev started again, slightly pissed with the insult to his strength even though they all knew it to be true. The only one who stood a chance was Caspian.

"Have you not thought about our children? It is not just Killian you are risking. It is the lives of our unborn children. The heirs. One wrong move Killian cannot just heal. One wrong move and they are dead. Think before you act upon such impulsivity."

"Please Rem. We won't let that happen. Just please let us try," Killian begged. Pure rage flashed in his eyes before his shoulders dipped in defeat.

"Nothing I say will stop you. You will not listen to me and you will call him regardless of what I say. Just do it. Do it and be done with it."

Killian didn't like his tone, didn't like his sagging shoulders, didn't like the utter defeat and betrayal in his eyes. But this was something they needed to do. If he was capable of controlling Beast, it would change everything.

"I am sorry," Killian whispered before commanding, "Beast, I would like to see you."

The change was quick when Rem did not fight it. So quick that it made the prince realize just how hard Rem fought to keep him under control. It was something he must suffer through day and night. An endless battle. He must be so tired of fighting.

Orange exploded in his eyes and the magix on his chest burned brightly.

Beast's head dipped toward Killian to kiss him. One of his less aggressive kisses. Killian smiled at him when they pulled away.

"Hello," Killian greeted.

He just blinked at him. Killian laughed.

And in that moment, he realized...he was still mounted on him. Rem had not pulled out even when he grew soft. And Beast...was easily distracted by sex. His member hardened up almost immediately and filled the prince once again.

Killian hissed, unprepared for it.

Beast's eyes narrowed with intent and a low growl rumbled from his chest. Killian looked at Zev with worry but he was focused on Beast, his expression inquisitive.

"Beast, no," Killian said trying to sound firm. He sounded calmer than he thought he would but his voice was still weak and shaky.

Beast doesn't respond to weakness.

He turned Killian over and shoved him down on the couch, face first into the cushion. Killian sputtered, trying to breath past the velvet but his hand was still gripping his head, keeping it in place. His rump was up in the air, knees spread, showing all that he could offer.

Beast growled again before shoving Killian's hips down, his stomach slammed into the couch and he cried out.

"Beast! Stop it! I am pregnant! I cannot do it this way!"

Beast roared and shoved him down harder.

He tried to wiggle his arm beneath him to relieve some of the pressure on his stomach, but he was held down so tightly, he wasn't able to manage it.

"Zev! Get him off! He is crushing my stomach!"

The Consorts

"Command him, Killian. Just like before," was Zev's only reply. He sounded calm and not at all worried. Did he seriously want to risk their babies?

"Beast! Stop!" Killian screamed.

But he was not listening. Instead, he pushed inside him forcefully, burying himself all the way to the hilt.

"Zev, please! He's not listening to me!" Panic lacing Killian's voice.

"You have to calm down Killian. Try to think of how you did it before when he was attacking Drek. You were panicked then too, but you kept your cool."

Killian screamed and fought but he could not get him off. He tried to make himself angry and summon all of the emotions he had before. He tried to think the same thoughts, but it wasn't working.

"Stop!"

Killian threw him off with his mind and his powers. Beast went flying across the room and slammed into the wall...hard. His body crumpled to the ground.

Killian watched him warily, breathing heavily. He was not unconscious, but he laid there, staring at him. His expression was docile...but...strange. Like he wasn't really there. Like a corpse.

"Come," Killian commanded.

He slowly staggered to his feet and walked over.

"Kneel."

He dropped to his knees before him.

Zev's mouth was open in surprise, his eyes wide.

Then he turned to Killian, with an incredulous smile. But as soon as his eyes fell upon Killian's face, the happiness turned to horror.

"Killian!" he grabbed at him, cupping his face and wiping under his nose.

The prince looked at him with confusion until his hand came away with blood. Killian gasped, bringing his own hands to his face and feeling the warm liquid spill from his nose.

"You are too far along in your pregnancy to be using your powers," Zev said sternly.

Killian glared at him. The nerve of him, to scold him when he could have helped.

"I had to get him off of me, he was crushing the babies."

"You should have compelled him, like I said to."

"It was not working! And I was not going to risk the lives of my heirs!"

"Look at him, Killian!" Zev shouted, pointing a finger in Beast's direction who still knelt, waiting for further instruction. "It already has worked!"

Killian backed away from Zev, betrayal in his eyes.

"I do not know why I listened to you. I should have listened to Rem, he only has my best interests in mind. My safety is always his priority."

Zev's face fell.

"Killian--"

Killian turned away from him sharply, focusing his attention on Beast who sat there through it all like an empty shell. It wasn't right to do this to him, to treat him like some feral animal. He shouldn't be forced against his will or treated like less than them. He was a person. He had rights. It wasn't fair.

Killian stroked Beast's face before leaning his forehead against his.

The prince whispered, "You don't deserve this."

Kissing him softly, before pulling back and saying, "Rem, come back."

The orange faded from his eyes and skin and Killian's heart ached as it went. Rem blinked, eyes darting around before zeroing in on the blood smeared across Killian's face.

"Killian," he breathed with worry. "What did it do to you?"

"Nothing, I am fine. It worked...sort of."

"What do you mean by 'sort of' and why do you bleed?"

"It is nothing."

Rem growled then whipped on Zev. "What happened?"

Zev's face was still crestfallen. He looked to Killian and reached out for him but the prince snarled at him. "Do not touch me!"

Rem watched the interaction anxiously.

"What did he do?" Rem asked, then turned to Zev, anger clear in his eyes. "What did you do?"

"It is nothing, Rem. Please, just drop it. Can you take me to Lorn? I want her to make sure the babies are alright."

Rem made a distressed noise in the back of his throat at the thought of something being wrong with the children and it being his fault. He stood, grabbing an opaque robe from the armoire and dressing Killian in it before scooping him up into his arms. Killian wrapped his arms around his neck and pressed his face into his chest.

"Killian, I'm sorry!" Zev said, but Killian ignored him.

Rem began to walk and Killian started thinking about Beast and how horrible it must of been to lose his will. To be controlled like a puppet. He pictured the blank look in his eyes. The vacancy. Hot tears spilled out of his eyes and he clutched Rem tighter.

"I am sorry. I am so sorry," he sobbed.

"Do not apologize," Rem said softly.

"No! I have to! I should not have done that, not to you or to him. I have been forcing both of you against your will. It is your body Rem! What right do I have to control it? I should have listened to you when you said no. Every time you said no. I promised you that your body was your own and I valued your consent, yet I have gone against my word. I have betrayed you time and time again! What right do I have to be your lover? I am horrible and selfish--"

"Stop," Rem said fiercely.

He stopped walking and pulled Killian back to look at his tear streaked face.

"I do not blame you for enforcing your will. Each time you have had valid reasons for doing so. You must understand, Killian, that in my village, those with magix have learned only to suppress. We do not embrace this curse as you have often made me do. We fear it. But if you have the power to control it, to eliminate the possibility of devastation, then I implore you to use that ability and maybe then, we will learn to coexist with our curse. Learn from it. You are helping me, Killian, I swear it."

Killian hid his face back in his chest and they walked the rest of the way to the medical wing in silence. When they got there, Titus, Pierce and Orion were just finishing up.

Orion was cramping a lot more than usual, so his attendant wanted to have Lorn look at him. Titus held him in his arms much like Rem was holding Killian.

Pierce glanced at Killian, saw the blood on his face. The young Lord's face twisted in worry, mouth opening to say something, before shutting and face hardening. Stubborn as always.

They left and Rem laid the prince on the examiner's table. Lorn took one look at Killian and frowned.

"You've been using your powers."

"Just once," Killian said. "It was important."

Lorn shook her head before getting a warm wet cloth and wiping his face clean of blood. She then continued her examination, making sure that everything was okay.

"You are fine. The babies--as I have been informed that you are having twins--are fine. Let's take a look at them shall we? It's been a while since your last ultrasound."

That last sentence was said with a hint of scolding.

She had been trying to get him to come for checkups for a while but he never got around to it, trying to avoid anyone seeing him lose control when the madness overtook him. Lorn would be able to sniff out immediately if he was troubled. And if she knew, then the King would know which is exactly what Killian was trying to avoid.

Suddenly the room filled with the sound of fluttering hearts. Three aside from his own. And on the screen he could see them. His precious twins, curled around each other. Killian smiled at the screen as Lorn brushed her glowing hand along his stomach, projecting an image of the twins at different angles.

"Can't tell the genders just yet, but come back in two more weeks and I should be able to."

Rem helped Killian off the table. The prince was unable to keep the wide grin off his face. Even Rem's lips quirked.

"You're in the beginning of your second trimester which is where you'll start to see a major growth spurt. It will cause a bit of pain and discomfort. Just a heads up."

Killian dipped his chin in acknowledgement before they took their leave.

Rem offered to carry him again, but he wanted to walk on his own. Though he did use his arm for support, leaning most of his weight on him.

"You should probably rest."

"I feel like that is all I do," Killian complained, though yawning against his will.

"You are pregnant, it is what you must do."

Killian didn't argue and just let him lead him back to the room.

Drek, Caspian, and Zev were sitting on the couch talking quietly while Faust was fast asleep in bed. Rem helped Killian ease in beside him and immediately Faust curled around the prince, arms around his waist, tugging him to his chest. Rem joined the other Consorts by the couch and Killian closed his eyes trying to rest.

Sleep was easy to achieve, but rest was much harder. He had a nightmare again. That same nightmare where he was in the bathroom, lying in the tub filled with blood, unable to move. But it was different this time.

He wasn't alone.

Rem sat in the tub across from him.

No.

Not Rem...

Beast.

He was leaning against the wall of it, arms propped along the ledge on either side. His head slightly tilted, expression blank...passive. But there was something off about him. Killian couldn't place my finger on it but his instincts were screaming at him. Danger. Danger. Danger.

Then suddenly...he could move. Though something told him not to.

Those eerie orange eyes watched him. Or they appeared to be watching him, but Killian couldn't even see a rise and fall of his chest.

Was he even alive?

Killian's lips parted and the beginnings of his name started to form, but the very moment his body even twitched, Beast's eyes zeroed in on the movement. Fast and sharp, and Killian knew that it was not wise to attempt it again.

He was alive. That was a relief...but he was not acting the way he normally would. There was something frightening about him.

Killian felt someone behind him. Their body was warm but it sent shivers down Killian's spine. The tiny hairs on his skin raised to attention. Killian was so afraid...wanting to look, wanting to move but knowing he couldn't. Because he was certain that Beast would attack him. He would attack and kill him. Killian felt scared and helpless.

And the whispering began, right in his ear.

Killian fought hard not to move, not to squirm away. Not to do anything because of the consequences that might ensue. The whispering grew louder and more guttural. He wanted to scream, every part of him already was, but he didn't.

Blood began to drip from his nose. He could feel it leaving hot trails in its wake. Then from his ears, his eyes, and dribbling from the corners of his mouth.

Killian held back the sobs he wanted to release.

You'll wake up Killian. It's just a dream. It's just a dream.

Killian kept chanting that over and over again, but the whispering only grew louder and he could feel his lungs filling up with blood. He choked and gurgled on it.

Was he dying?

Two shadowy hands crept along his neck. His eyes rolled down to catch a glimpse of the black talons, that could only belong to a monster.

And that's when he snapped. His vision flared orange and he did not know what happened after that. When he opened his eyes, he was being held.

No...restrained.

It was Rem who was holding him down. His face pressed firmly against his chest while his limbs were pinned down.

"Rem?" Killian croaked...his throat hoarse from what felt like overuse. And a weird coppery taste coated his tongue.

Rem hesitated before pulling back. Killian peered around him, gasping when he saw the destruction. The entire room was destroyed. Furniture splintered, holes in the walls, sheets shredded.

And blood. So much blood. There were guards everywhere, carrying bodies out of the room.

"W-what's going on?" Killian asked, his voice shaking. He looked down at himself and saw the red substance coating his skin.

No.

No.

"Rem?" Killian started to panic.

"Shh," he hushed, tucking his head back into his chest so the prince couldn't see anything.

And then he heard Drek's voice, low and solemn.

"Fourteen guards dead, seven in critical condition. Zev and Caspian are in surgery as we speak."

Killian squeezed Rem's arms and pushed his face even closer to his chest.

"I did not do this. Please tell me I did not do this. Rem...Drek...please," his voice cracked, even muffled against Rem's skin.

"Shh, Killian. You are okay. Everything is okay," Rem hushed him again, then to Drek he said. "How is Faust?"

Drek was quiet for a moment.

"Being the closest and getting the worst of it...he's not in good shape. The Healers haven't been able to stabilize him yet."

A strangled noise left his throat.

Rem hugged him tighter then addressed Drek again, "We will speak of this later. Take him out and stay with him."

Rem transferred the prince to Drek arms. Killian breathed in the scent of sandalwood and oak. He too held Killian's face in his neck, under the silky tresses of his golden hair so he could not see the damage done. He held him that way the entire time. Down the hall he could hear horrified gasps.

Drek's pace quickened and soon they reached their destination. It was the private bath in the lounge. He set Killian down on one of the short stools before peeling his clothes off his body. There was so much blood caked on, that it crinkled like paper. Killian winced at the sound.

Drek worked quickly, his face taut with concentration. His golden brow furrowed. And though he seemed fine, Killian saw the gashes marring his pretty green skin. One particularly bad one stretched from his temple to his chin.

Killian reached to touch it, but saw the blood on his hand and arm and froze, staring at it in horror. Drek pushed Killian's hand down and lifted him up before depositing him into the warm waters of the bath.

The clean clear water immediately went murky with all of the blood.

It reminded Killian of the dream and he immediately thrashed, screaming in protest. Drek held his arms and shushed him, climbing in behind him so he could better wash the blood off. It must have hurt him with all of the wounds he was sporting, but he didn't even wince. He acted as if he didn't have a single injury.

"I hurt them," Killian whispered.

"It wasn't your fault," he said automatically, running a soft cloth down his skin.

"I killed people."

Drek didn't reply.

"I did it again. I killed people. Hurt the people I love. I am a monster."

"You are not a monster, Killian. None of this is your fault. You have so much on your plate right now. Things happen that are not in your control. It's life. And you just can't control that."

"Drek...I do not think I can rule. I do not think...I should even have these babies."

Drek stiffened behind him.

"Don't say such things," he said in response.

"Ian would be a much better ruler than me. He is smart and caring and passionate. He would be the perfect King. He is much more like our father than I am. I am sure there are Succubae that would kill to have his heirs."

"Killian, stop it," Drek snarled fiercely.

Killian winced.

He stopped talking but his mind couldn't stop running.

Maybe...

Maybe he was better off dead.

Chapter 20

King Ellis Innis of Incubi had aged a few years in only a couple of horas.

When the news of the second massacre reached him and his son being the cause...the stress nearly crushed him.

"I can't keep this out of the news. People are going to find out," he sighed, running his fingers through his brown locks. His intricate golden crown crooked on his head and his gray eyes dulling as he read the casualty list.

"If only there were some way to help him through this," Queen Jessa said, sorrow in her voice. Her red eyes were dimmed and her full lips pulled down into a frown.

She too was worried for her son. For the mental state he must be in after all of this. She knew he had a habit of internalizing his pain and was probably beating himself up over this. Something he picked up from his father.

"We should tell him, Ellis," Queen Jessa urged.

The King shook his head sadly, squeezing his gray eyes shut. "We can't, Jess. He'll kill him."

King Ellis dropped his face into his hands, shoulders sagging.

Queen Jessa rested a hand of her own on his shoulder and together they wept.

Rem; tall, dark, handsome, and intimidating, marched down the halls of the palace with intention. His jaw was set and power rolled off his skin in waves. Servants and guards jumped out of the way when they saw him coming. He paid them no heed.

His long wild black mane flaring behind him as his powerful legs encased in black leather, carried him down the corridor. The gold collar on his neck told the people of the palace that he was owned but the black crown on his head screamed to the world that he is a King. Consort or not, he was a force to obey.

His sense of smell was impeccable and he scented his way to the room where Killian was staying. It was isolated...and safe.

Drek was standing outside the door. His green skin taut with rippling muscles. His thick arms folded across his broad chest, bulging everywhere. His golden hair was pulled back in a tight and efficient ponytail which also revealed the bandage on his face and exposed the golden collar on his throat that matched the crown he too wore on his head. He wore a pair of dark gold leather pants that matched his collar and tall brown boots. His incredibly toned torso covered in bandages similar to the one on his face.

He looked up at Rem's approach.

"Report," Rem commanded.

Drek's bright green eyes glanced at the door before he gestures to the tray of uneaten food beside him.

"He's still not eating," Drek said finally, though knowing Rem could deduct that from the evidence provided.

"He has not eaten in three days."

"He hasn't done anything in three days. He won't eat, won't sleep, won't talk. He just sits there in a daze," Drek grumbled, clearly worried.

"We cannot allow him to starve himself any longer. It is unsafe for the children."

"I'm aware of that, but what are we supposed to do?" Drek asked, worry clear in his tone. He was anxious about the entire situation.

"He must be forced. It is for his well-being."

Rem started for the door as he spoke but Drek stopped him with a hand on his shoulder. Rem paused and glanced at him curiously.

"We have already tried. He won't let anyone get close to him."

Rem's dark brows furrowed, but he continued to push the door open.

The room dark, and much smaller than what they were usually in. It had the necessities, a bed, nightstand, dresser, and there was the addition of a balcony that led to the stony path behind the palace.

In the center of the king sized bed, sat Killian. His shoulders were slightly hunched, lavender skin pale and not at all rosey with blush and saturated with color. His long curly maroon hair was tangled on his head looking darker in the dim lighting.

He was slender but still cut with muscles and what used to be rippling abs was now a swollen mound around his middle. The brown comforter was pooled around his waist as he stared forward at the blank, empty brown wall.

His hands were upturned resting on his lap and dried tears were caked onto his face, flaking at the corners of his eyes. His face that was once full, round, and delicate with a small button nose, big eyes, and full lips, was now pale, gaunt, and lifeless. His lips were dry and cracked, his normally bright red eyes framed with full long, curved lashes, were now dull and glazed over.

Seeing him this way caused physical pain for Rem. He couldn't help but feel responsible. If it weren't for him, Killian wouldn't have magix to be dealing with. He'd be normal.

"Killian?" Rem called softly.

Killian didn't respond, didn't move. It was as if he hadn't heard a word.

"Killian my love, you must eat."

He still didn't respond.

Rem made a move forward while Drek watched on.

He got as close as the edge of the bed before he was thrown back by an invisible force into the wall. Baffled by the incredible show of power, Rem stared at Killian, masking his expression of surprise.

Drek offered him a hand and the dark Consort took it.

"I don't even think he noticed he did it. He's been like this since..." Drek trailed off, expression uneasy.

"Since what?" Rem pressed, noticing Drek's obvious hesitation.

The past few days, Rem had been taking care of damage control with the King and Queen. As much as he wanted to be by Killian's side, he had to fulfill his duty as Rank One. But it killed him inside, not to be there for his beloved, not to hold him during his time of need.

"Since it happened. He hinted at...suicide," Drek said.

Rem's head snapped over to Killian, who still hadn't moved throughout the entirety of the visit.

"He would not do something so foolish."

"Like I said, he hinted at it but I don't think he'd go through with it. He just has a lot of pressure on him and he's scared."

Rem sighed. And the door to the room opened and Orion stepped inside. His red hair was lush and curly on his head framing his bronze skin. His stomach heavily swollen with child covered with a soft beige cotton tunic and loose matching pants.

"I'm sorry. I didn't mean to interrupt, I just wanted to see how Killian was doing," he said softly.

Orion watched the two men warily. He was aware that none of Killian's Consorts liked him. They hadn't liked him before when they were all Potentials, but now that they were officially chosen, it had become abundantly clear. They did not hold back their looks of contempt or the sneers on their faces. It made Orion want to shrink in on himself. But he did not.

Orion was used to being disliked.

His adam's apple bobbed as he swallowed back his discomfort. When he peaked around the two huge Consorts, he saw Killian sitting in the bed, looking awful.

His heart lurched as he set eyes on his friend. The one person who truly cared about him and had given him everything. No, he could not love Killian the way that Killian wanted him to, but he did still love him, in his own way.

"Prince Killian!" Orion gasped, running to the bed, before any of the Consorts could stop him. He vaguely heard Drek scream for him but ignored it. Then soon realized that that was a terrible mistake. He had not known where the force came from, but it took hold of him, and threw him far away from the bed. Drek caught him, absorbing most of the impact, in hopes of protecting the unborn baby in Orion's stomach.

Orion gasped and wheezed as his mind scrambled, trying to figure out what just happened. He looked at his friend on the bed who still hadn't moved.

A small trail of blood began to leak from Killian's nose down to his lips.

Rem swore then glared at Orion. It wasn't fair of him to blame Orion because it was not his fault, but he did.

"What's wrong with him?" Orion asked.

"Shock," Drek answered.

"So it's true then? He really did kill all of those people?" Orion asked.

Killian whimpered.

The sound drew everyone's attention as the Incubus on the bed made soft helpless sounds, his face twisted in pain. The reminder of what he did triggered something in him.

"Get out," Rem said harshly to Orion.

Orion sputtered in shock. Drek gave him a careful but hard shove toward the door. His face was not friendly.

"Leave," Drek said coldly.

Orion's eyes watered as he ducked his head in submission and ran out of the room.

Rem sighed, rubbing his hands over his face. "I should not have been so unkind to him. He was only showing his concern."

Killian's shoulders trembled and his whimpers grew. Rem wanted to hold him, but he was afraid that Killian would use his power again which would only worsen his health.

"Killian, can you hear me?" Rem asked.

Killian groaned before wilting into the sheets, falling on his side while his chest heaved. As he fell, the comforter around his waist shifted allowing the two Consorts to see the smooth expanse of his naked bottom and slender thighs.

"Gods above, have mercy," Drek swore.

It was not the sight of naked flesh that had stunned the men to horrified silence, but the raised swirls and jagged designs that adorned the back of his inner thigh that had caused such a reaction.

Killian had the marks of magix.

"That is not possible," Rem hissed.

Rem touched his ear where a new red jewel with silver plating pierced it. It glowed against his fingertips as he hissed a command to someone from the outside.

Almost immediately, the door opened and a silver haired Incubus stepped in. He was thin and lean muscled. The shortest of the men in the room, excluding Killian. His skin was a dulled silver, nothing like his polished and glistening short locks. And his eyes were like the edge of a blade, sharp and blinding, the same luminosity of his hair. His eyes were thin slivers and tilted downward. His nose was straight and long, His lips were a perfect bow shaped with the top lip much thinner than the bottom, but not in the pouty way Zev's was. There was something deadly about it, like he was hiding fangs.

He had three white horns and a white tail. His body was encased with the skin tight bodysuit and armored plating that all soldiers wore except his was adorned with a silver wolf in the middle of his chest with blue jeweled eyes. And fastened to his shoulders was two blue hooked claws. The hooks a symbol of a lieutenant. The emblem on his chest was a signifier of his faction and the color blue showed that he was one of Zev's men.

Zev's lieutenant; Arix.

He bowed at the waist.

"How may I be of service, my Lords?" His voice was slick like the scales of a serpent.

"I want eyes on the visiting family and attendants of Crown Prince Killian. Do not be seen, do not be heard. Report back to me and me alone."

Arix may have been Zev's lieutenant but everyone answered to Rem. He was their General after all. Arix bowed again. His silver eyes slid behind Rem to the now silent Killian.

When he disappeared, Drek frowned at Rem.

"You think they are behind this?"

"I am certain of it," Rem said smoothly, eyes trained on Killian's new markings.

"But it's not possible to give someone magix. So how would they--?" Drek started but the door opened and cut him off. He whirled around and then his jaw dropped.

"Faust?" he stuttered.

Faust, stepped inside the room and gently closed the door behind him. His hair was long and unbound, white as fresh fallen snow, straight as a blade. It blended in perfectly with his white skin which made the silver accents in his hair, crown, collar, and clothes that much more flattering. His black eyes were clear...something that no one had seen in quite some time.

He looked healthy, full bodied like he was when they first met him. If they hadn't known any better, they would have passed the previous weeks off like a dream.

Faust was healthy.

"How is this possible? Killian gutted you! Shred you apart like a piece of paper! You died four times on the operating table? How are you even moving?" Drek exclaimed, so flabbergasted he didn't think to keep his voice down. But Rem didn't scold him. He too was staring at Faust in surprise.

Faust should not have been standing there without a scratch on him. To be quite honest...he should have been dead.

From how badly he was injured and how the Healers struggled and failed to stabilize him, everyone assumed he was going to die. Even the King was preparing to call for a replacement. But there he was. He spoke very softly as he usually did.

"I do not know what happened. I felt like I was sleeping and then when I woke up, I was completely healed."

Drek started to say something else, but Rem put a hand on his chest silencing him. His eyes watched Faust, who had caught a glimpse of Killian. The white Incubus stepped closer to the bed, but not close enough to trigger Killian. He saw the markings on Killian's thigh and he didn't seemed shocked. It was as if he expected it.

Rem noticed.

"Poor sweetling," Faust said softly, then stepped closer to the bed.

"Do not go any closer," Rem warned.

Fause looked at the dark Consort with a soft expression. "It is fine." Then he stepped up to the bed. Rem and Drek tensed but...nothing happened.

Faust was able to kneel on the edge, fingers brushing Killian's skin where his marks now lay. He studied them for a moment, before he peeked over at Killian's face.

"He's asleep," Faust declared.

Drek and Rem sighed in relief.

"We should hook him up to a healing orb while we can," Faust continued and Drek immediately sent for a Healer to do so.

Once the healing orb was set up, Faust adjusted Killian more comfortably in the bed.

"He might have another nightmare," Faust said once the Consorts were alone in the room again.

"Do you think the beast in him will show up again?" Drek asked.

"It is hard to say. They are magic energy, they do not have minds. It will possess him if he allows it in," Rem said.

Faust was shaking his head.

"I do not think it is that simple. I think there are more to these 'Beasts' than we realize. They are people."

"You sound as foolish as Killian," Rem hissed. "Beasts are not people."

Faust frowned but didn't argue. He was staring at Killian.

"It will hurt, sweetling," he said softly to Killian's sleeping form. "It will hurt a lot more before it gets better."

"What are you talking about?" Drek asked.

But Faust shook his head, then stood.

"I must continue my research," he said, then left.

Drek stared after him. "He's acting strangely."

Rem's eyes narrowed. "Indeed he is."

For three days, Killian slept. Drek stayed with him, keeping watch to make sure that nothing happened. And for a while, nothing did happen.

But Faust was right...Killian had another nightmare and it was bad.

The Consorts

The prince felt sick to his stomach as the darkness blinded him and all he could hear were those whispers. His body remained immobile in that Gods forsaken tub. But it was not Rem who sat across from him in the bath of blood.

No...

It was Jax.

The Incubus who had assaulted him those months ago. The one that scarred him, made him afraid of his own bodily desires. With bright blue eyes yellow hair and creamy fair skin. He watched Killian with that twisted smirk on his face.

It was when Jax began to touch Killian's frozen form that he lost it. Screaming bloody murder. He couldn't see anything else but those menacing blue eyes and felt nothing but the intense sensation that he was in danger.

Danger.

Danger.

Danger.

Jax pulled a dagger from the bloody water and advanced toward the prince.

"How dare you carry another man's heirs? But don't worry my sweet Killian, I'll get them out and I'll fill you right back up," Jax purred.

The dark wispy shadows clung to Killian's shoulders as he watched in horror as Jax held the dagger up, positioning it so it was to pierce right into his stomach.

Killian screamed and screamed until his throat was raw and tears blurred the image of the male before him.

And the whispering in his ear grew so loud he couldn't even hear himself anymore. But the whispers that had always been so indistinct were now clear enough that he could pick up one word.

Safe.

He grasped at it. That word, that meaning, that feeling.

He wanted to be safe.

He pleaded to the shadows, begging them to save him. Desperate, he hadn't realized what he was doing. Hadn't seen that the dream had faded around him and he was in the room with his Consorts shouting at him.

No, he saw the shadowy figure at the door of the balcony and ran for it.

Safe.

Safe.

Safe.

The shadow disappeared but Killian could feel the pull. Pushing him out the doors.

His bare feet planted on the cool stone of the balcony ledge, the night air whipping around him. He stared down at his stomach through his tears.

"I am sorry," he whispered to it. "I am going to keep you safe. We are all going to be safe."

His body trembled, straining with power as he kept the figures inside the room from reaching him. He had to protect his children. Keep them safe from all that was trying to hurt them.

Everyone was trying to hurt them.

Blood was gushing from his nose and ears, but he paid it no attention. He didn't listen to the yelling around him, the whispers inside his head. He took a deep breath with a smile on his face.

And jumped.

Chapter
21

Killian was powerful.

But his power was no contender for Beast. Upon seeing Killian's form disappear over the ledge of the balcony, to the hard stone below that would ensure a quick, messy death, Beast tore out of Rem with absolutely no resistance at all.

Blood spurted from his back as his deep red wings sprouted without hesitation. His form was quick, a dark blur as he pushed past Killian's power that held them all hostage.

Like razor sharp blades, the power cut into his wings, shredding them in various places, forcing a ferocious roar to echo off the marble walls, reverberating throughout the palace, alerting everyone that something was happening.

Beast did not care about the pain. His focus remained on getting to Killian. Protecting him. It did not matter to him that he could not fly with his wings so badly injured. He simply leapt off the balcony after his beloved. Pistoning his body forward in a long graceful arc, blood staining the air in a bright red mist, willing his body to fall faster. His claws, reached out, grabbing hold of Killian's arm before pulling the smaller body into his chest and turning only moments before slamming into the stone below.

His body hit the ground with a sickening crack, bones crunching. His wings red ruin and body immobile. Bones had cracked, splitting his flesh and protruding from the wounds, glistening with gore. Blood began to creep along the dips and curves that decorated the stone path, spilling from his dark body. The pool steadily growing in size.

The impact from the fall had knocked the wind out of Killian but left him unharmed for the most part. His face was still covered in his blood and Beast's blood had soaked into his gown.

The path had been active with servants tending to the yards or running errands. The few that happened to be around at the moment screamed in horror as they watched their future Kings slam into the ground. The bloody mess had brought some to tears.

Guards swarmed them. Some grabbing the thrashing Prince, gently restraining him as he screamed and fought. The others gently picked up the mess that was Beast and hauled them both away.

There were shouts and commands and utter chaos going on in the palace. But one rumor had spread. The Crown Prince had lost his mind.

The rumor grew and spiraled out of control. There were some who began to question whether or not he was fit to rule. They began to protest and allies of the King were starting to question his judgement.

There was too much damage control to be done, the King had not a chance to even see his own son. His son who was sedated and chained to a gurney being treated for the few wounds on his back caused by his Consort's rib bones during the fall. His son who just tried to commit suicide.

Rem was in horrible condition. The damage to his wings shortened his lifespan...a lot. He would have to go through intense physical therapy in order to fly again. His wings were stitched back together, but they would never be the same. As for his other injuries...his skull was cracked in several places, his spine misaligned, the bones in his right arm and shoulder were shattered, a clean break on his left forearm. His right leg was broken in several places and his hip was cracked. Six ribs were also broken, one puncturing his lung, another only millimeters away from piercing one of his hearts. Rem's heart.

Had Rem's heart been pierced, he would have died and it would leave just Beast. Beast who could not comprehend control and would have been put down for the danger he posed.

But he would live. They both would.

Three of five Consorts were out of commission, including the top three Ranks. It was Faust now who was in charge. He and Drek stayed by Killian's side, keeping watch to make sure that he did not have another episode.

Until the King could regain control over his nation once again, Killian was kept sedated. Any more incidents would cause irreparable damage to his future reign and reputation.

The first time Killian woke up, he was mumbling nonsense under his breath. Begging for safety and protection. He was quickly put back under.

The second time he woke up, he began talking to someone that no one could see. Apologizing, begging for forgiveness and pleading to protect his children as if the person he was talking to was angry at him. The Healer sedated him again.

The third time he awoke, he was a bit more lucid than the first two times. He was aware of his surroundings despite being so heavily drugged that his speech was slurred and his eyes glassy. He begged Faust.

"Please...don' wanna sleep...please...no...more...please," he mumbled, tears filling those red jeweled eyes of his.

When he saw the Healer with a needle in her hand, his tears flowed more freely. His whimpers grew and his pleas made the Healer hesitate.

"Please...no...no..."

The hesitation did not last long and the Healer once again put him under.

Faust reached over and wiped the still flowing tears from his lover's eyes. His own eyes stinging as he did.

"We cannot keep doing this to him," Faust said finally to Drek.

"We don't have a choice, King's orders," Drek said softly, but he agreed with the white Incubus. Hearing Killian beg each time killed a little part inside him. He wanted to hurt someone, blame them for this. For bringing someone he cared deeply for, so much pain. "Someone is doing this to him."

"We already know who that is, we just don't know how," Faust said.

"Then we have to tell the King!"

"With what proof?" Faust challenged.

"I'm sure Arix has dug something up by now."

"He won't report to anyone but Zev or Rem. Both of which are out of commission at the moment."

"We outrank him. He has to listen to us," Drek growled, prepared to use force if need be.

"That's not how it works and you know it. He was given explicit orders from Rem to only report to him. He's not going to go against orders. Especially not after he was just hired."

Drek growled.

"So what are we supposed to do?" Drek asked.

Faust sighed, gently stroking Killian's hair.

"There is something I've been thinking about. I've only drawn up possible theories, so by no means is this reliable information, but I believe that our child and Rem are not the only Beast Holders here in the palace."

Drek frowned. "You can't think one of his cousins--?"

"No," Faust shook his head quickly. "There would have been record of that. Killian does not carry the gene. It is not in his blood. I believe it is someone that his cousins may be controlling. A servant perhaps."

"But what about the markings on his thigh?" Drek asked.

"I have another theory about that. I think it might be something that our child's Beast is gifting him. If you look closely, the marks are different than Rem's and they do not match any that were in the texts I found in the library. I think that also has to do with Killian's ability to use compulsion. I've read up on it, the theory that Zev presented to me, and I believe he is on to something. Killian's powers of compulsion are much stronger than what they should have been if he had just been a carrier of a magix user and not the one with magix himself. I believe it gives him the ability to push images into other people's heads. Meaning if someone is a magix user with that ability, they could be influencing Killian's dreams and causing these hallucinations," Faust explained.

Drek swore, leaning back against the wall in shock. His bright green eyes wide, trying to take it all in. It was a lot to digest.

"If you don't think the magix user is any of Killian's relatives, who do you think it could be?" Drek asked finally.

"That is what I am counting on Arix to figure out."

"This is a lot more than I signed up for," Drek sighed.

"Is it? He is royalty and these are problems they must face. Do you regret your decision in staying to be his Consort?" Faust asked.

Drek didn't hesitate in his answer. It was sure and confident, just as he was. "No, I don't regret it in the slightest. Killian is precious to me, he always will be and I will give my body, mind, and soul for him. He is my reason for existing now."

Faust grinned at that answer before looking back to the prince.

"I too feel the same as you do. He is my everything," Faust said softly.

A knock on the door interrupted their moment. After being allowed in, a servant poked her head in, giving a bow in greeting before uttering, "Lord Caspian has awoken."

Drek perked up.

"I'll stay with Killian, you go check on our fallen brother," Faust said.

Drek nodded and followed the servant out.

He had been so worried about Caspian. He knew the Incubus had been kicked so many times that he trusted no one. He hoped that Caspian did not begin to resent Killian.

Drek was quite fond of the bond he and Caspian shared.

He didn't want to have to choose between the two because...he would choose Killian. It would break his heart to abandon Caspian because Caspian was all alone. He had no one. And just the thought of that made Drek's chest ache. But he loved Killian and he would not put anything above that...not even a special friendship.

Drek made his way to the medical cot where Caspian lay, hooked up to all kinds of machines. His body covered in bandages. His right eye was swollen and his lip was busted, but he still had a grin on his face when he saw Drek approach.

"How is it that you aren't lying here on a gurney with the rest of us? Is it the steroids?" Caspian mused, though his voice was hoarse from lack of use. His glowing yellow eyes were slightly unfocused meaning he had quite a bit of drugs pumped into his system.

His curly orange and red hair was a messy nest on his head. And his golden skin still shimmered under the bright lights above. Injured yes, but still absolutely breathtaking.

Drek grinned at him before flexing his muscles obnoxiously.

"I can't help it if I've been blessed by the Gods. They probably didn't want to ruin such a beautiful body."

Caspian snorted but the grin stayed on his face. Then his smile faded.

"How is he?"

Drek's smile also faded.

"He's been sedated three times since the incident. King wants to keep him under until he can get the Kingdom under control. A lot of damage control needs to be done and if Killian has another episode, the people won't trust him as King."

Caspian's lips pulled down into a frown.

"Why is this happening to him? Someone as pure as he is should not be punished."

"I don't know. I wish I did," Drek sighed.

"And we can do nothing but watch. I don't like feeling so useless," Caspian hissed.

"Neither do I. Faust is doing his best to piece together the puzzle but it's going to take some time. Especially with Rem out of commission now."

Caspian's brow furrowed in confusion.

"What's wrong with Rem?"

Drek pushed Caspian's curtain to the side revealing Rem lying in the cot next to him. Unconscious and completely covered in bandages. There were twice as many medical vines attached to him than there were to Caspian, and he was linked to four different magic orbs. Not to mention his wings...they were painful to look at.

Caspian jolted as if he had been physically shocked as he gaped at Rem's completely destroyed body. Rem who had been untouchable. Rem who was all powerful.

Rem was utterly broken.

"Impossible," Caspian whispered. Then his wide frightened eyes turned to Drek. "H-how--?"

"Killian lost it and jumped off the balcony. Beast went to save him, but could not protect himself from the fall. He took the full brunt of it. Nearly killed Rem."

Caspian hissed.

"This is insane," Caspian gasped.

"Faust thinks that someone may be causing it. That there is another magix user besides our child and Rem in the palace. Someone that his relatives may be in cahoots with," Drek explained.

"But what's the point? Why kill off Killian?"

"Because he's the heir to the throne dummy."

Caspian scowled.

"I really want to tell the King," Drek muttered.

Caspian rolled his eyes. "That's the dumbest thing you've said so far."

Drek narrowed his eyes at him. "And why is it that?"

"Because we don't know who it is. We have an idea that it may be his relatives but we have no proof. And you heard what Killian said. His father lets his cousins get away with everything because he cherishes his baby brother, also known as their father. He will probably dismiss it."

"Not if it's his son's life on the line!"

"Judging from his reaction last time, I wouldn't put it past him."

Drek growled in frustration. He didn't want to believe it, but he had been there and he had seen that glint in the King's eye. And it was a huge possibility that Caspian was right.

And based off the relationship he had with his own parents, he could definitely see it being the truth.

"I should probably get back to Killian. I want to be there if he wakes up again," Drek finally said. "Get better soon. We need you."

"Aye aye captain," Caspian saluted with a lazy grin.

They stared at each other for a moment longer, sharing a look full of silent messages, before Drek dipped out of the room and back to Killian. Caspian sighed in his bed, looking down at his battered body before glancing over at Rem and wincing.

It could be worse, he thought. It could be a million times worse.

Chapter 22

Killian was swimming in a sea of darkness. Thick and heavy, his limbs were stiff, unable to move with the strength he desired. He was lost in the mass of nothingness. It numbed him. Relaxed him. He didn't want to leave, despite knowing that he should. That this sweet blackness was nothing but an illusion created to cradle his fragile mind. And in that blackness, he saw the occasional light, fighting to break through, fighting to reach him.

It didn't.

Because Killian didn't let it. He let himself succumb to the emptiness until it swallowed him whole. He didn't know how long he was there. Swimming. Waiting.

Until suddenly, he wasn't alone.

He wasn't frightened. He was simply numb to it all. Nothing could hurt him here, not in his sea of darkness. He was protected.

But this stranger, waited. Sitting perched on a single wooden chair one would find in the kitchen of a servant's house. Ordinary. Everything unlike the being that sat in the chair. A figure he had come to know so well. One he had feared and one he now worshipped as his savior.

The figure was made of nothing but shadows, dark and smokey forms, always moving, writhing against oneself. Indistinct, just as it's voice had always been.

"Who are you?" Killian asked.

His voice sounded strange, like it was garbled up by some unseen force. Slow and faint.

The figure didn't move from it's spot on the chair but it raised its head. From the dark wispy figure, he saw two bright orange eyes staring at him. Vibrant and familiar. He knew what it was.

"Beast? Is that you?" he called to it.

The form's head tilted.

No it wasn't the beast inside of Rem. This was another one. The one inside of him...Inside of his child.

"Have you been protecting me this entire time?" Killian asked.

The form quivered. The prince floated towards it, moving at such a slow pace, he wanted to be frustrated, but he wasn't. He couldn't be. Frustration required energy, required thought, and Killian did not have any to spare. He didn't want to spare it. He wanted to be numb.

"I do not want to fight anymore. I am tired," Killian told them. And with the words came an even heavier weight. One that made his shoulders sag. So so tired. His eyes began to droop. The figure's talons shot out and grasped his wrists, digging into them.

Killian blinked, then looked down at his wrists expecting to see blood. There was none. Nothing but the pin pricking sensation of the tips digging into his skin. Not piercing. Not breaking any flesh.

"Please," Killian whimpered. "I want to sleep."

The talons tightened around him, but still careful not to break any skin. Then a garbled voice reached out to him.

"No," is what Killian thought it said, but it was too guttural for him to be sure.

Warm breath spread across his face as the figure moved closer. He could smell the spicy scent of cinnamon, sweet and alluring. It stung a little as if wafted up his nostrils. His eyes, that he had not known closed, popped back open until he was staring into impossibly bright orange depths, gyrating against different hues, almost like the center of the sun. His eyes burned. Killian tried to turn away but the figure would not let him. Instead he stared until the numbness settled over him and his eyes no longer stung with pain.

"Wake," it hissed.

And as if he were being sucked into a void, his body ripped away, tumbling into colors and sounds. The feeling returned to his limbs, the pain. Emotions slammed back into him until he was sobbing awake.

"Killian?" a gentle voice called from beside him.

The prince gasped, trying to catch his breath but the aching in his chest and the endless tears that spilled from his eyes made that nearly impossible.

"Breathe, sweetling. Breathe. In and out."

Killian tried to listen, tried to calm his rapid heart beats. It took several moments, but finally, his tears slowed as did his breathing.

Two stark white hands cupped his warm cheeks and brushed away his tears. He blinked looking into Faust's black depths, so similar to Rem's.

Rem.

Killian's lip quivered as he relived that very moment where Rem's body met the stone pavement. He sobbed again, almost falling into another fit, but Faust gripped him harder and forced his attention on him.

"Relax sweetling, everything is alright."

"Rem," he whispered brokenly, blinking past the still falling tears. Faust's calm expression did not waver.

"He will be fine. Everything is okay now sweetling. You are safe and so is everyone else." Though his face was smooth, the bond between them did not allow for him to fool Killian. He was lying.

"I want to see him," Killian demanded.

"He is still sleeping. You do not want to wake him," another voice said. Deeper, huskier.

Killian turned his head quickly to find Drek standing against the wall with his arms folded over his chest. His bright green skin a welcome explosion of color to his eyes. His golden mane wild on his head, framing his gorgeous face. But those eyes...they were all wrong.

They were cold...distant. Much like when Killian first chose him to be his Consort. He half stumbled half crawled along the bed to get to him, but Faust's hands kept him from touching the ground.

"Drek," Killian called to him, reaching out for him, but he did not return the gesture. He did not come into the prince's arms. No...he glared.

"Drek," Killian called again, his hand dropping and his voice cracking...broken.

His tall imposing form pushed from the wall and he marched up to Killian. His face growing angry. His snatched the prince's jaw up until he was forced to stare up into those furious emerald eyes of his. He bared his teeth at him, his grip painful.

"Why the hell would you do something so stupid?" He snarled.

Killian blinked in confusion.

"Did you think of no one but yourself? You have the nerve to make us all fall for you, pledge our entire existence to you just so you could go off and kill yourself? And our children? Have you gone mad?"

Killian's face burned in shame. Faust appeared beside Drek and rested a hand on his shoulder.

"That is enough," Faust said to him lightly.

Faust who was no longer gray and gaunt. No longer lifeless and sickly. Faust who was healthy and pure just as the day Killian met him. His skin almost glowed, radiating with light.

Drek released Killian's chin and he wilted back onto the bed.

"I am sorry," he whispered.

Drek barked a harsh laugh before he shoved his face into Killian's, his forehead bumping against his a little painfully.

"I love you Killian. Does that mean anything to you?"

Killian's chest tightened.

"It means everything to me. I love you too, Drek. Truly," he told him. And he did. He loved them all.

"No. You don't. If you did, you would not have attempted something like that. You would not have done something so foolish," he bit back, backing up and pacing.

"I just wanted to be safe! I wanted everyone to be safe! I keep hurting people, hurting you! I just wanted to protect you all--"

"That is our job, Killian! We protect you!" he roared, whirling on Killian. The volume and ferocity of his tone forced the prince into submission. He sat silently, wishing he could take it all back.

Drek continued in a deeper tone, but with just as much venom. "You do not get to strip us of our purpose. King or not, that is not right."

"Drek," Faust said softly.

Drek took a deep breath and fell silent.

"I am unsafe to be around. I am falling into madness and I cannot stop it. I cannot fight it, not anymore. I am losing myself to it. It is better if I am no longer a threat. Ian will be a good ruler, I swear to you he will. You all will be cared for."

Drek shook his head again in anger and disbelief before walking out of the room, not wanting to hear another word. Faust sat next to Killian on the bed, while he stared after Drek.

"You are not falling to madness. It is not your fault that this is happening to you," he said.

"Then what is? What reason?" Killian begged for the answer. Something to make sense of all this insanity.

"We believe another magix user is here at the palace. Someone at your relatives' disposal. And that magix user may very well have the same abilities as you do."

The thought never crossed Killian's mind. He felt as if that would be information that he would be warned about, have some inkling of. But then again, with how many secrets have been kept from him, he was not so sure.

"A servant...do you think Velma..." Killian asked trailing off with the question but knowing Faust would pick it up.

"I do not know. We have Zev's lieutenant shadowing them and learning what he can. When Rem awakens, he will report his findings to him."

Killian winced again at Rem's name.

He did not think...he had not known he would...

Faust seemed to read his thoughts.

"You have no idea how much you mean to us all. We would all give our lives for you. Please don't make us have to prove it again."

His words stung.

"I am sorry," Killian whispered again, feeling like utter crap.

"It is done now, let us leave it behind us. We have much work to do."

He started to get up but Killian latched onto him. "Do not leave," he begged.

He didn't want to be alone. He had no idea what would happen left to his own thoughts. He needed to be distracted so he wouldn't think about all of the bad things happening. Killian needed a distraction to keep himself in check. And if he left him alone, he was positive the madness would come for him.

Faust sat back down, "I will stay," he said softly.

"Sing for me," Killian begged in a quiet tone.

Faust looked startled at the request, but complied anyway.

Faust's voice was everything Killian thought it would be. He sang no words in distinction, just simple soothing sounds, but his voice was so lovely it did not matter. Gentle and melodic with the ringing of bells, his voice was enchanting. It started out low but grew in sound, grew in strength creating a magnificent crescendo that sent shivers up Killian's spine and gooseflesh on his skin.

His eyes fluttered shut as he listened but snapped open only a moment later. The fear of what he might see shot through him.

But Faust's voice brought him back down from his peak of terror and into a calmness he had not known for a while.

And then, he felt something. A tiny flutter in his stomach. At first the feeling made him queasy, but the more it happened, the faster he realized what it was.

"Faust..." Killian started, placing a hand on his protruding stomach.

Faust stopped singing immediately and the flutters stopped.

"What? What is it?" He asked worriedly.

"The children, they were...moving. I could feel them."

Faust placed his hand on Killian's stomach. He stayed there for a while, but there was no movement. He frowned.

"Are you sure?" He asked.

"It was while you were singing. Sing again," Killian said, getting excited.

Faust began to sing, but his hand did not lift from his stomach. They waited until finally they felt it. The little flutters, gentle caresses. A smile spread across Faust's lips and his eyes drooped in happiness.

"They are strong," he said.

Killian grinned with him. "Yes, they are. Just like their fathers."

Faust smiled, pulling him under his arm until he lay tucked into his side, his cheek resting on his strong chest and he hummed a soft melody. His hand moving in small slow circles on Killian's stomach.

"Faust?"

"Yes, sweetling?"

"How long have I been unconscious?"

"About three weeks."

Killian sucked in a breath. "I have not fed in a while."

Faust's hand froze on his stomach, tilting his head down to him until he could see into his black eyes.

"Are you hungry?" he asked him.

He was afraid to reach for his *Haise* to truly confirm whether or not he was hungry, but even if he didn't have that gnawing sensation in his gut or the feverish heat that always seem to overcome him, he still needed to feed.

He stared up at him and really took in his health. How he seemed to be glowing. So different from how he was before. He was amazed and slightly worried.

"How are you healed?" Killian asked in astonishment, understanding just how crazy the transformation was.

"I am...unsure. But I never truly felt sick, despite what it seemed."

Killian tucked his head under his chin and closed his eyes briefly. "I am so glad you are alright."

"Your concern warms me."

Killian pulled back to smile at him, then leaned up to kiss him but just before his lips met Faust's, he saw his eyes flash blue.

Killian gasped in shock, jerking back.

Faust frowned.

"What is it?" he asked.

"Y-your...nevermind," Killian swallowed hard and looked away, thinking better of saying anything. It had to be his dreams. They were messing with his head in waking reality.

He stared up into the black depths, and with a quiet whisper, "Feed me?"

Faust smiled down at him before leaning to place a soft kiss on those begging cupid's bow lips. Killian groaned, pushing himself forward and up into his lap. Faust was hard, his length straining against the thin fabric of his pants. The tip brushed against Killian's butt, just shy of the special place he really wanted it.

The prince kissed his way down Faust's bright white skin, from the lightly stubbled jaw, to the gorgeous expanse of his neck. Faust's heavy breathing filled the silent room.

Killian's fingers danced along his skin, tracing every dip and groove of his lover's muscles through the fabric of his tunic before pulling it free of his pants and slipping his hands underneath to feel pure skin against skin.

Faust moaned, hands cupping the round globes of Killian's butt, the hold disrupted briefly when the prince tugged his tunic up over his head. Killian's mouth watered at the sight of Faust's smooth white chest and toned abdomen. He was as built and defined as Caspian with that same lean sleekness. His stark white nipples pebbled as the cool air hit the exposed nubs.

Killian's lowered his mouth to lick them.

Faust tossed his head back, "Oh, sweetling."

Killian grinned, trailing his lips downward eliciting more moans from his quiet lover. When reached the waistband of Faust's pants, he nearly tore it off, not bothering to be gentle. No part of him wanted to wait. He wanted his shaft down his throat.

Faust chuckled as he helped Killian remove his pants without too much damage. Killian continued his assault, latching his mouth onto the pure white member of his lover, stiff and ready to penetrate.

"Easy, sweetling. We have time," he murmured, fighting past his groans of ecstasy as Killian worshipped him. The prince was relentless, licking and suckling his rosy tip.

When he could bear it no more, he rushed to pull Killian up and place his shaft at his slick filled entrance. Killian made soft eager noises before he was slowly lowered onto Faust.

"Faust!" he moaned, closing his eyes and tilting his head back. His back arched as his lover filled him. Not wanting to wait, Killian began to move, starting that fluid dance that would have them both reaching climax way too soon.

Faust smiled, putting one hand on the back of Killian's neck, pushing their foreheads together. They panted, taking each other's breaths.

Killian's thighs quivered as he quickened his pace, feeling that lovely burn curl in his gut.

"Feed, sweetling," Faust urged but even he had a hard time getting the words to surface. His scrotum pulling up tight and brushing Killian's backside.

Killian opened his eyes and met Faust's gaze before he fed. Pulling but not too much. Even in the throes of passion, he still feared harming his lover. Killian screamed as his release hit him. Faust echoing him as the hot spurt of semen painted his insides.

Killian pulled back his *Haise*, sighing as he gently laid against Faust's chest.

He made sure not to take too much which allowed Faust to remain conscious. When their breathing settled, they began to pull back on their clothes, wiping off what fluids they could with that they had available to them in the room.

Killian cuddled against his lover once more.

"How are the others?" he asked softly, almost too softly, still basking in his afterglow. Hearing the answer frightened him to no end. How far had he gone in his madness? What damage had he caused?

"They are well for the most part. Drek and Caspian are fully healed. Zev is on the mend, but due for a speedy recovery and Rem is...alive."

Killian's heart skipped a beat at that last bit.

"Alive..." he did not like the way he said that. As if Rem was permanently crippled. As if Killian had done irreversible damage. But that could not be. Rem was strong. Beast was strong. He could not hurt them. Please, Gods Above. Please don't confirm his greatest fears.

"He is alive Killian. Just focus on that. We have not lost him," Faust said, almost as if he were reading his thoughts.

"That is not good enough," Killian whimpered.

"It must be. For now at least. He will heal sweetling, just give it time," Faust said smoothly. "Now let us get you out of this room. Things have calmed down with the rumors."

"What is it that everyone believes happened?"

"That you are undergoing too much stress with such powerful heirs and that it is a side effect of the pregnancy. They also believe it will end when the pregnancy is over."

"Will it?" Killian asked.

"It will end when we catch the one behind this and end their life."

He said it all with his calm and gentle voice, which made it all the more terrifying. It was hard to remember that Faust was a warrior. He had seen him fight, he knew he was capable of causing quite a bit of damage with a spear, but he had forgotten as he often did. Faust's personality was the complete opposite of what he expected a warrior to be.

"There cannot be many who truly believe that," Killian countered.

Faust breathed a sigh. "You are right. But none will speak against it, the King has spoken. To challenge his word is treason and none would risk it."

He was right about that. It was the same when the call for bachelor applications went out for his Consort ceremony. None would refuse the King, to do so meant death for defiance. But one cannot win loyalty through fear, not truly. They would lie in wait for any opening of betrayal.

Killian would not rule through fear. He would rule with love. He wanted his people to love him not fear him. And that might very well get him killed.

The prince slid to the edge of the bed, placing his bare feet on the cold ground, feeling the pinpricks of icy marble shooting up his feet through his legs. He shivered. Faust was there, placing an arm around Killian's waist while the other wrapped around his back and he pulled him up, taking most of his weight with ease.

Killian was a bit unsteady on his feet. He had been lying down for so long, he had to get used to walking again. He wobbled a bit as he stood but eventually was able to gain his balance once again. Faust grabbed some flats from a cupboard and slipped them onto Killian's feet. He held on to Faust's shoulders to keep his balance as he raised each foot. The shoes were comfortable and protected his bare soles from the cold floors.

"Where are my Warriors?" Killian asked Faust.

"Caspian is training with his unit, Zev is with Rem, and Drek...I am unsure of his whereabouts."

Killian's chest ached as he remembered how furious he had been with him and how his face twisted at his words before he stormed out of the room. Killian did not want to drift from him. Their bond had grown so strong, to sever that tie would leave him susceptible to Filo's advances.

"You said I had been out of commission for weeks...Does that mean they are back? My cousins and siblings?" Killian asked Faust carefully as they walked slowly through the halls toward his room.

"Yes," he answered smoothly.

His whole body went rigid. He was unconscious and they were running around doing only Gods knows what. How many traps have they lain? What kind of horror was he waking to?

The Consorts

A warmth and gentle hum radiated from his stomach and spread throughout his entire body until he was shaking with power.

"Keep it in, Killian. You will do harm to yourself and our children," Faust warned.

Killian fought hard to swallow it back but it was just like trying to shove back bile, it kept trying to force its way out and keeping it inside only made him feel horrible. For his children, he would. He would not lose control.

With every bit of strength he possessed, Killian pushed his power down and his unease away until he felt calm and more himself. Breathing in and out slowly, Killian regulated his breathing and continued on his way. Faust smiled at him brightly, clearly impressed with his show of restraint.

Learning how to control these outbursts of power was the first step in learning how to control the magix takeovers. At least...he hoped it was. His only option was to remain positive and hope that things would get better with a bit of stubborn will and whole lot of optimism.

As they walked through the palace, Killian began to realize how quiet and empty it was. There were no servants buzzing around, no laughter in the distance, no voices, no sound. The halls were absolutely deserted. Was it because of him?

"Where is everyone?" he asked.

"It is rather quiet. I suppose they are preparing for the Ball. The King has announced that it will officially be held in four days. Something positive after such a travesty. I believe it is also a way to show that you are sane."

Killian frowned at that.

If they were really preparing for the Ball, wouldn't the palace be buzzing with activity? There should be chatter and gossip. People should be running around all over the place. It should be busy. That is what it was like whenever there was a big event, nothing like this. Not so...empty.

"Relax, Killian. They could be out of the palace. I am sure there is nothing to worry about, sweetling. Everything will be okay."

Killian wanted to believe him, but there was something inside him that tugged at his gut, alerting him that all was not as it seemed and that there was something happening. Something bad. It was similar to when forests were empty just before a storm.

Could the palace dwellers sense something amiss?

Or were they just afraid he would end their lives in another fit of madness?

Not knowing drove him crazy. Was the damage done irreversible? If they did fear him, he'd just have to work even harder to get them to love him again as they had before his pregnancy and all of this madness happened. Though that was much easier said than done.

Sighing, Killian leaned into Faust's side, clutching his arm close. Faust smiled and started to hum, not minding at all about how slow they were moving. Carrying such a large weight was really beginning to take a toll on him. He couldn't see his feet anymore.

As confirmation, he tried to peek over the roundness of his stomach but it stuck out too far and he could see nothing but the swirling designs in the white marble tiles they walked on. He couldn't even tell what color the flats were that Faust put on him. He didn't think he liked being pregnant very much.

Faust froze abruptly, bringing Killian to a jarring halt. Killian frowned, opening his mouth to protest until he noticed the serious look on his Consort's face. Faust's black eyes darted back and forth, searching with his gaze and straining with his ears.

Killian didn't hear it at first and made a move to continue on but the moment he took a step, his ears perked. There were small groans coming from down the hall, in the direction of Killian's rooms.

He wondered if it was his other Consorts even though Faust assured they were away from the room. Then the sounds of a scuffle grew louder until screams and shouts of guards grew in volume. Killian and Faust looked at each other briefly before hurrying toward the noise, Faust being careful to keep Killian a step behind him in case of danger.

The scene they stumbled upon confused Killian.

Guards were hauling a thrashing Drek away while Marza held Filo in a tight embrace, murmuring quietly in his ear. Killian's head swam as he noticed the disheveled state of his youngest cousin and lack of clothes on his Consort.

"What is going on?" Killian asked softly, brows furrowed and head tilted, trying to understand the scene that was playing out.

"Cousin! Your lover assaulted Filo!" Marza said with a sneer. She sent a venomous glare to Drek. Drek who was still thrashing wildly. But there was something off about him. His movements were crazed yet they didn't reach his eyes. His emerald green eyes that were dull and void.

"Why were you in my rooms, cousin?" Killian asked, his gaze directed at Filo.

Ever so slightly, Filo smirked, but it was gone before anyone else could notice. His face twisted into a pitiful expression.

"I was trying to find you, cousin. I heard what had happened and wanted to check up on you. I saw your lover there and asked him where you were. But he...he..." Filo choked on a rehearsed sob. Marza hugged her brother tighter, cooing to him.

Killian turned to the thrashing Drek. He approached him slowly, Faust shadowing his every move. He leaned forward and peered into those vacant green eyes.

Was he being...compelled?

Killian reached for him with his mind but was met with darkness.

"Drek," he called out.

No answer.

"Drek," he said again, this time with his mind.

There was a spark. A glimmer of something but it was gone too quick, fading into the darkness. Killian had not had much practice in using compulsion, but if it could work on Rem and Beast, it would work on Drek. Besides, they were deeply connected. The bond he shared with Caspian and Drek was different than the ones with his other

Consorts. Their bond was interwoven with magix. He needed to channel it, tug on it, to reach Drek.

He tried again, forcing his magix to arise and wrap around that small green tether that kept the two bound.

It was hard to get a grasp, but once he did, he held tight and jerked.

Blinding green light burst through the darkness, clearing it away. Drek gasped, then coughed, crumbling to his knees. The four guards on him looked confused, but did not release him.

Drek blinked, looking around.

When his eyes landed on Filo, they burned with murderous intent. His whole body tensed before he leaped with a swiftness, none were prepared for.

Before he could reach Filo, Killian stepped in front of him placing one hand to his chest. Faust was there with a hand to his arm. Both were gentle in their restraints and Drek would not harm either one of them.

"Filthy fucking snake!" Drek spat, glaring at Filo.

"You shut your mouth!" Marza hissed. "Dirty little bottom feeder needs to learn his place!"

Killian's gaze was glacial as he fixed it on his cousin. "Speak to my Consort in such a manner again and I will cut your tongue from your mouth."

Marza huffed incredulously. "You would defend that monster after what he did to your own flesh and blood?"

Killian looked at Drek, "What happened?"

Drek met Killian's gaze and crumpled in despair. "I'm sorry Kill, I swear I wasn't in my right mind. You know I would never."

That, Killian knew all too well. The problem was, who had the power to tamper with his mind.

"Never what, brother?" Faust asked softly.

Drek's head dropped. He didn't answer.

He didn't need to. It was obvious. Which was the point.

"We must take him, Your Highness. By order of the King."

Killian's eyes tightened. He looked at his lover, gently cupped his cheek and forced that green gaze to meet his.

"I know," Killian said. And it was enough.

They hauled him away while some servants came to attend to Filo. The prince watched him with a calm expression. They would not get away with this.

Killian made his way to the study knowing that is where his father would be after ordering Faust to follow Drek. King Ellis was there, sitting at the large round table with Uncle Netter and Aunt Kendra sitting across from him. A guard was whispering his ear no doubt feeding him whatever lies that Filo had fed everyone else.

Father glanced up at his son, his expression hard, then he nodded slightly and dismissed the guard. Killian watched the guard as he left and closed the door behind him. Then he focused on his father who was watching him with that same hard expression.

"He did not do it, Father," Killian said evenly. "Release him."

"There are eye witnesses that object to that statement."

"Like who? Velma? She's a snake, just like the rest of them," Killian glared at his uncle and aunt who looked shocked at his verbal attack.

"Killian," Father hissed in warning. His eyes narrowed dangerously.

"Perhaps it is best if we leave," Uncle Netter said starting to stand, but Killian flicked his hand and his uncle slammed back down into his seat.

"No. You will sit here and listen to it all," the prince said evenly. Uncle Netter didn't object. He genuinely did not want to upset Killian and probably did not even know what transpired, even though his son was involved. It was always the same. Every time that Filo or any of his children did something wrong, he was conveniently not present when it all blew up. Killian couldn't tell if he was in on it or if he was honestly that clueless. But he would not miss out on this one.

"Your son and the rest of your children have been tormenting me for years and I have dealt with it, never speaking up because I knew that my own father would not hear me out. My father valued your children over me and that is why they have gotten away with everything they did to me. But I will not stand it. Not any longer."

Killian looked back to his father, mustering all the anger he felt into his eyes so that when King Ellis looked at them, he would burn with his rage.

"You said you knew all that was happening in the palace, dear Father, but you do not know anything at all. You are blind and misguided."

"Watch your tongue," King Ellis hissed, getting to his feet.

"You did not even know that there is a third magix user in the palace."

Killian expected shock and surprise in his face. But he saw none. Instead, he saw a hint of fear and guilt. Then his expression changed to sadness and despair.

"Take this as another lesson, son. Sometimes things are not as they appear but you must treat it as so for the greater good."

Hurt and betrayal coursed through Killian like a vicious river tearing around a bend. He turned away sharply, so the King wouldn't see the hurt in his face and as he was about to leave, the King called out, "One hundred lashes."

Killian jerked to a stop.

"I will give him one hundred lashes, but he will not die tonight. And he is not to be seen anywhere around Filo."

Killian bit his tongue and silently left the room, knowing any protest would fall on deaf ears.

One hundred lashes...he said it like it was a mercy. Drek didn't deserve to be punished.

Killian made a beeline for the palace dungeons, in hopes of consoling Drek and maybe getting a little more from him in order to find undeniable evidence that he was not at fault.

The basement of the palace was everything that a dungeon was supposed to be. Dark and dreary with cement walls and flooring, dewy air, musty smell, and little to no lighting. Just the eerie glow from the torches lighting the walls. There were rows and rows of reinforced steel bars. Most cells were empty but there were a couple that were occupied.

A few shifters looking ragged, covering in blood, dirt, sweat. Shackles around their ankles and wrists. They glared at the prince as he walked, but he paid them no heed. Some imprisoned nymphs had the nerve to shout out lewd remarks. The guards that followed Prince Killian barked at them to shut them up.

Killian kept walking with his head held high, until there was one cell in particular that made him stop before it. The utter coldness and dread that filled him was stifling. His heart beat out of control and it was so hard to breath past his fear, but he forced himself not to show his abrupt fear.

Something compelled him to look inside the cell even though he really didn't want to. It was dark inside, but he could very faintly make up a figure curled into a ball in the far corner.

It was a male with shaggy white locks and deep brown skin. Killian wanted to see his face but from the lighting and the angle that he held himself, he could not.

"Who is he?" he asked the prison guard.

"Yehwin. Your great great great Grandfather's familiar. He went feral after the King passed away. He's been locked away down here ever since."

"Familiar?" Killian asked. He had heard about them before but did not know any still walked this plane. After his great great grandfather, the Clouds never sent any more.

"Some say he is a spirit trapped in an animal's body. Some say he is one of the Fallen Gods, in an animal's body. But familiars are animal companions used to guide and protect their charges. It was a practice that ended after Yehwin went feral. Many were too afraid to risk it happening again so they stopped bonding with familiars."

"You say animal but what I see is a male."

The guard looked at him funny.

Killian frowned and looked back at the cell. Where the male had been now sat a white tiger with glowing blue eyes. They watched him without blinking. He shivered under the stare.

"My mistake. My eyes were playing tricks on me," Killian mumbled. Then forced himself to keep walking. He felt those eyes on him the whole time.

It was only when he reached Drek's cell that the prince forgot about him.

They hadn't touched him yet, but he was still shackled like some animal. When he saw Killian approaching, he rushed up to the bars.

"Killian," he breathed.

The prince touched his cheek.

"You do not deserve this," he said.

Guilt was clear in his eyes.

"I managed to get your sentence changed to one hundred lashes instead of death," Killian told him.

Drek winced, but gulped and nodded.

"I will not end it there, Drek. I swear it. I will get them to release you," he vowed but Drek shook his head.

"No, Killian. I will accept the lashes. I need to be punished."

"No you do not. It was not your fault!"

"Compelled or not, I touched him. I touched him when I am yours. My body has been sullied and I must repent for that. Let me have the lashes."

"Drek--"

"Enough, Killian. I made my decision," he barked sharply. Then he leaned in to kiss him but froze and backed away.

Killian wanted to pull him closer, to press himself to his planes, but the guilt in his eyes would not allow that to happen. He was punishing himself for something he had no control over.

"Drek."

He backed away from the bars and receded to the farthest corner of the cell.

Killian frowned but turned away and left the cells. As he passed by Yehwin's cell again, he heard a soft voice call out to him.

"You smell of his blood, child."

Killian froze.

He turned to the cell and peered inside.

The tiger appeared from the shadows, melting into the dim lighting until he was mere inches from the cell.

"You smell of his blood," he repeated.

Killian looked around to see if the guards had heard the voice too but they were looking at the prince with confusion, unsure of why he had stopped walking.

"They cannot hear me if I do not will it so."

Killian blinked at the tiger who sat there calmly. Where was the feral beast that they were talking about? He seemed perfectly docile.

The tiger's tongue flicked out, licking his nose before his blue eyes zeroed in on his stomach.

His eyes narrowed before he said, "That child will scream."

Killian looked down at his stomach then back at him, gasping when he saw a male again. A very comely male with strange white markings on his face and arms. Tribal marks, thick and thin bands of white. His eyes were just as eerie as they had been in his tiger form and his hair was as pure as his markings.

He watched Killian the way a predator would watch their meal. The prince staggered away from the cell, bumping into one of the guards behind him.

A tiger once again, Yehwin laughed. Loud and bellowing. The sound raised the hairs on the back of Killian's neck. It resonated in his head even as he rushed out far away where he could no longer hear the sound physically.

He sought out Faust and found him in the bedroom, talking to...Caspian.

"Caspian!" Killian ran and flung himself onto the golden skinned Consort.

He winced, but smiled, wrapping his tail around Killian's. He dipped low to scoop the prince into a long, tender kiss that made his toes curl and every worry just disappear.

Killian wanted to squeeze him tight but from the way he winced earlier, he was still probably too injured for it.

When they broke apart, he stared up into his bright yellow eyes.

"I keep hurting you," he said with tears beginning to brim.

"I can take a beating," he said softly, brushing away what started to spill out of his eyes.

"But you should not have to, not from me."

"It's in the past. Right now, I am fine. Still kicking ass. You don't need to worry. Now more importantly, what's going to happen to Drek?"

Killian sighed, deflating a little.

"I managed to get his sentencing down to one hundred lashes. I wanted to do more but Drek won't let me. Says that he needs to be punished."

Caspian hissed in annoyance.

"Sounds just like the meathead. I swear, all those steroids are messing up his brains," he muttered.

"Perhaps it is best if we start the hunt for the magix user on our own until we can get the confirmation from Arix," Faust said softly.

"Why don't we just compel the answer out of him? Save us the trouble," Caspian suggested.

"It is an invasion of privacy!" Killian hissed, traumatized after what he had done to Rem and Beast. And now what was done to Drek. Compulsion was a horrible power that he wished did not exist.

"Does that really matter right now? We're kind of desperate and none of that will mean a thing if you're dead."

"He has a point," Faust added.

Killian sighed, rubbing his temples. They were right though. They were running out of time and they had no leads. Maybe, if they could find out who it was before tonight...before Drek's punishment, they might be able to save him from it. And save all of them from Filo. Killian finally nodded in agreement.

Caspian sent for him and Arix appeared within ticks. He bowed graciously as soon as he saw the prince.

"My Prince," he greeted with respect even though his voice was slippery and snakelike.

"You may rise, Warrior."

He raised his head, his silver eyes glinting in the light.

"Have you found anything out about my cousins?" Killian asked.

He shifted in place, looking uncomfortable.

"With all do respect, My Prince. I have been ordered to relay that information to Lord Rem only."

"But I am Crown Prince, soon to be King. I outrank him. Do you wish to defy me?" Killian said simply, seeing if he would crack without the need for the prince to compel him.

But he didn't budge, instead saying. "With your recent illness, the King has declared all of your orders void." Rage filled the prince but he bit it down. It was a problem for another time. He sighed, pushing his mind into Arix and forcing his will.

"Tell me all of the intel you have gathered," he commanded.

"There is no suspicious activity to report. All sightings have been normal," Arix stated mechanically. The silver in his eyes dulling with the compulsion.

Killian frowned about to push him but then he continued.

"I am being followed."

Caspian swore in frustration.

How could they possibly catch on? How could they know they were being shadowed? Arix was good. Beyond good. Killian read his file, so he knew it could not be his lack of skill.

And then it hit him.

"Was Drek in the room when you were given the order?" he asked Arix.

"Yes," he recited.

Filo probably got his magix user to compel the information out of Drek.

Damnit!

There was a knock on the door.

"Enter!" Killian called out after snapping Arix out of the compulsion.

A servant stuck her head into the room and offered a timid bow.

"The King has requested your presence for the lashing," she said quietly.

"Already? They have just sentenced him! He should have until the night!" Killian shouted in anger.

The servant trembled in fear. He cleared his expression and softened his tone to something much more soothing.

"Thank you, you are free to go."

The servant bowed again then hurried out. Killian looked to his Consorts. Each wore solemn expressions.

"He will live," he whispered, trying to remain positive.

Just barely...but he will live.

Chapter 23

The lashing had been brutal. It very nearly killed Drek but he endured. His eyes burned with rage and determination as he took his punishment, not uttering a single cry. Killian cried all the tears for him but kept it together in front of his gleeful cousins.

It was only afterwards, when the onlookers departed from their entertaining show of bloodshed, Drek let the pain consume him, passing out in a pool of his own blood. Killian ran to him, holding him close. They carted him off to the medical wing and Killian had not left his side.

Caspian's lieutenant, a pixie named Mirabel with long flowing pink hair, tiny features and lilac skin stepped into the room. She bowed lowly to Killian, her big pink eyes full of respect. The prince acknowledged her with a nod. She rose and turned to Caspian, leaning up to whisper something in his ear.

"Zev has awakened, Killian," Caspian told him.

Killian's ears twitched and he felt his heart beat faster.

"Go to him. Stay with him. Inform him of all that we have discovered. I will stay by Drek's side."

Caspian nodded before he and his lieutenant disappeared behind the door.

The babies began to shift within Killian, kicking a little. The little flutters pushing in time with his hand.

He smiled, placing his free hand on his protruding stomach. Thinking of his children brought him back to the cells where Yehwin stayed. He said his child will scream. Singular. Which one was he referring to? Did he know anything about magix users or beasts in general? Should he risk asking him? Would he even tell him? Should he ask him what he meant by it?

His child will scream.

What does that mean? He had to know something. Maybe he should--

Pain like no other exploded in his skull.

The stabbing sensation pierced behind his eyes causing his vision to blur. Bewildered, he nearly passed out from the initial force of it.

It hurt terribly, much worse than any headache or migraine he had ever experienced. And it was so sharp, so intense, he couldn't even find his voice to scream. It was still lodged in his throat.

Tears sprang from his eyes as he fought to take a breath.

Killian's chest heaved with the effort but another wave knocked away any sense of control he thought he might have.

It was excruciating.

What is this?

That child will scream.

Killian fell out of his chair, crumpling onto the ground as another wave hit him.

He vomited, choking on the action.

The rancid smell only wafted into his nose forcing yet another wave of vomit and pain to wrack through him.

That child will scream.

Over and over again. He wanted to pass out, just to escape the pain, but every time he was on the verge, his body jerked, keeping him conscious throughout it all. Footsteps that were too light to be anyone he knew approached his crumpled figure.

He tried to tilt his head up.

And he saw the beginnings of large white paws. They led up to the form of a white tiger. One he was soon becoming familiar with.

Yehwin.

How did he get out of his cell?

"H-help," Killian wheezed.

Yehwin cocked his head. His blue eyes glowing even brighter.

"I told you so," he said, his voice thick with an accent he couldn't quite place. Not from anywhere near the south of Astoria, that was for certain.

"Please," Killian begged.

"You are in charge, no? You make it stop."

Another wave hit him and finally he could scream.

Yehwin hissed.

"Silence, boy. They will hear you."

"I want it to stop," Killian said weakly, vomiting again.

Yehwin peeked at the gross pile Killian created with disgust. Well as much disgust as one could imagine a feline expressing.

"You will never gain control of your child if you cannot control her Beast."

Her?

The magix user was male. Had to be. All magix users born from S-Level Incubi were to be S-Level Incubi. They were to be male.

Yehwin tsked, shaking his large head.

"Not always."

Another wave hit Killian and he cried out but bit his lip in order to hold the sound in so no one would discover as Yehwin instructed.

"Make her stop, boy. Or she never will."

Stop, Killian commanded weakly in his head. In retaliation, another wave hit him. He screamed again.

Yehwin swiped at the prince with his paw. Not hurting him, but a warning that he could.

"Make. Her. Stop."

Again and again the pain hit him. He could feel something within the pain, as he reached forward trying to escape it. It would brush his palm and dart just out of reach. Desperately, he curled a finger around it and yanked with all his might. Bright orange light cocooned around him, holding him in a protective embrace.

"Stop it!"

The pain vanished.

Yehwin smiled with feline grace.

"Good."

It took several moments for him to catch his breath. The aftershocks of pain still haunted his body in phantom spasms. Killian tried his best to regain control and as soon as he could, he regarded Yehwin. Yehwin who remained unfazed by it all, sat there licking his massive paw, leisurely.

"Why?" Killian choked out.

Yehwin's ear twitched but he did no more than that to acknowledge the prince.

"Why was she screaming? What had I done to upset her?" Killian questioned further, needing an explanation for what just occurred.

"She is responding to your pain," Yehwin finally responded. "She cannot see, so you are her eyes. She cannot feel so she feels through you. Your pain is her pain. Both of your children's' pain. And when you cannot keep yourself in line...neither can she. You do this to yourself."

"But why now? Why is she lashing out now? I have been in pain for far longer."

Yehwin blinked at him slowly. Killian waited for him to answer.

With a sigh, he said, "She is developing. As all babes develop in the womb. And as she develops, she gets stronger. She can do more, she is more powerful. You can only expect it to get worse from here on out now that she can attack. It was coming all along, something you should have known."

Worse?

How much worse can it get? Had he not been dealt enough in his share of misfortune and misery? How much stronger must he become to weather this storm so catastrophic that the very foundation of the kingdom shook with unease?

This was too much.

"Enough of that boy," Yehwin snapped. "It is unbecoming of a King."

Killian sucked in a deep breath, trying to shake the near gutting of his chastisement. Though harsh, there were never truer words.

"Get up," he commanded.

The prince pushed himself to sitting position with the weak limbs that felt so detached from his body, wiping the drying vomit from his lips.

Wrinkling his snout in distaste, Yehwin swiped his paw at him. A surge of power wiped the mess from his face and the floor.

"Disgusting," he hissed.

Killian struggled to stand, swaying occasionally before finally conceding to the support the wall offered. Staring at the massive feline before him, Killian wondered aloud.

"How is it that you escaped the confines of the holding cell?"

Yehwin made a sound between a snort and a sneeze.

"You mortals cannot confine me," he hissed. Then his expression calmed into smooth indifference. "I am Cloud born."

A gasp of surprise left Killian's lips as he hastily dropped down in a bow, choking out a shocked, "Blessed!"

Yehwin ignored him and sauntered to the door. "Let's go."

Killian scrambled after him, but not before shooting Drek's unconscious form one last look.

"Be well my beloved," he whispered.

Yehwin hissed impatiently and Killian quickly followed suit, closing the infirmary door swiftly and firmly behind him.

"Where are we going?" he asked as they walked down the hall, cautious that they might run into any guards or servants who would find fright in the large feline whom was supposed to be confined.

"Relax, child of his blood. They cannot see if I do not will it so," he said, ignoring Killian's question.

Child of his blood?

Did he mean his great great great grandfather?

"Why do you call me that?" Killian asked.

"You share his blood, no?"

"Who?"

Yehwin's body arched gracefully as a sweet secret smile split his feline face. His eyes fluttered closed as if remembering a fond dream before he said softly.

"Liaelliuwei," his voice a gentle caress. A quiet purr making his entire body tremble.

Killian had heard the name before but knew very little of the male who bore it. For this he was certain, his blood ran through Killian's veins.

Yehwin settled before continuing his easy strut down the hall.

"You were his familiar?" Killian asked, though already knowing.

"Don't ask fruitless questions, boy."

"Why are you helping me?" the prince asked.

"Because I refuse to watch Liaelliuwei's empire crumble. You lot are destroying his life's work with your antics."

"You know who the other magix user is? The other beast?"

Yehwin said nothing.

"Who is it?" Killian pushed.

Yehwin whirled on him, blue eyes blazing.

"I am a Guide, not some source for pilfering information. You must figure it out."

Killian sighed. Of course it wouldn't be that easy.

Yehwin led Killian back to his room. He opened the door and found both Faust and Caspian waiting there. They stood upon his arrival.

"You called for us?" Caspian questioned.

Killian frowned in confusion then looked at Yehwin who only yawned and licked his paw. He sauntered further into the room settling himself on one of the chaises.

"Feed child. You are starving," he said.

Killian's frown settled even more. But he was right. He had to feed even if he was not hungry for that particular thing. He hadn't in so long he could only imagine how adversely it was going to affect him. He also noticed that Yehwin wasn't allowing his Consorts to see him, if the confused looks on their faces were any indication.

"I need to feed," Killian told them softly.

The look on Caspian's face was serious, something Killian was not very familiar with. It frightened him. Glancing over at Yehwin, he noticed he wasn't moving.

"You are going to watch?" Killian asked him incredulously.

"Nothing I haven't seen before child. I care not for your modesty," Yehwin answered with another yawn.

Killian didn't know how comfortable he was with that, but the looks on his lovers' faces were a bit more important. They couldn't see Yehwin, couldn't hear him. To them he must look every bit like a lunatic.

Killian cleared his throat and ignored their confused looks, taking each of them by the hand and led them to the bed. Caspian sat on the ledge of bed, pulling Killian by the waist until he fell on his lap, straddling him. His yellow eyes were intense as they searched his. Faust sat a little distance away, his black eyes just as intense.

Killian caressed the side of Caspian's face, tracing his jaw with his fingertips. His eyes drooped but he did not close them. He was still watching the prince with a tenderness that made his heart pound viciously in his chest.

"So beautiful," Caspian whispered.

Killian wrapped his arms around Caspian's neck and kissed him. A kiss full apologies, of desire, of overwhelming passion. He kissed him until his lips were flush with blood, tingling with a faint tinge of pain from the intense pressure. He kissed him like he'd never hold him in his arms again.

"Killian," he whispered, sensing his distress.

"I love you," Killian whispered, wanting to cradle him in his arms. Remembering the wide frightened eyes of the child that still lived within him. That had been hurt so many times. That he hurt so many times. One that he'd probably hurt again seeing as things were going to get worse. "I love you," Killian whispered again.

Caspian stroked his hair gently. "I know," he said. "I love you too. Very much."

"I do not want to hurt you," Killian whimpered as his hands slid down his sides to his butt, gripping and kneading the globes lovingly.

"I can take it, Killian. I'm not fragile."

"I do not want you to leave me," Killian finally admitted. The fear had been gnawing at him.

Caspian was skittish in a way. He lived on the streets most of his life. He was born with the instinct to flee when his life became endangered. It was the only way he could survive in Faltaire. His life was his top priority. Killian wouldn't blame him if he decided to leave. But the look in Caspian's eyes was dangerous. Anger swirled in those glowing yellow depths. His smirk was...scary. Not at all his usual warm and playful.

"Do you think so little of me, sweet Killian?" he purred. His voice poured down Killian's body like honey and liquid sex.

Killian pressed his face into Caspian's cheek and clung to him unable to bare his gaze any longer.

"Never," Killian whispered. "It is my fear of losing you that speaks. You should leave, for your own safety."

Caspian pulled back.

"For someone who is constantly begging to end their loneliness, you have a surprising habit of pushing those closest to you away."

His gaze was unwavering. Searching and piercing. Killian's defenses stood no chance. He kissed Killian then. Slow and sweet. Faust let them have this moment. Let Caspian take Killian first. Let him feed the prince until he fell limp onto the bed with a satisfied smile. Still conscious, just barely.

Killian kissed him again, softly.

"Thank you," Killian whispered to him.

Then he looked over at Faust. The Consort opened his arms for him. Killian crawled onto his lap and settled there, feeling slightly shy and not really knowing why.

He had been with Faust a couple times before, so it seemed kind of silly to be so self-conscious, but he definitely had not been with him as many times as the others. What with his declining health, he was afraid of taking too much of his strength away. Strength he could be using to fight off his strange ailment. He guessed that was pointless seeing as he was fine and probably always had been.

But the nagging suspicion that something was wrong, wouldn't release him from it's clutches no matter what proof was displayed before him. Faust's straight white hair was baby fine and softer than silk. Killian's fingers glided through them, feeling each lock slip from his grasp like water. Faust was smiling sweetly at him.

"It has been a while, sweetling," he said kindly.

"It has," Killian said softly with a frown.

"I know you meant no harm by it. I know I have your affections."

Killian kissed him softly.

"You do, you always will."

His smile was radiant then. Blinding the prince with the absolute perfection of it. He was so so beautiful. The way his skin glowed like the sun was caught beneath his pale white skin. Like he was born from the Clouds. Like he was a God.

He twisted Killian, gently laying him down on the bed, until his lean muscled body hovered over the prince. Killian ignored the ache of his weighted belly and stared up at him adoringly. He was still smiling. Even as he slid down and parted the prince's legs, exposing Killian to his gaze. His smile only broke when he leaned down to kiss the ring of wrinkles that cried slick in response.

Killian shivered, immersing himself in the feeling.

"Faust," he moaned when his tongue found him, caressing his most sensitive part.

He feasted on Killian and the prince loved every second of it. Every twirl and plunge of his tongue. His gentle ministrations had him panting. Breath left him in gusts.

"Faust, please. I need it. I need you."

Faust pulled back, his white lips glistening before his pink tongue flicked out and licked the remains from his face.

He reached over and kissed Killian. Kissed him again the moment his unsheathed member pushed inside. The moan caught in Killian's throat and his head flung back into the bed.

Faust trailed kisses along the newly exposed flesh, leaving him heated and begging.

Killian's thighs trembled around his waist. And Faust waited. Waited until Killian could breathe again before starting to move. Thrusting into him. Over and over again until the prince was literally sobbing in pleasure.

And that moment right before he hit his peak, Killian fed. Drained Faust of all he had to offer. Drained him until his inevitable climax coated his insides.

Now normally, Faust would pass out after Killian fed from him. He always passes out.

This time he did not.

Instead, he lay beside Caspian, limp and content. They both wore happy smiles on their faces with glazed eyes. Killian wanted to be worried about it. He wanted to question it. But he could not. Why? Because he was still starving.

Feeding had woken up a hunger in him. One that surpassed all hungers before. One so strong that his eyes began to tint orange as the beast inside him tried to take over.

No.

No.

He will not let him hurt anyone. Not again.

"Calm yourself boy. You'll work yourself into a miscarriage," Yehwin drawled, strolling over.

But this time, his form was of a male again. Dark golden brown skin, electric blue eyes, blinding white tribal markings on his arms, chest and face, and equally white short but messy hair.

His walk was smooth, graceful, like liquid.

Killian's heart beat wildly in his chest and he could hear the animalistic growls that burst from his throat, coming out in short spouts. His breathing ragged. he was fighting it. Fighting so hard to stay in control. Why is this happening? Why was he still starving?

"Because you haven't fed in a week. Two Consorts is not enough. Not when you're pregnant and not when you've been fasting. Stupid boy."

Yehwin leaned close to Killian's face. The prince could see every perfect inch of his. He flinched away. Yehwin grabbed his chin and forced him to look at him.

Killian was swallowed up in those glowing blue eyes. So bright they almost looked white themselves. He leaned closer until he was only a breath away, the closeness making Killian uncomfortable.

"Get over it. You need to feed and you need to be full. Come now, feed on me," he said. Killian recoiled.

"No!"

Yehwin snorted and rolled his eyes. "I will not join with you that way, I have no interest. We will share the warmth of lips and that is all. It will not harm me. You must feed. Feed or murder your entranced lovers and the seventeen guards in the hall. Your choice."

Killian growled but leaned forward.

With reluctance, he pressed his lips to Yehwin. His lips were warm and soft. Kind of like Rem's. Very precise like Rem too.

He squirmed a little.

Don't just move boy! Feed!

Killian gasped at the command then released his *Haise*. This feeling. It was like nothing he had ever experienced before. It was even stronger than when he fed on Beast. He was full in ticks. Stuffed even. He could take no more. But as he tried to pull away, Yehwin grabbed his wrists and pressed harder. The lust became painful.

Killian writhed, fighting against his hold but Yehwin was Cloud born. A God even. Killian could not even hope to contend with that power and strength. He forced Killian open, keeping his channels wide. His being felt like it was expanding. His skin pulled so tight against his bones. Resisting the tautness. Killian couldn't take anymore. He was going to explode.

No more! he begged. Please! No more! It hurts!

Take it all child, you need it.

Not this much. He was already full. It felt like it was killing him.

When he truly felt like he might pass out from the pain, Yehwin pulled back.

"Do not let even a tiny bit slip. Hold it in," He commanded with a sharp hiss. His blue eyes narrowed at him.

"I...cannot...Too...much," Killian gasped between pants.

"Hold it," Yehwin growled, then stood and turned briskly to the door. "Come."

Killian tried to move but stumbled. Yehwin hissed in annoyance before snapping his fingers. He was immediately dressed and flying toward him on some invisible current.

"Walk," he snapped.

Managing to do so but swaying the entire time. His vision, no longer orange, was blurring.

"Faster."

Killian pushed his body faster despite its urge to completely break down. The energy he fought to hold in was eating away at him, making everything so horribly uncomfortable.

He didn't even realize where they were until he was pulling back a white curtain and revealing Rem's broken and unconscious form. Yehwin stood beside Rem's bed and turned his sharp gaze on Killian.

"Now give it to him."

"What?" he choked.

"Give it to him boy. Heal him."

"I cannot do that! I do not know how--"

Yehwin clicked his tongue at him, annoyed.

"You're expecting a child yet you don't even know how to feed another? Halfwit."

Killian stared at him with wide eyes. Vision still blurring at the edges.

"Give it to him as you would take in during your *Haise*. Your body will know what to do instinctively."

"I-I-I cannot!"

"Enough with that! You can and you will! Do it now!" Yehwin snarled.

Killian could think of no other way but shoving his lips against Rem's cool, unresponsive ones and releasing.

He did not know exactly what he was releasing but he knew that it provided relief for the tightness in his being. Like sand pouring from a bag, draining him. It felt so good to let it go. And Yehwin was right. His body knew exactly what to do.

Rem's body jerked off the bed. His skin began to glow, gyrating colors as it does when he was in the throes of passion. His magix lit up like a flame, burning where Killian's skin pressed against it.

It was only when he was contentedly full and no longer uncomfortable with the tightness that he pulled back with a sigh. Rem coughed, leaning over the edge of the bed to vomit. After he was done, he sagged back into the bed, breathing heavily. He blinked his eyes and they went from black to orange to black again.

Yehwin made a disgusted noise before cleaning the vomit up with a wave of his fingers.

Rem sat up in bed.

"Rem?" Killian gasped.

He was looking at him bandages in confusion before his head snapped up and his eyes met his. Killian threw himself at his beloved, hugging him close and sobbing.

Rem held him tightly, caressing his back but not saying a word.

"I am sorry! I do not know why I did something so stupid!"

"Enough Killian. It is alright. Do not cry."

Killian didn't listen, still blubbering into his shoulder, successfully drenching him in his tears.

"Enough with the dramatics boy, we do not have the time. Tell him to go to your bedroom and wait with the other two." Yehwin snapped his fingers. "Come along now."

Killian turned to Rem.

"I have to go, but go to the room and wait for me with Caspian and Faust."

Rem was still confused but he followed the order without a word. Yehwin must have made him compliant because Rem would never just follow orders blindly. Even if it was from Killian.

He followed Yehwin to another room. Drek was still unconscious. Yehwin turned to him.

"Feed on me again."

He did so this time without hesitation. Taking as much into him as he could hold before immediately releasing it all into Drek.

Drek thrashed on the bed. He had to hold him down even though it took all his strength and a little bit of his power to do so.

He too, vomited, which Yehwim quickly cleaned up.

Killian told him to go to his room and wait for him with the others. When he nodded in compliance and disappeared, he looked to Yehwin.

"What now?" Killian asked.

In the brief moment that Killian blinked, Yehwin switched forms again, back to a tiger. Another blink and he shrank to the size of a housecat.

With a graceful leap, he landed on Killian's shoulder then laid himself across them, making himself comfortable.

"Now to the library."

"What about Zev?" Killian asked.

"He is already waiting in your room with the others. Now hurry up."

Killian headed for the library.

He gave the prince instructions, telling him where to go and what documents to pick up. He seemed to know exactly where they were and all of the content it held.

"What's this for?" Killian asked as they made their way back to the room where his Consorts waited for him.

"Don't ask stupid questions."

Killian huffed in annoyance.

Cloud born or not, he was very rude.

"I can be whatever I want. I am a familiar," he purred lazily, reading Killian's mind. That trick was getting old and fast.

When Killian opened the door to the room carrying the documents and books, he saw his Consorts all jump to attention. Caspian and Faust were back to themselves, if not a little exhausted.

"Why is there a cat on your shoulder?" Zev asked.

Killian was surprised to see him completely healed. Especially without his help.

"His injuries were healed by your servant Gestina," Yehwin yawned after stretching.

"Why is there a talking cat on your shoulder?" Zev said again looking very wary. "It is talking right? That's not the meds?" he asked the others.

"Nope, it's talking," Caspian confirmed.

Zev nodded satisfied. Yehwin jumped from Killian's shoulder. And another blink later he was a tiger again. His Consorts looked very confused then.

"I am Yehwin," the tiger said. "And I am here to help you...not die."

The looks on their faces were quite comical. Each Consort stared at Yehwin dumbfounded. Well except Rem of course who kept his face as unreadable as ever.

"Not as much as you might think, child," Yehwin said to Killian.

Reading his mind...once again. Killian glared at him for it and he sneezed then licked his paw.

"Where did you come from?" Faust asked quietly.

Yehwin stopped licking himself and stared at Faust. His eyes were narrowed intently, then he yawned and ignored him.

"Put the documents on the table," he commanded.

Killian did as he was told, spreading each document out on the coffee table by the little area of couches. All of his Consorts came to gather around.

"Each one of these documents has information you need in order to figure out what is going on and how to stop it," Yehwin told them.

Faust frowned, picking up a few pages.

"I've looked through these quite a few times and could find nothing that would prove to be of any use. Most are just old stories."

"Not stories," Yehwin hissed at him. "That attitude is why you haven't figured it out yet."

Faust cocked his head, then stared down at the pages intently as if the answers would suddenly leap out at him. But Faust was smart, he knew that would not happen.

Yehwin sighed then padded over to the table a slammed his paw on one piece of paper. "Read it," he snapped.

Caspian picked up the page and began scanning the contents written in their ancient language Vern.

"Read the fourteenth paragraph from the top," Yehwin told him.

Caspian began reading aloud.

"Ipill la yokun drolic ver peen ah van dris ouy'all mer valen. Vo ter Clued sa meno friyand. Somaastri er visterdin'ya ah la kin."

Yehwin was pacing. Then he held up a paw to stop him.

"Stop. Now what does that mean?" he prompted.

"It's just an excerpt about the Gods," Killian said confused.

Yehwin was getting impatient, pacing again.

"Yes, yes. But what about the Gods?" he continued to push.

"That the Gods are created by the Clouds and reside there. They watch us and may influence us but do not directly interfere," Drek said, supplying the answer this time around.

"Good, now why don't they interfere?" Yehwin continued.

"Because they are forbidden?" Killian said though it came out as more of a question.

"Why? Boy! Why are they forbidden?" Yehwin hissed.

Killian frowned. "I do not know."

Yehwin sighed then looked at Caspian.

"Next sentence. Keep reading."

Caspian frowned but did as he was told.

"Baayi non foed ni basan."

"Yes! Basan! What does that mean?" Yehwin stopped and stared at them all intensely.

"The word is unfamiliar to me," Killian admitted.

Yehwin sighed then looked at the Consorts.

"Anyone?" he drawled.

Rem spoke for the first time. "Corrupt."

He said it so softly Killian barely heard him.

"Again. Louder," Yehwin pressed, leaning forward.

"Corrupt," Rem said a bit louder.

"Yes! Corrupt! The Gods cannot directly interfere with the world of the living because they will become corrupt if they do."

"How is that relevant?" Zev asked.

Yehwin lost all his excitement. Killian could literally see him deflate. With an exasperated sigh, he shrank back into a housecat and went to curl up on the couch. "Read and find out. It's right in front of you."

"Are you serious? You're just going to stop there? If you know, just tell us!" Caspian shouted.

"Be grateful he gave us that much," Killian said softly. "He is a Guide. He does not give us all the answers, he leads us to them. He has been generous in giving us this much." he gestured to the documents on the table. Caspian sighed but let it drop.

Everyone got to work. Each Consort and Killian himself spent horas reading and rereading the documents over and over again for some sort of clue. But they did not know exactly what it was that they were looking for. What did the Gods have to do with anything? Were they cursing them? Was there some sort of loophole that allowed the Gods to interfere with their lives?

It did not seem possible but from the little information that Yehwin supplied, it seemed like the only answer. And none of his Consorts were coming up with anything better.

Killian sighed, leaning his head on Caspian's shoulder as he sat next to him on the floor with documents spread out all around him. He had his own hefty pile in front of him, none of which he could make any sense of. It was starting to frustrate him.

Caspian paused for a second before leaning down and kissing his temple. Killian closed his eyes at the feel of his soft warm lips on his skin.

"Do you want to rest?" he murmured lowly to him.

Killian shook his head and stretched his back a little bit, wincing when it ached. Drek, who was sitting on the couch behind him noticed his discomfort and grabbed a pillow for him to sit on. It helped a tiny bit but not much. Killian rubbed the small mound of his stomach. The twins have been pretty inactive, made him wonder if they were sleeping.

"They giving you any pain?" Zev asked.

Killian shook his head again, before looking down at his stomach. "I think they are asleep."

Killian couldn't be sure though, he was still very fresh in the pregnancy. Their movements were hardly noticeable as they were still small and still developing.

"Yehwin says the magix user is a girl," Killian said softly.

Everyone--except for the cat on the couch--stopped and looked at him.

"A...girl? I thought the offspring of a magix user and an S-Level Incubus had to be an S-Level Incubus themselves?" Zev questioned.

"That is a conclusion I had drawn as well," Faust said gently. "It is written here."

He pulls out a couple pages from one of the documents.

"It says that 'the intertwining DNA of one with the blessing of blood and an S-Level Incubus will inevitably spawn S-Level Incubi with the blessing of blood.'"

Yehwin, who had remained silent this whole time tsked with disapproval.

"You mistranslate. 'The intertwining DNA of one with magix and an S-Level Incubus will inevitably spawn S-Level Incubi and those with the blessing of blood.'"

"And with Killian having twins..." Caspian started before trailing off.

"One is with beast and the other an S-Level," Zev finished for him.

Yehwin snorted. "This term beast. I have adapted it as I have heard you speak it, but I do not truly understand why it is that you call them that."

"Those with magix have beasts," Killian said slightly confused by his admittance.

Yehwin's feline face contorted, contemplative.

"What is it exactly that you believe blessing of blood is?"

Rem spoke this time.

"The blessing of blood is large sum of power that develops into an alternate form of the holder composed of only base instincts."

Yehwin was quiet, his face twisted even more. He sat up and stared intensely before asking.

"And what do you believe determines who is gifted with the blessing of blood?"

"A genetic component in our blood," Rem answered but for the first time, hesitantly, he seemed unsure of his definition.

"Who taught you this?"

"It is in the books, the records," Killian replied, a bit confused.

"Wrong! All of it!" Yehwin exploded. And with his outburst came the abrupt transformation into a male. So quick that as usual, Killian didn't see it happen. Yehwin began pacing around the room, his expression angry. Furious even. Killian was a bit startled by the sudden change.

"Wrong?" Rem asked.

Yehwin stopped and whirled on us. "Yes! Wrong. Everything you have just said is completely and utterly wrong!"

Rem's eyes widened in shock.

Killian got up and went to him, grasping his hand tightly. The topic of magix was very sensitive to him, especially his lack of knowledge about it. Everything he knew was his only reassurance of himself and to be told that it was wrong? To be told that he literally had no idea of what he was, what he carried? It was soul shattering.

Yehwin stormed over to them. He peered up at Rem, who towered over him slightly, then snapped his fingers and Rem's tunic disappeared.

Yehwin studied the raised swirls and jagged lines that decorated Rem's chest and arms. Rem watched him, let him probe around until he was satisfied.

Yehwin took a step back, then turned to Killian, "Call him out."

Killian's mouth popped open in confusion.

"W-what?"

Yehwin grew impatient. "Call his 'Beast' out, boy!"

The prince looked over to Rem unsure. He didn't want to do anything without his permission, he didn't want him to be any more uncomfortable than he already was.

"Any day now!" Yehwin hissed.

"Is it okay?" Killian asked Rem.

He looked torn.

Killian turned to Yehwin.

"His Beast is very aggressive, especially around others--"

"I am Cloud born boy, or have you forgotten?"

There was a collection of gasps and soft, "Blessed" heard around the room amongst the Consorts. Rem stared at Yehwin a little differently, more unsure than before, but eventually he nodded to Killian.

Killian nodded back before taking a deep breath and whispering, "Beast, I would like to see you now."

The change was instant. The magix blazed brightly and his eyes glowed that brilliant orange. It was moving, like lava in his eyes, barely contained.

He immediately yanked the prince toward him, his nostrils flaring before he dug his face into Killian's neck. Killian could feel him sniffing around his skin. His eyes were wide. The movement in them, like there was a whole world trapped behind them, and it became more and more unstable.

This was the first time he's seen Killian since the jump. He was probably worried. Killian reached up and cupped his cheek, forcing him to stare into his eyes, knowing Beast could break his hold easily if he wanted to. But he didn't. Instead he looked at Killian and whined. The prince placed a hand on his chest, feeling the blistering heat of his magix and the frantic thumping of his heart. Just his, not Rem's. Rem's was slow and steady.

Beast was anxious.

"It is alright. I am fine. You saved me," Killian told him.

Beast whimpered, then tugged Killian closer, rubbing his cheek all over him. He gave Killian little licks on his cheeks and neck.

Yehwin just watched it all.

"You are a lot more developed than you should be...Sotershai."

Beast froze.

His entire body stiffened in Killian hold. Then slowly...very slowly, he lifted his head up to look at Yehwin. His expression...Killian couldn't read it. But there was an awareness that he had never seen before. Not with Beast.

"You even responded to your name...that's not good at all," Yehwin continued, his voice hard and extremely solemn.

His name?

Beast had a name?

Sotershai.

It sounded so familiar. Where had he heard that before?

Faust suddenly dropped the papers he was holding, his eyes wide with unbridled shock. His mouth hanging open with it. "Clouds have mercy," he whispered.

Beast's eyes flew to him for an instant before returning to Yehwin. Slowly and with a gentleness that he had never used before, pushed Killian behind him. The prince peeked from around his back, confused as to why he was assuming a protective position.

Yehwin's blue eyes glowed even brighter, such a stark contrast to his dark skin. The corner of his lips curled in a deadly smirk as his eyes glinted.

"Can you speak?" Yehwin asked.

Beast...no, Sotershai, growled lowly in warning.

"Not yet, but close to it, right? You've gained some awareness...and produced offspring."

Yehwin's eyes flickered to Killian and he felt a chill go down his spine. Yehwin's voice...it was so cold. Not at all like before. Killian was...afraid.

Yehwin was quiet then suddenly he appeared behind Killian, yanking him away from Sotershai and shoving him down on the couch.

Sotershai roared in fury, aiming to lunge for him, but bright gold chains appeared, slithering across his body and successfully restraining him.

"I can't move!" Zev growled.

Killian glanced at his Consorts and watched them as they struggled to move but were frozen in their positions. The prince turned his attention back to Yehwin who stared back with an unfriendly face.

He yanked Killian's pants down and spread his legs. Killian yelped in surprise.

Yehwin's fingers grabbed at a particular chunk of flesh on his inner thigh. It was small but there were markings there. Markings that Killian hadn't even realized existed. They were raised swirls that looked similar to Rem's but had subtle differences. Like a variation of his magix markings.

Yehwin hissed then turned to Killian's snarling lover.

"You bound this vessel. You were aware enough to do that much. You have broken so many rules, Sotershai! The Clouds will not be happy."

Sotershai thrashed against the chains that held him.

"I do not understand what is going on. How do you know his name? What do you mean?" Killian asked frantically.

But this time Faust spoke.

"Beast isn't a beast at all...He is a God."

Chapter 24

A God?

How is that even possible?

His name.

"Sotershai...the God of Fate, Destiny, and Protection."

It was Drek who spoke, looking just as shocked as he sounded. Yehwin stood, releasing Killian's legs and snapped his fingers. Killian's Consorts could move again but Sotershai was still being confined. The Consorts watched Yehwin warily, unsure if he was actually a threat to Killian but the familiar paid them no mind.

"Correct, the God of Fate, Destiny and Protection. Except Sotershai no longer exists. Should not exist."

Yehwin said before that Gods were not allowed to interfere with the world of the living because they become corrupt. When breaking the rules, especially of the Clouds, there were severe consequences. There had to be. Could it be that their punishment was to be wiped from existence?

"Why? Why shouldn't he exist? He's clearly right there." Drek asked.

But this time Killian had the answer.

"Because he is corrupt," he whispered.

Yehwin smiled.

"Precisely, child of his blood."

"But I still do not understand. Why is there a God in Rem's body?"

"I told you before that what you knew of the blessing of blood was false. What they have taught you is all wrong. The books you have read, the history you think you know, is false. Someone has hidden the truth from you. Someone is trying to rewrite history."

"So how will be able to figure out who the other person with magix is if we don't even know anything about it?" Zev asked with frustration.

"I will tell you," Yehwin said.

"I thought you said you wouldn't give us any answers, that you were only a Guide?" Drek questioned.

Yehwin sighed. "That was before I knew how poorly informed you were. I will not tell you who the other person is but I will tell you one thing. Those with the blessing of blood are vessels for the corrupt Gods. It is their genetic makeup, their natural power that ensures that their bodies are capable of holding the immeasurable power of a God. When Gods become corrupt they are stripped of what they once were and their base essence is sent into a void. When a child in the world of the living who bears the genetic makeup compatible with a God's power is conceived, the bare essence of a corrupted God is released from the void and inserted into the vessel and then grows with that child. Their awareness dormant so that they might never corrupt again."

"Why not just kill the corrupt Gods? Why put them in another body?" Zev asked.

"You cannot kill a God, foolish boy. They are immortal. That is something not even the Clouds can undo. Gods typically cannot exist within a mortal body. The mortality will taint them and trap them in the vessel they inhabit. That is why the Clouds chose to put dormant corrupt Gods in

"Does that mean that all those with the blessing of blood actually have corrupt Gods living inside them?" Caspian asked. Yehwin nodded once.

Killian felt sick. He gripped his stomach. There is a God inside of him. He was carrying a God.

Clouds have mercy.

"Not quite, child of his blood. The child inside you is a Half God. A demigod if you will. If an aware or awakened God conceives or sires a child, that offspring is bound. Meaning that no God's essence can enter that vessel because a new God has been created. In your case, the new God of Fate, Destiny, and Protection, assuming the position the spawn's sire once held."

"How did Sotershai awaken then? If he's supposed to be dormant?" Caspian asked.

"The vessel's original essence is the component that keeps the God's dormant. When that is disturbed the line gets blurred. Sometimes, but very rarely, the consciousness of the God can be awakened if the vessel endures a traumatizing or life threatening event, one that brings the God's essence total control of the vessel."

Killian suddenly remembered the little boy from his dreams. Rem. Running away from that inky blackness. He said he was almost killed by a pod of Sirens when he was younger. Could it have been that? Could that have started the awakening of the God inside him? And was that why he kept seeing it? Was it possible that Rem's beast...no...Sotershai was showing it to him?

"Children with the blessings of blood undergo many tragic events in their lifetimes...it comes with the curse. Would that not cause many of the corrupt Gods to awaken?" Faust asked softly.

The Consorts

Yehwin looked at him slowly...calculatively, before his eyes narrowed and his attention turned back to Killian. The prince did not expect him to answer, but he did.

"There are other...qualities to consider. It is not just any child with magix that can trigger the awakening of their corrupt Gods...but ones with natural and raw power. Levels that would normally kill them at birth. These children are so powerful that their bodies should not be able to hold it. And in rare cases, their vessels do and they live. There is no word for them...but they are special. And with so much power...it tends to...leak. Young Killian, when I fed you to heal your Consorts...you held much power. Much much more than you normally do and it was uncomfortable, yes? You wanted to release it somewhere...anywhere to rid yourself of the pressure. It is much like that for these special children. And when these children are endangered and have these traumatic experiences, that excess power is fed to the Gods inside them and it is like giving a starved male food for the first time. That is what triggers the awakening. It is a risk, yes, when the corrupt Gods are placed within these special children but it is one the Clouds are willing to take because there is nowhere else for them to go."

Sotershai snarled, practically foaming at the mouth before he gave one sharp yank and the chains snapped. He wouldn't hurt him, Killian knew that, but still he panicked.

"Stop!" he shouted.

Sotershai froze. His eyelids drooped as he stared at him with vacant eyes.

No...Killian didn't want to do that to him. He promised he wouldn't do it to him again.

"Rem, come back," Killian whispered shakily. The glow of magix slowly faded and the orange bled to black in his eyes. Rem blinked then looked around, confused by all the face still dumbstruck with the new information.

"You found what you were looking for?" Rem asked Yehwin.

Yehwin nodded.

Rem waited for anyone to clarify. No one did. The room was uncomfortably silent.

"Rem," Killian said softly holding his hand out to him. "Come have a seat."

Rem stared at him suspiciously, then did another glance around the room, noticing all the eyes on him. His face wiped clean of any emotion before he came to his side and sat next to him on the couch. Killian interlaced their fingers together and rubbed his thumb against his knuckles.

Killian took a deep breath and then told him everything they had learned. He watched his face through it all but he hid his reaction well. His eye didn't even twitch. He gave nothing, just simply stared at him stoically, quiet.

"Say something," Killian begged.

"I am...processing."

The prince squeezed his hand and to his surprise Rem squeezed back.

"So now that Sotershai is awakening, what will you do?" Zev asked Yehwin, standing up and coming to Rem's other side. There was something about his movements and positioning that made him seem just a little bit protective over Rem.

Yehwin pursed his lips and narrowed his eyes in thought.

"Nothing right now. There are more important things to be focusing on. You all need to figure out who the other magix user is and fast. They will strike again very soon."

Killian tensed at the new information. He wanted to know what their goal was. What did they hope to accomplish? What threat did Killian pose to them that they would so viciously come after him?

What had he ever done to his cousins to make them hate him so much that they would go out of their way to find someone to torture him, his loved ones, and finally kill them all? Besides a few petty arguments as children, he could not think of anything that would warrant such hatred.

"Do you believe the God within the other magix user is awakened as well?" Faust asked.

"You all better hope not because the within the other user is Perseth."

Perseth.

The God of Destruction and Chaos.

Caspian groaned, "Are you kidding me?"

"You lot have no idea how deep this goes, how much trouble you are in. It is why I could no longer sit back and watch. And if it is another awakened God that you are facing, if it is Perseth awakened, I would focus on getting your own God under control. Or else that is it for the lot of you."

And with that being said, he vanished.

"What are we going to do?" Killian whimpered, the panic starting to settle in. "I cannot fight this, I am pregnant and barely holding on to my sanity as is!"

"This is not your battle alone, Killian. It's all of ours," Drek reminded him. "And we need to look at the positive aspects. We have a God of our own on our side. And Rem on his own is incredibly powerful. Then there is the rest of us. Your Consorts. We are powerful too. The best of the best because in the event that you needed protection, your Father wanted you to have the most secure. And Sotershai is literally the God of Protection. We can handle this. You need to believe that."

Killian took a steadying breath.

"You are right. Panicking is not going to help anything. And as future King, I need to be prepared to deal with situations like this and remain calm. Gods above, it is like all my training went down the drain these past few months." he sighed.

"We can prepare all we want for disaster but when it actually happens, you'll never really be prepared. It's just the way life works," Caspian said softly.

That wisdom came from experience. Killian could see it in the clouded look in those bright yellow eyes. He just wanted to hug away all of his fears, doubts, and pain. He wanted him to smile and be carefree. He wanted him to actually mean it.

"We need to assume that Perseth is already awakened as worse cast scenario. I think our best bet is to fully awaken Sotershai," Faust said.

"And how are we supposed to do that? We didn't even know he was waking up in the first place," Drek pointed out.

"Well we do know that he has some sort of attachment or infatuation with Killian. I think in order to really push him into waking up, we need to call him out more. Have him interact with Killian more. Killian can draw him out until he's fully awakened."

"But what about Rem? What will waking him up do to Rem?" Zev asked.

"If he takes over than Killian can always just call Rem back. We have witnessed him do it not even twenty moments ago."

Zev looked unsure. Rem remained silent. Killian was worried about him, he seemed so detached from the entire situation despite the fact that they were discussing his fate. The news of what he held inside him was probably still ruminating in his mind.

"I think we are forgetting something really important," Caspian said with a level a seriousness that drew the attention of everyone in the room.

"What?" Killian asked.

"What did Sotershai do that corrupted him?"

The room fell silent. The tension thick.

"We could be unleashing a monster and not even realize," he continued.

Rem flinched.

Actually flinched.

Killian looked up at him with worry but his gaze was downcast and clouded. He was receding into himself, becoming more distant.

"You are not a monster, Rem. It does not matter that Sotershai is inside you because you are not him and he is not you. You are your own person, Rem," Killian told him softly.

Rem closed his eyes and tilted his head back with long exhale. Then without another word, he got up and left the room. Zev got up to follow him but Killian grabbed his hand and shook his head.

"He needs space. Let him collect himself."

Zev looked torn but eventually sat back down, placing a hand on his knee and rubbing anxious circles into his skin. Killian frowned at him but continued on with the conversation.

"We cannot do anything that Rem does not agree to. It is his body and his fate. We have taken advantage of him enough already," he said firmly and made sure every Consort was clear on that rule. Rem wasn't a pawn. He is a King. His King. His lover and his partner. Though he may need some reminding of that.

Killian felt a little nudge on his insides. His hand fell above it and he soothed a few small circles above the stretched expanse.

"It is alright little ones. Everything is fine," he whispered sweetly to them.

And it would be...he just had to keep believing that.

Killian and his Consorts continued their research in hopes of finding any clues about who the other magix user could be. They had their meals sent to the room and ate in silence. Well all except Zev who refused to eat. He was antsy beside Killian. His bright teal eyes periodically darting to the door in hopes that Rem would waltz through it.

He did not. They did not see him for horas. When they finally decided to turn it for the night, Killian saw Zev head for the balcony instead. He watched him through the window sadly.

Faust, Drek, and Caspian were tucked into bed, in the beginning stages of slumber. Killian crept past them and out of the room in search of Rem. He had an idea of where to find him and was happy when he was right.

He was in the garden, sitting on a low tree branch. The same one Killian found him on those many weeks ago when he was so convinced that he was a danger to him and that he needed to send him home.

Thank the Gods he didn't.

Killian cupped his underbelly and sat beside him on the branch, looking up at the night sky.

They were silent for a few long moments. Then finally, Killian reached over and touched his knee. He flinched again, but Killian did not move it. He squeezed it instead.

"Zev is worried about you," he told him.

Rem didn't say anything.

"He would not eat and now he will not sleep. He is waiting for you to come to bed."

Rem looked up toward the sky. The moon's light glinting off his perfectly angular face. His long straight nose, full lips, high sculpted cheekbones, and sharp jawline illuminated.

There wasn't just a God in him...he was a God on his own.

Killian cupped his cheek and forced Rem to look at him. He stared. His black eyes intense. So close Killian could see all of the crazy colors that make up that perfect blackness, just bouncing off each other, full of fear and anxiety.

"You speak of Zev, but not yourself," Rem says softly.

"Because I am not worried. I have never been worried. Not about you."

"I am a monster, Killian--"

"Enough," Killian snapped at him sharply. His tone even and finite. "I forbid you to utter such nonsense again, do you understand me?"

Rem did not answer.

Killian narrowed his eyes and squeezed him harder, jerking his chin toward him. "I said: Do you understand me?"

Rem's eyes flared and jaw clenched. He saw that rage, that fire in his eyes and a wave of relief went through him. This was Rem. He did not like being dominated. He did not like being ordered. Not by anyone...not even Killian. This is the male he loved.

Killian smiled.

"Say it," he whispered.

"I understand," he said...his voice cool and even.

Killian smiled wider and kissed him softly.

"You are not a monster, Rem. I know that you do not believe it now and I do not expect you to. It will take time to change your mind, but I will. We all will. We will make you see just how incredible you are. We will show you what we have known all along."

Rem's stare was intense.

Then suddenly, he grabbed Killian, smashing his lips against his. Rem's hands ran along Killian's body, tugging him closer until every inch of their bodies were touching. His kiss was passionate, fiery, fueled by so much, Killian was overwhelmed. He pulled back and panted breathlessly. Taking a deep breath, he stood and offered him his hand. "Come."

Rem grabbed Killian's hand and led him to the lounge. On the way, he stopped a servant and had her request for Zev to meet them there.

Killian pulled Rem to the bed and caressed his face as he kissed him fiercely. Only moments later did Zev burst into the room looking frantic. When his eyes landed on Rem he released a sigh of relief and headed over. He sat on Rem's other side and searched the dark Incubus's face.

"Are you alright?" Zev asked.

Rem gave a short nod.

Zev released another breath then nodded to himself. " Okay," he whispered.

"I told you he was worried," Killian laughed softly.

Zev glared.

"He had been gone for horas!"

"I am a grown male, Zev. I do not require a keeper," Rem said to him, looking at the flustered blue male.

Zev shoved himself to his feet angrily, "Well excuse me for caring!"

Rem snatched his hand, stopping him before he could stomp away. Zev looked back at Rem in surprise.

"Thank you," Rem said softly, then kissed Zev's knuckles lightly.

Killian had only seen Zev blush once before, but it was not as intense as it was this time. Rem released his hand and Zev sat back down beside him quietly. The prince chuckled, then kissed Rem's cheek. He kissed Killian's lips in return. And that aggression returned. Killian could see it in his eyes, he wanted to ravish him. He wanted him hard and fast. He wanted to release it all on him.

Gods above, Killian wanted it too!

But he was pregnant.

Rem's hands trembled along Killian's skin as his began to glow. Zev watched in amazement. A deep growl rumbled in Rem's chest, his eyes electric, full of passion.

He was incredible.

His fingers dug into Killian's hair before tightening into a fist at the nape of his neck and yanking. Killian's head flew back, exposing his neck where Rem nipped at the exposed flesh.

"I want to ravage this body of yours, sweet Killian," Rem growled.

Killian made eager sounds in the back of his throat.

But Rem pulled away, breathing heavily. His erection straining in his pants. He got up and paced.

"I cannot. You are pregnant and I will not be able to hold back. Clouds above, I need you!" he roared, his skin still glowing, even brighter now with each passing moment. Everything was so pent up inside him and it needed some type of release.

Gods, if only he could give it to him.

"Take me."

Both Killian and Rem's heads snapped over to Zev.

He was staring up at Rem with determination in his eyes.

"Take me," he said again.

It was silent for a long while but Zev didn't back down. He stared Rem down.

Rem's eyes flitted over to Killian. He made a sound of approval. His eyes hungry in anticipation. And then Zev stood. He walked over to Rem slowly, his eyes never breaking contact. Rem stared right back. Then slowly, Zev reached up and ran his fingers through Rem's hair. With one hand locked at his nape, Zev leaned up and pressed those pouty lips of his against Rem's.

Rem didn't respond to the kiss at first, but then slowly, he began to move his lips against Zev's. The blue male melted against him and the fire in Rem sparked again at the submission. Zev wrapped his arms around Rem's neck as Rem deepened the kiss.

Killian stood up and grabbed a chair, placing it at the edge of the couch so he could watch and give them the space they needed.

Zev pulled back from the kiss and tugged Rem by the waistband of his pants to the bed. Just as they reached the edge, Rem took a hold of Zev's thighs and hiked them up around his waist. Zev gasped as Rem now held him in the air and their erections pressed against one another.

They kissed passionately for a while until Rem tossed Zev back on the couch roughly. The blue male bounced looking shocked but strangely pleased. Killian purred in contentment.

Rem glanced over at him, his heated gaze fixated on the prince intensely. Killian moaned in pleasure at the attention, wishing so desperately he could join them, but knowing that was not a possibility.

"Rem," Zev whispered breathlessly, drawing the dark man's attention back to him.

Rem crawled over Zev and lined his torso with kisses until meeting his lips in a fierce claim of dominance. Zev met Rem's ferocity digging his hands into his hair, raising up to meet Rem's kisses. They battled like it was a vicious war to be won, and the inevitable victory fell to Rem.

Zev's breath came out in heavy pants as he stared up at Rem who had completely dominated him, had him pinned with two knees and one hand.

Rem growled down at him.

Still Rem though, not Sotershai. The God had yet to surface. He gave this moment to Rem.

Killian was completely mesmerized by the movements of their bodies, seeing the blue hues slide against the gyrating colors that made up the glowing black. There was something...poetic about it. Killian wanted to capture the beauty of it.

He could see the way Zev's body tensed, as if fighting the urge to dominate, to top. He would not top Rem. He knew he couldn't. And Killian noticed it in every shudder and every tremble.

It excited him.

Their bodies were like ice and onyx, sliding and writhing against one another. The soft lighting from the shining moon, sprinkling in through the sheer lavender colored drapery illuminated their bodies. Sweat glistened off their muscles, as he watched them strain to contain themselves within the heat of their passion.

Rem dug his hands into Zev's hair roughly, eliciting a moan from the man, then shoved his head down until the blue male was just inches from Rem's raging hard on.

Eagerly, Zev unfastened Rem's pants and freed him from the confines of his leathers. The long thick length of the dark male sprung forward, exposed for both Killian and Zev to enjoy.

Rem's head tilted to the side as he gazed down at Zev expectantly. There was a sort of power and Kingly aura surrounding him, in his behavior. It coaxed a whole new wave of slick from Killian's body. Zev needed no further encouragement before he bent forward and took Rem's impressive length down his throat.

Killian watched as he bobbed his head up and down swallowing Rem's rigid member with pure adoration. He worshipped him, so desperate to please. It was incredibly arousing. Killian had never seen Zev act that way before. He was always so confident and sure of himself. It was a nice change to see him at Rem's mercy.

Rem's eyes flicked up to Killian. His gaze hungry and fiery. Chest heaving with raging passion he had yet to unleash.

The prince smirked at him and bit his lip, opening his legs a little bit wider on the chair to give him a sneak peek of what was in between. Though it's not as if he hasn't already seen it before. Or tasted it...

Rem disappeared like smoke then reappeared before Killian. He gasped in shock. Rem leaned over him, arms caging him as he braced himself on the armrest of the chair. His face so close, Killian lost himself in those swirling black depths.

"Rem," he breathed.

He kissed the prince before he could even finish exhaling. His lips devoured Killian's. The prince whimpered in the back of his throat, trembling as Rem pulled him against his body. His hands slithered down until he reached Killian's entrance. He moaned as his Consort gently rubbed his fingers along his skin, soaking his hands in his slick.

Once his hand was practically dripping, he pulled away with one last chaste kiss and disappeared again. He solidified on top of Zev who lay naked on the bed, waiting. Rem's fingers traveled down the blue male's body until he found the spot he was looking for. He circled the ring of puckered skin, wetting it with Killian's slick, before pushing one lubed finger inside.

Zev hissed, back arching off the bed.

Rem leaned down to kiss his neck, whispering something in his ear.

Zev's legs spread wider, allowing Rem better access.

And gave Killian a better view.

Slowly, Rem's finger pushed in and out, coaxing heavy pants from Zev whose eyes were screwed shut and fists clutching the sheets beneath him.

Rem's eyes danced over to Killian and he saw the very rare smirk on his face. It was very slight but for someone who has studied this male's face for months now, he could catch even the tiniest of expressions.

Killian was elated Rem was enjoying himself. If there was anything to take his mind off the pain and stress of what was happening, Killian would give his life to get it for him.

Zev gasped loudly as Rem stuck another finger in. His hand moving smoothly now that Zev's entrance was coated in Killian's slick.

Killian's mouth watered when Rem finally turned Zev over, pushing his face into the bed and lined his shaft up with Zev's hole.

Killian leaned forward in his seat, hungry with anticipation. He watched the slow push of Rem's body and the utter bliss on Zev's face as the male he loved slid inside of him. Killian squealed in delight.

Rem's eyes flickered over to the prince, drawn in by the sound. Then with slow precision, he began to thrust. It must have taken a lot for him to remain as gentle as he was in the beginning, when Killian knew he wanted nothing more than to screw Zev into the mattress. But he was patient and steady letting the other male get used to the intrusion.

And Zev...Zev was a sight. All of those muscles quivering with strain, a light sheen of sweat coating his skin, the very faint shadow of those long blue lashes casting over those high cheekbones. He was an incredible sight to behold.

Rem knew it too, angling back to give Killian a better view. Then without much warning, he snapped. Rem's thrusts were powerful, hard, quick and it left both Zev and Killian breathless.

Where Killian was vocal in bed, Zev was not. He took it silently, with his mouth hanging open in soft pants. His eyes stayed closed but it was obvious from the euphoria on his face that he was enjoying himself.

Rem held nothing back from Zev now. It was all aggression, all untamed passion. He was a machine, in the way his body moved, unyielding. When he grabbed Zev's dark blue tail roughly, yanking it, eliciting a loud yelp from Zev, he noticed the orange flicker in his eyes.

Sotershai did not surface, but he was there. Rem's pleasure was his own. And it took no more than a few moments for the dark male to explode inside of Zev. The sensation proceeded to bring Zev to completion only moments afterward. And like a chain reaction, seeing the males he loved release inspired his own climax.

Killian's body quivered with the aftershocks of release.

Zev had completely melted into the bed, his body limp with the afterglow. Rem was still breathing heavily, his chest moving frantically, but the aggression was gone and the brightness of his skin began to dim to it's normal blackness.

Killian sighed in contentment, a happy grin on his face.

"Wonderful," he whispered.

Zev gave a tired smile. "I agree completely."

When Rem slowly eased himself out of Zev's body, the latter let out a soft moan at the loss.

Killian's Rank One sauntered over to him, cupping his face between his large hands.

"Feel better?" the prince asked.

"Much."

Chapter 25

Killian was feeling particularly unwell today. It was obvious from the way his stomach rolled through the night, forcing both his Consorts and himself to wake up various times so he could vomit.

It most certainly didn't help that the twins were starting to become a lot more physical turning what used to be gentle flutters into sharp jabs.

"This is only the beginning," Lorn told him. "It's only going to get worse from here on out."

Comforting.

"Deep breaths, Kill," Drek reminded softly rubbing gentle circles along Killian's back as he hunched over a bin puking his guts out.

It was horrible, the worst he's felt so far.

Killian choked on another wave of vomit, tears burning his eyes as nothing but acid pushed through his lips. Drek's face twisted in pain as he watched him suffer.

Caspian was there with a warm cloth and a glass of water for Killian to wipe his face and rinse his mouth out. The prince leaned against Drek's shoulder, panting and eyes tearing up, hating how he felt.

And it was only going to get worse.

S-Level Incubi suffered the worst through pregnancy. In the past, the symptoms were so terrible that the survival rate was significantly lower than it is this day and age with modern magic. He counted himself lucky enough to be born in this era but unlucky for having to endure this.

When his stomach finally settled, fatigue overcame him. His whole body went limp with exhaustion. Drek brushed a sweaty lock of hair from his face, tucking it behind his pointed ear.

"Shouldn't he start getting better? I mean he's in the middle of his second trimester right?" Drek questioned aloud.

Caspian shook his head sadly. "No. Not with S-Levels. Unfortunately it's only going to get a lot worse. Only Succubae have their morning sickness recede when the in their second trimester. S-Level Incubi gradually increase with their symptoms all the way up until it's time to deliver. He'll have to be bedridden a whole month before his expected due date. Too much movement can create unnecessary complications. And being pregnant with twins..." Caspian trailed off sadly, but it said enough.

Drek raised a brow.

"You sure know a lot about this."

Caspian's expression went dark. "I was born in a brothel, it comes with the territory."

Drek's face grew sad, but Caspian simply smiled at him. "It comes in handy though. I'll know what to do when the time comes, it helps to be better prepared, yeah?"

Drek nodded. Then he glanced down at Killian. The prince's eyelids were heavy, weighing down on his eyes. He could barely see through the slivers of vision he was granted.

"Don't let him sleep. He'll have another episode," a familiar voice said.

Yehwin appeared on the bed, in full tiger mode. His huge body taking up a portion of the large bed as he lay sprawled on his side, completely relaxed with those glowing blue eyes trained on Killian.

Drek gently shook the prince until he blinked sleepily.

"I want to sleep," he mumbled.

"Sure. Sleep. And kill about twenty more people," Yehwin said flippantly, licking his massive paw.

Killian glared at him weakly.

"I'll go get you something to eat," Caspian said softly before silently disappearing from the room.

Drek gave Killian a quick kiss, once on the lips and another on the forehead.

"Stay awake, Kill," he murmured against his skin.

Killian groaned in protest not realizing his eyes had closed completely.

"So I see you all have made no progress with finding out who the other magix user is yet," Yehwin tsked. "The longer you wait, the worse your futures will become."

"If you're so all knowing just tell us," Drek growled in annoyance.

Yehwin hissed at him.

"I am not all knowing. I know much but not all, brat. And I am not permitted to tell you. There are rules that I must follow as well and I refuse to be punished by the Clouds because you lot are too dimwitted to realize what's in front of you. I have provided too much already."

Drek opened his mouth to retort but Killian squeezed his arm and shook his head.

Turning his attention to Yehwin, "Thank you. We are grateful for your guidance and all that you have risked for us."

Yehwin purred in approval.

Drek huffed, not very happy with the circumstances. Killian couldn't fault him, it was incredibly frustrating for them all.

Faust swept into the room. His silver collar shining, matching the silver crown on his head and sparkling against the stark white of his straight baby fine hair. His black horns looked polished, glistening just as much as his accessories. He had an aura...different from before. Powerful even.

It was...strange. It made Killian uneasy.

"My dear sweetling, it is time for your fitting," he said to him gently in that musical voice of his that seemed to melt his very being. His big black eyes showed nothing but warmth and kindness as he knelt before Killian, grasping his hands. "Are you well enough to move? I can reschedule."

"No. Make him go. It will keep him awake and alert. We do not want our dear Aaia causing a fuss."

Aaia?

Killian raised a brow at Yehwin in confusion and he could see his Consorts doing the same.

Yehwin yawned. "Tis what you'll name the girl."

Aaia.

It was strangely perfect.

He glanced down at his stomach, placing a hand upon the bump as if he could touch her.

"Go now, or she'll start screaming again," Yehwin sang in warning.

Killian flinched and jumping to his feet immediately, wobbling when the weakness overcame him. Faust and Drek both jumped to catch him. He staggered but caught himself and waved them off.

"It is alright. I am fine. Just got up too fast. Let us go," he said quickly. Faust and Drek shared a look while Yehwin chuckled.

"I'll tell the other lover to bring your food to you," Yehwin called to their backs as his two Consorts escorted him out of the room.

Killian was brought to the royal fitting room in the seamstress's wing where his brothers and sister were all being fitted. Servants and seamstresses all flitted around with a purpose. Orders were being barked and fabrics carried. Gilra was chatting away with her attendant, gushing about the two fabric choices. One of glittering gold that would go wonderfully against her dark brown hair. The other a saturated cream that would look lovely against her lavender skin.

Ian was having the final alterations of his ensemble done. He looked absolutely stunning in his white tunic with gold embroidery along his chest and stomach, slim fitting sleeves, and high collar with dark brown pants tucked into gold boots.

Pierce looked incredibly uncomfortable as his own white vest was being fitted. He too had gold embroidery along the mid section of his vest but it was intertwined with red jewels. He was still wearing his black leather pants that he trained in. Killian was positive they hadn't gotten that far in the creation of his outfit.

But he was amazed at how captivating his siblings were. Though they all shared traces from their mothers, Killian's more prominent, it was still very clear who their father was. He showed in all of them.

As soon as his sister's gray eyes glanced in his direction, a high pitched squeal pierced the air. Ignoring whatever conversation she was in the midst of, she hurried over to Killian, her hands immediately flying to his stomach.

"Oh Killian, look at you!" She gushed, then cooed incoherently at the bulge at his abdomen. She was careful not to physically touch him, wary of the warning looks his Consorts were giving her. More so Drek than Faust. But Faust did look a little bit worried.

She looked up at Killian with hopeful gray eyes, hands poised over his stomach, "Can I?"

He smiled slightly and nodded.

Her first touch shocked him a little. He was used to having his Consorts put their hands on him. His body had become accustomed to their touch. He even became used to Lorn's hands on his stomach. But having someone foreign...startled him. Made him uncomfortable.

And he hated that he was referring to his sister, his own flesh and blood as foreign, but she was. This distance that he was forced to keep when growing up has estranged him from his siblings. As much as he did not want to admit it, it was affecting him.

He fought the urge to flinch when her hands made their way around his stomach, softly prodding, hoping to feel any sort of movement. But his twins were sleeping peacefully now, being rocked to sleep by his movements.

"It's still a bit too early for others to feel them moving," he told her softly despite knowing that Faust was able to feel them once they heard his voice. Maybe if she sang for them, they'd move for her too.

After all, his sister had an amazing voice.

"Lady Gilra, we have to finish fitting you for your gown," her attendant called out to her.

Gilra smiled brightly at Killian before straightening up, placing a kiss to his hand, and practically skipping over to her attendant. He smiled fondly after her. How easy it must be to live so carefree.

"Stop that. I can tell what you're thinking and it doesn't make sense to compare. It won't change what's happening," Drek said quietly.

Killian sighed.

"I know," he agreed sadly.

Lisa approached with her parchment pad in hand.

"Prince Killian, Lord Drek, Lord Faust, this way," she said, gesturing to behind a curtain where countless servants waited. Ethel was there with a kind and nurturing smile on her withered face. It would be strange now, to have her dress him without Kara. It had been the both of them for so long, he barely knew one without the other.

And knowing he was the one to take Kara's life? It made him sick to his stomach.

"Nervous? Your first time having other servants see you undressed," Ethel said jokingly. She knew what he was truly thinking of and this was her way of diverting his attention. He hadn't thought about the others that would see him. His whole life he'd been covered up with only Lisa, Ethel and Kara being able to see him in any state of undress. But now that he had his Consorts and he was no longer "pure" of body, it did not matter who saw him. Of course, it was improper to go sporting around immodestly, but there were less restrictions.

"A little," Killian admitted with a small smile.

"Don't fret. When you were just a babe, you used to run around the palace naked. Lisa here almost had a conniption every time."

Lisa glared at the older female before hissing, "It is improper."

"He was a child," Ethel said with a playful roll of her eyes. Lisa huffed.

"Come now, let's get you out of those clothes so I can get your measurements. You two Lord Drek. Lord Faust, Lady Gilra has already sent the designs for your ensemble, we just need to make a couple of adjustments," Ethel said.

Killian raised a brow at that.

Gilra?

Why would she be designing Faust's outfit for the ball? Since when did they talk?

Killian was still frowning as Faust was pulled in one direction by a servant while he and Drek were pulled in another.

"How has the morning sickness been?" Ethel asked as she pulled the measuring tape around his waist.

"Awful. This morning was the worst."

"I have a couple of remedies I could cook up for you, it will help with some of the symptoms."

He smiled at her gratefully.

"I remember when the Queen was pregnant with you. His Highness has no idea what to do. I was called in the wee horas of the night when the Queen felt ill and His Highness was too panicked to be of use," Ethel continued fondly. "I'd make honey ginger porridge at three in the morning just so Her Highness could settle her sickness and get a couple horas rest."

"I am in dire need of that," Killian laughed.

Ethel continued on with his new measurements, telling him stories about his mother's pregnancy and his Consort mothers' pregnancies and how their symptoms differed. How they dealt with their discomforts differently and how his father panicked the whole time. Apparently, he even fainted when Gilra was born. Couldn't handle all of the blood.

The Consorts

Killian was still laughing when Zev entered the room, looking regal in his silver crown and matching collar, striking against his blue skin. His navy and white streaked waves were piled high on his head and out of his face. He was dressed simply in a dark tunic and black pants tucked into black boots.

He approached Killian immediately, giving him a swift kiss on the forehead.

"It's nice to hear you laugh again. See your smile," he murmured in his ear.

Killian blushed and smiled inwardly, turning his face into his Consort's neck happily.

"Lord Zev, this way for your fitting," a servant said.

Zev gave Killian another kiss before following the servant. The prince watched him go.

"You are so smitten," Ethel teased.

Killian blushed even harder and looked away but couldn't quite keep the grin off his face. He was smitten. With all of his males. Each one of them brought him such happiness and joy, he couldn't ask for more in his lovers. And they each were different, adding to this relationship in many ways. Some nurturing, some humor, some friendship, some protection, some intelligence. He could only hope that their children inherited these traits from them all.

The small smile found its way back on Killian's lips as he chuckled quietly to himself, counting himself lucky to be with such incredible males. Ethel grinned widely at him, as if she could read his mind and knew exactly what had him so giddy.

Could you blame him?

Look at them, they were wonderful.

Killian glanced over at Faust who just finished putting on his tight white leather pants with a gorgeous gold embroidery tucked into calf length yellow gold boots. His upper half was clad in a white tunic that had gold floral designs along the front. His collar was short and straight but did not hide the gold collar encrusted with red rubies, decorated with gilded foliage. Around his stomach was a gold belt tied tightly and on his head a stunning gold crown that looked like small curved antlers interweaving into a circlet.

Killian's jaw dropped with how amazing he looked. He had never seen a more regal being in his life. Even his other Consorts were awed.

Killian opened his mouth to call out to him but the words caught in his throat as he saw him wince, gripping his head. His once clear black eyes glazed over and watered slightly. He rubbed the center of his forehead, right between his horns.

A frown turned Killian's lips as he stared at him and deepened when he saw a servant girl rush up to him with a cup of steaming tea.

"Thank you," he said softly with gratitude to the servant with his lovely musical voice.

The girl bowed and rushed away.

She had short brown hair and caramel colored skin. Her eyes were big and golden framed with thick lashes. Her features were cute, youthful. She couldn't have been any older than Pierce's seventeen years. But he had never seen her before.

"Ethel," Killian said lowly. "Who is that girl?" His eyes never leaving the servant who went to stand at the edge of the room, her gaze never leaving Faust.

There was something off about her.

Something in her eyes that seemed...empty.

"Her name is Maya, she's the daughter of one of the palace chefs," Ethel replied quietly as she followed his gaze.

"Why have I never seen her before?"

"She's been attending your extended family."

Killian's brows shot up and his reaction was instinctual. He flung his hand out, sending the cup of tea in Faust's hand flying across the room where it hit the wall and shattered into hundreds of pieces, spraying tea everywhere.

Killian's eyes shot to the servant. He pushed Ethel's hands away and started toward her.

"Leave," he commanded.

She stared at him blankly.

His anger flared and with it, his left eye tinged orange. "Leave."

She blinked startled before dropping into a deep apologetic curtsy before hurrying out of the room.

All of the servants stared at the prince in fear and confusion, not knowing what just transpired. His Consorts looked on with concern.

Killian waved his hand, ordering them to carry on with their tasks. Slowly, they followed suit and continued their work.

"Lisa," Killian barked.

She was at his side immediately looking wary.

"Yes, Prince Killian?"

"Anyone serving my visiting relatives and their attendants--cooks, maids, guards, anyone--they are not allowed anywhere near myself or any of my Consorts. Is that clear?"

Lisa stared at him for a long time and he stared right back, daring her to challenge his authority, before she nodded.

"Yes, My Prince."

He dismissed her then stalked up to Faust who was staring at him with confusion.

"How long has she been serving you?" Killian demanded.

"Sweetling, I don't underst--"

"How long has she been serving you?" He snarled. The anger not directed toward him as he knew it had nothing to do with Faust, but at his cousins because he knew they were up to something. He would not let them harm another one of his Consorts. Not Faust. He would protect him.

Faust stared at him silently for a while, searching his face. Anger bubbled in Killian and his vision flickered orange again.

A gentle hand came around Killian's waist as a warm body pressed against his side. "Best to answer him, mate," Caspian said to Faust as he clutched the prince close, drawing circles into his hip. He was staring at Faust intensely, in warning while simultaneously trying to calm Killian down. He was communicating with that stare, to let Faust know Aaia's Beast was lurking and would arise if pushed.

"For quite some time now, a bit after the announcement of your pregnancy," he answered softly.

And right around the time he started getting sick.

The connection was so obvious, how had he not known better? Faust wasn't naive...he was the most intelligent Incubus Killian knew. So why...

"And she has been giving you this tea?" he asked.

"Yes. It was a new brew that was offered to me and I was interested in trying," Faust said softly. A hiss of annoyance slipped from his lips. He couldn't believe this!

"You are not to drink it anymore, Faust."

Faust gave a slight nod, "If that is your wish, sweetling."

Killian peered up at him.

"You are feeling ill again," he accused.

Faust smiled gently, "It is just a tiny headache, nothing worth worrying about."

"Faust, please. You have to tell me these things. Stop trying to carry all of this on your own, let me help you."

"I swear to you sweetling, there is nothing for you to be worried about," he promised.

Yeah right.

Killian turned to a servant, "Go get Rem."

"My Prince, Lord Rem is in a meeting with the King--"

"It was not a request," he said quietly, cutting them off.

"Yes, My Prince," the servant said, bowing, then disappearing.

"Is everything okay?" Caspian murmured down to him, his words barely more than a whisper of breath against his ear.

"No," he said simply and waited until his Rank One materialized in the room in a puff of smoke. His dark eyes sought him out immediately. Blank expression, all business. He did a swift survey of the room, making note of the obvious tension and the mess of glass that was currently being cleaned up.

"Leave us," he called out to the servants.

They began to scurry out of the room immediately, fearing the prince's wrath. The rumors that had been floating around about him most likely contributed to their speed.

"Ethel, Lisa. You stay," he said.

They both bowed and stayed put.

"Yehwin!" he called out.

He blinked and suddenly the male was standing in front of him in tiger form, his glowing blue eyes fixed on him. Ethel and Lisa gasped in alarm. Killian looked at everyone before speaking.

"I have been silent and I have been passive and they are getting cocky because of it," he stated with barely contained anger.

Ethel and Lisa looked confused. As expected seeing as they knew nothing about what was going on. Ethel had some inkling, she knew how his cousins treated him growing up and often came to his defense when he was blamed for their poor behavior. And she was smart, intuitive, and perceptive. She must have picked up on something.

"I have no doubt in my mind that that tea is what made Faust so sick. My guess is, they are trying to kill him. Just as they have tried to have Drek killed with their framed rape case. And Caspian when they urged me to shatter his soul. I am sure Zev and Rem are next. I am not going to let it happen."

Killian watched as some faces twisted at the mention of the attempt on Caspian. Many of them hadn't known about it. Killian did not tell anyone and neither did Caspian.

"I do not know how they are doing it. I do not know why they are going to such lengths in the first place. But these are not childish games anymore, these are attempts on my life, the life of my heirs, the lives of my lovers and that is treason."

Killian had everyone's undivided attention.

"I am done waiting. I am done letting them get away with it all."

He made eye contact with each and every one of them.

"It is time to make our move."

"We should alert the King--" Lisa said quickly, panic in her voice.

"No," he said sharply. "This must be handled on our own. Unfortunately, my father is too blind to see what is happening right under his own nose."

"But--" She started.

"Lisa, this is a King's order."

Her lips snapped shut and her eyes widened in shock behind her thick black framed glasses before she bowed deeply.

"As you command, My Prince."

Killian looked away and back to the rest of the group, "Tomorrow night we will have a meeting in my private chambers. I want each of your lieutenants present. Do not speak a word of this to anyone. Ethel and Lisa, I want you both present as well."

"Should we inform your siblings as well?" Ethel asked, concern lacing her voice.

Killian shook his head. "My siblings will be fine not knowing. They are not targets."

Yehwin tsked.

"Are you sure about that, child of his blood?" he sang.

Ethel and Lisa gasped, unaware that Yehwin could talk.

The familiar barely spared them a glance. His glowing blue eyes were trained on the prince.

Killian frowned. "What are you saying?"

Yehwin's head cocked to the side. "They are after your life, yes? You are future King. If you die, who is to take the throne? Ian, no? They will go after him next."

Killian's eyes widened in horror.

"Are you saying this is about taking the throne?" he asked.

Yehwin rolled his eyes before glaring at him, "You will be King, boy! Everyone is after your throne and you are foolish if you do not know that already."

"They would have to massacre our entire family in order to get the throne. The line of succession is too grand for a takeover."

Yehwin sighed. "You are naive. People will go to many lengths to take the crown. There will always be a target on your back. As there is on your father's and every King or Queen before him. That is the price you pay for your kingdom."

Killian frowned. Were his younger siblings really in such danger? Ian? Gilra? Pierce? Pierce was still a child.

Killian cleared his throat uncomfortably before speaking. "Even so, it is best to keep them out of it. We will be discreet in our approach and they will be safer with the less knowledge they have of the matter. Besides, I have no intention of dying. I will be King and I will remain King until my heir is old enough to take the throne from me. I will not be intimidated and I will not be overthrown."

Yehwin didn't say anything else.

"Allow the servants back in and do not speak a word of this."

There were several nods before the room filled again with servants. It was quiet as their outfits were designed and fitted.

The food Caspian brought was not nearly enough to satisfy his hunger so they all shared a meal out in the garden. It was actually really nice. Killian rarely got to spend time with all of them together besides when they went to bed. Though with his incessant morning sickness, it was short lived.

Ethel made him some of her famous ginger honey porridge which helped a bit with his stomach. He had some more right before bed to sleep longer. And Gods knew he needed as much rest as possible with the Ball tomorrow.

He was cuddled between the strong chests of Rem and Drek while Caspian hugged his waist underneath the comforter and Zev spooned Rem's back. Faust slept peacefully on the other side of Drek.

Sleep actually came to him. His dreams were full of bright vibrant colors. It was a nice change from the dark wispy shadows he was so used to.

He dreamt of his future children, running around giggling, causing mischief in the palace and driving their fathers insane. He dreamt of a gorgeous little girl with red jewel eyes and onyx black skin and curly black hair with random strands of maroon. Her face chubby with youth and tiny button features. Always beside her is a little boy with the same chubby face and button features, brilliant red eyes, and straight maroon locks. His skin a familiar pale blue. They both had identical maroon horns and tails. They were adorable.

In his dream, they were tickled and twirled by Drek, sang to and read to by Faust, playing tricks and causing mayhem with Caspian, spoiled with treats by Zev, loved and protected by Rem, and pestering Yehwin. Killian saw this complete family. And it was so real. He didn't want it to be just a dream. He wanted that reality. And he wanted it badly enough that he was willing to fight dirty to get it.

He would not let his family be destroyed before it even truly began. If he had to bathe in blood, it will be done.

That morning he woke up early but well rested and determined. There was a fire in his veins that he hadn't felt in a while. He felt invincible.

Waking each of his Consorts with a kiss, they bathed and started the day with a meal. The palace was buzzing with excitement as the preparations for the ball were being finished up. Killian still had some time to himself before he had to get ready. He spent that time doing as much research as he could and wasn't any closer to finding answers.

Ethel came to fetch him when it was time to start preparing for the Ball. His attendants buffed and polished every inch of his skin until he was practically glowing. His scalp tingled after being tugged and curled so many times. His hair was braided and styled into a high bun wrapping around his gold and ruby crown. He was dressed in his white chiffon harem pants with red shorts underneath and a gold chain belt that jingled when he moved and felt heavy on his hips. His torso was clad in a heavy gold and ruby encrusted bodice with a slight protrusion for his raised stomach and high collar. His family crest was clear in the middle.

His feet were covered in soft leather shoes that soothed the ache as his body accommodated the extra weight. On each shoulder, a pendant was clasped holding in a place a long deep red velvet cloak with gold embroidery. It too was heavy but bearable. Killian was used to such things.

When he was done getting ready, he found his Consorts also dressed and looking drop dead gorgeous. Drek was stunning in a cream and gold tunic and pants tucked into gold boots that matched his crown and collar.

Caspian nearly blended in with his all gold ensemble trimmed with red fur and red boots. His crown and collar sparkled with red rubies.

Zev was striking in his white and silver ensemble with several cut outs covered in mesh along his sides and chest. His silver boots were shiny and freshly polished matching his collar and crown. Killian had already seen Faust's outfit but he still looked more breathtaking with it on.

And Rem...

He was absolutely divine.

They covered his broad shoulders in a black fur mink linked together with a single silver chain. The chain was clasped together with a red ruby pendant. The rest of his smooth black torso was bare, letting the world feast upon his rippled abdomen. His legs were clad in black leather, so tight they were nearly pasted on and blended with his skin. His boots were a dark silver with black and red accents. Much like his belt that hung low on his hips with Killian's family crest in the center. His collar was the same dark silver, tight against his throat and it matched the gorgeous black and silver crown on his head.

The Consorts

He braided his hair back to show the sharp angular features that drew Killian to him like a moth to a flame.

He was as beautiful as he was deadly.

"Prince Killian, you will be announced soon," Lisa said to him.

He snapped out of his gawking and nodded to her in understanding. That meant that his Consorts would be leaving now. They were to make an appearance first before his Rank One escorted him out. And they did, once they received the cue from Lisa.

Drek, Faust, Caspian, and Zev each placed a chaste kiss on his lips as they passed to enter into the ballroom. Rem stayed by his side watching the small waiting room clear out. His hand slipped around Killian's waist comfortingly.

Lisa peeked behind the door before closing it and motioning them forward.

Killian could hear the buzz of the crowd, but he tuned it out because he didn't like the way it made him feel. That nervousness that sank into his gut whenever he was in front of a large crowd. It would only cripple him in the end and he could not show weakness. Not as a King and most certainly not in front of his visiting relatives who were waiting patiently outside that door. Waiting for him to show any sign of failure so they could exploit it.

"Relax," Rem said softly.

Killian took a deep breath and let it out slowly, feeling a calmness settle over him. Rem nodded in approval before offering his hand. Killian took it and the doors opened, the room quieting.

He saw the hundreds of faces of many kinds, dressed up in their best formal wear. Unfortunately, the whole Kingdom could not fit in the ballroom so only allies and friends could attend, but there were so many that it was not lacking in any way.

His visiting family sat to his left while his Consort mothers, siblings, mother and father sat to his right. And in between were his four Consorts kneeling on either side of his throne. Drek and Caspian on the left, on one knee with one fist resting on the ground while the other was tucked behind their back. Their heads bowed in respect. On the other side, Zev and Faust mirrored them.

Once Rem and Killian approached them, he stopped and Rem continued forward, kneeling beside Zev closest to his throne. Killian proceeded forward, caressing each of their cheeks lovingly. Each one leaned into his touch, nuzzling his palm or placing a kiss to his wrist.

He turned and sat on his throne, smiling at the crowd, who then began to resume their chattering. Killian nodded to his Consorts who stood and took their respective seats on either side of his throne, just one step below where his was perched.

He hated the setup of their thrones. He knew it was important to show hierarchy but once again he was isolated. Too far from his family and too far from his lovers. He couldn't talk to anyone.

And until he gave birth and had his official Consort King declared, he would remain alone on this pedestal. Killian sighed sinking into his seat.

Caspian glanced back at him, hearing his sigh. He stood suddenly, walking over to the musicians playing with his catlike grace and smooth movements, his tail sashaying with every step.

Killian watched as he leaned over to the composer and whispered to them. They nodded then bowed. Caspian glanced over at him with a wicked grin before he strolled back up to their seats, then past his own and up to Killian's.

The prince stared up at him with wide eyes.

He bowed deeply, peeking up from his bow with mischievous yellow eyes and a naughty smirk. When he straightened, he offered his hand.

Killian smiled at him and took it.

He helped the prince up and out of his seat before escorting him onto the large white marble dance floor. People backed up and parted at their approach. Once in the center, Caspian pulled him close, taking one hand in his, before placing the other around his waist. Killian placed his hand on his chest, where he could reach since Caspian was so tall.

Caspian nodded at the musicians and a soft melody began.

Caspian was an amazing dancer. He led with grace and confidence. Each movement bled into the other. Killian was swept away, twirled and dipped but all with enough caution that it did not put too much stress on his weighted belly. He supported nearly all of Killian's weight as they danced along the entire floor.

People watched on in awe. So entranced they didn't dare join in.

It was only when the King and Queen came sweeping onto the floor that the spell was broken. More and more joined in until several couples were waltzing.

"Thank you," he whispered to his Consort.

"Of course," Caspian replied happily. "You need some fun after all this crap."

He laughed and clutched him tighter.

"You are so good to me," he murmured.

Caspian hummed.

Eventually his dance with Caspian was interrupted as each of his Consorts stepped in to dance with him. All except Zev, who remained seated with an arrogant pout failing to hide his angry blush.

Killian hadn't been able to spend much time with those one on one lessons. He wanted to drag him on to the floor anyway to get him to loosen up but that wasn't the way to deal with Zev when he's like this. It would only make him angrier and throw more of a fit if he messed up in front of all these people.

Killian chuckled quietly to himself. He's such a child.

"Can I have this dance...cousin dearest?"

The sickly sweet voice jolted Killian out of his thoughts. He blinked in surprise at Filo who stood before him with a smile on his sinful red lips. He was decked out in a red velvet tunic with gold embroidery and the family crest on his gold belt. His legs were clad in soft beige pants and in gold and red boots. The red was so vibrant that it matched his hair perfectly.

He looked divine. And Killian hated it.

His head cocked to the side, smile never faltering. Killian gave him a diplomatic smile back and nodded slightly. His whole body was tense as Filo slid his hand around his waist. His other gripped his hand. Filo's skin was still soft with privilege, as if he never lifted a sword or did any work his entire life. And Killian suppose that was accurate. He was spoiled rotten.

The prince placed his hand on Filo's chest and they began to move. Being so close to him sent every hair on the back of his neck on high alert.

"Are you enjoying the ball so far, cousin?" he asked, voice honied to perfection.

"Yes, thank you. And you?" Killian asked politely, feeling more and more uncomfortable.

"Oh very much. It's a splendid reception. I'm glad we came all this way to be a part of it. I look forward to many more once the move is complete."

Killian stiffened.

"Pardon?"

Filo's smile widened devilishly.

"Oh have you not heard? Our gracious King has offered us permanent residence in the palace. We are family, we shouldn't be so far away from each other. Don't you agree, cousin?"

Killian masked his face completely and offered a joyous smile. "That's wonderful news. With more exposure to the monarchy, you'll finally be able to learn your place."

Filo's eyes narrowed slightly but he didn't lose that smile. Instead, he jerked Killian closer until he was flush against him. Filo was shorter than him, so it was a bit odd. He was forced to maneuver his hand from his chest to his back. Killian placed his hand on Filo's back shoulder blade and through the thin fabric, he felt something underneath. Something lumpy.

His brow furrowed as he felt around but his attention was diverted by the snaking hand that caressed his back lower and lower until it nearly grazed his bottom.

Anger flooded through him but before he could react, there was suddenly a looming presence towering over them. Filo and Killian glanced over and saw Rem. His face was hard. Killian could almost see darkness hazing around his form like smoke. Filo was gaping at him but Killian felt nothing but relief.

"I am afraid I must steal the prince," he said in his impossibly deep voice.

Filo shivered, but on his face wasn't fear.

It was lust.

Killian wanted to claw his face off but refrained, untangling himself from Filo's arms and into Rem's instead.

"Cousin," he said with dismissal.

He bowed and sauntered away.

"Thank you," Killian whispered to his Consort.

He nodded once.

Killian noticed him leading him back to his throne where everyone was already seated. All except one.

Killian glanced around trying to locate his soft spoken Consort. He spotted him with his sister and Killian could see how well their outfit complimented each other. It made the prince a bit...jealous.

Strange.

Faust was actually on a small stage next to the musicians with Gilra. Everyone was quieting and moving off the dance floor, giving them their full attention.

Gilra's voice came ringing out, echoing around the vast room.

"I want to thank you all for coming tonight to celebrate my dear older brother's Consort choosing and Ranking Ceremony. As well as congratulations for his pregnancy. As a gift, his fourth ranked Consort, Faust, and I have worked to prepare a special song. This is for you, Prince Killian."

Two microphones were brought out and placed in front of Faust and Gilra. Faust looked over to him and smiled sweetly. His black eyes twinkling. Killian leaned forward in his seat, eager with anticipation.

The orchestra began to play an unfamiliar melody and then they began to sing. It was the most beautiful thing he had ever heard in his life.

Gilra's voice was as perfect as Killian had always known it to be. His sister was a singer, it was what she loved doing and traveled all over to perform.

But Faust?

He had heard him sing softly and had dreamed of hearing his voice. But to hear him full out? Killian was mesmerized.

His voice was enchanting and lovely and so Faust that Killian started to tear up with how amazing he sounded. The both of them together was otherworldly. They complimented each other perfectly; the harmonious sounds bewitched every person in that room.

They sang in Vern, bringing forward their roots which made it special in a different way.

Faust didn't take his eyes off of him. And Killian's eyes didn't leave his either.

Because he was so focused on him, he noticed the slight shift in Faust's expression. His twinkling eyes became tense and less serene.

Killian frowned at the sudden change. During Gilra's solo, the prince studied him. Something was wrong. He could sense that he was in pain. No one would be able to tell but Killian could. He was hiding it. Was it another headache?

Faust's eyes flashed blue. A vacant expression overcame his face.

"Rem," Killian whispered. But his Consort could not hear him over the loud music.

Damn it. There was no way to be subtle.

Killian didn't want to make a scene and draw attention to him or disrupt the performance but he couldn't shake the feeling that something bad was about to happen.

He glanced over at Filo. But he was looking at Faust. Intently. Marza looked relaxed but Bennett. He was staring right at Killian.

Killian looked away and back to Faust only to see his face twisted up in pain. Gilra was looking at him in confusion. And then he started screaming.

Killian had never heard Faust scream like that. Like the agony was so intense he was dying.

The prince jumped up and started running for him.

His Consort collapsed on the stage, gripping his forehead, writhing in pain and screaming at the top of his lungs.

"Faust!" Killian cried as he ran, stumbling but trying hard not to fall.

Why was no one doing anything? It was like everyone was just frozen, staring in shock.

Blood was dripping down his arm, spilling from the cracks between his fingers. Killian made it to him and tried to pull his hands away.

"Faust, please!" Killian cried, not knowing what he was pleading for or what he could do to help. "Someone get a healer!" the prince commanded.

And like the spell was broken, people started moving, rushing around. Gilra collapsed down beside them, helping Killian hold Faust down so he didn't thrash and hurt himself.

His hair and tunic were stained with blood. Finally, a healer got to them and his Consorts were there helping move their fallen brethren.

Along the way Faust passed out from the pain.

Killian followed him all the way to the infirmary, but as they were leaving the ballroom, Killian glanced at his cousins. Each one of them had a smile on their face and they were staring right at him. Killian hissed in fury.

They transported Faust to a bed in the medical wing. Killian helped the Healers clean away as much blood as they could. When Gestina brushed the hair away from his face, everyone in the room gasped. Right in the center of his forehead, where the blood streamed from, was a tiny black horn.

Faust, who had two horns upon his arrival to court, now had three.

That was impossible. People didn't just gain power out of nowhere. Not unless...

"Cover it up and tell no one of this," Killian snapped at Gestina.

She blinked in shock, still surprised by the discovery.

"Now!" he shouted.

Gestina jumped before getting a wrap and quickly bandaging his head, making the cover thick enough that one could not tell there was another horn underneath.

He turned to Zev, "Make sure no one saw anything."

Zev nodded and disappeared out of the door.

"How could he have--?" Drek started but Killian whipped his head toward him with a growl.

"Do not say another word. Do not speak of this, we do not know who is listening."

Drek closed his mouth.

Killian turned back to Faust, holding his hand.

They could hide this. They will find out the reason why another time, though Killian had an idea. But they had to hide it.

"I am not letting them take you. Not you too. I am going to protect you," Killian swore to his unconscious Consort.

Those damn bastards, he was not letting them get away with this.

They would get the horn removed. It would be risky but it was worth it. It could be hidden and they wouldn't have to worry about the consequences. No one would know. It could be hidden.

Faust groaned in the bed.

"Faust?" Killian said softly, brushing Faust's cheek with the hand that wasn't holding his.

His eyes fluttered.

It will be okay Faust. I won't let them get you. We can hide it, he thought.

Faust's eyes opened. And what once was pitch black now had an electric blue ring in the center. Those glowing blue irises slid over to Killian.

We can't hide it.

"Shit," Drek swore.

Faust stared up at them with his strange blue ringed irises, confusion clouding his features.

"What is it? What's wrong?" he croaked, voice hoarse.

Killian took a deep breath, not quite knowing how to explain.

"I think I know why you have been feeling sick, my love," he started. "But we cannot discuss it now. We are going to have you moved to our personal chambers, but I want you to pretend you are asleep. Do not open your eyes at all until you are told."

Faust frowned.

"Gestina, arrange for his bed to be moved immediately."

Gestina nodded.

Killian couldn't trust that she wouldn't open her mouth to his father. He looked over to Drek with a serious gaze. "Stay with her," he mouthed. Drek nodded and got to work making the arrangements.

Once another person came in, Faust closed his eyes and remained still, breathing even. It was the perfect show. If Killian hadn't known better, he would have believed him asleep as well.

Killian motioned for the rest of his Consorts to clear out of the room.

Ethel was waiting for him at the end of the hall, a new outfit in her arms. The prince quickly followed her and changed out of his bloody clothes into something fresh before he made his appearance back into the ballroom. It was buzzing with activity and gossip.

It quieted once Killian arrived.

"I apologize for the disruption. My Consort is doing well and recovering as we speak, so please, continue the celebration without worry," he announced.

The crowd clapped before settling back into a peaceful atmosphere. Gilra ran up to him immediately.

"What happened? Is he okay?"

"He had not been feeling well for a while now."

"But the blood--"

"Was just a scratch he inflicted on himself during the ordeal."

Gilra's lips pursed but she nodded, buying it completely.

"I hope he's okay."

"He is," Killian reassured. "And thank you for the song. It was lovely."

She beamed at him, successfully distracted. "We've been working on it for a while now. It was so difficult not to tell you about it. You know how I am with surprises. Can't seem to keep my mouth shut."

Killian laughed a bit forced, "I know that all too well."

"Oh Father wants to speak to you. You should go see him."

Killian stiffened but nodded. He still hadn't figured out what to tell people but he was going to have to make something up on the spot. He spotted the King sitting on his throne, speaking to an ambassador from the Dragon clan. They bowed at his approach before dismissing themselves.

Killian watched them go before bowing to his father.

"Father, Gilra said you wished to speak with me."

His father was quiet, just staring at him, scanning him head to toe. Killian was a little put off by it and slightly annoyed but he didn't let it show on his face.

A part of him was still upset with him for the punishment he dealt Drek unfairly. A large part. When he still didn't say anything, Killian let the impatience show on his face.

King Ellis finally spoke then.

"You handled that well."

Killian nodded in thanks.

"I see the rest of your Consorts are well. Healed. Even those in critical conditions. Strange isn't it?"

His gray eyes flicked up to Killian's. He couldn't read his expression.

"Yes, well I had help. No thanks to you," Killian snapped, losing his calm composure.

The King's brows narrowed, but then he sighed.

"I know that you are cross with me, but there is much you don't understand--"

"Which could easily be fixed if you would just tell me," Killian interrupted.

"My hands are tied," he said and there was something that flashed in those gray eyes of his. As if there were something more he was trying to tell him.

"You are King. Untie them," Killian said harshly before bowing and walking away without being dismissed.

The prince searched the crowds until he found the person he was looking for. Filo was flirting with the son of the Fae queen. Killian interrupted. The Fae Prince bowed in respect to Killian before walking away to give him privacy with his cousin.

"Cousin! I hope all is well with...what was his name? Faust?"

Killian gripped his throat in a crushing motion, moving close to hide the action from onlookers. Filo choked as he leaned into his ear.

"I have caught you now," Killian sang before releasing him.

Filo glared at him, rubbing his throat.

"Better watch your back, might be a target on it. Later cousin dearest," he said happily before walking off.

Killian found Titus standing by the door wearing his Guard uniform sporting a green lion insignia, symbol for Drek's faction. Killian walked over to him.

"Do you have the girl?" he asked him.

"Yes, My Prince."

"And the sample?"

"Yes, My Prince."

Killian smiled. "Good."

There was no way that Filo was going to get away with this one. Finding out who the magix user is that they have on their side is important yes, but with that being their entire focus, they weren't going to get anywhere.

No, it was time to try a different strategy and that was to attack Filo directly.

The magix user will make themselves known eventually but they just had to smoke out Filo, Marza, and Bennett first. Then the rest will fall into place.

Killian hadn't been thinking clearly with everything that was going on, but he was becoming desperate. He didn't want any one of his people getting hurt again. He needed to protect them and he needed to step up as their ruler. Sitting back and waiting for someone else to solve his problems, relying too heavily on his Consorts, finally having people he was close to...crippled him. He became too dependent and forgot who he was. Who he is. He is strong alone and even stronger with them. But his strength is not limited to having his males at his disposable.

It came from years of training and lessons. It came from the loneliness he loathed so deeply. He realized that Heirs start off alone to build themselves up, strengthen their defenses, sharpen their minds until they are a force to be reckoned with by themselves. And then with the addition of strength from their Consorts, they become unstoppable.

That's what it is to be a ruler. That is a King. And now that his head was on straight, it was time to put some plans in action.

First, he had to figure out what to do with Faust. There would be no hiding his obvious upgrade in power, which means he will inevitably be put to trial.

But that's where Killian could turn this around. This differs from Drek's case because he never had a trial. Assault of a Royal eliminates that possibility. Killian had no hope in really saving Drek. But as long as he had evidence of foul play, Killian could still win this and keep Faust safe.

The Consorts

Killian stayed at the Ball, talking to everyone and keeping up appearances. No one suspected anything. And when he felt he spent enough time there, he excused himself politely with the excuse that carrying has made him weary.

And that was not entirely a lie. The weight of the twins left him a bit tired and fighting back the constant waves of nausea was exhausting.

As quickly as he could, he made it back to his personal chambers. He found all his Consorts there. Killian sought out one in particular.

He was standing before the large dressing mirror, expression a mix of horror and sadness. But most of all: defeat. He knew what it meant now...that his life was in danger.

"Faust?" Killian called to him, coming to brush his arm.

He turned to him and tried to smile for him. When he reached for him, Killian saw his strange blue ringed irises flicker to his arms.

Killian followed his gaze and noticed the light blue veins that were slightly apparent through his skin. They traveled all along his arms and shoulders and even up his neck, but none really on his face.

His gentle face turned into a frown.

"Faust, I will not let anything happen to you. I promise."

Faust touched his palm to Killian's cheek and smiled again, weakly.

"Sweetling, there is naught you can do for me. I have committed a great crime."

"You have committed no crime!" he hissed. "Do not delude yourself into thinking you are anything but a victim. This is not your fault!"

"The King will see no different--"

"I will make him see. Something I regrettably could not do for Drek before but am able to do for you."

"You have a plan?" Caspian asked, coming to his side.

Killian nodded.

"Things have been set in motion."

Faust's brows raised.

He focused all of his attention on him. "I will not let you die, Faust."

Faust leaned down and kissed him.

"Thank you, Killian."

Killian nodded. Then turned to the large cat that was sitting on the couch.

"Yehwin, can you help Titus guard the evidence please? I do not want my cousins learning of it and trying something with their magix user."

Yehwin yawned before standing and disappearing.

"Titus?" Drek asked. "What need do you have for him?"

"Everyone plays their parts, Titus included. Even Orion," he said.

"Orion?" they all said in unison, some with surprise others with disgust.

"What could a heavily pregnant Incubus possibly do?" Drek exclaimed.

"Orion is not only an incredibly skilled fighter, but an amazing strategist. I've been working with him and Titus," Killian admitted.

It was something he had thought of recently. Around the time of Drek's whipping. Those slivers of sanity Killian had were used to formulate a plan to smoke out the culprit. He didn't want to involve his current Consorts because he knew they'd be watched and could be manipulated just as Drek was.

His safest bet was to go with someone he was rarely seen with and that no one would suspect. And just as Drek had said 'what could a heavily pregnant incubus do.' It was perfect. No one would ever think of Orion.

Or Titus really for that matter. He had no special ranking aside from being a soldier in Drek's faction. One of the footmen. Most didn't even remember that they both were in the running to be his Consorts.

"So what is this plan of yours?" Zev asked.

Killian shook his head.

"I cannot say yet, but I will tell you soon. It is imperative that this works and timing is important."

Killian glanced at Rem who hadn't said a word this whole time. He was staring at Killian...intently from across the room. The prince stared back, trying to figure out what he was thinking. And of course he couldn't because this was Rem. No one ever knows what he's thinking.

"Is something wrong?" he asked him.

He didn't respond just tilted his head slightly, gaze narrowing. Then he broke contact and stared at Faust. Killian sighed before saying, "Physically, how do you feel, Faust?"

"A slight headache but other than that, perfectly fine."

Killian gave him a hard look and he chuckled lightly.

"I mean it. There is nothing else beside that."

He let out a soft breath of relief.

"Okay, in that case, I will let my father know what has happened. Be prepared for a trial."

"Is that wise?" Zev asked.

"Do you trust me?" Killian asked.

"With my life," he answered immediately.

"Then trust me," Killian said before heading out of the room. "Rem?"

Rem's gaze flickered to him.

"Stay with Faust no matter what."

Rem stared blankly before nodding once.

The prince swept out of the room. By this time the Ball would be over and the King should be in the throne room, but instead Killian found him in one of the studys with his mother, aunt, uncle, and General Lee. Killian started for a moment. Why would his aunt and uncle be in a meeting with his father and the General of the Astorian Army? It hasn't even been an hora since their last guest left. What was so important that they needed to meet now? And more importantly, why was Killian not called to this meeting?

"Father," the prince greeted stiffly.

"Killian, now is not the time," his father said dismissively.

Killian narrowed his eyes.

"I believe you will disagree," he said tartly.

Father sighed and opened his mouth to speak but Killian cut him off.

"A crime has been committed."

Father stilled.

"What crime?"

"My Consort has been poisoned by Filo, Marza, and Bennett."

Father let out an exasperated sigh. "Not this again. Killian I don't have time--"

"With the blood of Kappa hearts. They are responsible for the murders."

That stopped them dead.

"They couldn't have-" Uncle Netter started.

"They are and I have proof."

"Proof?"

"Yes."

"And where is this proof?" Father questioned.

"In a secure location. General Lee, if you'd excuse us for a moment? I'd like to speak to my family in private."

General Lee stood and bowed deeply to him. "Of course, My Prince."

He bowed to the King and Queen before taking his leave.

Once he was gone, Killian faced his family. Taking a seat at the table when the twins reminded him that they were alive and kicking...literally.

"Now what is all this about, Killian?"

Killian took a deep breath. "Do you know the history behind the blessings of blood?"

Uncle Netter glanced at King Ellis who stared directly at Killian. He did not break eye contact.

"There is little on those with magix. Their history lost," his father said mechanically.

Killian cocked his head to the side. "Is it?"

"Killian, sweetheart, what are you getting at?" his mother questioned.

"Yehwin, could I borrow you for a moment?" Killian called out.

Yehwin appeared instantly.

"You ask me to do this then that. Make up your mind boy," Yehwin hissed annoyed.

Killian looked at his family who were looking at him strangely.

"Can they see you?" Killian asked Yehwin.

"No."

"Can you let them see you?"

Yehwin sighed before the room erupted into gasps of surprise.

"He was locked up!" The King shouted in alarm.

"Your cages can't confine me, mortal," Yehwin spat at the King.

"Yehwin, can you tell my family about the real history of the blessings of blood?"

Yehwin looked at him. "I can only confirm what you have already discovered."

"That is fine," Killian concluded, knowing he would say something like that. "Can you confirm that those with magix hold another being in their body?"

"Yes."

"That the beings they hold are none other than dormant Gods?"

"Yes."

"And that these Gods allow for certain powers to be passed along to their vessels?"

"That is correct," Yehwin said.

"Can you confirm that some of these powers include manipulation of the mind?"

Yehwin looked at Killian with a particularly feline grin. "Yes, child of his blood."

Killian turned to his family, "You are aware that Yehwin is--"

"A familiar," his father continued.

"And Cloud-born," Yehwin added smugly.

"And what are familiars sworn by the Clouds not to do?" Killian edged.

"Lie," his father said tightly.

"That is correct. And Yehwin, can you confirm that besides myself and my Rank One Consort, there is another magix user in the palace?"

"Yes."

"Thank you, Yehwin. Can you go back to guarding?"

Yehwin disappeared as quickly as he came.

Killian focused his attention on his Father and stared him down.

"They have a magix user and they are using them against me."

No one said anything for a while until Uncle Netter finally spoke up, though not to Killian. To King Ellis.

In his soft voice, he said, "Maybe it's time we tell--"

"Not another word, brother," the King snapped, shutting Netter up.

Killian had never heard his father speak to him that way.

"What are you hiding?" Killian demanded.

"It is none of your concern, Killian."

"It is my concern when my life and the lives of my children are being threatened!" He snarled. Something flashed in the King's gray eyes. Not shock...or fear.

No...come to think of it, he didn't look surprised about any of what Killian had revealed to him about the blessings of blood. And in his eyes was...guilt. Which meant...

He knew.

"You knew," Killian said aloud.

Father's face was composed completely. He wasn't letting anything slip. But it was too late...Killian already saw it.

"You knew about the history. You knew what magix users were capable of," Killian accused.

"Killian--" Queen Jessa started but Killian paid her no mind. He had all attention on his father. His too calm father.

"You knew about the third magix user too."

His face showed nothing. And then it clicked.
"You know who they are."

Chapter 26

"Who are they?"

The King did not speak.

"Tell me who they are!"

Still silence.

"Tell me!" Killian screamed, slamming his fists against the table, shattering the wood to splinters. His eyes were tinting that familiar orange and he could feel the half-God inside him coiling up, ready to spring at the slightest opening.

"Ellis-" Uncle Netter said with panic in his voice, evident on his face as he stared at Killian uneasily.

"Enough," King Ellis said.

He wasn't going to tell him. It was the most baffling revelation in the world. His father cares not about the life of his son or the lives of his heirs. He would sacrifice them all to keep Killian in the dark.

"You made me believe that the possibility was inconceivable but in reality, you were hiding them. Protecting them. Well then, if you will not tell me, then I promise you this. I will find them and I will kill them. I will slaughter them and you will do nothing to stop me."

A promise was made and so it shall be.

The King ignored his declaration and said, "Show me your proof and I will pass judgement. Let us be done with this."

Killian's vision went orange again for a moment but he took a deep calming breath.

One step at a time.

He stood and led them out of the room briefing them on what he was about to show them.

The Consorts

They reached a room in the far corner of the palace close to the servant quarters in an area that is rarely frequented. Titus was standing outside the door. When he saw them, he went down on one knee and bowed his head in respect.

Killian brushed his shoulder, "Any complications?"

"None, My Prince," he confirmed.

"Good. Rise."

He stood and moved to the side remaining on guard with his arms clasped behind him. Killian gestured them all inside the small chamber. Maya sat in a chair in the empty room, Yehwin lying at her feet.

"Do you recognize this servant?" Killian asked his aunt and uncle.

They both nodded, "She had been assigned to Marza," Kendra said.

"This is the same servant who has been serving my Consort, Faust, tea. The same tea that poisoned him."

"That is not enough to conclude it was your cousins who did it. As suspicious as it makes them, it is not hard proof--" the King started but Killian raised a hand.

"I am not finished."

And with impeccable timing, there was a knock on the door.

"Come in," Killian called out.

The door opened and Orion came in carrying a case with Gestina in tow.

"I had Orion fetch a sample of the tea."

Orion opened up the case and presented the King with a couple of documents.

"This specific tea is only grown in the Southern region of Kerbis. More specifically in the gardens of the Royal Keep that can only be accessed by someone of Royal blood. And what you have in your hands shows the traces of Kappa blood mixed in the tea. Which Gestina is here to confirm."

To that, Gestina gave a nod.

"Gods Above," Queen Jessa gasped.

"You said he was poisoned. How so? Was he killed?" King Ellis questioned.

Killian shook his head and turned to Yehwin who nodded. Moments later the door opened again. Killian's Consorts filed in. And one was cloaked.

When he pulled back the hood of his cloak, his face was revealed. The room gasped as they took in his strange blue ringed eyes and third horn.

"They poisoned my Consort with power. Knowing that one look at him would have him put to death for treason. They have been coming for all of my Consorts and they have been coming for me. You let them get away with it every time. Enough is enough. If you don't accept this proof that I have delivered to you on a platter, then I will take matters into my own hands."

Killian watched his father. His face was tense.

"Come with me, Killian," he said then started out of the room.

"Not until I know my Consort is safe!"

Killian's father stopped and sighed. "I will not charge him. He is safe. Now come."

Killian looked to Faust, then to his father. "Swear to the Gods, because your word alone no longer means anything to me."

King Ellis looked like he had struck him. The prince didn't care. His behavior was inexcusable. To allow attempted regicide, to his own flesh and blood? Despicable.

With hardening features, he said "I swear on my blood and the Gods Above, that Faust Akili of Sapientae will not be prosecuted."

Killian let out a breath of relief. This had been easier than he thought it would be. Killian rushed toward Faust and kissed him fiercely before saying, "I will be back. Keep the girl here until I come back to release her from their compulsion."

His Consorts nodded and Killian followed his father out of the room, down several halls until they were in his private chambers.

He ordered the servants that were cleaning, out. They closed the door, leaving the two of them alone and in silence. The King did not speak, just kept his back to him. When he turned around, his expression was full of pain.

"You are angry with me and you have every right to be," he started. But the way he spoke, there was something different in his tone. Desperate.

"I know what I did to your Consort was unforgivable--"

"You nearly killed him," Killian accused, his voice catching at the end.

The memories came back to him. The blood, the sounds of whip hitting torn flesh, his screams of pain, the helplessness Killian felt at being unable to save him, the disgusting look of glee on Filo's face.

"He almost died and the whole time he thought he deserved it, that he did something wrong. Everyone looked at him like he was a monster but what monster feels remorse for a crime he didn't even commit!" Killian screamed, hot tears blurred his vision.

Stupid hormones.

"I know. And I know that nothing I do or say will make up for it, but I need you to understand--"

"What, Father? That my own flesh and blood will not defend me and mine? Or that my own flesh and blood is out to kill me?"

His father took a deep breath.

"Have you not wondered why I allowed Rem to be your Consort?" he said suddenly.

Killian looked at him confused.

"You said it was because I needed someone to keep me calm like Mother does for you."

Father shook his head. "No, that was why I allowed him to stay even though he lost control of his beast several times."

"Not a beast," Killian said softly. "Sotershai is not a beast."

"Sotershai?" his father repeated with a raised brow of confusion.

Killian shook his head and waved it off. He continued.

"It was because I knew he could protect you."

"What does that have to do with anything?"

"I am aware that there are forces beyond our means at work here. But I need you to understand that there is a bigger picture here. I am doing what I can to protect everyone I love. And I know it doesn't seem like it but that includes you. I just need you to be stronger Killian. I need you to remember how strong you already are."

He had that look in his eyes again, like he was urging Killian to read something more into his words. But he didn't understand.

What was he trying to tell him?

Killian wanted to ask him outright but there must be a reason for the secrecy, why he hasn't already come out and said it straight because that was more of his father's style. He really wasn't acting like himself.

"One King alone may have his hands bound, but another King may have the key to unbind them."

With his words came the full force of those intense gray eyes. He stared back at Killian with just as much intensity.

"I understand," Killian told him.

The King looked at him levelly, "Do you?"

Killian paused then shook his head, "No, but I will."

His father let out a breath of relief.

"Now we must keep this incident to ourselves. Your Consort will not be punished but you must not speak of any accusations again."

"You are letting them get away with it again?" Killian screeched, not believing what he was hearing. He thought they just went over this.

His father tensed again. "Bigger picture," he repeated.

"So what are we supposed to tell people? He cannot hide it and people will ask questions," Killian demanded, placing his hands on his hips and letting the exasperation show on his face.

He was pregnant and tired. He wanted this whole thing to be solved so he could relax with his Consorts in bed after a nice and thorough feeding. But more importantly, he wanted to be sure that all his Consorts were safe. He wanted to get Faust's story straight.

"We'll flip the script," the King said.

Killian frowned.

"What?"

"Change the story. Many people don't know what actually happened and they will continue to be in the dark until we give them a story. So we'll say that your Consort was always this powerful and instead used a cloaking spell to hide how much power he does have."

"Cloaking spells are forbidden. That is substituting one crime for another and my Consort is innocent. I will not have his name pulled through the mud because you want to protect your precious demon incarnates. And say we did go with that ridiculous reasoning, why would he cloak himself? People are going to question him about that. It's a strange thing to do considering how power hungry the world we live in is," the prince pointed out.

King Ellis sighed.

"There are some sacrifices--"

"My Consorts and I have made enough sacrifices. Try again," Killian snapped.

"Then use a cloaking spell."

"So now you are telling me to make my Consort break the law?" Killian raised a brow at his father.

He couldn't be serious. Killian worked this hard to prove that his Consort committed no crime and he wouldn't have it solved by actually breaking the law. Where was the logic?

"You don't have a choice. Keep it hidden and no one will know. After all, if anyone suspects, I will deny. I am King and my word is law."

Killian shook his head.

"I do not trust you, Father."

"Killian--"

"How do I know you will not change your mind? How do I know you will not sacrifice him to protect your precious kin?"

"You are my kin, Killian! That includes protecting you."

"Rich, considering you let me nearly die more times than I can count these past few months," he sneered.

"Because I knew you were strong enough to overcome it! Something you keep forgetting!" He bellowed.

Killian flinched. The King looked on angrily.

"I raised you the way I did for a reason, Killian. There is a reason for everything. I raised you to be strong on your own. Remember that you can be!"

Killian's heart was pounding in his chest and he looked down in fear that he would see the expression on his face. He didn't want to prove him right.

But he was weak. He knew he was. He didn't know why, but everything he had learned has flown out the window. He knew this! But he didn't want it flung in his face. He didn't want someone else to tell him what he already knew. It just made it all the more real. And it made him realize how terrible a King he'll be.

Killian's eyes watered and he clenched his teeth fighting to hold them back.

Stop crying Killian! You cry over everything and it doesn't solve a damn thing! All you are doing is showing how weak you truly are and proving everyone right.

You're proving your father right about you. You can't protect your Consorts. You can't protect your own servants. And you probably won't even be able to protect your own children. All you're doing is proving to the world how poorly you're suited to be as King.

Killian's eyes burned even more.

Don't cry.

Don't cry.

Don't you dare fucking cry!

"Killian--?"

"I understand," the prince said, his voice void of any emotion despite all that was roiling inside him.

He bowed slightly to his father and exited the room, heading back to the chamber where everyone waited. He could hear his father behind him, his concern nearly palpable, but he didn't say a word and neither did Killian. They didn't need to.

The prince approached Faust silently. Then without a word being said, Killian spelled him. He gasped. And suddenly his form blurred before clearing back up to the Incubus everyone recognized him as. His third horn gone, his eyes completely black, and the blue veins under his skin no longer visible.

He was back to normal. On the outside at least. They couldn't undo what had already been done. He was more powerful now and that wasn't going to change.

"Killian, what did you just--" Queen Jessa started in shock.

"No one will speak a word of this. Faust fell ill from lack of sleep and that is what caused his episode. Please inform those who know the truth this new story. Now, if you'll excuse us," Killian said blandly. He motioned for his Consorts to follow him. They did without making a sound. It was only when they got back to their room that they began to ask their questions.

"What is done is done. Let us not speak of it any longer," he told them.

"But--" Zev started.

"Enough," he snapped, shooting him a stern look.

When he quieted, Killian softened his expression.

"I need to feed." he looked to Faust, "If you are feeling up to it?"

He nodded and stepped closer to him.

Killian glanced over at Rem. "I may need more later."

He nodded solemnly. Killian led Faust to the bed and ignored the others who made themselves sparse.

Faust sat on the edge of the bed and looked at Killian gently. He reached out a hand to him. Killian took it and climbed onto his lap, wrapping his arms around his neck.

"I apologize," he whispered to his lover.

Faust just smiled and kissed his nose once before moving to his lips. His kisses were passionate but gentle and so very sweet. It took nothing to bring about his slick. Killian pulled him free of his pants and undid his own before quickly sliding him inside all the way to the hilt. Killian tilted his head back and moaned.

Faust's lips fell to his neck seamlessly. And they made sweet love. It was slow and sensuous. He let Killian feel everything, savor every moment of it before the pressure became too much and he nearly climaxed.

"Feed, sweetling," he whispered.

And he did. Killian drained him dry, trembling with the force of his ecstasy. Amazing. He felt extraordinary. Even more so when he came, exploding his hot cream and drenching Killian's insides. Killian shivered at how full he felt...in all ways. Faust panted lightly, his white skin covered in a thin layer of sweat, slightly flushed from the physical activity. He looked at Killian and smiled widely.

"Full?" he asked in that soft musical voice of his.

Killian nodded numbly, still trying to catch his own breath.

"Should I get Rem?" he asked.

Killian nodded again. Faust had done well in feeding him but the full feeling was temporary. Killian knew he needed more.

Faust kissed him before gently pulling him off. Killian whimpered at the loss. He laid him on his side before disappearing. Killian could feel his essence leaking out of him and he groaned. Soft lips littered kisses on his shoulders. He trembled at their warmth, turning his head slightly to peer up at his dark Warrior. Without another word, he slid right inside.

Killian's entrance still wet with slick and Faust, Rem had no problems pushing in completely. A shaky cry left the prince's lips and he closed his eyes, just enjoying the feeling of him, and how he stretched Killian so completely.

"Rem," he moaned, curling his arm up behind him to wrap around his neck. He kissed any part of the Consort he could reach. His shoulder, his neck, his jaw, his lips. All of him.

He moved gently, caressing the skin on his stomach, but cradling him carefully so he didn't put any unnecessary stress or pressure on the babies. Rem brought Killian quickly and he fed as much as he could until he was sure he was completely full.

Rem groaned lightly as he came, stuffing him even more. And he passed right out, with his breath on his ear.

Killian's dream was strange. He was in the throne room wearing his outfit for the Ball but there was no one there. He looked around, curious. There was something off here. He closed his eyes, took a deep breath, then opened them again. When he did, he was no longer alone.

Filo stood before him, naked as the day he was born. Killian snarled at him instinctively but he didn't respond to it. And that's when Killian knew there was something wrong. He...was crying.

He stared at the prince with tears in his big gray eyes. There was fear, unbridled fear in them, enough to make Killian pause. He stepped toward Killian and he took one back, suspicious.

"Killian?" he whispered.

Even his voice was different.

"Help me."

Killian's eyes widened in shock. The tears were endless and his shoulders shook.

"Help me!" he cried, stepping toward him again. Killian backed away.

"Help me!" He screamed and was suddenly being hauled back by some invisible force. He fought and clawed but couldn't break free.

Killian couldn't even move, just watched as he screamed and cried, his eyes never leaving his.

"Help me! Help me! Help me!"

Killian gasped, eyes flying open to his own darkened room. His breath came out in pants and Killian took a few deep breaths to calm himself. Filo's screams still ringing in his ears.

Help me.

Killian didn't mention the dream to his Consorts. It wasn't something he thought they should stress about considering all that they had on their plate, but his curiosity did spike.

Was it another one of their tricks? Were they trying to get him to let his guard down to strike?

It was a possibility but there was something different about it that made Killian hesitate in drawing that conclusion. He tried not to let it distract him as he held his meeting. He wanted to keep it brief, informing those who needed to know who to watch out for, who to keep an eye on, what to report and what to do when approached about the situation.

Some of the group looked shocked, namely Ethel and Lisa but others were more informed and knew that this was happening. Namely his Consorts and their lieutenants. Even Orion and Titus had been previously informed. It made the meeting easier.

Now that Killian had his team, he relayed to them the plan. Some things had to be altered due to incoming obstacles, namely his father. He was an unknown factor. Killian couldn't tell if he was truly an enemy.

He answered a few questions he received swiftly before ending the meeting, stressing that no one was to speak a word of it.

After getting their confirmations, they filed out.

Killian sighed, exhausted, even though he had just woken up from a nap.

"Yehwin," he called to the large cat.

He tilted his head in Killian's direction.

"Can I have a word with you in private?"

He nodded and led the way out of the room. Zev looked at Killian with confusion, probably wondering why he didn't want to say it in front of them.

And Rem...was staring again. Killian couldn't read his expression...but then again, when could he ever? He followed Yehwin with an "I will be back" to his Consorts.

Yehwin took Killian to the library where there was a little set of chairs and a table. Killian thought he would curl up in the chair as he normally did but instead he transformed into a tall dark skinned male. It was rare that he used this form. Killian studied him as much as he could.

He took a seat on one of the chairs and Killian did the same opposite of him. He looked at the prince with those glowing blue eyes and motioned for him to start talking. Killian told him about what his father said to him in private and he told him about the dream.

"And you think they are related?" he asked in that deep accented voice, much more pronounced than when he was in either of his feline forms.

"Maybe, I'm not entirely sure. It just seems strange to me to receive that dream right after my father tried to send me a discrete message."

Yehwin pursed his lips. "Perhaps. Or maybe your Father is in on it and they are trying to manipulate you as they have done so many times in the recent past."

Killian sighed.

"That is what I am afraid of. I do not know what to think or who to trust anymore."

"One of the many difficulties when being King. It is something that will always pose a problem for you."

"I know."

Killian just couldn't figure out why his father wanted to protect them so badly. If they were committing a crime, it's his job--their job to handle it. They punish those who defy them. So what was it that made him accepting of their misdeeds? It had to run deeper than just blood ties. Killian refused to believe that to be the case because he wouldn't sacrifice his son for it. Killian was more his blood than they were.

Unless they were somehow being coerced? Maybe it was the other magix user that was pulling their strings? Because for the life of him, Killian couldn't figure out why they would hate him so much. He had done nothing to them. Nothing to warrant such extreme measures, nothing to bring about a death wish. They were a family first and foremost and that used to mean something once upon a time.

Sure, they bickered and fought. They weren't the nicest of cousins, but it was always silly childish things. It was never that serious and until these threats on his life started happening, he would never believe them to commit such heinous acts.

So why?

Why damn it?

Was the corruption from their magix user's dormant God spreading? Could it affect other people? And what does one have to do to become corrupt? And then Killian thought about Rem.

Would he become corrupt? Will the rest of the Consorts and himself become corrupt from the exposure of a corrupt God so close in their vicinity?

Will it affect his children? His demigod daughter? His S-Level son? Are they in danger as well? More than they realized? Then he stopped to think for a moment. It probably wouldn't get him anywhere, but it didn't hurt to ask anyway.

"Yehwin?"

"Yes, child of his blood?"

"I do not know if you can tell me this but...how did Sotershai become corrupted?"

Yehwin paused, his expression pensive.

"I suppose it would not do any harm. But I warn you, it is not some complex story, it is quite cliché really," he said.

Killian leaned forward in his chair, eager to gain any new knowledge about him. This God he had come to love.

"Very well. Sotershai is the God of Protection first and foremost. It is what pulls to him the most and affects everything he does. His urge to protect is all consuming and sometimes his need to act is impulsive and relentless."

Yehwin paused to frown a little.

"Around the time of your Grandmother Illya's reign, this land was full of discord and war. It was not the peaceful land you know it as and more importantly, Incubi did not have complete control over the land. It was divided by species and there were several battles for territory. Many died and no one lived as long as they do in this era. You are quite fortunate for that, boy. Faltaire now would be a safe haven in comparison."

Killian shivered, thinking of what he saw of Caspian's experiences growing up. He did not know it could get worse than that. And for the whole land to be swallowed up in that strife? Incomprehensible.

"When so many needed protection, you can only imagine what it did to Sotershai up in the Clouds. He could watch but not interfere. His light influences from above were not enough to amend the issues to stop the fighting. It would take a more direct approach and that he was forbidden to do. So he watched. And waited for it to end or at least show signs of getting better. It did not.

Now for your Grandmother's reign, it began in blood and ended in blood. There were revolts left and right. It wasn't until the battle of the Fae that moves were made. Now I'm sure you know enough from your history books to know just how horrible that revolt was. Fifteen years of the most brutal battle in history. And as you know already, the Incubi won. But how? Well that was kept a secret.

Because no one could know a God interfered. Sotershai grew fascinated with your Grandmother, watched her grow up and watched her develop into a fine Warrior and an even better Queen. And soon he came to love her, despite it being absolutely forbidden. Well, it was not the feeling that was forbidden but more so the desires that came with it. She could not know him and he could not know her. Not without coming to her and that would be direct interference.

But...well...he did so anyway. He manifested to her as an Incubus and became her leman. And together they fought in the Battle of Ranya which you know was the final battle of the revolution and ended the war. It was also the battle that killed Illya. With her death Sotershai went into a rage and revealed his true self. Destroyed all of Riktara, Yande, and Akimar, now known as Rhettick, Kerbis, and Heltzig, where we now reside."

Killian gasped.

Those were the three largest countries in all of their land.

"He would have done more if the Clouds did not force him back and stripped him of his consciousness, sending him to the Void where he waited until your dear Consort was born. It is no wonder that your Rem was drawn to you. You have her blood. Sotershai would find her and has found her, through you."

Killian stared at him wide eyed taking it all in.

"But if he was her leman, does that mean my family shares his blood?" Killian asked.

He hoped that Sotershai was not kin, that would make things incredibly uncomfortable.

"Nay, Sotershai was not a Consort, he came to her as a General made leman. She bore a child on one of her Consorts and that is where you are descended from."

"Was that allowed? I thought sovereigns could only mate with their Consorts?"

"Things were much different back then. Rules have changed."

That's how he became corrupt. And it makes sense now why there was such a pull to him in the beginning. They were drawn to each other because of the love shared in the past.

But it is only his blood he is drawn to, not him as an individual.

Killian was not Illya.

Killian frowned in sadness.

"Does this mean he does not truly love me? Does he love only what I remind him of?"

Yehwin shrugged.

"That I do not know."

Killian nodded.

"Thank you Yehwin, this has been most enlightening."

Yehwin dipped his head before fading away into nothingness. Most likely going to lounge about until they needed him once more.

Killian stood, processing all the new information before making his way back to his rooms. It was empty, save for one.

Rem's back was to him as he peered out into the night sky through the open doors to the balcony. There was something strange about him, he was giving off a different...aura.

"Rem?" Killian called to him.

But as he turned, he saw it was not Rem he was looking at, but Sotershai. His eyes were blazing orange and the marks in his skin glowed in the dim lighting. Killian let out a soft yelp of surprise but otherwise schooled his shock and slight anxiety.

"Hello...Sotershai."

He closed his eyes and let out a soft hum that came from deep within his chest. Like a purr. Killian took a few slow steps towards him, watching him carefully because he knew he still had to be careful around him. Once Killian was right before him, his eyes snapped open and they stared at each other silently. A wave of sadness overcame him and he found himself frowning.

"Do you love me?" Killian asked him.

He blinked at him cocking his head slightly.

"Or do I just remind you of the one you truly love?" he added softly.

Sotershai whined lightly, sensing Killian's distress. He pressed himself to Sotershai's chest, burying his face in those blazing marks and relishing in the near uncomfortable heat, listening to his two hearts beating thunderously.

"Kill..."

His head snapped up at the sound. It was guttural and difficult to understand but he swore it sounded like...

"Kill..."

Sotershai was looking down at him with his brows scrunched up in what seemed like determination but Killian honestly couldn't be too sure.

"Did you just...speak?" he asked incredulously.

He growled in response and it might have been in agreement.

"Do you...understand what I am saying? Are you trying to communicate with me?" Killian asked searching those bright eyes.

He nodded his head once and the prince nearly fainted.

"You can understand me," Killian whispered in shock. "You can talk."

He grunted in reply.

"Are you...waking up?"

Sotershai opened his mouth but incomprehensible noises came out. He grew frustrated and hissed loudly. Killian flinched.

"It is okay, do not push yourself too hard," he told him brushing his cheek with the palm of his hand, letting his fingertips linger on his skin as he pulled away. But Sotershai didn't let him go far, snatching his hand up and pressing it back to his skin. He nuzzled the prince, closing his eyes.

Killian closed his own just swimming in his warmth. Then he heard it.

"Kill...love."

Chapter
27

Killian had the dream again.

Standing in the empty throne room wearing his Ball best. This time there was music. Faintly in the distance he could hear its melancholy tune, low and haunting, making it seem very much like a nightmare.

He looked around him, searching for the inevitable presence of his cousin, but he could not see him. And the music grew louder with each passing moment. A sense of urgency overcame him.

Where was the music coming from? And who was playing it? Someone had to be there. And suddenly there was. Not one but two someones.

In the center of the room they waltzed. And as graceful as the movements were, there was something off about the pair.

One was a dark mass of shadows, one he had come to recognize as a corrupted God's essence. The other, his red haired cousin. Though he was not himself. His expression blank, void of any emotion or sense of life. His movements were stiff and robotic.

Familiar.

Their circular movements were small and contained. Killian drifted closer to them watching them carefully. They didn't react to his presence, it was almost as if they didn't even know he was there. Well that was until Filo looked at him.

His expression still blank and vacant. But there was a lone tear that spilled from his left cheek on to his creamy fair skin, staining it. Killian watched the drop fall before his gaze flickered up and back to his.

And though he didn't say it this time, he could still hear it.

Help me.

Killian awoke with a gasp, pushing frantically through bodies and leaning over to vomit. Hands came to pull his hair back, while more rubbed slow circles on his back.

The Consorts

When he was finished retching, his body was shaking. Killian couldn't even take the glass of water someone handed him. The trembling in his hands had him spilling it all over.

"Killian? Are you alright? Did you have a night scare?" Faust's soothing voice asked.

Killian shook his head.

No.

It wasn't frightening. It was sad. Killian never felt such overwhelming sadness and utter helplessness. It was crippling.

A finger slid over and jerked his chin up until he was staring into Rem's pitch black eyes. His searched Killian's thoroughly.

"Not afraid. Sad," Rem confirmed for the others.

"Sad about what?" Zev asked.

Killian tried to take deep, calming breaths but the trembling did not cease.

"It is nothing," he tried to say.

"That won't work on us," Drek said cooly.

"Tell us what's wrong," Caspian added, tail flicking with concern.

Killian sighed before saying, "I had a dream about Filo. He was in a corrupted God's thrall and crying. And I just stood there and watched. It is as if he is asking me to help him. But I cannot tell if its real or not."

"It's probably another one of his tricks," Drek said angrily.

"Is it?" Killian countered. "What if he really needs help? What if the magix user that is in hiding is the one pulling the strings? What if Filo is being manipulated the same way Drek was? Or the servant girl Maya?"

"Then that would change things immensely," Faust said softly.

"It would make sense though. Especially with how his Father is acting," Caspian pointed out.

"That would imply that His Highness knows about the other magix user," Zev said.

"He does," Killian said.

Everyone stopped and looked at him.

"He knows?" Zev exclaimed incredulously. "Then why has he not done anything?"

"That is what I keep asking but he keeps saying there is a bigger picture. And every time he does, he looks at me as if he is trying to tell me something else. Except I do not know what he is trying to say. My Father is always straightforward and blunt with everything he does. I am not used to his subtlety."

"Do you believe the Queen would know something about it? Or perhaps one of your Consort mothers?" Faust asked.

"She may or may not, but my mother is obedient to my father. She will not tell me anything if he does not wish it."

"But he does want you to know, he just can't tell you himself. Maybe the perfect solution is to ask the Queen," Caspian said.

"I will ask then," Killian concluded then looked down at his hands.

They were still shaking. Then he felt the familiar tingles and dizziness. He fell limp. Rem caught him before he could completely fall back into the pillows. He gently laid him down before brushing his hair out of his face. Sweat began to coat his skin and his mouth ran dry.

His *Haise* was here. He had done well with keeping himself fed enough where each time it was bearable. He didn't understand why it's so strong again.

"His *Haise* already? He fed twice last night," Drek said.

"It could be the fast development of our children. The further along he gets, the more he has to feed to accommodate their growing bodies," Faust suggested.

What he said made sense, but the look on Rem's face told Killian it was something different. He was staring at him again with that strange unreadable expression. Intense enough to make Killian shiver. Rem's eyes flashed. Just for a second, but it was enough to know that he was right there. Slick oozed out of him.

"Sotershai," Killian whispered.

And like a summoning, he ripped out of Rem and to the surface, completely taking control with blazing eyes and brilliant magix marks that flared with heat.

"Kill..." he growled.

Killian saw the fear flash in his Consorts' eyes.

"Did he just say 'kill'?" Drek panicked, then made a move to grab the God but Zev threw out an arm and held him back. His eyes never leaving Sotershai's form.

"Wait." Was all he said.

"Sotershai," Killian whispered again with slight pleading. His hips slightly raising on their own. Sotershai growled again, hovering over him with a hand on either side of his head. Killian wrapped his legs around his waist and pushed his hips up, begging for friction.

"Kill...love," he grumbled.

"I love you too Sotershai. I love you so much," Killian whimpered.

"I...give...Kill...love," his guttural voice promised.

"Yes. Yes. Make love to me, Sotershai," he begged, rolling his hips to urge him on. He roared, slamming his hips against him. Killian jerked with the movement before weakly turning over to offered his slick soaked backside.

Sotershai slid right in with no resistance. His thrusts were powerful and dominating. His magix was burning brighter than ever. Killian screamed his moans, meeting him thrust for thrust, throwing it back as hard as he could without endangering the babies.

Feeling his sword pierce him over and over, heating up inside like an iron rod was like nothing he had ever experienced. The prince begged and moaned, pleading with him to breed him again. He was getting close. So close to completion.

And then his thigh started burning. Killian screamed and this time not from pleasure. But Sotershai reacted, going harder.

"We have to stop them," he heard someone say.

"No!" Killian yelled at them. Though he wasn't sure who he was speaking to.

And it hurt so badly, the burning, but Sotershai inside him felt so good he couldn't stop. Not when he was so close. So he kept going.

Harder.

Faster.

Until he was sobbing with pleasure and the burning sensation began to grow unbearable, traveling down his leg.

He could see his vision tinting that familiar orange color, nearly blinding him. And it was almost like something inside him was expanding. Killian couldn't quite explain the feeling.

"His eyes," someone whispered.

Then something popped within him. Sotershai roared with his climax and Killian came with him but the pain was so intense he could barely feed. Sotershai's breath was erratic and uneven.

"My leg," Killian whimpered.

He turned over and Sotershai slid out of him as he did so. Zev came over and pulled Sotershai back gently. Killian was surprised when the God let him. Faust was there in an instant, pulling his leg away. He heard several gasps before he looked down at himself and saw what everyone was staring at. His eyes widened at the discovery.

His leg.

It was covered with raised marks of magix. The small ones that had been on his inner thigh had now expanded down to right above his knee.

Killian gaped at it. Then he looked at his God lover. He was staring back. And then he did the strangest thing. He smiled. Killian frowned at Sotershai.

"Sotershai? Do you know what this means?"

Sotershai's smile widened.

And it was even stranger seeing it on Rem's face as he had never seen him do it before. At least, not like this.

"Ready...soon."

Ready soon? What does that mean?

"What do you mean by that?" he asked him, voicing his thoughts aloud but right when he opened his mouth, his eyes and chest immediately went dark and Rem was back. Rem gasped, taking in a deep breath before panting heavily. His eyes were wide with shock.

"What just happened?" Zev asked.

"Did you try to get control again?" Caspian asked Rem.

But Rem shook his head.

"Something shoved me to the forefront," Rem said gravely when he was able to catch his breath.

"What do you mean?" Killian asked cautiously.

"I do not know how to explain it, but I felt a presence with me, aside from Sotershai. It has never happened before."

"Was it malevolent?" Faust asked, concern lacing his voice.

"I do not know."

It wasn't like Rem to be so disoriented.

"Let us discuss it later. We have too much on our plate already," Killian told them, starting to get up but wincing from the pain in his backside and on his leg.

Killian didn't want to overwhelm Rem. He needed a moment to collect himself and reanalyze what happened. He'd be able to tell them more when he was better composed. Killian examined the marks again and frowned. This was going to be hell to cover up.

He stood and headed for the bathroom to wash himself off. Rem joined him but didn't say a word or touch him. It should have concerned him, but he didn't think anything of it. He needed time and space and Killian would give that to him.

Killian put on fresh clothes and ate some breakfast. He had a checkup with Lorn in a little bit and was about to head over to the medical wing when he was stopped by his uncle.

Uncle Netter was the spitting image of his father. Despite a few differences, they could be identical twins. Sometimes one was mistaken for the other, at least that's what his father told him happened often in their childhood.

"Uncle, what brings you here?" he asked politely and a bit confused.

"I wish to speak with you in private, if you have a moment?" He asked him.

Killian's brows furrowed but he nodded anyway.

He followed him to his rooms. When Killian entered, it was empty. Not even Aunt Kendra was there. Turning to his Uncle, he spoke.

"What is it you wished to speak about, Uncle?"

Netter looked nervous but suddenly there was a determination in his eyes like someone lit a fire in him. It left Killian a bit surprised. Then he spoke with urgency.

"I think there are some things you need to know. I was not allowed to tell you, but I can see how this might be important to your immediate future."

Killian stared at him intensely.

"Do you know who they are?" Killian asked him.

Uncle Netter stared at his hands, wringing them before he said. "Yes."

Killian blew out a breath and took the nearest seat.

"Will you tell me?"

Netter looked uncomfortable but nodded. "There are things I must tell you first. So that you might understand where your father is coming from."

Killian glared.

"So you are siding with him," he accused.

Netter frowned.

"It is not as simple as that."

"Explain please."

Netter nodded, "Very well then. I think the first thing you should know is my brother Ellis is not the eldest."

Killian frowned.

"What do you mean?"

"I am the eldest son of Queen Gina and proper heir to the throne of Incubi."

Killian's jaw dropped.

No. There's no way. He couldn't be.

He opened his mouth to speak but Netter held a hand up and spoke.

"That's not all. It is also important that you know that the blessings of blood runs deep in our family tree."

His stomach sank. There are no records...

They couldn't hide something like that.

There is no way that this wouldn't get out earlier. They couldn't have kept so large a secret. Why would they?

"I do not...understand," Killian finally admitted feeling numb.

"I know it is hard to take this all in but I need you to understand that things are much different when you are Royal, especially when being King. My mother, your grandmother, hid her pregnancy with me because she knew what I would become. Her symptoms were much like yours and it grew worse when I was developed enough in her womb to influence her actions."

Killian froze.

"Are you...are you saying it is you? You are the other..."

Netter shook his head and raised his palms up in defense.

"No, no, no!"

Killian took a deep relieving breath.

"But I used to be."

Killian stiffened again.

"Used to be?" he repeated.

"It is difficult to explain but based on what you said earlier, you appear to be well informed about the nature of those with blessings of blood."

"I have to be. My lover is a bearer," Killian reminded him slightly upset that he was taking so long to reveal everything.

Uncle Netter nodded nervously and cleared his throat.

"Right. Well I was a bearer and what you have not been told is that if a child with the blessings of blood were to ever appear in the Royal bloodline, they were to be executed at birth. Queen Gina knew this and knew that I would not stand a chance, so she hid me. She hid her pregnancy and my birth. I was kept confined to a secret chamber in the bottom of the palace with few knowing of my existence. I lived alone for the first few years of my life until my brother, your father, was born. Upon his birth the lie was woven. She was said to have had twins. I was the 'second' born son, my appearance cloaked. This lie enabled me to live and my brother to take the throne. He was unaware of my origin.

He thought me his younger brother and treated me as such. At my mother's orders, I followed along with the ruse. And for most of his life he believed it to be true until his very own Ranking Ceremony. I happened upon one of his Potentials having a less than proper conversation about my brother for which the being inside me did not appreciate as they were incredibly protective. At least, I assumed that was the case, but really he fed off the chaos of it. And I had an episode, similar to what you have recently experienced. Thankfully I did not cause too much of fuss but enough that Ellis was forced to drive a sword through my chest.

It did not pierce my heart but instead the heart of the being that shared my body. And that is why I no longer have the blessings of blood. But the loss has diminished my power and shorten my life force considerably. I have only a year left of life. My brother knows this which is why we have been invited to stay in the palace."

Killian hadn't realized tears were falling down his cheeks until his uncle smiled gently and bent to wipe them away.

"You are dying," Killian whispered still in shock.

"I am already dead," he said softly.

More tears spilled from Killian's eyes completely blinding him. His uncle nothing but blurred colors before him.

"I know this is hard for you to hear, but there is more I must tell you."

He nodded for him to continue, wiping away more tears.

"That is how my brother found out about me. And at first he was angry. He had quite the temper back then, sort of like a certain someone."

Netter smiled and nudged Killian's side with his arm. Killian didn't smile back.

"But when our mother explained to him the reason for keeping it a secret, he suddenly became extremely protective over me. Even more so when he found out how long I had to live. And so he too began to work to hide it. That is, until another was born into our line."

Killian knew before he spoke another word. But he needed his uncle to give him the verbal confirmation. Tell him that every hunch he had was correct.

"Who is it?" he asked.

"Filo."

He knew it but it still bothered him. How it was possible for the gene to be in their bloodline? And how could everyone just let that little bastard get away with everything he had done?

Killian's chest felt tight and breathing suddenly became difficult.

I am going to kill him, Killian thought. His intent must have showed on his face because Netter was quick to utter, "Wait! It's not Filo's fault!"

Killian whirled on him, the incredulousness blatant on his face.

"Not his fault? All of this is his fault! He has come for my life and the lives of my lovers more times than I can count! I almost killed my own children because of him! His life is mine, there will be no debate."

Netter grabbed Killian's arm before he could storm out again. His expression was pleading, knowing that what he was capable of and knowing that he would make Filo suffer before he killed him.

"Please, nephew. It is not Filo's fault. He is being enthralled."

Killian's mind flashed back to the dream he kept having. The look of helplessness on Filo's face, his voice cracking, pleading for Killian to help him. To save him. No, he would be a fool to fall for it. He was not going to put himself or his lovers in danger anymore. Looking for the good in someone is a complete waste of time. Especially when they've wronged him so many times. He could only be naive for so long.

"Uncle, I understand that he is your son, but the crimes he has committed is unforgivable. For the safety of our family and the safety of this kingdom, he must die."

Netter's eyes grew wide and desperate.

"Nephew, I beg of you, don't condemn him. He is innocent, I swear it! The real Filo is kind and gentle, it is the beast within him that makes him a monster. Don't punish him for the acts of another."

"You mean the way my father did when your son accused my Consort of raping him? Do you know how severe such an accusation is?"

Netter opened his mouth to speak but Killian cut him off before he could utter a word.

"My lover nearly died. My lover would have died because of it and my heirs would have had one less father to care for them, one less father to protect them, one less person to love them. Now tell me again why I should not punish him? Rip him apart for all of the pain and suffering he has caused?"

"Because you are not cruel," his uncle said softly. "You are pure, the purest of mind that this Kingdom has seen yet. And you may view that as a weakness now but it is because of that that your Consorts love you. It is because of that, you will build a monarch without bloodshed."

Killian shook his head.

"I am not pure as you all continuously claim. One thing I've learned since gaining my Consorts, is that there is no such thing as purity. There is naivety and stupidity. I refuse to be either anymore."

Killian made a move to step around him but he stopped him again. Killian felt his nostrils flare and eyes flashed orange as a familiar heat ran through his body. Taking a couple of deep breaths, Killian willed himself to calm down.

He's trying to save his son, it's understandable. It was better to be a patient King than a reckless one. Killian took another deep breath and relaxed his tense frame. Killian gave his uncle a leveled look.

"How do you suppose I handle this situation then? I cannot just let it go the way you all have been. The more he gets away with it the more confident he will get."

"That is what your father is planning on."

Killian frowned.

"How would that be beneficial?"

Netter glanced around the empty room anxiously before lowering his voice.

"The God has been using the real Filo as a shield. Whenever Ellis tries to confront the God, it shoves Filo's consciousness to the forefront."

Killian snorted.

"What good will confronting the God be? Is there any sense reasoning with a being who cannot talk?"

Uncle Netter sighed almost guiltily.

"The God inside Filo is already awake."

A cold chill went down his spine, raising every little hair on the back of his neck to high alert.

If that's true, they are in big trouble. If memory served him right, Yehwin said the third magix user was the vessel for the God of Chaos and Destruction.

Perseth.

And if Perseth was awake...that would mean war.

"He is not fully awake but he is very close to it. He has almost full control of his vessel."

Killian brow furrowed in confusion as something he said hit him.

"You said Filo was enthralled. How can that be?"

"I'm sure you are aware of the powers these Gods possess. Your Consort was a victim of the same power. Filo has been manipulated since he was a child. It is the main reason why we moved to Kerbis, to keep him isolated. We did not realize it would get this bad."

"But how can he be enthralled if he is the vessel?"

"The same way the Gods can compel you and I, they can compel their vessels."

"So you're saying...the God in Rem can compel him? And the demigod in me can compel me?" Killian asked him.

Uncle Netter gave him a serious look.

"Yes."

Killian's stomach dropped. This was a lot worse than he first imagined. He could only hope that the demigod in him was too underdeveloped to make such a huge move. But as for Sotershai?

Killian worried about that.

Sotershai is strong already. He was waking up at a much faster rate than they anticipated. He's already able to talk. And he's been forcing himself to the forefront of Rem's consciousness more often.

Could it be that Killian's presence and Sotershai's infatuation and desire to be with him may be accelerating his development?

Was Killian a danger to Rem?

But he guessed the real question is if Sotershai is a danger to Rem. If he had the power to compel him, and he was able to destroy three of the biggest regions in all the land, then maybe he proves to be a bigger issue than Perseth. But who was worse to have loose?

Sotershai or Perseth?

And they won't be able to defeat Perseth on their own. They needed Sotershai. They needed him to wake up if they had any hope of winning this and protecting their loved ones. Could they get Sotershai to cooperate? Can he get Sotershai to cooperate?

What happens afterward? They couldn't risk leaving him with so much power or else it would endanger Rem and it must truly be unfortunate to share a body with such a powerful being. Rem already has issues as is, Killian didn't want to add any more stress for him.

It was one huge mess that he had no idea how to clean up.

"There is more you must know," his uncle said.

Killian gave him an exasperated look.

"More?"

Netter gave a solemn nod.

"You know it is Perseth in Filo, but I must inform you that I was the original vessel of the Corrupt God of Chaos."

Killian sat back down with a sigh.

There should be a limit to how complicated this mess can be.

"Continue," the prince urged with another sigh, feeling as if he had aged a couple more years.

Netter nodded then proceeded.

"When I had the blessings of blood, I shared a vessel with Perseth. Sometimes I felt myself blacking out, being trapped in a dark room with no one around and shrouded in darkness. The older I grew, the more it started happening. I later learned that it would happen every time that Perseth would take over. My family dealt with much of what you are experiencing. It was hard for them to cover up the horrible acts I committed, especially when I awoke not knowing what I actually did.

It was part of the reason that your father's Potential and I were at odds. I did not have control of my vessel at the time and as strange as it sounds, Perseth is actually fond of your father. When the Potential said some less than pleasant things about Ellis, Perseth snapped.

If your father did not pierce Perseth's heart, than Perseth would have awakened. Unfortunately, Kendra was newly pregnant with the triplets and Perseth jumped from my vessel to Filo, who was a bearer of magix, before the God's heart was completely destroyed. In entering a new mortal body, Perseth was forced back into dormancy. And while Perseth is the true sire of Filo, he did not bind Filo's vessel. It left the underdeveloped half-God vulnerable. The destruction of Filo's other half was the catalyst needed to beginning the awakening of Perseth again.

Because we both have shared the God of Chaos, I have a connection with my son. I can reach him in that place he is trapped in within himself when Perseth takes control. I have been with him through his entire life and I can promise you the Filo you have encountered is not the real Filo.

I do not have enough power left to help him and I will not live for much longer to be with him, so I beg of you to help him. Help him so I might hold my son again. I know this is a lot to ask but you have the power to help. Please."

When his uncle got down on his knees and bowed, Killian's chest felt so heavy it made him nauseous.

"Please help him. He needs you."

"Why me?"

Netter looked up from his bow.

"Because your father is right. You are much stronger than you realize."

Killian shook his head and stood.

"I do not know what you want me to do."

"Talk to him," Uncle Netter pushed, getting to his feet.

"How am I supposed to do that?"

"You have been seeing him have you not? He has been coming to you."

The dreams.

Killian turned a suspicious eye on him.

"How do you know that?"

Uncle Netter met his gaze and it was a bit strange looking into a face, into eyes that were near identical to his father's.

"Because I am the one who sent him to you."

"You sent me those dreams? How?"

"I only bridged his mind to yours, what happened I had no control over. I still have some remnants of power left when I was the bearer of the blessings of blood."

Could Killian trust him?

Was this true?

Was that the real Filo he saw in his dream? Has he really been trapped in there? Has he truly been calling for help?

"Why now?"

"What?" Uncle Netter questioned in confusion.

Killian unleashed his full gaze on him.

"Why am I just seeing him now? Why have you not done anything before this? Or why have you not tried to get me to help earlier?"

Uncle Netter sighed.

"Because I began to realize that your Father does not have it under control. He has been trying to keep you out of this, but it is not possible. You are involved because Perseth is targeting you. For what reason, I do not know. But now that he's on your trail there is naught we can do to hide you. You will be in crossfire regardless."

And that was lovely to hear.

"I have to think. I have to figure this all out."

"I understand."

The Consorts

Killian walked toward the door and this time Netter didn't stop him. With one hand on the golden knob of the door, Killian stopped and turned his head back to his uncle.

"Thank you. For telling me."

He nodded and smiled. Killian always did think it was strange that a male so kind had children so evil. But if Filo was the bearer of the blessings of blood, what was Marza and Bennett's excuse? Were they being compelled as well? Or were they just rotten?

A headache came along as he walked down the halls back to his room. Killian was about to turn the corner down the corridor until he felt eyes on him.

He glanced over his shoulder and noticed a pair of eyes peeking around the corner. Hidden in an area where the lights of the hall had trouble illuminating. But he knew who it was. He didn't say a word, but his eyes were trained on Killian's every movement. The prince stopped and turned to face him.

If he was alarmed at being caught watching him, he didn't show it. Killian walked toward him. When he was only a few feet away, he stopped and crossed his arms. Meeting his gaze head on. Maybe he would be able to tell the truth from lie on his own.

"Which one are you?" Killian asked him.

He didn't say anything, just blinked.

"Are you Filo or are you Perseth?"

His head cocked to the side.

Killian stared at him, before opening my mouth to say something, but saw his gray eyes flicker to something behind him.

A low dangerous growl came from right above Killian's shoulder.

Killian didn't bother glancing behind him. He could feel the warmth nearly burning his back. He reached behind him to caress his cheek but didn't take his eyes off of the male before him. His breath tickled his skin.

"Sotershai," Killian breathed softly, voice as gentle as his touch.

Filo's nostrils flared.

"Stay...away," Sotershai growled in that guttural baritone of his that sounded more like snarls than actual words.

Filo's eyes flashed.

And Killian had his answer.

Chapter 28

Killian couldn't get out of bed.

The cramping had become much worse. Lorn stayed by his side the whole day, checking to make sure that nothing was wrong. Queen Jessa also insisted on being there, sitting on one of the couches having tea with Faust.

Caspian assisted Lorn in caring for the prince as he had the most experience with pregnant S-Levels. He knew what to do and how to help. He was the perfect assistant. It was strange seeing him in serious mode. Killian was used to him and Drek joking around all the time.

Drek on the other hand was in and out of the room under Rem's orders. Killian didn't know what for but he was in too much pain to really care. He'd worry about it later.

Yehwin laid on the bed on the pillow next to his in his smaller cat form. He kept giving purs of approval but Killian had no idea what for.

"Do you know something that we do not?" Killian asked the lazy cat when he was well enough to catch his breath. The pain came in waves and it was best to take advantage of any moment he wasn't suffering.

Yehwin blinked at him and if he didn't know any better he'd say he was smiling too. He definitely knew something. Killian's glare was sharp.

"What is it?" he demanded.

Yehwin didn't say anything but his smile widened.

"He likes your voice," Yehwin said in a light and cheerful voice, his tongue rolling with his heavy accent.

Before Killian could stop it, a frown twisted his features. Partly from the confusion in his words and another from the onslaught of pain that was once again bubbling and building in his abdomen. A soft and slow hiss left his lips as the pain increased and Yehwin was soon forgotten.

Lorn informed Killian that there was a point in all pregnancies when the fetus's power began to develop and infuse with their bodies. And Killian had twice the amount of power working in him. Whether increasing or decreasing, they wouldn't know until the twins were born. But they were boiling with power inside him. And it hurt like Hell. This process is what killed most S-Levels before modern medical magic.

Inhaling sharply, Killian tried to control his breathing, focusing on everything and anything other than the pain. But it was so forceful, so blinding, he could not see--feel past it.

A slow exhale was the only sound that could be heard. Gods above he needed a distraction!

A soft knock resonated on the door. Everyone's head snapped to the sound.

Rem glanced at Killian first and he gave him a slight nod. He opened the door and Trina--one of the attendants that he assigned to care for Orion-- popped her head in.

With wide eyes, frantically searching. She seemed to notice the tension and his face crunched in pain.

Falling to her knees she bowed, pressing her head to the white marble floor.

"Forgive me, My Prince. I did not mean to interrupt."

"Rise and speak your piece," Rem commanded, his words crisp and full of authority.

Trina rose, her big brown eyes were wide. Worry and age had wrinkled her lovely brown skin and her gray hair was wild, some tendrils stuck to her face as sweat beaded at her hairline.

Something was wrong.

Oh Gods, not again. What is it this time?

"Speak," Killian wheezed.

She nodded.

"Lord Orion has gone into labor."

Killian shot up from the bed, his own pain forgotten.

"He is not due for another month!" Lorn hissed, standing.

Trina's eyes dulled with worry. "I know. He's been complaining about sharp pains for a few weeks now. I thought he was going through the power development stage of the pregnancy but..." she trailed off. "We need help."

"I am attending our Crown Prince. I cannot," Lorn snarled at the Healer. "You are trained for this!"

"I know and I apologize for interrupting but we haven't been able to stabilize him. If we don't act soon, we'll lose him and the baby."

The tenseness in the room fell on us all thick and heavy. Stifling.

"Go," Killian told Lorn.

"Killian--" Caspian started, concern twisting his features. The prince held up a hand to stop him before he continued.

"I will be fine. Caspian, you have more than enough experience with this and you will do just fine helping me."

"Killian, I'm not trained! I don't know what I'm--" he stopped him again, looking into those wide yellow eyes, pupils swallowing up his irises from his panic.

"I trust you," he breathed, not breaking eye contact. "I trust that you will not let anything happen to me. I am fine."

Killian switched his gaze to Lorn, jerking his chin toward Trina. "Go. Then report back to me."

Lorn's eyes flickered to Caspian then backed to him and she finally bowed, walking swiftly out of the room with Trina, murmuring lowly to her. Most likely demanding the details of what happened. Killian watched them leave, lightly closing the door behind them.

The room settled into silence, until a sharp pain shot through him and he hissed again, clutched his stomach, closed his eyes, and gritted his teeth.

Caspian made a noise of distress in the back of his throat, looking worried as he came to his side. A cloth dipped in a bucket of cool water slid across his brow, wiping away all of the sweat that began to gather.

"What's wrong with him?" Zev asked.

"It's not anything to be worried about. Aaia is just having her fun," Yehwin yawned.

"Can you tell her to stop?" Killian growled as another wave hit him.

Yehwin laughed.

"I won't. But you can, child of his blood," he purred.

The urge to smother the cat with a pillow was overwhelming. Caspian ignored him and continued to wipe Killian's forehead.

"You'll be due soon," he whispered, not really looking him in the eye, but his eyes roamed all over his face.

"How can you tell?" Killian asked him.

He sighed before smiling at him, "I can smell it."

Strange.

Killian stroked his cheek gently. "Thank you."

Caspian gave him a half smile before pulling back and wringing out the water from the cloth. The soft sound of water trickling back into the bucket was soothing. Killian let it lull him into a meditative trance. It was only disturbed when there was another knock on the door. A lot louder and more demanding than before.

Rem glanced at Killian again, debating whether or not he was well enough for another visitor. Killian nodded at him. He stared for a moment, searching his face deciding whether or not he was being truthful. He opened the door a moment later. Killian's eyes narrowed in confusion and in shock.

Pierce.

His white hair was wild and blue eyes red rimmed. Even his tunic was wrinkled and disheveled. He looked scared.

"Brother," he greeted. His voice shaky, more like a boy then an adult.

He was terrified. Killian sat up concerned.

"Can I speak with you?" He asked, stepping further inside the room.

"Speak freely," he told him, concern lacing his voice and his features.

He had never seen him this way before. It worried Killian.

"Privately," he rasped.

His Consorts tensed but seeing that pitiful look on his baby brother's face had Killian patting Caspian's knee so he could help him up.

Faust grasped one of Killian's hands while Caspian wrapped an arm around his waist. He cupped underneath his swollen belly as they helped him stand.

"Let us go," Killian told his brother.

Killian waddled, hoping that the pain wouldn't remain. Pierce offered his arm for him to take. Killian smiled at him gratefully before grasping it and giving him his weight. Killian could tell from the way his Consorts' lingered with their touch that they didn't feel wholly comfortable with leaving him with his brother. Killian shot them a look, reassuring them that he'd be fine.

"Let one of us come with you. You don't know when the pain will strike again. Something could happen to the bab--"

"Caspian, I'll be fine."

Caspian sighed before stepping back.

Killian glanced at Rem before he left and noticed how tense he was but he let him go. Killian smiled at him and left.

Walking through the halls, they were silent. Killian waited for him to speak but didn't want to push in case he was gathering his thoughts. But he had an idea of what he wanted to talk about.

He was worried about Orion. It was finally becoming real for him. And he was realizing that he's not ready to be an adult because he was still a child himself, how could he possibly raise one of his own? He was probably even more scared that it was happening so fast.

Killian was not entirely sure about their relationship but if he had any feelings about Orion, then he was probably worried about his health and what this meant for him and his child. He could lose them both.

Killian could only imagine what was going through his mind. How he might be feeling. His poor baby brother.

They walked out to one of the many balconies that looked out to the vast forest around the palace. Stone walls with bordering pillars and a small lounge couch that overlooked the mass of green. They sat down beside each other. He was gentle in helping him down. He waited, listening as he took a deep breath.

"I'm sorry," he whispered.

Tears were glittering in his eyes.

"I'm so sorry."

Killian wrapped an arm around his shoulders and kissed the side of his head, feeling the dampness of his tears on his shoulder where he tucked his head.

"It is alright, brother. I forgive you. I knew you never meant any real harm."

His shoulders shook.

His head twisted side to side.

"I'm sorry."

He kept saying it over and over again.

I'm sorry.

I'm sorry.

I'm sorry.

The first couple of times Killian didn't think anything of it. Pierce had never been malicious so not only was it surprising when he first showed Killian that ugly side but also uncharacteristic. He was probably beating himself up over it. It broke Killian's heart.

But he kept going. Over and over again. And it became clear that there was something more happening. Killian could feel it in the tightness in his gut, the heaviness in his chest.

I'm sorry.

I'm sorry.

I'm sorry.

Even more so when he felt the coolness of a blade press against his back.

Killian breath hitched softly, body stiffening but he didn't dare move.

"Pierce," he whispered. "Think before you act."

Pierce was still trembling. Tears were still streaming down his flushed lavender cheeks as he pulled his head back, the blade pressing deeper into Killian's spine. The prince winced, feeling the sharp edge cutting through his thin robe right into skin.

"Pierce," Killian said sharply.

"You can't be King. He won't allow it," Pierce sobbed.

"Pierce...I am your brother. Will you really kill your brother? Your own flesh and blood?" Killian said slowly, carefully, not taking his eyes off of him.

"He won't make it stop unless I do!" Pierce shouted, the blade at his back trembling.

"Put the knife down and let us talk about this. Let me help you."

Pierce shook his head.

"I can't. I can't. He's going to kill them if I don't."

He didn't need to say anymore, Killian knew who and what he was talking about immediately. Somehow...someway...Filo was behind Orion's early labor.

"He will kill them anyway. Once I am gone, he will go after Ian...then Gilra...then you. It will not stop until we are all dead. So put the knife down and let us figure this out together."

Pierce shook his head again before taking a deep breath and meeting his eyes.

"I'm sorry," he said again.

Before bringing the blade down.

Chapter 29

Killian could not forgive him for this. He would not forgive him for this.

To turn his own brother against him? Using not his compulsion, but the weakness in their relationship. It was a wicked plot. He knew Killian would not harm his baby brother intentionally. But he also knew his instincts of self preservation were higher when carrying.

And as that blade came down, Killian's instincts took over, forcing him to strike. Swiftly, his power surged, flicking out and knocking Pierce away with such force, he slammed into the stone walls, cracking them. Blue eyes lost focus for just a moment, before he whirled on him with a vengeance.

Even with the force of the collision, he did not lose his grip on the knife. There was determination burning in his eyes like a wild flame and Killian knew this would not end well. It became clear what that bastard wanted.

If Pierce couldn't kill him, Killian would be forced to kill Pierce.

Curse him for not allowing his Consorts to accompany him. He should have known better. It was Jax all over again.

Killian dashed for the entrance to the hall, hoping that he could get to a nearby guard on duty, but he was ripped back and tossed into the marble pillar, just inches from the ledge of the balcony.

Pain sang through his bones, as his knees buckled. He slid down the pillar unable to stand. His stomach...Gods above it hurt.

Pierce came for him again, blade glinting off the sun's light.

Killian through a hand out to keep him back but the pain wracked through him so thoroughly it was hard to breathe. Damn it!

With clenched teeth, he tried to blink past his blurring vision only to see white when the earlier cycle of pain came back to haunt him.

Aaia please! Don't do this to Daddy!

He begged the child inside him to leash her power, but she did not listen and it only increased. Pierce struck the invisible wall Killian cowered beneath, again and again. Each strike pushing him lower and lower onto the ground. The cramps in his gut grew harsher with each ragged breath he took. Wet warmth spilled over his top lip into his mouth where he could taste the metallic tang of blood.

"Pierce, please. Stop this!" Killian panted, desperately, barely able to get his voice above a whisper.

He couldn't keep this up. The pain was too much. With his vision dimming, he knew he did not have long until he blacked out. His sight blurred, warning him of his slipping consciousness.

"Yehwin…" Killian whispered, so softly, it was barely a sound.

It was all he could manage to get out, but he hoped. Just hoped that he'd hear him. His power flickered out and there was nothing between his brother and him any longer. Killian closed his eyes, unable to stay awake under the blinding pain.

He waited for the inevitable blow from the blade that no longer had obstacles.

And waited.

And waited.

But nothing.

Daring to crack his eyes open again, he saw his beloveds. All of them. Rem and Zev had Pierce pinned to the ground, knife yards away from his grip. Caspian and Faust by Killian's side, wiping the blood from his face and checking for any wounds. While Drek stood by the door, barking orders to those he could not see.

And Yehwin.

He stood off to the side and out of the way, but those glowing blue eyes were trained on him.

Thank you.

Though Killian did not say the words aloud, he heard them, and gave him an imperceptible nod of acknowledgement.

Knowing he was safe, he let himself succumb to the darkness.

When he awoke again, he was in his bed. Lorn and Caspian just a few feet away murmuring quietly to each other over a few pieces of paper in Lorn's hand.

Faust sat on the couch with a cup of tea, reading over some documents while Drek sat across from him. Long legs stretched out and ankles crossed just like his arms. His head was tilted back and eyes closed. Resting but not completely asleep. That much Killian could tell from the rigidness in his posture. And Rem was standing guard at the door, still as a statue.

Blinking a few times, Killian slowly moved to sit up. Dizziness heavy. All eyes turned on him. His gaze trained on Lorn and Caspian, hand resting on his stretched stomach.

"The babies?" he asked, voice hoarse.

"They're fine."

"My brother?"

Caspian and Lorn shared a look before Caspian answered this time. "He is fine. Being questioned by the King as we speak."

Killian wasn't quite sure how he felt about that. Who is to say they did not plan it together. Or his father might make it go away as he had a habit of doing.

"And what of Orion?"

Lorn smiled.

"He has given birth to a female. Your new niece, Gwendolyn Innis. She's a bit small but healthy and Lord Orion pulled through as well. They are both being tended to."

Killian released a breath of relief.

Everyone was okay, thank the Clouds.

"You should rest. Your body underwent a lot of strain," Caspian coaxed softly.

He didn't feel like resting but Killian knew he was right. He came really close to losing everything. That demon almost won. Killian shivered at the thought.

Closing his eyes, Killian let himself drift again. This time dreaming of the days that were sure to come. Well if they didn't die first. They were filled with color and laughter.

He saw them again. his precious children, running around in the palace driving their fathers insane. He could smell their innocence. They will be here soon.

When he awoke, his bladder was near bursting. Thankfully, Rem woke instantly and helped him to the bathroom. And much to his discomfort, stayed there while he relieved himself.

"You do not have to watch," Killian grumbled.

"I am not letting you out of my sight again," he replied blandly.

Killian rolled his eyes and didn't bother fighting him on it. After washing his hands, Killian headed out of the bathroom and instead of the bed, headed for the door.

Rem was there in an instant, giving him his signature blank stare as he blocked the door. Killian glared up at his pitch black eyes.

"Let me pass."

"Where is it that you are going?" he asked.

"To see Orion and his newborn."

"They are all asleep."

Glancing out the window, Killian took note of the freshly set sun, then turned back to Rem with an even fiercer glare.

"Liar," he hissed.

"You are unwell."

"Rem, let me pass."

"Nay."

"Rem!"

Rem blinked at him.

Killian huffed in aggravation and waddled back to the bed, sitting angrily at the edge with his arms crossed, not caring if he woke the others with his jostling.

Drek's arm slid around his waist and tugged him back, forcing him to lay on his side, tucked into his chest. His lips were on Killian's ear as he sleepily mumbled, "Stop pissing Rem off."

"Pissing Rem off? He is pissing me off!" the prince hissed.

Rem said nothing and climbed back into the bed.

"Sleep," was all the black Incubus said.

Killian growled in reply.

He couldn't sleep, he slept all day. His body was well rested. He was full of energy, brimming with it actually. And he wanted to leave the confines of this forsaken room! He was sick of being here all the time.

He wanted to see Orion and Titus, see how they were doing and maybe find out more information about what happened with Pierce. Did they know? Did Filo approach them too? Was Pierce acting weird beforehand?

How were they taking Pierce's disappearance after the birth? Because if Killian were in their shoes, he would definitely be alarmed if a parent wasn't there for the family. Or were they expecting this behavior from him after all he's done before?

Killian hadn't seen Pierce in a while, he wasn't quite sure if he changed, or if his mentor has been helping him adjust to his new role as a father. And Killian didn't know what the relationship was like between the three of them.

He supposed if he were a good brother and a good ruler, he would have been there for them more. Then maybe all of this could have been avoided. Maybe he would've seen the signs.

Killian wanted to talk to him. He wanted to see his brother and figure out why he was desperate enough to kill his own brother? What did Filo say to him to make him attempt regicide? Because there is a part of Killian that believed he was not under any compulsion. He was free of mind control and knew what he was doing when he tried to kill him.

To be willing to kill him? Murder him when he was not only his brother and King but with child as well?

The stakes must have been high. Killian had to know the full story. He had to know why. Because it would break his heart if he couldn't even trust his own brother.

"Go to sleep Killian," Drek mumbled against Killian's neck where he had buried his face. "I can feel your worry lines."

Killian rolled his eyes at him, knowing Drek couldn't see it. He couldn't sleep. Not with so much on his mind. So he waited. Waited until Drek's breathing evened out then slowed. He waited until Rem's chest was moving steadily. He waited until all of his Consorts were deep in their slumber before slipping carefully from underneath Drek's arm and tiptoed to the door.

It would be a miracle if he managed to escape without Rem noticing.

The Consorts

Sometimes Killian didn't think he really slept, there was no way someone could be that aware of everything all the time. Nothing got past him.

Killian hands shook as he reached for the handle on the door. So close. As he turned the knob, he felt someone behind him.

Damn it!

"Rem please--" he started, turning around to face him.

But Rem was still fast asleep in bed.

The male before him, shouldn't have even gotten in. Not undetected.

"Hello cousin."

Bennett.

"What are you doing in here?"

He hid the tremor in his voice well.

How did he get in here? Especially without alerting any of his Consorts? Killian didn't even open the door. He glanced around him at his sleeping lovers. They hadn't stirred at the presence of an intruder. They were all still. Way too still.

Killian focused his attention back on his cousin, heavy with suspicion. Something was definitely not right. Marza was a backstabbing slut. Filo was that and evil incarnate.

But Bennett?

He was the quiet one. Marza and Filo were the ones that enjoyed tormenting him his entire life, but Bennett, always following along, laughing along, playing along, never actually did anything to him. He was the silent bystander that let everything happen without lifting a finger to stop it. He was still wrong and Killian didn't like him, but he didn't fear him.

He was never worried about him.

So why did his stomach drop at the sight of him? Every tiny hair on his body raised to attention. Even the demigod inside him began to stir restlessly, sensing a threat. His aura was dark, thick and clouded like murky smoke, almost choking Killian with its intensity. The feeling was uncomfortable, stifling. It made his heart race and not the way his Consorts did.

He felt off.

Wrong even.

Killian's first assumption would be that he too was being compelled, but it different from the others. From Maya, from Drek, and from Filo. Did Bennett always have this aura and Killian never noticed?

"What do you want?" Killian questioned, on full guard, looking at his cousin suspiciously. From his muddy pink eyes, pale lavender skin, to his wavy brown locks. He was normal enough in appearance, nothing that really stuck out. Not like Filo's devastatingly gorgeous features and brilliant red hair or even Marza's dainty features and curvaceous body. He was the most invisible of his siblings.

Maybe that made him the most dangerous. And here he thought Filo was the worst of it.

"I came to warn you cousin."

Killian's brows furrowed.

"Warn me about what?"

"There will be four deaths in the next twelve horas. Three will be very dear to you. You will not be able to prevent it, but you must not let it break you. He'll be waiting for it."

Killian's blood ran cold.

Deaths?

"What are you talking about? Who will die? Who will be waiting for what? What is going on?"

Bennett just stared, his plain face pulling into a disappointed frown.

"I will not get involved further. Consider yourself warned."

He held up a hand, drawing Killian's attention to his long fingers before snapping. The prince blinked startled and he was gone. Shifting around with searching eyes, Killian inspected the room, trying to find any trace of him but he completely disappeared.

He rushed over to the bed, gripping Drek's shoulder and shaking him. He popped up immediately, awake and alert, dark green eyes scanning the room for any sort of threat. His frame tense and prepared to leap into action.

"What's wrong?" he demanded, his voice still thick with sleep, not at all matching the awareness in his face.

Rem was up too, staring at Killian intently.

"Bennett. He was just here," he said, his voice shaking and mind still reeling from the information. "He said he came to warn me. Four people are going to die in twelve horas. He said three would be dear to me."

Rem's eyes narrowed before he disappeared in a puff of smoke. Drek's eyes continued to scan the room before he frowned.

"I did not sense him at all. Are you sure?"

"Of course I am sure!" he snapped.

Dead.

Someone would be dead.

He already lost Kara, he didn't want to lose anyone else. He couldn't lose anyone else.

"What's with all the racket?" a liquid voice groaned. The sheets rustled and Caspian emerged with heavy lidded eyes and flushed cheeks, still half asleep.

"Worst guard ever," Drek muttered under his breath.

Caspian blinked then quickly read the situation. His pupils dilated before he was immediately alert, nostrils flaring rapidly and eyes darting around the room.

When he looked at Killian, his pupils had nearly swallowed the yellow in his irises.

"What's wrong?"

"Killian says Bennett was here. Warned him about four deaths that are supposed to happen in the next twelve horas."

"You sure he was telling the truth? He could be just saying that to riled you up. It could be another one of their plots."

Killian shook his head.

"No. It was different this time. I don't think it was Filo's doing. Bennett was..." he couldn't finish his sentence. He was too busy building a mental list of who might be the next target. He has tried and failed several times to get his Consorts. He wouldn't go for them again, would he?

What about Ethel and Lisa?

They already got Kara, they could be after them next. That's two people right there. But what they gain from that?

Ian and Gilra?

They were his siblings and the next in line for the throne. Yehwin said they would be in danger. Could they be after them?

It was likely considering they already got to...

Pierce.

Killian was moving before he even realized. Throwing open the door he raced down the halls, as fast as his feet could carry him with the extra weight of the twins.

He followed the trail by instinct alone, reaching the cells where his brother was being held, dismissing the guards who tried to stop him with a hand.

Funny how his father would throw his own son into a cell for attempted regicide but not his nephew.

Killian's brother was curled into a ball, his face in his hands. He looked so small, hunched over like that. It made his heart break.

"Pierce," Killian whispered.

His shoulders jolted, but he didn't dare look up.

"Pierce, look at me," Killian pleaded.

Finally his brother raised his head. His white hair plastered to his face, blue eyes red rimmed from crying. His gaze was dull and void of emotion.

"Why did you do it?" he asked him. "What did he say to make you do it?"

Pierce looked away, shoulders sagging.

"It doesn't matter," he said, voice hoarse.

"Pierce. What did he say to you?"

"A life for a life."

Pierce lay down, curling into a ball on the small cell bed with his back facing Killian.

"Pierce," he called again.

But he didn't turn around. No matter how many times he called his name, he did not answer.

"Let us go," a deep voice from behind him and suddenly the world went black.

When the darkness finally cleared, he was back in his room. Killian gasped, feeling the bile rise up his throat. Rem was behind him, rubbing small circles into his back.

"I threw up the first time he transported me," Zev said reassuringly, from his perch on the edge of the bed.

"We need to do something," Killian insisted to his Consorts. "I cannot let someone die, not again."

"You need to calm down. You don't even know if he was telling the truth," Drek said, repeating what was said earlier.

"But what if he is? Isn't it better to be safer than sorry? I cannot risk losing another life. Not when I have been given notice prior."

Faust walked into the room with a steaming cup in in his hands.

Killian thought it was for himself, seeing as he always had a cup in his hand, but instead he offered it to the prince with a comforting smile.

"Drink up sweetling, it will calm your nerves. You'll be able to think clearly after a nice cup."

Killian took it gratefully and offered Faust a weak smile. He took a sip, moaning at the sweet spicy taste. It was like nothing he had ever tasted before.

"This is delic--"

His world tilted, dimming around the edges.

"Sleep sweetling, everything will be okay when you wake," he whispered before the world went to black.

When he awoke, it was morning.

Rem was sitting at the side of the bed, one hand stroking Killian's exposed thigh.

"You drugged me," the prince growled.

Rem's eyes flickered over to him, but he didn't say anything. His expression was strange somehow. Contained.

"What is it?"

Rem still didn't say anything. Instead he leaned over and kissed Killian softly. His lips were like flower petals. His tongue pushed against Killian's bottom lip, gently coaxing him to open his mouth to him. Killian did without hesitation.

But it was strange.

Rem did not initiate intimacy out of the blue. He wasn't acting like himself. Killian pushed away from him and opened his mouth to voice his questions of concern but Rem pushed him back and sealed his lips to his again. His movements more aggressive but not forceful. It was full of the passion Killian begged him to give him for so long.

The passion he was used to seeing from Sotershai, not Rem. And Sotershai was nowhere to be found. His eyes did not glow. His magix did not heat. His skin did not brighten. And his hearts did not race.

"Rem-" Killian tried again, but the Consort wouldn't let him get a word in. He was relentless, tongue dancing with Killian's, body curving against his tasting like everything sweet and wonderful in the world.

The Consorts

But Killian would not be distracted. Because that's exactly what this was. A distraction.

"Rem, stop!"

Rem stopped immediately, breathing ragged, chest heaving, and his jaw locked. He wouldn't meet Killian's gaze.

He had never seen him act like this before. It wasn't like him.

"Tell me what is wrong."

Rem still didn't look at Killian, instead at his hands, where he clenched and unclenched his fists. It was scaring Killian.

"Rem, tell me."

One hand reached and gripped Killian's cheek, swiping back and forth right beneath his eyes. His forehead pressed against the prince's and he squeezed his eyes shut.

"Rem."

"I am sorry," he whispered.

"Sorry?"

He wrapped his arms around Killian's waist and pulled him against him, one hand pressing the prince's head into his neck.

"Tell me," Killian mumbled against his chest, desperate now.

"Pierce is dead."

Chapter
30

He couldn't have heard him right.

There was no way. Pierce was not dead. Not his baby brother. Killian shook his head. "No."

"Killian, I am sorry."

Killian squirmed, beating against his chest, needing to break away from the cage of his arms, from the confinement. he needed to see his face when he told him this.

"You are lying!" he screamed.

Rem doesn't lie.

"No!"

Rem looked down, his expression tortured. He actually looked ashamed. As he well should!

"I told you someone was going to die! He warned me and you all did not listen to me! And now he is dead! My baby brother is dead!"

It wasn't fair to blame Rem. After all, he was the only one of his Consorts that actually jumped into action when he told him of the warning. Though he disappeared, Killian knew he was trying to get answers because that's what Rem does.

"Lorn told us earlier that you might start hallucinating. She said it was a side effect of the drug Ethel has been slipping into your meals to help reduce the pain of your pregnancy. She said that it would induce a fit and potentially trigger another episode that could cause a miscarriage. We were instructed to give you that tea whenever we sensed you might be.

I searched and I did not find any trace of your cousin. His scent did not linger and not even Sotershai felt another presence. I checked on your cousins and they all were fast asleep in their chambers. I thought that it might be...It was a foolish assumption. And after you fell unconscious, I went to check on your brother to be sure his life was not in danger.

It was as if he were waiting for my arrival. I saw your brother with a dagger. I witnessed him push it against his throat. I tried to save him but fifty guards had been compelled to gut themselves if I interfered.

I did not know what I should do. I did not know what choice to make. I have failed you," Rem said, his voice, full of that rare emotion that he never liked to share.

Killian tilted his head back, letting the tears stream down his face as he thought of his baby brother and the last conversation they had. How pitiful and miserable he looked. How he was thrust into problem after problem, none of which a seventeen-year-old should ever have to go through.

His brother was dead.

Who would be next?

"I want guards on all of my siblings as well as Ethel and Lisa. Trustworthy ones. I know that it may not be of any use seeing as they could just be compelled, but it would make me feel better to know that they are not alone if anything should happen."

Rem nodded once, still refusing to meet his gaze.

"And I want guards with Orion, Titus, and Gwendolyn. They are not out of the clear either. He might try to finish them all off." Killian turned to Rem. "Do they know?"

Rem nodded again.

"How are they?"

"Orion is...distraught. Titus is doing his best to console him."

Killian sighed. He guessed that answered his questions about the nature of their relationship. They managed to work something out. And it wasn't just an unfortunate circumstance that bound them together, but a budding relationship.

Now it was gone.

This had to stop.

"When will you finally make your move? What are you waiting for, child of his blood? How many more people does he have to kill in order to realize that he must be stopped. Stopped by no one but you," a thick accented voice said from off to the side.

Yehwin.

He was in his tiger form, sitting by the door with his back straight and blue eyes glowing. He looked...disappointed.

"But my uncle--"

Yehwin roared. The ferocious sound piercing Killian's eardrums making them ring. It startled both him and his Consort.

"Enough with your excuses! Are you King or aren't you, boy?" he hissed.

Killian shook his head. "I am not King yet--"

Yehwin snarled. "Weak. You are all weak. You tarnish Liaelliuwei's blood." With another growl, Yehwin disappeared.

What was he supposed to do?

He didn't know what to do!

If there ever a time where he wished he was not the first born, it would be now. The pressure was so heavy, like a rock pressing into his chest, cutting off his airflow, distracting him from any possible thoughts that might free him from this hell. He never felt more useless in his life.

Killian wanted to act but he just didn't know what to do. He was so confused. Because any wrong move can cost someone their life. Clouds have mercy, please.

He had been given so many different answers for why he couldn't do this or that and it caused him to sit there, frozen, not doing anything while the world around him went up in flames. The more he waited the worse it got, but the wrong move could ruin everything. Was his cousin really behind all of this? Or was it the corrupted God? Who was in control of the vessel?

And how could he end them?

Was it even possible to end the life of just the God or would he have to kill Filo too? What does Filo even want? And what about his other cousins? Marza and Bennett? What would he do with them? Were they being compelled too or were they just wicked?

Killian didn't know what to do and he couldn't wait on his father anymore, not when there is so much at stake. He had to act before the next one is dead.

And he only had six horas left. A lot happen in six horas.

He would forgive his Consorts for their blunder. Being at odds at such a crucial time was hazardous and probably their enemies' intention. They will not show weakness and they will be unified. He'd deal with the issue at a later time. For now, they had to work together.

He cannot wait anymore.

Filo had to die.

Killian was sure that he would want to end his suffering if it is true that he is trapped in there. And it will be unfortunate to have to kill his kin, but is necessary for the good of the people.

They could not have this maniac on the loose, killing as he pleased.

And it was even more terrifying, knowing that Perseth was so close to being awake fully. They had to stop him before that happened.

Or else, they wouldn't stand a chance.

Killian stood.

Rem watched him, uncharacteristically worried.

"Let us go," Killian told him, his voice hard and hoarse. Lingering evidence of his crying.

Rem didn't ask any questions. Killian walked to his closet and wadded through the endless silks and garments until he saw it, perched on the wall, still shining.

His sword.

The hilt, gold and ruby encrusted, glimmering in the light of the closet. The blade was well kept. The edges sharp and metal polished.

He grabbed it, mounting the sheath to his waist before sliding the sword inside.

Rem was standing at the entrance of the closet, eyes fixed on the blade he had strapped to himself.

"You plan to fight? You are with child."

"I can handle my sword. I am no stranger to the art of combat. You will do well to remember I have trained just as any of you have and I am skilled with my weapons."

Rem opened his mouth to protest but Killian shut him up with a sharp look. He closed his mouth and stepped aside.

On the way out of the closet, he grabbed Caspian's bow and quiver of arrows. While all his other Consorts always have their weapons on hand, Caspian rarely carried his around unless for formal events. He said it was too bulky and uncomfortable when he slept. Which he did...all the time. One would think that he would be used to it since he had to do it most of his life when he stood guard in the trees, but Killian didn't question it and let him have his way. He was deadly with or without it anyway.

They left the room, Rem following close behind him. At the nearest guard, Killian handed the bow and quiver to him.

"Get this to Caspian immediately."

The guard bowed deeply before hurrying off with the weapon.

He wanted all his Consorts armed in case Perseth--who he was now officially dubbing the culprit of this mess--decided to hunt them again. They needed to be able to protect themselves.

Heading to his cousin's chambers. Killian traveled through a couple of halls, stopping when he heard a noise. Something that closely resembled whimpering.

Killian's ear twitched as he strained to listen to the faint sound.

A scream pierced the air.

In the direction of Gilra's rooms, he hurried as fast as he could, Rem disappearing behind him. When Killian reached the room, panting, stepping over several corpses, he nearly vomited at the sight before him.

Blood.

It was everywhere, in thick puddles on the marble floors, staining the rugs, streaking across the sheets of his sister's bed.

The threat had been apprehended by Rem. A guard whose expression was dull and void of life in a way he was all too familiar with.

He didn't struggle as Rem restrained him with a blade against his throat.

Instead, he slammed his neck into the blade, slicing his own throat open. Blood squirted out of the wound, spraying Killian in the face.

He couldn't even register the suicide. He was still stuck on the lump on the ground.

A mass of bright red hair that darkened at the tips by the blood it was surrounding it on the ground. A few feet away, a slender body, crumpled in a bloody gory heap with small lumps of red ruin littering the floors around it. The copper skin that was so similar to...

Orion.

But it was not Orion who laid there.

The body was female.

Jo.

Orion's little sister, who he brought here from Rhettick to join his personal army and managed to earn the role of Drek's lieutenant. The girl who followed around his Consort with eyes full of young admiration bearing a crush that all could see. Jo, who was the exact opposite of her brother, full of energy and spark, always seeming to be happy. And even more so when she found out she was going to be an aunt.

Jo, who was only fifteen years old.

Younger than Pierce and dead, just the same.

This was going to break Orion's heart.

Killian looked over to his sister who was cowering on the bed with blood soaked clothes, eyes wide, still staring at the young lieutenant's decapitated corpse in horror.

Tears were an endless stream down her lavender cheeks. Killian swept her up in his arms, not caring about the blood.

"You are safe," he promised her. "You are safe now."

"She's dead," his sister wailed. "She's dead."

Killian didn't say anything to that, just held his sister tighter, shielding her from the gore that decorated her room.

"Let us get you out of here. Then you can tell me what happened," Killian told her, pulling her close to his side and supporting the majority of her weight as they stepped outside her room, past all the dead bodies.

Killian saw out of the corner of his eye, Rem grab a sheet, spread it out on the ground before carefully lifting Jo, placing her head and her body on the sheet. Then gently, he wrapped her body and lifted her into his arms.

He would thank him later for that. She did not deserve to be left there.

Killian brought his sister back to his room. The castle was bustling with guards as the news spread. Killian wouldn't let any of them in to question his sister, he wanted her to gather her bearings first.

She sat on his bed in one of his robes, with haunted eyes, cupping a steaming cup of tea between her palms.

"She was protecting me, said that you were assigning your guards to protect us. I didn't question it with all the craziness that's been going on lately and with...Pierce--" she broke off with a sob.

Killian rubbed her back slowly, as the pain of their loss hit them both.

She inhaled shakily.

"And everything was fine. Until one of the guards just started attacking. Then all of them were. And Jo probably would've survived if she didn't have to protect me. I only got in her way. She was quickly overwhelmed when more and more of them came in. One of them got by her and attacked me. I would've died but she...she threw herself in front of me and didn't have enough time to defend herself. It's my fault! I should have died!" Gilra started sobbing.

Killian held her closely and assured her that it wasn't her fault and that Jo was doing her job, protecting her. Eventually, he let the guards in to ask his sister questions. When they were done and his sister cried herself to sleep, Killian left her side.

"Stay with her," he commanded Rem once he returned from taking Jo's body to the healers. He didn't argue even though Killian could tell he wanted to. Rem didn't want to leave his side.

Killian headed to the medical wing and walked in just in time to see Titus leading Orion into the morgue. Not even a second later, Orion was screaming.

High piteous, heart wrenching screams. Titus pulled the distraught Incubus into his chest and held him tight, whispering comforting words to him but it couldn't possibly be heard over the screams.

Orion fell to his knees and sobbed, slipping out of Titus's grasp and practically crawling to the table where Jo's body lay. Her head at an unnatural angle, lifeless golden eyes, staring out into nothingness. Gestina was preparing the thread and needle to sew the head back on.

Orion shouldn't see this.

"Jo! Jo! Jo wake up! Wake up please! Please!"

He grabbed her head from the table, not even noticing that it detached from the body, and cradled it to his chest. Whispering to her words that Killian couldn't hear and rocking back and forth.

Gestina made a move to take the head but Orion snarled at her viciously, teeth bared and tail whipping. His expression deadly and full of warning. Gestina held her hands up and backed away slowly. Then looked to Killian for help.

"Let him mourn," he said softly, then left them.

He gave a solemn nod to Titus on his way out, which he returned sadly. He would take care of Orion. And Killian would take care of Perseth.

There came a time where one must make a decision. A life altering, unforgiving decision, that just might change their very foundation and all that they once believed in.

Killian hadn't come to that point yet, but some people around him have. He watched them struggle and watched them suffer. Keeping his mouth shut because that was what he knew how to do best.

Be silent, little Prince. Your words mean nothing.

He tried to be understanding. Truly, he did. But there was one thing that they needed to understand. He let the words reverberate in his mind.

I am a sword and I am a crown.

And I will paint the world in red.

There was a part of him that would die tonight, right along with his cousin. There is a part of him that has stayed hidden, quietly biding time until the perfect moment to strike shone like a beacon. And there will be a part of him that stood tall even as his very being crumbled.

I guess this is what it means to be King, he thought.

Killian unsheathed his blade, listening to the soft slice of metal against leather. The blade's edge gleamed dangerously in the soft light of the hall, lit only by the flickering flames that danced on the tips of each wick of each candle that sat perched in the alcove of the wall.

He was waiting for the prince in the garden, as if this very moment had been destined to happen on this night at this time. Perhaps it has been.

Would Killian live to see another day or will this be the end of him and all that was his?

His body was covered in the tight leathers of his armor. Small plates covering his vitals. His sword rested in his sheath at his hip.

With his back to him, Killian was able to examine his small frame and minute musculature. He was dainty and made more for the art of bedwarming than battle. But Killian had no doubt that he would peel the skin from his very bones if he let his guard down.

He was not weak and he was not defenseless, despite his fragile appearance.

His hair was as red as a freshly bloomed rose, curling in soft natural tendrils, seeming so much more saturated against his pale white skin.

His pointed ear twitched before he lifted his chin and slid his gaze over his shoulder and at him. A soft chuckle left his sensuous lips.

"So you're finally growing a pair?" his cousin said, turning to face him slowly.

His expression full of cold amusement. Those gray eyes familiar but so very wrong. Everything about him was wrong. He was like a curse and to lay eyes on him was an instant hex of misfortune and misery.

"And you are finally done hiding?" Killian snapped back.

Filo--no--Perseth tipped his head back and laughed. The sound chafed against Killian's skin, leaving him raw and stinging.

Everything about this creature was so wrong.

Of course it was. Because he was not meant to be here. Not in his palace, not in his cousin, not in this world.

What would the Clouds do? Would It leave him here? Would It not interfere? Would It not break It's laws despite how many have already been broken? Would It leave them here to die by this creature's hand?

"Hiding?" Perseth purred, his lip curling in a wicked smile. "Such an interesting word. Hiding implies running. Cowering. Fearing. Hiding is not something I've done at all. But you?"

His gray eyes glinted, flashing a bright orange before dulling back to gray.

"You have been hiding your entire life."

Killian bristled at the truth. He knew that much but to have it flung at his face by him no less, made his blood boil.

The demigod rose like a crashing wave inside Killian, slamming into the walls of his control. Killian took a deep breath and let it out through his nose.

He could not let him rile Perseth up, not this early on. He had to keep a cool head and do what he came here to do.

End him.

Killian stepped forward.

"Then maybe it is time I came out to play," the prince mused before lunging for him, sword raised and ready.

The move was swift and well practiced, but just a tad too slow as Perseth drew his own sword and brought his blade to Killian's, staving off the blow. The sound of metal clanking against metal reverberated through the prince with almost as much strength as the vibrations from the forceful blow. Childbearing has made him slow.

Killian would have to make up for in skill.

Perseth was quick, sweeping under with a swing of his sword aimed at Killian's stomach. The prince side stepped and met him with his sword, blocking his blade and forcing it upward.

Putting some distance between them, Killian shuffled a couple steps back, but didn't take his eyes off of his opponent. He was still grinning with that madness leaking orange into his normal gray. He darted for the prince again, intent clear in his gaze. His eyes darted left but Killian could see the obvious calculation, and knew he would come for his right. When he did, Killian was ready, spinning out of the way, sending his blade slicing into his side.

The blow so quick, blood didn't have enough time to touch his sword.

Only a few ticks later, did it begin to seep from the unguarded part of his armor.

He was a fool if he thought that armor would stop him. He was there when the designs were being developed. He knew all of its strengths and weaknesses. It would not stop him nor would it stop his blade.

Perseth growled lowly.

Killian let the sound wash over him, coaxing that fear that would normally paralyze him, into action. Let that fear be his guidance as he fought to win. Let his motivation be his cousin's salvation, the revenge for his brother's death, the suffering of his lovers and family, and the lives of his unborn children.

Let him be the end of Chaos.

In a second, they were at it again, breathing heavily, slashing and spinning. Dodging and striking. Sweat coated Killian's body in a light blanket and the heaviness of his weighted stomach was beginning to press down on him but he didn't let it break him.

It would be his loss of focus, the humiliation of forfeiting that would be the end of this fight. Killian could not let that happen. He had to keep fighting, keep pushing.

The adrenaline was pushing through, making his veins pump viciously with blood, flooding his face and his limbs. Making him loose and full of false stamina. Killian should've been done for ages ago but his body's natural reaction kept him going.

They were panting, both covered in shallow cuts, sweat, and blood. He had been on the offense these last few rounds and his defense was getting weaker and weaker.

Killian had to end this soon or else he was going to run out of steam.

The tension was thick and suffocating. And Killian could tell he was not the only one winded by their battle. Perseth was still not at his peak, despite how developed he seemed. And the body he inhabited was not cut out for this sort of physical labor. He was untrained and sloppy, and he was suffering for it.

But there was a part of Killian that believed he was holding back. Some of the moves he was making and openings he was leaving just seemed a bit too obvious. And Killian couldn't help but notice the breastplate of his armor was substituted with a much weaker metal. One that would not protect him against a sword.

Killian could tell it was carefully painted to match the original materials, but his sword nicked it in the corner and a part of the paint came off.

Was Perseth being set up?

Or was Killian?

Killian watched him with careful eyes, drinking in any movement and every breath he took or made. He would not let any of his behavior escape him. He refused to stupidly follow his plan as he had been these past months.

Perseth lunged again and they were submerged in battle. It was more intense this time, but Killian was able to see his maneuvers more carefully with better eyes. He was definitely making it too easy for Killian to get the upper hand. Is that what he wanted or was he setting Killian up for a trap?

Or could it be that the real Filo is interfering and trying to give him opportunities to end this fight? He was still in there and it was still his body that was being used so there was a very strong possibility.

But Killian was uncertain. And that uncertainty cost him.

Perseth managed to get a deep cut in Killian's thigh that had him staggering. The prince hissed in pain and the burning sensation began. A warm wetness soaked through his torn soft pants.

His legs trembled as his structure was compromised. While he was distracted by the pain, Perseth lunged again. In a rush, Killian side stepped him, kicked out with his injured leg, ignoring the burning sensation and knocked him to the ground. He was on him in a second with his sword poised over his heart.

Not Filo's...

Shouldn't he have two hearts?

Why had he never heard Filo's heart beat?

It was there, he knew it was. It had to be. Netter said that Filo would have been a vessel himself if Perseth hadn't jumped in him first, which meant that he had another heart. But Killian had been close to Filo a couple of times and he never heard two hearts beat. It was part of the reason why he convinced himself so thoroughly that he had not been the magix user.

That he couldn't be.

What was going on?

Killian's blade quivered with unease as it halted just above the single heart that beat in Filo's chest. Killian stared at the being inside his cousin.

His gaze was fixed on the blade, but he wasn't struggling. Instead, he looked eager.

Filo...

Are you even in there?

The dreams...were they real, or were they too an illusion?

Do it.

End him.

Strike the blow.

He's right there!

Killian shook his head, clenching his eyes shut as if that would quiet the vicious voice in his head. He needed to think.

He couldn't think.

"Killian, don't!"

Killian's head whipped up and around. The King was staring at them with horror in his eyes. His clothes were torn and covered in blood. His sword, dipped in red, in his hand.

"Don't kill him. It's what he wants," King Ellis said carefully.

Perseth snarled beneath him.

"Why?" Killian asked wary.

"Because he will do to you what he has done to Filo. If you make the killing blow, he will jump from Filo's body to yours."

Chapter
31

"I have been working this whole time to find a way to seal him so that you might be spared," the King said to him.

Killian glanced down at the Chaos God beneath him. He leered.

"How is it possible? I do not have the magix mark. I was not born with a second heart. My body is not compatible," Killian countered.

"It is true that you were not born with a second heart, but you do have the mark of magix. And your vessel is carrying four hearts right now. Any of which can be overtaken. And should it be your heart or the heart of your S-Level child, yours or his life would be forfeit."

Killian's chest seized.

He couldn't kill him. He was right under his fingertips and he couldn't kill him.

A roar of frustration left Killian's lips, echoing into the crisp air. Filo...no Perseth laughed maniacally beneath him.

"What will the little Prince do, hm?" Perseth grinned.

Killian's hands moved on their own accord, tossing away the blade, latching around his thin neck and squeezing tightly. Not tight enough to kill him but a warning not to push him. Killian didn't have to kill him to hurt him.

Perseth coughed, wheezing a little but the grin was still plastered on his face.

Killian's gaze flickered from his father back to Perseth.

"Yehwin!" Killian called out. The cat materialized instantly just across the balcony. His expression calm and level. It was clear he was still upset, but there was something else. Like he was waiting for something.

Killian filled him in quickly, tightening his hold on Perseth's neck so he didn't get any ideas. "What should I do?"

Yehwin was quiet for a long moment. Long enough that Killian was worried he would not say anything.

"Are you so sure he has that power?" Yehwin said softly.

Killian's brow furrowed as he looked at him. He was staring at the prince with such intensity, it was as if there was a hidden message in his words. But he could not decipher it.

"You are not that susceptible. The truth is there, but you must remember what I have told you."

Killian frowned at him.

What was he talking about?

Perseth threw his head back and laughed. The sound full of mania, it sent shivers up Killian's spine.

Was the real Filo in there? If he was, what state would he be in if released? Surely, having someone so deranged inhabiting his body would have some lasting trauma. Would he ever be able to recover? Could he live a normal life after this? However long it might be?

If he somehow managed to free Filo and rid him of Perseth, he would surely lose a large sum of his lifespan, just as Netter did.

"Come on, little Prince! End me like I ended your pathetic brother."

Killian froze, his blood running cold.

Perseth bared his teeth in a way that was much too aggressive to be considered a smile.

"Oh yes, it was so easy. The young ones are gullible. And he was so ready to betray his older brother, it hardly took any influence. A few words to push him in the right direction and he was practically begging to slice you up."

"Shut up," Killian growled, feeling the rage curl in his gut like something alive and writhing. Power swelled in his veins. He fought to hold it back.

"He hated you. He hated your power, your influence, your privilege. He wanted you dead."

"Shut up!" Killian snarled, squeezing his neck tighter.

"Don't let him bait you," his father cautioned.

But Killian could barely hear him over the blood rushing in his ears.

"He suffered you know. I made sure of it."

Before Killian could even register his own movements, he had the blade in his hand, shoving it deep into his cousin's chest. Filo's body jerked. A light flared in his eyes before they watered.

"Killian no!" a familiar voice screamed. It took Killian only a moment to realize it was his uncle, who just burst onto the balcony.

He waited for the inevitable rush of power to spear toward him and corrupt his heart or the heart of his child.

But nothing happened.

Killian frowned in confusion, staring down at his cousin who was coughing up blood, the rivers staining his cheeks.

"Not...me..." Filo whispered.

Killian watched in horror, head turning in what felt like slow motion.

His uncle stood there, grinning at him. But it was not his uncle at all. Not with those glowing orange eyes. It had never been Netter at all.

Perseth had been in Netter's body all along.

King Ellis stared at the God with fury and anguish in his eyes, tears streaking down his face.

"You killed my brother."

Perseth grinned wide. "No, dear brother. You did. The moment your sword pierced this chest many years ago. And you so stupidly believed every lie. I didn't even have to compel you as I had done all the others."

In a flash, they moved, engaging in a vicious battle. Killian's eyes could barely follow their movements. They slashed and parried, switching seamlessly from offence to defense and back again. He was so transfixed, he hadn't even realized the body beneath him twitch.

Killian zeroed in on his cousin. Filo's lips were parted and blood dribbled out. His eyes were open, blinking slightly as he looked up.

The realization of his actions finally hit him.

He killed the real Filo. He was being compelled this entire time...

"Yehwin!" Killian called desperately. Looking at the cat with burning eyes. "Please, I need to heal him!"

The cat remained seated, eyes sad.

"Yehwin!" Killian shouted again, not understanding why he wasn't moving. He needed to feed him. Filo was dying. He was dying. "Yehwin, please!"

Yehwin slowly made his way to the sobbing Prince who tried to keep the blood from spilling from his cousin's chest.

"I tried to warn you, child of his blood. He cannot be saved."

Killian sobbed harder, "No! No, there has to be something you can do! We can't let him die!"

"Kill...ian."

A blood soaked hand brushed Killian's cheek weakly. Killian focused his attention on his cousin, grasping that bloody hand tightly.

"I am here, Filo. I am so so sorry. I did not--" Killian choked as another sob bubbled from his lips.

"Kill...ian...I-I'm...s-sorry," Filo rasped.

"It is alright. It was not your fault, cousin," Killian whispered, pressing his forehead against Filo's.

"L-lo...ve...you," he whispered so softly, Killian was only able to hear it from being so close to him. And the hand in his went limp.

The prince pulled back horrified and was met with vacant gray eyes.

He wanted to mourn but this battle was not yet won. Killian turned in time to see Perseth's blade plunge into the King's chest.

No.

No!

The King's bright gray eyes widened. He stumbled back, slowly looking down at the silver sword jutted from his chest. He looked over to Killian, sadness in expression before he collapsed.

Dead.

Blood curdling screams ripped from Killian's throat. Perseth stared at him with a maniacal smile, eyes alight with the death and chaos surrounding him. A crazed laugh left him.

But it was short-lived.

One second he stood there full of glee. Another, and his head was rolling on the ground.

Blood and innards splashed across Killian's face, some even getting in his mouth. Netter's body crashed to the ground, delayed. It was as if it too hadn't quite registered what had just occurred.

Behind him stood Sotershai, bloody sword poised.

The God was breathing heavily. His body covered in cuts and gashes. But it didn't look like it bothered him in the slightest.

Killian was too busy in shock to notice Yehwin leap in the air, plucking something that Killian couldn't see with a soft, "Oh no you don't."

Somehow, Killian knew he had grabbed Perseth's essence. But it did not overcome his body. He guess because Yehwin was Cloud born and had powers they could not comprehend.

The prince's gaze darted from Yehwin to Sotershai to his father's lifeless corpse. Killian released Filo from his grip and stumbled to his father's body.

"Father?" he rocked his still form as if he was simply sleeping and Killian meant to wake him from his slumber. But he did not wake.

"Father wake up! Please! Father do not leave me! I cannot be King! I am not ready!" Killian sobbed, shaking him over and over.

"Child, he is dead," Yehwin said softly. "Whether you believe it or not, you are ready to rule. And you are King. No more hiding from your Destiny."

Killian wailed, pulling his father into his arms.

Sotershai came behind him, wrapping his arms around the prince's shoulders and pressing his face into his back.

Filo.

Netter.

King Ellis.

Pierce.

Dead.

"Killian," Yehwin said, commanding the prince's attention.

His head snapped up and he stared at the male.

"I must take Perseth back to the Clouds."

Killian nodded numbly, looking down, not really registering his words.

"And Sotershai."

Killian's head snapped up again, alarm clouding his features.

Yehwin was looking at him sadly.

"You know he cannot stay here. He is meant to be dormant."

New tears welled in his eyes.

"Please...I have lost so much already," Killian whispered brokenly.

"And I'm sure you will learn to lose more. Such is the fate of a King."

Killian looked to Sotershai, who had stood, tall and imposing. His eyes were blazing, fixed on Killian.

"I'll give you a moment to say your goodbyes."

Killian gently placed his father on the ground as he stood on shaky legs. His body trembling. He staggered to Sotershai, nearly falling against him.

He caught the prince easily.

"You knew," he accused him.

And to Killian's surprise, he nodded. "I am not of this world. I have broken the rules too many times. They will not let me stay."

His voice was deep, smooth, and clear. He was fully awake now. Of course he was. Right when he was leaving, he wakes up.

Killian sobbed, clutching the fabric on his chest. He held him close, breathing in deeply with his nose buried in his hair.

"I love you, Killian. And I will be with you. In our child."

"I love you too, Sotershai," Killian hiccuped, clutching his stomach with a trembling hand.

Sotershai leaned back slightly, lifted Killian's chin with a finger, and kissed him so deeply he felt light headed. Their entire relationship went into that kiss. Killian dug his fingers into his thick black hair, holding him as close as he could. They kissed with every memory, every touch, every breath of their being.

"Sotershai," Yehwin called.

Sotershai pulled back, stared into Killian's eyes before kissing his forehead.

He released him and Killian felt his power caress his skin as he left Rem's body in a shimmering golden light. The light danced in the air before curling around Yehwin's outstretched hand.

With a small smile, Yehwin disappeared.

Rem let out a slow breath, his black eyes blinking rapidly. He looked lost. But then he stared down at the three bodies before looking down at him.

He sank gracefully to one knee.

"What are your orders...King Killian?"

Chapter
32

After the Battle

Clean up was messy.

It took several weeks to get the palace back in order. Those who died were given proper burials and memorial for the living to mourn the dead.

His Consorts survived the carnage fairly unscathed, which was a blessing. Faust had hidden and protected Killian's siblings with the help of Killian's Consort mothers.

Drek and Caspian were dealing with the compelled guards, trying to incapacitate and not kill them. Zev had been horribly injured while trying to protect Ethel, Lisa, and Lorn. Thankfully, Lorn was there to heal most of the damage until Gestina was able to get to them.

They all survived. Throughout this entire ordeal, they were always the first to end up in the worst shape, taking the brunt of most attacks. Of course, half of the attacks originated from Killian himself. Something no one would forget anytime soon. It made dealing with other diplomats a bit difficult, but he could handle it.

He was handling everything a lot better than he imagined. But it was not because he had an epiphany and sudden burst of confidence. It was because he had to.

Because Kara, Jo, Pierce, Netter, Filo, and his father died for this throne, for this family. Killian had to protect it.

It was the only way to honor them.

Funerals for Pierce, Netter, and King Ellis were held a few days after their deaths. His Consort mothers were distraught, especially Queen Jessa. But Consort Mother Mae was hit the worst with grief.

Losing her lover and her only son nearly drove her mad. She was currently undergoing extensive therapy with Aunt Kendra who had also faced the same loss. Even more when she realized she had lost two children.

Bennett disappeared without a trace.

After he gave Killian that warning, he fled. He wasn't sure why, but he'd get to the bottom of it soon enough. He had troops on the lookout for him. He'd show up eventually.

Titus took Pierce's place and became the new General. While Killian liked having him in his personal army, he thought that position would better suit him.

He took great care of Orion as he mourned both his sister and Pierce. Together, they were sure to take amazing care of Killian's niece Gwendolyn. They promised that she would grow up knowing how wonderful her father Pierce was before he died, despite the crimes he committed.

And amidst the chaos of rebuilding the empire, Killian gave birth to the twins.

Aaia and Marsh.

Aaia was a sight to behold with stunning curly maroon hair, four black horns, and bottomless black eyes like Rem. Her tiny tail was black too as well as her delicate little wings. Her mark of magix curled around her stomach. Her brother, Marsh, took after Zev with light blue skin. His hair was was bright white with streaks of maroon. Four dark blue horns protruded from his forehead matching his dark blue tail. His eyes, were ruby red, just like Killian's, with red wings to match. Drek was brought to tears when they decided his name.

The twins were spoiled rotten.

Yehwin didn't come back for a while. But when he did, Killian wanted to be mad at him. He couldn't though. He knew he was only doing his duty, but it still hurt.

Zev didn't take it well when they told him Sotershai was gone. Killian knew they shared a bond, he just didn't know how strong it was.

Rem and Killian took the time to comfort him, hold him when his grief took a turn for the worst.

Yehwin promised that Sotershai was safe and it was for the best. He also informed them that Perseth could always be reborn into another vessel and that it was impossible to truly get rid of him, but the Clouds would take extra precautions next time he's placed in a vessel.

Killian wondered if Yehwin was going to stick around. When he asked him outright, the familiar said the Clouds assigned him a new charge. Two to be exact.

He rarely ever left Aaia and Marsh's side.

It made Killian feel better knowing they had his extra protection. Yehwin would guide them well.

Killian kept his family close. Aunt Kendra and Marza stayed at the palace permanently. Velma was dismissed immediately and sent into exile. Killian knew Ian loved to travel and he couldn't take that away from him, but once he moved his lover Thomas, a blacksmith, into the palace, it became easier to make him stay.

Gilra became fast friends with Orion. They stuck together, mourning Jo's loss. Witnessing such brutal carnage left its mark on Killian's younger sister, but she was strong and didn't let it stop her from doing the things she loved and spreading that joy.

Killian was also happy to see her ask Faust for sparring lessons so she could fend for herself. She didn't like being vulnerable and didn't want to cause another death because of her helplessness. He gladly obliged.

Overall, things were getting better.

They would be better.

Killian would make them.

He was King Killian Innis of Incubi.

Father.

Lover.

Friend.

King.

And he would always have his Consorts.

Epilogue

One Year Later

The sun was setting, painting the sky in vicious reds and fiery oranges. The taverns were beginning to fill with their normal rowdy crowds preparing for the night of drunken stupor that was frequent in town.

Amongst the partygoers was a cloaked figure, weaving in and out of the crowd seamlessly. One might not have noticed the expensive cloth his cloak was made of, or the lack of weapon on his person and that was the point. They hid in plain sight. Easy for the eye to skip over. Harmless.

Only if one didn't know what to look for.

Another cloaked figure, with the same unassuming aura traced the shadows of the alley, following like the night in the sky.

The first hadn't realized they were being followed until a hand clamped down on their shoulder.

The figure spun. Curly brown hair spilled from the hood and muddy pink eyes were revealed.

When his assailant pulled back their hood, his eyes widened.

Maroon locks tumbled from their perch on slim shoulders. Bright ruby red eyes practically glowed in the dimness.

King Killian Innis.

Bennett glanced around and noticed he was backed into an alley.

He sighed and placed a hand on his hip before a humorless smirk tilted his thin lips.

"Your Highness, what a surprise to see you away from the palace."

Killian cocked his head, his glare relentless.

"My Consorts can handle things in my absence."

"Another surprise, not seeing them at your side," Bennett remarked.

"I am not alone."

A dark figure appeared out of the darkness. Like thick smoke into solid form, so dark he was almost indiscernible from the deepest shadows.

Consort King Rem Brangwen.

"Ahh, so you finally learned something after Perseth," Bennett remarked cooly.

Killian's face remained impassive, not revealing a single thought.

"Why did you leave, cousin dearest?"

"If you thought I was staying during that bloodbath, you're crazy, my dear King. Marza might not remember being compelled but I do. It'd be foolish to put myself in that position again, don't you agree?"

"You abandoned your family?"

Bennett let out a laugh.

"It's a rough world, cousin. People die. You should know this well by now. If you're smart, you survive. Hence why I'm still alive."

"Did you not think I would find you?"

Bennett looked pensive for a moment before he shrugged. "I supposed you would. When you would...not sure. Seeing as you have your hands full with the twins and another on the way?"

He glanced down at Killian's midsection. Though it was impossible to tell from underneath the cloak, the King was pregnant again in his second trimester.

Killian's eyes narrowed.

"How did you know what was going to happen? Back then."

"I'm not sure what you mean, My King."

Killian's lips thinned ever so slightly.

"The deaths, Bennett. How did you know they were going to die?"

Bennett smiled.

"You are not the only one the Clouds sent help to."

Killian's brow furrowed.

A figure dropped into the alley from the roof of the nearby building.

Silver hair, silver skin, and serpentine eyes.

Arix.

Zev's lieutenant.

He bowed to Killian before shifting into an albino snake. Slithering up Bennett's arm, he remained perched there, alert and waiting.

"You're a familiar," Killian stated.

"Correct," the snake hissed not unfriendly.

"My job was to watch, report, and not interfere," Bennett said. "Tasked by the Clouds Above. I am but a humble servant to my Gods."

Killian snorted.

"Is that all cousin? I must return to my travels now."

Killian stepped back and dipped his head, conceding.

Bennett bowed and backed away. Rem and Killian watched him disappear.

"What will you do?" Rem asked his King.

Killian sighed, rubbing his temples. "Nothing. Who am I to challenge the will of the Gods?" The King tilted his head back to stare at the burning orange sun dipping that much closer past the horizon. "Trust Yehwin to keep that bit of information to himself. I will be having a word with him about this and Zev is going to need a new lieutenant."

Rem chuckled, taking Killian's hand in his, before they disappeared in a huff of smoke.

About the Author

N. A. Moore was born and raised in New Jersey. She began her creative journey early in life, reading whenever she could or filling up notebooks with fantastical stories. She started posting her stories online in 2008 on Wattpad where The Consorts was first introduced. She works as an artist, selling her works under the name Nerrealz Art. She has an unhealthy obsession with coffee, anime, and The Sims. Visit her online at neriahalmahdi.com.

Follow N.A. Moore on:
Instagram: @author_namoore
Facebook: @AuthorN.A.Moore
Twitter: @author_namoore
Goodreads: N. A. Moore
Patreon: Firelipz

Also available as an e-book.

Made in the USA
Middletown, DE
07 February 2020